THE ART OF BEING JONNY

james sismanes

WHAT IF I TOLD YOU, YOU COULD ROB A BANK AND
NOBODY WOULD KNOW?

HUTCHINS
HP
PRESS CO.

For Monique,
My muse, even when she didn't know it.

1

THE COMMUNITY CHEST CARD

in the beginning, it didn't feel like stealing.

It was more like fate, you know? Like the old *Monopoly* windfall, a fortuitous bank error in the player's favour. Now I know what you're thinking: you've barely been here for more than six seconds – four, if you're speed reading like Wile E. Coyote on Xanax – and I'm already trying to wash this red paint off my hands. But if we're being honest with ourselves here – and I don't mean the kind of *dishonest* honesty like when a politician runs for president or when a big business tells you it's launching some eco-friendly initiative; I'm talking about real, godforsaken, cerebral *honesty* – only an asshole would surrender the possession of a pot of gold… right?

In a utopia, any such error would be quickly confessed and corrected, the plague of a guilty conscience intolerable for any saint behind a picket fence.

But not in this world.

This world that we inhabit hardly enjoys the luxuries of benevolence and righteousness. We're entrenched in a never-ending Groundhog Day where acts of trickery habitually pollute the very air we breathe like a colossally lethal minefield clogged in soot.

I'm going to level with you: it's not that I'm dishonest by nature;

raised by the stern right hands of an unyielding mother and father, I'm probably the furthest thing from it. But that devilish temptation, the urge to warp the realms of illegality and luck was just far more salivating than an unwritten code of do-goodism.

Besides, what if *I* told *you*, you could rob a bank and nobody would know? Would you do it? It's literally a million dollar question – multi-million, even – right? They've always said that if you give a man a loophole he might rob a bank.

But what happens if you give a man the bank?

* * *

Liquor poured while dodging spotlights swarmed themselves in the blow of cigarette smoke. The air was thick and murky as a toxic poison of evaporating perspiration and endorphins contaminated the atmosphere. The room's evenly populated male-to-female-ratio was made up of the town's most gregarious residents, its most desirable inhabitants as an unbalanced pandemic of pretentiousness and self-loathing plagued the nightclub and its regulars.

This was 'Minx.'

This was Allentown's finest socialite-laden establishment.

This was an isolated world, a black hole far removed from the existential wilderness that hid out on 17th Street and beyond.

Jonathan Jinks swayed and rowed, ambling to the head-knocking rhythm of a subwoofer as he approached the counter.

"I'll get a lager," he ordered, brushing the collar on his creaseless, blue and white chequered shirt.

The bartender – pushing up on her tight leather blouse like the lead in a raunchy alcohol advertisement – snapped the cap from the green plated bottle before pouring it's contents into a frosted glass.

"Thank you," he acknowledged, his eyes boggling and bouncing as the bartender winked with allure.

"Don't mention it," she whispered above the club's deafening sound system, moistening her lips to make certain her provocation was discernible.

Same old Minx. Lucky I stayed away, apparently.

A Saturday night at Minx was the mandatory order for twenty-to-thirty-something year-olds who longed for a provisional relief from their superficial misfortunes. At Minx, one could avoid the displeasures that lingered in the outside world, temporarily basking in the raptures of gratification as they chased their every desire in a mystical alter ego.

The place was a little like Las Vegas – whatever happened there, stayed there – and all affiliations and memories were deemed unofficial, unconsciously erased from the mind like a bright flash from an intergalactic 'Neuralyzer' device.

"Boys," Jon blurted as he flattened his backside on a leather barstool and planted his glass beside him. "Listen, you didn't hear this from me but have you *seen* the women in here tonight? Have they been spiking something in these glasses 'cause this place looks it could've made Jerry Sandusky an honest man!"

Levi, Marcus and Zeke revelled in the molesting misfortunes of the former *Penn State* assistant coach before surveying the room and combining their powers to assign numerical grades to each woman within their radius.

"She's a straight ten," Marcus calculated as he sipped on his bourbon and pointed in the direction of a supercilious dark-skinned woman.

"Now, now, Marcus, you know what they say... you *never* wife up a ten," Zeke preached as they clinked their glasses and guzzled their liquor in one speedy swallow.

"Why do they say that anyway?" Levi asked with naivety.

Zeke extended his forearm and dropped it around the shoulders of his pal.

"Because, my intellectually and socially challenged friend," he patronised, drawing blind smirks from the rest of the crew. "A ten is *always* crazy. There's no such thing as a gorgeous woman with the mind of a scientist. They're either a seven or an eight with a rewarding tendency to clean your dirty drawers or they're a full blown, supermodel slash porn star 'suck me like a vacuum'-type ten with a half-chewed hazelnut for a brain."

Descriptive, Jon thought.

"You paint quite the picture, don't you Z?" he quipped, condemning the explication of the remark.

"What can I say? It's this vivid imagination; surely by now you can call on me to give you a helping hand the next time you're asked to paint a nude portrait or something?"

Jon hardly relished these sorts of derogatory exchanges and often sought for ways to divert the offensive subject matter off course.

"Alright, alright," he pleaded. "Maybe I shouldn't have brought it up but what's so difficult about actually complimenting a woman *without* being an asshole?"

Jon had a particular way with verbal expression. On face value, his choice of words offered the impression of a youthful yet conservative goody-two-shoes. His kinesics, however, rarely pivoted from the conventional physical standards of the group's social fraternity.

"Okay then," Zeke huffed and puffed as he gobbled his tongue and cleared his throat before preparing his finest Shakespearean accent. "Did my heart love 'til now? Forswear it, sight!"

A silent pause ensued for a second, two.

And then, a rumbustious exclamation.

"For I've ne'er seen true beauty 'til I see her pussy tonight!"

The boys erupted in a lively applause, clinking their glasses as they snickered like hyenas at an after-dark zoo party.

"You don't look impressed, my friend," Zeke poked. "I guess Mrs. Sawyer didn't teach you about that recently salvaged passage from *Romeo and Juliet* when we were in high school?"

"Yeah, yeah," Jon conceded. "Whatever, asshole."

The pair exchanged a series of winks, Jon grinning as he waved a breezy approval.

"Y'know, speaking of which, Sandusky could've really benefited from a fake ID and a *Romeo and Juliet* ruling if he'd just gotten that fetish out of his system like fifty fucking years ago," Marcus lectured, reminding the coltish crew that only he alone had a degree in law.

For Zeke and Levi, Marcus' counsel shifted the conversation away from the frivolity and into an academic study of law and order, a topic they hardly cared to discuss with a lager in hand.

"Hey, yo, Levi," Zeke barked, clearly bored by his band of brothers. "Log in to 'PLiNKER' and check to see if those girls are online."

Levi whipped out his *iPhone* like a cowboy in a fast draw, swiping against its lock screen as he tapped on a blue application icon.

"What the hell's a 'PLiNKER'?" Jon asked naively.

"Oh my sweet, socially deprived comrade," Zeke jested, lampooning Jon's 'under-the-rock' lifestyle before an audience of his closest high school companions. "PLiNKER is where you go when you're fishing at a lake bodied by trout and you're the only one not getting a nibble."

"It's where you go when it thunderstorms and you're the only one left in the cold without an umbrella," Marcus added in what appeared to be a pre-rehearsed sales pitch saturated with prosaic metaphors.

"It's the fucking goldmine, Jon," Zeke unveiled, snatching Levi's smartphone out of his paws as he rotated it one-hundred-and-eighty degrees and illuminated the PLiNKER home screen in Jon's direction. "This baby right here gives you direct access to any girl at any club and at any party across the country."

Zeke toggled through the mobile platform, scrolling with his fingertips as he offered Jon a brief and gratuitous operational tutorial.

"So you basically enter a mobile room that syncs with your GPS-location and then you search for and interact with the digital profiles of people that are standing like four feet away from you?" Jon repeated, scoring an A- for information retention. "Seems a bit perverse doesn't it? Why don't you just walk up to them and introduce yourself?"

The three musketeer-bachelors sniggered, the obvious answer known only to each of them.

"No umbrella," Marcus admitted.

For the hours that followed, Jon and his closest college companions surged their way to uninhibited intoxication, the only deterrent being a futile attempt to seduce the nearest female.

"So Jon, tell me something," Zeke slurred, as he brushed his mousey wig. "Last night when the guys and I took a trip to that big, white abandoned house near Jordan Park and you decided to stay home and canoodle your girl, did you actually have any fucking idea on the epic-ness of what you were gonna miss out on?!"

The property in Jordan Park was infamous to Allentown locals. A once-lavish home formerly belonging to Thomas Strauss – the first man to harvest wheat in the state of Pennsylvania – Strauss, his wife and fourteen-year-old daughter perished under suspicious circumstances inside the expensive property in 1913 and the residence had remained vacant ever since.

"Let me guess," Jon probed. "Some artificially paranormal incident that could have gotten you all thrown in jail for the night while I relaxed, feet up on the couch with a beautiful woman in my arms?"

"Oh, get off your moral high horse, Jon, you do that *every* weekend!" Zeke sniggered. "It's by the grace of all that is both pagan *and* Godly that we even managed to get you out here tonight in the first place."

There was a not so imperceptible hush amongst the group as a ring of bass-heavy dance beats drowned out the silent tension.

"But to get to the point, not quite; so we get there at around eleven o'clock, right? And we pass by this dark owl hooting from a tree right nearby the place. We get to the front yard and this place is covered with overgrown weeds and vines and we're thinking we're in some kind of *Tomb Raider* type of shit right now. We walk around to the rear of the property and Marcus reaches out to a window and..."

Fancying his own contribution to the hair-raising anecdote, Marcus balanced his hand atop Zeke's shoulder and interjected, sustaining the suspense like an episodic television writer as he picked up right where Zeke had left off.

"So I reach out towards this dingy window and pull apart these frail wooden panels that are covering it up," he narrated fervently. "It's crazy, we jump through this window and travel up a staircase that leads us to the top of the second floor of the house. Levi has this fucking flash light with him like it's going to save his life and his hands are shaking like a dude with Parkinson's!"

The trio guffawed in tandem, recounting the events of the evening as Jon remained attentive, unmoved.

"The upstairs is still roughly furnished with this old, rusted table, a chair and a burnt out fireplace and every damn step we take feels like this creaky-ass floor is going to collapse beneath our feet. We walk around at least three rooms before we start to hear these loud banging noises against the walls. We panic and as we get the fuck out of there, I see this dark silhouette at the edge of the stairs!"

"And I swear to you man," Zeke admitted. "I hear this deep, 'Barry White eat-your-heart-out' type voice whispering 'who's there?' in my ear as we're running for our lives!"

The boys shared in the thrilling moment.

"Get the fuck out of here," Jon cried, clearly unconvinced.

"Fine," Zeke said bluntly as he sharpened his fingernails. "Believe whatever you want, my man. We're just trying to encourage you to have a little bit more fun, you know? Live life on the wild side just for a moment or two…"

Jon needed no such subjection to the untamed merriment that defied both his legal and moral imperatives. As far as he was concerned, the pressures that coexisted with his precarious employment status provided him with more than enough 'wild life' than an explorer stranded in the Amazon rainforest.

"Hey, I'm out here tonight aren't I?" he shielded, deflecting the truth with his gladiatorial helmet.

"Dude," Marcus replied as if it were his turn to carry the load. "This is like the second time you've been back to Minx with us since you guys began dating; like, what was it now? Four years ago?"

Four years, four months and nineteen days.

The day Jonathan Jinks met Maya Ververs marked a wrinkle in time, every bit as spellbinding as the fabled introduction of John Lennon and Yoko Ono in the *Indica Gallery* – only more kosher. The twosome were optically unbreakable, their gazes permanently in synch like the scope of an unwavering sniper rifle on a vulnerable target. An exchange of sweet nothings was peripheral – Jon only needed one look to determine that she was the perfect kind of trouble: a good girl who knew exactly when to be bad. From that moment on, Jon and Maya were inseparable, their romance incrementally blossoming into an intimate and steadfast devotion.

"Something like that," Jon acknowledged. "It's just not really my scene anymore. I mean, I have other motivations now that take me to different places; it doesn't mean I don't *want* to be here, just that my life has changed since Maya and I began dating and I changed jobs."

"Well, speaking of which," Zeke interjected apathetically. "How's that all going, anyway? Still 'pull your hair out and turn your ball hairs grey' kind of unfulfilling?"

Jonathan Jinks had dedicated his adolescence to academics, creativity and communal altruism. The son of a teaching principal and a highly reputable civil engineer, Jon and the Jinks family were historically ingrained in the very fibres of the Allentown community. As a descendant of one the operational founders of the Allentown-Kutztown Traction Company, the patriarch of the modern-day Jinks' – Gordon Jinks – chronicled the family's legacy as chief engineer of an assiduous team led by visionary and affluent business tycoon, Harris Weinstein.

Harris Weinstein had just purchased *'Dorney Park,'* the renowned Pennsylvanian amusement park when he approached Gordon with the mouth-watering proposition.

"I want to expand this once small, family-run business into the 'Disneyland of the Northeast,'" he professed, proffering a strategic proposal that would accelerate Gordon's career at the helm of engineering and design operations for the following seven years until the business' eventual absorption by the spirited development conglomerate *'Cedar Fair Entertainment Co.'*

Gordon celebrated his retirement by hand-delivering the cotton candy sprinkled keys to the *Dorney* castle to his offspring. Jon had been groomed like a theatrical understudy, undertaking a selection of part-time handyman duties at the park that included grounds keeping, planting vibrant petunias, repairing damages and touching up rusted paintwork while on mid-semester breaks. But for reasons never to be discussed over *Thanksgiving* dinner, Jon refused his father's offer like a fearless shopkeeper under the duress of La Cosa Nostra, instead, opting to invest his aptitude in a career that was far more speculative… and far less remunerative: the arts.

"It's been better," he confessed bluntly.

The group silenced, anticipating something supplementary.

Nothing.

"And…?" Marcus jiggled, his bushy eyebrow squinting and tilting.

"Well what do you want to know?" Jon burst, reaching aimlessly to disguise his trepidation. "Right now we're pretty low on work; and by pretty low, I mean I'm spending mornings buying bagels instead of painting houses. The commercial contracts we had have expired and the domestic opportunities just aren't there anymore seeing as this broken fucking economy apparently means that people can't afford to paint their Goddamn drywall anymore. And now my boss is talking about having to shut everything down if we don't pick up a new contract in the next four-to-six months. So, to put it lightly, 'scribbling on an expensive blank canvas to hang on a wall in *The Louvre* while millions of admirers flock from around the world to revere my work' isn't really the same as being crucified by a customer because her dog found its motherfucking way into the heavy-gloss paint tray."

Through the dimmed light, one could almost conceive the rolling of awkward tumbleweed as it became clear that Jon's outburst had overstayed its welcome.

"Well you know what, man?" Zeke responded, switching the mood like a quick-thinking live television host, "Let's drink to that then; to Jon the *Painter!*"

A swelling of uncertainty drowned the chorused echo as the crew clinked their glasses in a hollow celebration.

"I've got next," Jon declared, observing the four empty glasses on the stainless steel bar table as he ruffled through the contents of his dark, leather wallet.

"*You've* got next? What do you mean? We dragged *you* here," Marcus declared, assuming his own responsibilities.

Even in the most involuntary of circumstances, the noble act of 'giving' would often engross Jon. No matter the resistance, he was invariably disposed to do 'good' things.

"And this is my way of saying thank you," Jon feigned through a fickle smile, still rummaging through the trifold wallet as he sought for a bill or four. "So… we all having more of the same?"

The boys nodded.

But Jon's search had come up empty-handed. Inadvertently – and perhaps as a result of the unfamiliar territory that Minx now occupied – he had either overspent his budget or was far too impaired to differentiate between a ten-dollar bill, a credit card and a library card.

Great. I don't even want to be here, and now I need to fork out more cash, he recognised, recalling the automated teller machine that stood against a bricked façade beside Minx's entranceway.

His disinclinations notwithstanding, Jonathan Jinks could never have known that a seemingly predetermined pilgrimage to the ATM on 17th Street would bring him to a moral standstill; a destructive crossroads that would forever challenge a deep-seated honesty he only thought he possessed.

2

PINNED

INSERT YOUR CARD.

ENTER YOUR PIN.

The instructions could not have been clearer; *even* to a twenty-something-year old Pennsylvanian under a toxic influence.

Jon unleashed the powers of his wallet, slid out his savings card from its pouch and inserted the plastic through the vaginal-like opening on the front of the teller machine. The machine's clunky PIN pad made keying in his four-digit access code more laborious than applying a rubber contraceptive to a flaccid penis as a violent gust of wind twirled and flung an empty soda can over the mid-section of his right sneaker.

6174.

On a more ordinary November's evening in Allentown, an outbreak of pre-Christmas snowfall might have forced road closures and inner-city chaos, shifting nightclub regulars away from Minx and towards the enchanting Pocono Mountains for a recreational weekend of fall-on-your-ass alpine skiing and snowboarding. But the ever-arguable introduction of climate change meant the *only* thing preventing club-goers from slicing their vapid routine was spasmodic rainfall, vile winds or an onerous trip down south for *76ers* basketball in the *Wells Fargo Centre*.

WHAT DO YOU WANT TO DO? The machine beeped, impelling Jon to tap the withdraw button on his savings account.

He hesitated as he calculated just how much longer he fancied depriving his heavy head from the tranquillity of a flannelette pillow before pressing the corresponding button marked '$50.'

The machine's internal computer murmured, processing the request, contemplating its user's demands.

Until it reached a startling verdict.

YOU HAVE INSUFFICIENT FUNDS TO COMPLETE THIS TRANSACTION.

He could hardly believe the untimely nature of his error. Jon had long employed an almost bulletproof, ritualistic process like church-going Sundays or *Netflix*-binging Tuesdays. The routine was simple and uncalculated: commonly, at each month's end, he would utilise the bank's cloud-based transaction system to transfer funds to and from his spending account – and, by associated, his linked credit card – to his long-term savings account. Next, he'd periodically lodge deposits from his everyday spending account to his long-term savings account, replenishing these funds through a supplementary account. Not only did this practice preserve his financial independence, but it also restored a limited selection of funds for the purpose of daily expenditure.

Simple enough, right?

Wrong.

On *this* week, Jon had neglected to commit to the routine, effectively leaving his everyday spending account emptier than a banker's heart – with a remaining account balance to the glowing tune of only eight-dollars.

You have got to be kidding me.

It wasn't as if Jon was broke – he wasn't overly wealthy, either. But the limitations placed on his savings account meant that he was unable to *physically* withdraw funds from any American ATM.

A sensitive and unavoidable humiliation beckoned... until Jon remembered the limitless powers of his almighty *MasterCard*.

All I need to do is debit the $50 from my MasterCard account into my savings account. Then I'll withdraw that, get through the rest of the night and transfer the funds back first thing tomorrow morning.

The strategy was elementary, something Jon had effectuated at least once or twice before. Appropriating funds between various accounts was commonplace in The Information Age with ATMs and networked mobile devices providing the means to access, modify and withdraw any form of legal tender. The ATM was man's modern-day butler and for better or for worse, he was being forced to oblige and engage in the ever-evolving daily lifestyle that technology now dictated.

Jon obeyed the on-screen instructions, punching the appropriate buttons that would command the machine to relocate fifty dollars from his *MasterCard* into his savings account as a heavy Pennsylvania breeze began to funnel, formulating a mini-hurricane from a clump of dust and trimmings of assorted foliage.

The machine's secure cryptoprocessor scanned the information and grumbled once again, apparently taking longer than usual to reach an outcome.

TRANSACTION CANCELLED.

The message flashed in a large, bold, bright red font as it spat out Jon's card in repugnance.

What the hell? What happened to my money?

Jon ejected the plastic from the card reader's loosened grip. Puzzled and a little vexed, he brushed the jagged edges of the plastic with the inline of his fingers and used his mouth to blow a *Nintendo*-cartridge current of air onto its surface before reinserting it for a second attempt.

A faulty, blinking lamppost mimicked his quick-ticking brain as Jon hit the key on the ATM's control pad that propagated the associated codes for an account balance request.

This time, the machine was expeditious in its response time.

BALANCE UNAVAILABLE AT THIS TIME.

Jon was nonplussed, his right eyebrow peaking like The Rock at *Wrestlemania* as he leered intensely at the message before a time expiration command vanquished the text from view.

Wait, what?

The message's fleeting appearance forced Jon into a double take. He recalled the balance once again via the ATM's function keys, seeking an explanation as he glanced over both his shoulders to make certain he was not being watched.

Club-goers occupied the space behind the velvet rope at Minx, the line spanning around the block while the next in succession – a pair of petite, distracting blonde women in mini-skirts – patiently waited for their cue to enter.

Out of sight, out of mind. Out of mind, alright.

Jon disconnected from distraction, refocusing on the machine's suspect display screen as he released a heavy, nervous and frosty breath.

BALANCE UNAVAILABLE AT THIS TIME, the ATM's display screen revealed in its encore, leaving no lingering uncertainty.

What the f…

A mental skirmish materialised, Jon battling his wits as he fought with the nerve cells in his brain over what he was certain he had seen. Had his mind deceived him? Or perhaps it was the ATM that had become the master of a stranger deceit? The answer was about as clear as his handicapped vision.

Well, what are you waiting for? Why don't you just try it and see what happens?

Jon checked his surroundings once again before hitting the corresponding withdraw button on the ATM's keypad system.

Without protest, the automated teller machine spat out a small denomination, stamped with the face of President Ulysses S. Grant on the observe. Jon yanked the bill from the machine's cash dispenser, shaking and stretching the valuable paper before flipping it to its reverse side to gaze at a printed graphic of the U.S. Capitol building.

Holy shit…

It was about as likely an occurrence as a miner striking coarse gold on the first attempt… without the aid of a metal detector. Jon succumbed to the moment, embracing the unexplainable triumph for a millisecond before the incertitude returned.

Is this my money? How damn drunk am I? This is what happens when you never drink…

Jon's leather wallet peeled open as his trembling fingers – on account of both the frigid temperate and his untimely angst – helped to insert the note into its designated pouch.

Irrespective of any plausible explanation, Jon defined himself as solvent – he had withdrawn funds from within the limits of his possession to finance an atypical evening of open-handed spending.

As far as he was concerned, he was too far-gone and had relinquished all control over his faculties. But in the unlikely event that an inadvertent act of misconduct had transpired, he was fully prepared and willing to atone for any such miscalculation.

Or so he thought.

3

FOUR YUENGLING'S, GENTLEMEN

Indecision loomed over what was brighter; was it the light emitting from the candle-glowing chandelier? Or perhaps it was Levi's foolish grin that reflected at obtuse angles off the face of four filled glasses of finely fermented lager as he perused down the bartender's tank top?

"Four *Yuengling*'s, gentlemen," she said sweetly, placing each glass on a round table as her cleavage exposed the design flaws of both her low-cut garment and accompanying bra.

"This has got to be up there with one of our finest local exports," Zeke lauded proudly, his head and shoulders swaying from side to side in precise rhythm with the bartender's hips as she returned to her vocational duties. "I mean, we're talking about one of the largest fucking breweries in North America here, don't you think?"

Zeke was right. *Yuengling* was America's oldest brewery, founded when David G. Yuengling arrived from Wuerttemberg, Germany to settle in the sleepy, coal-mining town of Pottsville, Pennsylvania.

"What a worthy toast," Marcus mocked as he raised his glass like King Arthur to *Excalibur* and smirked in Zeke's direction. "And thanks Jon, you didn't have to pay for these."

"Happy to," Jon lied.

"Hey, what took you so long anyway?" Zeke queried, Jon's

prolonged absence apparently sounding an intoxicating alarm bell.

Honestly... I don't actually know.

Jon was still baffled by the strange happenings at the automated teller machine on 17th Street.

"I think that fucking machine is broken," he implied, avoiding a cotton-web of details. "I had to insert my card like two or three times over just to get the thing to recognise that something was actually in there."

Cue the comedic parade:

"So," Zeke sniggered, winding up for a trademark quip. "Kind of like what happens when you and Maya are having sex, right?"

Marcus and Levi broke out into wild hysterics, striking the table with closed fists as they spilled the contents of their glasses on their shoes and wriggled around like a couple of obstreperous twins.

"At least I can get pussy whenever I want," Jon snapped impetuously, opting for the first strikingly uncharacteristic but entirely environment-appropriate remark he could muster.

Somewhere between forty-seven and sixty-eight minutes later, Jon's exhaustion began to take over.

"Anyway," he said as he slipped his backside upwards and off the leather barstool. "Thanks for a great night gentlemen, but I'd say I'm just about to pass out if I hang around in this dungeon any longer."

"Oh, c'mon, Jon!" Marcus grunted, disappointed. "It's not because of what Zeke said before about Maya is it? Because you *know* that he's just a moron. Just stay for one more round."

Marcus' plea was genuine.

But Jon hardly needed to deliberate.

"One more round and I'll be sleeping with my own legs wrapped around my head on that couch over there," Jon jeered as he pointed to the soft-cushioned, red velvet loveseat, adorned with *Pimp-My-Ride-*

styled black-furred pillows.

After an unrehearsed enactment of goofy goodbye handshakes, Jon made for the 17th Street exit door, his legs practically supporting his upper-frame as he glided like a stoned swan navigating through a frozen lake.

Now... which way is home? he wondered, stepping forward and into the open-aired Allentown abyss as the stench of spilled lager and burnt out cigarettes became unpleasantly apparent.

Jon was in need of a cab. The problem? He had just blown the remainder of his cash withdrawal on a final round of lagers.

His faculties were beginning to fail him as a sense of enervation consumed his very being.

After taking shelter from the knife-sharp Pennsylvanian breeze, Jon recollected his bearings and pondered the necessary course of action.

One thing was for certain: he needed to hail a cab. In order to hail a cab, he required the obligatory payment to cover the travel expense. And in order to possess said obligatory payment, Jon needed to find an ATM.

It seemed as if the luck of the Pennsylvanian Irish was with him. Providentially and, as *this* luck would have it, Jon Jinks already knew the whereabouts of one tremendously close by.

4

PINNED 2.0

INSERT YOUR CARD.

ENTER YOUR PIN.

A bloodthirsty breeze spiralled and twirled an empty soda can over the mid-section of his left sneaker, the incident jogging Jon to recount the identical experience at that very same ATM on 17th Street somewhere between forty-seven and sixty-eight minutes earlier.

Jon poked and probed as he challenged himself to jigsaw the plastic debit card to the insert of the card reader.

6174.

WHAT DO YOU WANT TO DO? the machine asked as Jon emerged triumphant, gesticulating an emphatic fist pump in celebration of his unexceptional achievement.

Jon scanned the available options like a putative witness at a police line-up. Seeking clarity over the events of his last visit, he began in his own miniature-inquest. The goal – intoxicated or otherwise – was to deduce whether or not the 'TRANSACTION CANCELLED' and 'BALANCE UNAVAILABLE' transcripts were in error – the corollary of a damaged and defunct computer teller – and his fifty-dollar transfer and subsequent withdrawal had in fact processed flawlessly.

Jon thumped the grubby key on the ATM's control pad that propagated the associated codes for an account balance request as the machine's secure cryptoprocessor scanned a string of comprehensive binary code.

The theme music from *Jeopardy* ticked between his ears as he used the lag as a catalyst for vigilance. He glanced over each shoulder – one at a time as if he were wearing Batman's cowl atop his neckline – in an attempt to neutralise any unsuspecting onlookers.

Club-goers that had populated the three-room nightclub complex at Minx were steadily vacating the premises as a line of taxicabs began to approach the curb awaiting passengers, instructions, abuse or a combination of all three. Jon appraised that approximately fifteen to twenty foot-long *Subway* subs could be placed in a straight line beginning from his exact position and ending at the foot of the nearest Minx patrons – a pair of brunette women in mini-skirts stumbling in stilettos as they prepared to wage war against any foe that could rain on their cab-hailing parade.

Jon's lascivious stare was interrupted by a bold and bright white text that flashed once before remaining static on the ATM's display screen.

BALANCE UNAVAILABLE AT THIS TIME.

It had appeared again.

Holy shit! What happened!?

Jon flailed his arms in a frantic collapse, instantly attributing the persistence of the automated message to his very first transfer and withdrawal.

They've suspended my account! I knew it!

Jon evaluated his alternatives as he braced for a consequence. The repercussions would have to wait; Jon had another more pressing matter to resolve: his wallet was as empty as the stomach of a Santa Monica vagrant. He needed to find a way to load up his lightweight leather wallet with a dollar... or fifty. And if he couldn't, a distance barely achievable by a long-distance *Boston Marathon* runner would be the immediate concomitant.

Let me try something, he pontificated, wanting nothing to do with an Allentown footslog. *What if I tried it again? Would it work?*

Jon did not want to contravene the ATM's terms of use, but at a juncture as merciless as this, any possible breach of conduct seemed more than equivocal. Had his actions warranted an account suspension? Or had he prematurely incriminated himself over something that did not actually ever occur?

Jon geared up for a second trial. He exited the cancellation screen and obeyed the new set of on-screen instructions, hitting the corresponding buttons that would command the machine to relocate twenty dollars from his credit card and into his savings account.

The automated teller machine scanned the requested command as it murmured belligerently this time around.

TRANSACTION CANCELLED.

The identical response flashed again in its familiar bold, red type as the machine discharged Jon's card, the plastic reflecting the glare off the piercing Pennsylvanian moonlight.

However, on this occasion, the cancellation message was not anywhere near as puzzling as it was anticipated. The process had repeated itself verbatim, Jon's eyebrows slanting as he awaited his cue to execute the succeeding action.

Jon ejected the plastic from the loosened grip of the magnetic card reader. So as not to divert from ritual, he brushed the jagged edges of the card with the inline of his fingers – first, his thumb and then his index finger, as he had done so before – and then used his mouth to blow a pocket of air onto the card's front and back surfaces before reinserting it into the card slot.

The moment of truth.

Jon hit the button that hovered beside the word 'SAVINGS' on the illuminated display as he froze like an undressed Eskimo, ceasing all bodily movements, cautiously waiting for the machine to process the account balance request.

BALANCE UNAVAILABLE AT THIS TIME.

To a scientific researcher conducting an experiment on psychology, the lab report would have been exceptionally underwhelming. The machine behaved *identically* as it had during Jon's first visit, somewhere between forty-seven and sixty-eight minutes earlier. The result had culminated into a singular, seminal diagnosis: that an appeal to his earlier mantra of stupefaction and uncertainty was his only play.

A swelling scruple jingled in and around his North Pole-made sweater. It seemed that inebriation was not the most apt of human conditions to discern such a strange and unexplainable set of circumstances. But through the howling winds and the burn of winter, Jon had no time to wait for sobriety's check-in. If it were answers he so desired, Jon was clearly poised for a far lengthier wait.

He hit the withdraw button on the ATM's keypad system and checked the pre-set button marked '$20'.

A second or four – or eight – chimed away as the ATM's commands were being authenticated before the machine slipped out a perfectly conditioned Jackson from the cash dispenser.

Holy shit. It did it again.

Jon forced his throat to swallow a whale of saliva as he swiped the bill from the clutches of the machine, admiring the viridescent paper like a golden nugget at the foot of a translucent rainbow.

What. Is. Going. On? I can't think; I need to rest.

Jon signalled in the direction of the Manhattan-esque cab-line outside of Minx's shadowed entranceway before magnetising the attention of a reactive driver.

"Heading to Coopersburg," he reported as he wriggled into the car's back seat and attempted – rather fruitlessly – to clip the belt's tongue into its buckle.

Not this trick again… he groaned in silence.

The driver complied, nodding amiably as his curly, oversized moustache twitched back at the woolly passenger in his rear view mirror. As he zoomed west, the driver snapped and shifted gears, hastening at a speed that disregarded the legal limit after determining that Jon's stench was quickly contaminating what clean air remained in circulation.

Jon was dog-tired. As he stared out the taxi window and watched the limbs of towering sycamores and shady oaks jerk and sway to the modulation of a heavy gust, he softened his eyelids and succumbed to their forceful retraction. Through the vehicle of cognitive remembrance, Jon relived the strange events that had occurred that evening at the automated teller machine on 17th Street.

And as the memory of an ejected fifty-dollar bill replayed at the very forefront of his mind, Jon faded into a heavy blackness.

5

SLEEPLESS IN PENNSYLVANIA

If the screeching cry from his galling alarm clock did not force a sudden recoil, she could.

"Jon, wake up," uttered an idyllic yet absolute voice by way of his bedside. "It's almost eleven."

Maya Ververs was the anti-banshee, her indelible whisper evoking an unbridled pleasure that was a far cry from the terror of a traditional howling spirit.

The soothing timbers in her command marshalled Jon to cram his cranium in a blender as it gyrated in a coup to regain its senses. He was still a little muzzy and this distraction outweighed his need for coherence, making the incoming message appear rather intelligible.

Maya flattened and then arranged her half of the bed linen, fluffing her flannelette pillows like choking flamingos as she smoothed each section of the sheeting.

"What time did you get in last night?" she asked, carefully avoiding a feather-ruffle. "I didn't hear you when you came to bed."

Jon grumbled beneath his breath as he wiped a drop of saliva from his dry lip.

"I'm not too sure," he admitted, stretching his arms as a yawn caused him to fumble his elocution. "Might have been two or three. I really can't remember."

"So you had a *bit* to drink, then, hey?" Maya probed as she sat upright beside him and dropped her unwrinkled hand on his bear chest.

"I mean, I guess. You know what those guys can be like, and they'd been breaking my balls for months. I didn't want to disappoint them."

Maya scoffed at his reasoning.

"Typical Jon Jinks," she snickered, slipping him beneath the bus of a flaw that had forever perturbed her. "Always the crowd pleaser."

"Hey!" he refuted. "That's how I won you over, right?"

"Whatever helps you sleep better at night, baby," she giggled, leaning forward as she tongued his upper lip before clamping the bottom with her sabre-tooth as if it were a delectably fine cut of butcher's meat. "Now get out of bed; I'm making you scrapple with apple butter and scrambled eggs on toast."

"You're too good to me, you know that?"

"Who said you were getting it for free?" Maya jabbed mischievously as she pounced from the bed mattress and jetted to the kitchen of their Tudor-style home.

The Jinks and Ververs residence drew parallels from that of the antiquated English cottages of the semi-gothic. The home, built from light brick and stucco – with decorative half timbers exposed on both its exterior and interior – was covered by a steeply pitched gable roof while rubblework masonry and long rows of casement windows underscored the property's dramatic influences. Its ceilings were lined in patterned drywall while an array of ornamented functional pieces acted as the hallmarks of the structure's ecclesiastical architecture.

Jon massaged the skin on his forehead in a continuous loop, a vain attempt to mitigate the swelling, numbing sensation.

What time did I actually get in last night?

Memories of the preceding hours were jumbled in his recollection like an unpacked *Scrabble* box. Everything mostly blurred in an elusive smog, except for a small insert in his cognitive memory.

Jonathan Jinks – almost absolutely unclothed had it not been for the dark boxer-briefs that supported his crotch – gingerly slid his body from the solace of the bed linen. As he shot upright, wobbling like *The Leaning Tower of Pisa* in a Pennsylvanian tempest, he stretched his arms outwards and then reached for a pair of trousers from a chest of drawers.

"So what'd *you* do last night?" he asked, sauntering towards the marble kitchen bench top before resting his backside on a stool.

"Oh, nothing," Maya replied as she paced around the kitchen like a *Masterchef* contestant, heedful not to burn her fingertips on the edges of the metal skillet. "After I paid the last of our bills, which, might I add, we're still behind in…"

"Jesus, more bills?" Jon brooded, juggling through the trash-pile on the kitchen bench.

"It's like we were *born* to pay them," she satirised and sighed.

"Anyway," Maya resumed, shooting the subject with a semi-automatic. "My night was filled with adventure… I fell asleep on the couch during a movie."

Jon was hardly in the mood to review the couple's oppressive monetary situation, either.

"What'd you watch?"

"What'd *I* watch? Well, *Sleepless in Seattle* actually watched me; ironic isn't it?"

Maya tittered winsomely as she raised and flicked her whisk in a concentric circle.

"Sounds like that's what I should've done. I feel like absolute shit right now."

"I'm not surprised," Maya admitted. "You smelt like a little bit of everything when I woke up this morning."

Jon inhaled his own scent as he deliberated over the existence of Maya's G-rated accusation.

"Yes, babe," Maya asserted. "I can still smell it."

"I'd shower now, but that'd mean I'd miss out on this amazing freaking breakfast you're cooking up here."

"Yeah, yeah, you're excused."

As Maya systematically set cutlery and plates for two, Jon ambled around the marble and towards the stainless steel fridge, removing a carton of grape juice before spotting it on the kitchen counter.

"You know, the strangest thing happened to me last night," Jon recounted as he poured the contents of the carton into a highball glass.

"You mean besides the fact that you wandered around a nightclub in the freezing cold at a time when normally, you're passed out on the couch?"

Jon retraced his steps as he attempted to distinguish between actuality and fantasy.

How much of this can I actually even tell her?

"Well that, *of course*; but I had this really *weird* experience at an ATM," he divulged as he systematised his thoughts like a postal worker tracking and sorting through piles of zip codes and delivery addresses. "You ever had any issues withdrawing money before?"

"From an ATM? I don't think so… I mean, there was this one time where it wouldn't read my card and just kept spitting the thing out but that was more of a problem with my card, I think. Why? What happened?"

Great question.

"Honestly… I'm really not sure," he admitted. "I ran out of cash…"

Maya stumbled and stopped like a speeding truck at a school

crossing, evidently alarmed by the 'Jon And Maya's Financial Review' newsflash.

"…So I went to the ATM on 17th to withdraw a fifty but the damn thing declined my transaction. Turns out I forgot to move some money around last week and I was left with like eight-dollars in my account."

Jon narrated the anecdote in a measured prose as Maya struggled to keep up. He conjured a mental checklist, ticking each box with every expression to make certain each detail was veracious in nature.

"So I tried to transfer fifty-dollars from my credit account," he continued as he scrambled to recount each chess-move. "And then…"

Jon slammed the breaks as he scrunched the wrinkles on his forehead.

"Or did I?" he back-pedalled, his brain now grinding like a grandfather clock on cocaine.

Maya's expression indicated a similar hesitancy.

"Babe…?"

A silence trembled.

"Maya!" Jon blurted after an apparent epiphany forced an unnatural spray of verbiage. "Save that breakfast for me, I'll be back in a second."

Shit. I need an excuse. I have to get back to that ATM.

Jon scurried towards the bedroom, seeking an upper garment and a pair of shoes as Maya mimicked his footsteps, evidently bothered by his change in behaviour.

"What do you mean you'll be back in a second? What's wrong? Did something happen?"

"Nothing's wrong, I promise; I just need to head out to pick up some supplies and I'll explain everything when I'm back," he lied as Maya's focus jumped towards the walk-in wardrobe, its metal clothes hangers affixing a contingent of suspended paint tubes, brushes and other assorted materials from the hooks of its wires.

Jon sensed that his exposition would not suffice as he sought a more intelligible explanation.

"And *also*," he continued as if he had planned to all along. "I honestly can't remember what happened to my money last night and if something went wrong, I need to find out."

His stomach murmuring, he jetted back to the kitchen to slice out a piece of freshly fried Pon Haus before digesting the appetising dish in a guzzling mouthful.

"Absolutely delicious as always, Maya. Love you," he praised his lover-turned-chef as he licked the dripping oil from the ends of his fingers and planted a soft kiss atop her forehead. "Charge me double if you have to."

It was as if Maya were the victim of a cruel daytime television prank as she hobbled after him, her toes fumbling in her slippers. Something wasn't right; this wasn't the conventional Sunday morning she had grown accustomed to.

"Are you going to the bank? Or are you going to the art store?" she probed as she tried to decode whatever she could from Jon's ambivalence. "You know that they're not open on Sundays, right? The bank, that is. Why don't you just call them instead?"

Jon, apparently with welding wax drummed in both ears, swiped the car keys from a side table by the hallway mirror as a he tip-toed on the damp concrete outside and towards the four-door station wagon parked in the driveway.

Before the sensation of a sharp, thin chill could penetrate Maya's fragile skin, a vacuum of engine exhaust gas had already begun to form a dissipating trail away from the moving vehicle as it navigated speedily towards downtown Allentown.

"Jon!" she shouted hopelessly from the upper step of the wide-open

Tudor-style door. "You need a freaking shower!"

But it was too late. Jon was already long gone.

* * *

Thump!

The door slammed shut behind her with the force of a lightning bolt launched by a mythical Greek god. She shook the cold off her shoulders before dripping her fingers in a running funnel of warm water by the kitchen sink. Maya pressed her eyelids together, reflecting in a silent meditation over what had eventuated. His actions were unexplainable, his demeanour uncharacteristic.

Jonathan Jinks had disappeared like an incarnated phantom on return to the Promised Land, bathing in a glass tub of milk and honey as he left behind a trail of stupefaction and oblivion.

Everything seemed out of place, yet she knew that she had to retrace his steps in order to find some answers. She crept through the elongated hallway, bypassing the limestone fireplace en route to the couple's bedroom.

Jon's behaviour was certainly abnormal, but the configuration of the room suggested that at least one characteristic had remained unchanged. Deep in the pocket of the empty room, a scribbled matte-white notepad beside a drying paintbrush offered a state of marginal calm. Inscribed in fine cerulean blue brush strokes, an expression accompanied by a familiar illustration could be spotted from even the furthest of distances. As she ambled closer to the edging of the bedside table, she raised the notepad to eye-level and began to read.

I exist in two places. Here, and where you are. Don't worry.

A single-tone sketch of the Earth and a coloured heart succeeded the text. Maya did not need to repress her smile; at least, of course, until

Jon had returned. And although he was not present, Jon could not quite be ascribed for the originality of such incandescent wordplay. What was patently misconstrued as an expression of love was in fact, a daring passage from a more melancholy poem.

I did not become a tree or a constellation/

I became a winter coat the children thought they saw on the street corner/

I became this illusion, this trick of ventriloquism/

This blind noun, this bandage crumped at your dream's edge/

Jon had stumbled across the passage in an art class, adding the excerpt to a binder folder penned under the category of 'artistic inspiration.' But from this day forth, its message – deceiving in its ultimate meaning – would illuminate a far more prophetic warning.

Pray for me… Not as I am, but as I am.

6
PINNED 3.0

INSERT YOUR CARD.

ENTER YOUR PIN.

Jon had been here before, that much he *could* vouch for.

He checked the time on his smartphone before holding down the device's power button until a black reflection faded in: 11:57 am - 2% battery remaining.

Looks like that breakfast is going to become lunch.

A narrow crevice of sunlight battled to penetrate its beam through the crowded cloud while droplets of precipitation continued their intermittent descent through the Earth's gravitational maze.

A man – clothed from head-to-toe and protected by the shade of a patterned umbrella – walked his Yorkshire Terrier behind him, his scruffy canine sniffing and grunting at his trousers. Suddenly, Jon was very aware of two mortifying actualities: he *still* reeked… and now the rest of Allentown knew it, too.

Jon's eyes followed the wagging tail as the pooch – pounding at its paws and hastening the footsteps of its companion – leered back at him and groaned in revulsion.

Jon angled his head back towards the ATM. As he turned at the shoulders, a familiar and recognisable article flattened up against the side of the asphalt stole his attention like a golden ticket to *Willy Wonka's* chocolate factory.

It was the remains of a levelled, empty soda can.

A recollection he *could* remember.

After loading the plastic debit card in the rigid insert of the machine's card reader, he pressed the button on the ATM's control pad that commanded a balance request on his linked credit account.

6174.

The ATM did its thing, displaying an indexed list of deposit and withdrawal transactions on its weatherproof screen. He sorted through each withdrawal, eliminating – one at a time like an assassin with a long list of outstanding debts – every transaction he could verify.

Jon pointed and then pressed the tip of his index finger against the surface of the grubby display screen, sliding its position upwards as he crossed off each entry that dated back by at least a fortnight.

Until he arrived at yesterday's date.

Yesterday's date: the post-apocalyptic beginning of a spooky 17th Street parallelism. Somehow, the information overview screen that documented a chronological pattern of credit card spending indicated no such transfer activity.

Hang on a minute, Jon thought. *Of course! The bank's closed today – they're not going to have recorded any of my transactions just yet... right?*

Jon exhaled in a smoky sigh of relief as the wind's chill transformed the moisture in his breath into a foggy cloud of vapour.

If Jon had been feeling any kind of contrition, it appeared as if this could now be rectified through the handy implications made by the ATM's transaction records.

Jon fiddled with the zippers on his jacket pocket before navigating the ATM back to its primary start-up menu screen. You could say that he was about as content as an equally loved and loathed pair of neon-coloured *Crocs*; convinced by his own standards, even. But Jon's persistent, earnest nature wasn't buying the bandwagon routine. With the scent of scrapple thumb-printed against his nasal, Jon decided that he *had* to be politic.

And that meant cross-examining the accomplice of his alleged misdemeanour: his savings account.

SELECT YOUR ACCOUNT the machine's command prompt burped, drawing yet another skittish snort from its operator.

Once again, he commanded – with the weight of his magical money-mongering fingers – the machine to blurt out a calculated balance request on his savings account as he waited heedfully.

Come on, just give me a balance... just give me a balance!

This time around, the ATM *did* deliver a *numerical* figure.

But it wasn't the kind that Jon was hoping for.

ACCOUNT BALANCE: $-62

WHAT THE F...!? Negative sixty-two!?

A drowning panic ensued as the trepidation he had fought to suppress emerged as a conquering, preeminent warrior.

With a deep breath – or eleven – and the mental hypnotics of coercive persuasion, his consternations were tamed as he paused, dedicating a frozen moment to reflect on the evolving playing field.

Apparent was the need to employ a state of calm.

Jon suspected that this outcome did, in fact, make *some kind* of logical sense. Somewhere around twelve-or-so hours ago, Jon's savings account had registered a figure of eight dollars. After two consecutive withdrawals of fifty-dollars and twenty-dollars respectively, Jon channelled his inner-Archimedes to calculate that a deduction of the integers of twenty and fifty – which, of course, for those that could not find the light at the end of the first grade mathematical tunnel, combined to equal seventy – from the pre-existing amount of eight dollars equalled minus sixty-two.

But why, exactly, this particular equation had even occurred was a mystery worthy of a forty-minute *Twin Peaks* special.

So wait? My account isn't suspended? My balance is back?

Jon brooded over the upshot, twitching his fingers in agitation as he stared intensely at the diabolical display screen. What seemed at least marginally ostensible was that the machine's cryptoprocessor had accused Jon of involuntarily overdrawing his own account. But given that the *very same* ATM could not verify the existence of an outstanding transfer transaction on his *MasterCard* summary, something about this 'Stephen-Hawking-would-be-disappointed' theory did not quite compute.

If I transferred seventy-dollars from my credit card account, my savings account should have been seventy-eight-dollars in credit at the time I made the withdrawal. Doesn't that mean that I should have been left with the eight-dollars I started with after I took the money out?

Despite mathematics not being Jon's forte, his hypothesis seemed plausible. If the bank had not recorded the transaction on his *MasterCard* account, why had the balance been altered on his savings account?

In any case, if any violation *had* occurred, it seemed to be one deemed under the category of a minor offense; an accidental act of misconduct by which exoneration would be granted by the bank's governing body. At worst, Jon surmised that an adequate repayment penalty to recompense the missing funds might be the necessary course of action.

But all this, of course, hinged on Jon's admirable rectitude and his ability to declare these strange happenings to a banking representative.

As Jon removed his card from the ATM's insert, he pondered over the severity awarded to the man wearing his sneakers. What was expected of him next under such a rare culmination of events? The trivial answer, right or wrong, was reserved deep in the fissures of his abdomen.

There was a plate of sliced scrapple about nine miles south with his name on it. Anything else could wait until after his starvation had subsided.

And besides, the bank was closed on Sundays, anyway.

* * *

Discount drug stores lined 17th Street with the frequency of Douglas Firs on a wintery Christmas tree farm.

All Jon had to do was to take his pick.

Now I gotta get something. Need a distraction.

A haze of irony forged an interconnecting link between him and the '17th Street Daily Discount Drug Store,' Jon's consciousness feeling adversely vitiated by the mind-morphing effects of an illicit substance he was certain he had never consumed.

"Welcome, sir," the sales attendant greeted, her hands wandering in a pool of banknotes as she locked the cash register in place.

Jon offered a lukewarm smile, his senses distracted by the bewitching scent of a burning soy candle.

"Paint supplies?" he croaked diffidently, halfway between a question and the early beginnings of a statement.

"Ugh, yes, sir," the attendant responded as she shook on her eyewear and signalled with her index finger. "Down aisle three, sir, against the back shelves."

Jon expressed his gratitude as he slithered – his sneakers sweeping the floor dust like a wet mop on a mission – by shelves of Taiwanese replica sculptures and down a narrow passageway.

Their range was limited, tawdry and overpriced and offered little variety for any heavyweight artisan.

But the moment did not call for Jon to wield his virtuous hand of craftsmanship; something, anything would have to suffice.

"Something I can help you with, sir?" the four-eyed assistant uttered, startling him from behind as if she had followed him on a leash.

Jon rummaged through the selection before him using nothing more than his ocular senses in a process of elimination.

"I'm looking for a different kind of canvas piece. Something I can paint on that can add *character* to my work?"

The sales attended pressed her fingers against her lips as she scanned the products with her reading glasses.

"What about something like this?" she suggested, reaching over to unhook a white but not so plain plastic mask from above a sales shelf. "Kids normally use it for school projects. You know, art classes and the like. But they're totally versatile and extremely flexible."

She handed the blank mask into Jon's open palm as he read the brief documentation outlined on the product's navy description tag.

White matte crafter designer PVC mask, 9.75". Full-face coverage with moulded moustache and white elastic band.

"As you can see, this one's got this added detail right here, which can be used for illustrating protrusions and stuff," she peddled, eyeing off a measly commission as she ran her index finger atop the bulging indent of facial hair. "Or, you can just leave it how it is if you're planning on dressing up as Rich Uncle Pennybags for Halloween this year."

The sales attendant tittered but drew a stare from her customer as blank as the very plastic mask before her.

"Rich Uncle Pennybags?"

"You know, with the top hat and the cane and the moustache," she elucidated, piling together a pack of unhelpful clues. "You *don't* know... The *Monopoly* guy!"

Wait, what? Since when did he have a name?

Jon was about ready to convince himself that he was under some kind of psychedelic spell as he bobbed his head around the drug store like a pigeon on methamphetamine.

First the ATM tells me I owe money on my savings account and now the Monopoly man has a name. It's true: the world really has gone bananas.

"Oh, I'm so sorry," Jon apologised, immediately connecting the dots upon a second examination. "You're right, it definitely does look similar."

"You know *Monopoly* was actually invented here, right?" the attendant apprised as if she were reciting answers from a pop quiz. "Well not *here*, here, exactly, but still in Pennsylvania."

"Fascinating," Jon mumbled passively as he scoured the mask like a hawk to a squirrel.

"Yeah! I remember reading something about it a few months ago; something about this struggling salesman from Germantown who was inspired by this ancient board game that taught you how to cheat on your taxes."

The sales clerk was partially correct but wholly ironic as she mulled at the intersecting parallels of a struggling sales attendant looking for a brighter tomorrow. Originally designed by Elizabeth J. Magie Phillips in 1907, *The Landlord's Game* was a patented board game in which property values and rent collection were the key components for its thrilled player. But through the white magic of creative and innovative amelioration, Pennsylvania's own Charles Darrow evolved – or, as some fanatics would often argue, *stole* – what was originally conceived as a board game for economic aristocrats into a globally recognised pastime with the kind of unforeseen reach of a *Game of Thrones* fan base.

Jon rushed the mask against his frozen face as if he were re-enacting a scene from Jim Carrey's *The Mask* in an accelerated time-lapse.

"How do I look?" Jon muttered inaudibly, his voice muffling against the dense plastic of the facemask.

"Just like Rich Uncle Pennybags," the assistant flattered, stroking at an embryonic ego that Jonathan Jinks never knew existed.

7

HOME IS WHERE THE SCRAPPLE IS

A grave and spontaneous questionnaire beckoned as Jon's foot throttled to the floor, racing like a rally driver for his Coopersburg home. The four-door station wagon – pit stops included – clocked in for a total lap time of just over two hours, his body yearning for a disinfecting sponge and a spoonful of scrapple with each ticking digit.

Jon swung the vehicle and parked it on the sloping driveway. He fidgeted with his keys for a moment as he activated the locking mechanism, brushed his shoulders off and sauntered up the final four steps before the front door.

Jon had some explaining to do and boy, did he know it. It was as if he had just finished a round of hide-and-seek with the *Bananas in Pyjamas,* catching Maya unawares with a heedless and groundless disappearance. But in a haste of persuasive calculation, Jon was able to conjure up a story with far more plausibility than a banal 'dog-ate-my-homework' excuse.

"Got it!" Jonny roared, bursting through the front door of their Tudor-style home in a grand yet equally exasperating entrance. "Now just imagine it full of colour, like an American capitalist version of the Carnival of Venice, you know?"

Jon suctioned the plastic mask against his face with both hands as if a jovially non-verbal 'ta-da' would follow, this time deriving not nearly the same kind of reaction as before.

Maya appeared blankly inscrutable, her arms criss-crossed like threaded wire as she tried not to blink.

"Okay, okay," he conceded, detaching the mask from his skin as he placed it atop the side table. "So I think the banking system malfunctioned when I was getting cash out last night."

Jon decompressed and released an injection of candour as Maya's incredulous leer suggested that his sideshow distraction was an implausible motive for a not-so-magical disappearance.

"So you burst out of here, half-naked, without saying where you're going," she scolded, venturing on an isolated tangent. "You didn't even answer my phone calls – so what? You switched your cell off?"

Jon removed the cell phone from his left pocket, its blackened display screen refusing to illuminate at the push of its home button.

"Ugh, shit, my stupid phone died. And half-naked? What are you talking about? I put a coat on!" Jon snapped, his voice shifting from the timbre of a fluffy panda to that of a fearsome dragon.

"Is that really the only point you took from what I just said? Forget the coat – why'd you do that, Jon?"

Maya's tone twisted from vexation to desolation. After more than four years of companionship, Maya had never experienced an episode quite as unusual as this. And while Jon's behaviour *was* unprecedented, such an erratic change in conduct seemed a clear cause for concern; one in which Maya now coveted *any* kind of explanation for.

"You've never kept anything from me before, let alone walked out on me like that," she said, relinquishing her arms from their interwoven position as she stepped forward and into Jon's cloaked circle. "And to feel as if you needed to come up with that ridiculous excuse as to why you had to leave…"

Maya waved towards the lifeless plastic mask resting desolately on the side table, its elastic drooping off the edges in a sliding diagonal.

"Maya, I know, I'm sorry," he apologised. "I'm not going to lie to you – I'm still a little hung over from last night."

"So why'd you drive, then?"

Jon softened his gaze as he began to think like a courtroom suspect without a lawyer.

"One issue at a time, Maya, please. Listen, the reason I didn't tell you where I was going was because I didn't really *know* where I was going myself."

Maya squinted, her ponytail drooping as she searched Jon's eyes for a hidden and sound reasoning.

"I wasn't thinking straight this morning and I know that was totally not like me to just up and leave like that. I don't know what came over me – I'm truly sorry if I upset you."

A pause ensued as both parties bounced off their suggestive bodies in an attempt to level their emotions.

"Okay," she pardoned, sniffling before cleaning a trickle of snot with the back of her hand. "But don't do anything like that again, okay?"

Maya offered a playful bop on the shoulder as she hinted at a quirky forgiveness.

"Now, do you want to tell me what *actually* happened?"

The couple congregated in the kitchen, Jon taking up a whole episode of *The Bold and the Beautiful* to divulge near every detail of his 17th Street experience over an improvised brunch. He chronicled his encounters with the Nations of Jefferson American Bank automated teller machine and how the ATM's internal computer had incorrectly computed each of his transfers and subsequent withdrawals.

"So I don't get it?" Maya admitted, the information overloading her brain. "If you transferred seventy-dollars from your credit account, doesn't that mean that you should have been left with the eight-dollars you had originally when you first made the withdrawal?"

"That's exactly what I said!" Jon cried, pleased that he was not plummeting into a floorless well of insanity. "So given that my account balance says it's owing money, does that mean I've just overdrawn my account? Like a standard line of credit?"

"Well, I guess," Maya surmised. "But I've never seen anything like that before. You can overdraw your credit balance but your own funds? I don't even know if that's possible. Maybe we should just go down to the bank and get it all sorted out just in case?"

It seemed that Maya had forgotten the very informative-counsel she had provided Jon with earlier.

"Did you forget what day it was?"

"Oh, fuck!" Maya cursed, her memory clicking into gear as she shoved Jon's ATM anecdote into a separate bucket of internal memory. "Well just make sure you go in first thing tomorrow morning, then."

Jon gasped like a child who had just overheard his mother curse for the first time.

"We're gonna have to censor you, girl. It's God's day today, remember?"

Like Jonathan Jinks, Maya Ververs was raised a devout Catholic and consequently, any disinclination to attend Sunday morning mass was met with an unyielding admonishment from her immigrant father. But having extricated herself from the rigours of his austere governance, Maya was hardly as disposed to engage in acts of piety unless a grim calamity called for her attendance.

"Well, he's going to be pretty pissed we didn't go to church this morning then, isn't he?" she jested in return.

"Don't worry, we'll just tell him I was hung-over. That's not a sin, right?"

"Well, the bible says 'drink your wine with a merry of heart,'" Maya preached as she quoted a passage from the Psalms. "Besides, Jesus drank wine like all the time so who is *God* to say otherwise?"

The pair tittered as they sipped from their grape juice-filled glasses and returned to their forks.

"So what's on TV?" Jon asked, his mouth full as he reached across the bench for the universal remote.

"Ugh, what the..." he grumbled, shaking the unresponsive controller like a rag doll. "Maya, we got any batteries? I think this remote is dead."

Maya reached for the top shelf of her wooden kitchen cupboard, sorting her fingers through an assembly of articles.

"Sorry, hun, we're out. Can you just operate it from the box for now?"

Jon shrouded his displeasures.

"Sure."

He pressed on the box's hard buttons to scan through the digital channel guide before selecting one from the entertainment classification.

"At the Nations of Jefferson American Bank, we *know* America," boomed a sonorous voiceover artist during a commercial break, his baritone voice trembling the television speakers as an animated graphic advertisement of the financial conglomerate's logo flashed before the screen. "... The Nations of Jefferson American Bank: where the world is at your fingertips and our bank in the palm of your hand."

Jon continued to sort through the channels categorically, scrolling between action movies and sports featurettes before his desultory surfing landed on a peculiar programme airing on the *History Channel*.

Narrated by a British broadcaster whose accent bore a striking resemblance to David Attenborough – the only British television personality that Jon recognised – the documentary flashed a contingent of not-so-PG-13 visuals across the screen that explored demonic, female nymphomaniacs as depicted by century-old sculptures and oil-painted canvases.

"According to medieval legend, the succubus – a demon in female form – would often appear during its victim's dream state, taking the form of a seductive temptress in order to fulfil her sexual desires," the narrator elucidated to a gothic score as the on-screen content interchanged between John Collier's *Lilith* and Henry Fuseli's *The Nightmare* in an attempt to provide context. "The succubus – once only known to have copulated with the sleeping and unsuspecting male – now assimilates the hyper-sexualised female and the hyper-empowered predatory state. She is a captivating enchantress, capable of the kinds of wickedness only disguised by her obvious beauty."

Jon's fascination with the arts made the occult documentary a popcorn-worthy experience as he leant back and absorbed the footage in awe.

"Hey!" Maya interjected, midway through a swallow. "Can you put it back on *Pretty Woman* or something? It's way too early to be watching this kind of shit."

"Again?" Jon sighed. "We watched it last weekend. Don't you ever get tired of gawking at Richard Gere, the ass?"

"Do you ever get tired of gawking at Julia Roberts' ass?"

"Touché," he commended.

This was the kind of banter that Jon thrived upon as he drew on the dichotomy between his Sunday morning and Saturday evening exchanges.

Whatever. I can catch the rerun, I suppose, he considered as he switched the channel.

"Hey baby, what's your name?" he smirked, mimicking in suave

Edward Lewis vernacular, moments before the suggestive scene played out on screen.

Maya tingled, engendered by the remark as she swallowed her scrapple and joined the role-play.

"What do you want it to be?" she charmed in character, offering the kind of irresistibly sultry gaze that reeled Jon in like a freshwater squid to rod-bait.

Jon was far from certain that his actions had been pardoned and Maya was hardly sure that she had given any credence to his explanation.

But irrespective of theses lingering suppositions, their Sunday would recommence beside a make-believe ignorance, with sixty-or-so-minutes of uncensored, unrivalled fornication.

* * *

The sun had dawned and the moon was alight well before Jon and Maya crowned their carnal crescendo in a euphoric discharge. Their physical bodies convened as one, their souls conjoined as another as they exhaled heavily and caressed in each other's arms.

"That was…" Maya panted breathlessly. "…Amazing."

Jon rubbed her fingers and planted a kiss on her forehead.

"Hold out your hand for a minute," he whispered, as if stunned by an unforseen epiphany.

Maya sat upright, lending her hand to her beloved as Jon reached across his side-table, holding the stems of the bed sheet across his crotch with the other. With a single hand, he squeezed the sides of a cerulean blue acrylic paint tube into a dried plastic tub before collecting a pointed-round paintbrush and dipping its bristles in a splotch of acrylic.

"What are you doing?" she asked in anticipation.

"Just watch."

Jon rotated her palm, ensuring its backside was facing the sky-high ceiling as he cushioned the underside of her fingers for support. He waved the paintbrush by the handle before touching the tip of the brush's bristles against her silken skin.

"It's cold!" she squealed as Jon's silent giggle broke his momentum.

"He carries stars in his pockets…" he began to dictate, stroking the brush against her skin in synch with each spoken word. "…Because he knows she fears the dark…"

Jon's words were tranquil, his soft murmurs sending Maya into an exotic trance.

"…Whenever sadness pays a visit…" he continued, dipping his shoestring thin brush in the exposed acrylic. "… He paints galaxies on the back of her hands."

Jon blew a warm vacuum of air atop her hand, drying the crumbling paint in the process. Aligned like a Milky Way across her skin, the backside of Maya's hand was covered in an acrylic galaxy, sparkling and twinkling like a cluster of wishing stars on a hopeless night.

Maya Ververs stared at her painting before gazing back at Jon in perpetual wonder, her eyes illuminating with the twinkling reflection of a hundred blue-tinted stars.

8
PINNED 4.0

Jon seldom saw the moon through the crisp, Allentown fog on a Sunday. His exhaustion had returned, a gaping yawn escaping his dry lips as if he were forging smoky shapes from the exhaling of tobacco. Smells of pitch pine and fig cluttered his nostrils as he wiped a line of mucus from the tip of his nose.

How, in God's name, am I back here... again?

Jon's dream-machine would have to wait; his mind unyieldingly opposed to the soft tissue of a bedroom pillow until it could learn more. Was his conscience wrapped in a scrapple-filled sandwich of sin, or perhaps it was a compulsion, a fascination with the unfamiliar that gravitated him back to the automated teller machine on 17th Street?

A Sunday loaded with food, film and copulation had enervated the pair. Jon and Maya's vitality had been sapped, the warmth of their flannelette bed sheets acting as a rejuvenation chamber as the pair snored their way through the six o'clock sunset.

Maya – dormant like a hibernating bear in the wintertime – would not wake up until *at least* sunrise. But after catnapping through a period of snuggle and separation, Jon was not feeling quite as tranquil.

A distracting qualm floated within his organs, contaminating the very memory chip assigned to recall the details of the dubious ATM episode. Despite inconclusive conjecture, Jon had refrained from an admission of bother, slamming the lid shut on any such perusing that might have suggested otherwise.

But it nibbled at his insides like a starving lab rat to a leftover plate of Pon Haus. He dared not discuss it with Maya, but he *needed* something unassailable.

So, at the very juncture he could determine that not even the slightest of movements could wake his sleeping beauty, he rose from the cushioned mattress, dressed himself in silence and ignited the station wagon in preparation for the short voyage to 17th Street.

Jon angled his head forward, his eyes firmly gauged on the screen of the automated machine as its glaring reflection lit up Jon's face like a scary storyteller at a teenage campfire.

The self-adjudicated could begin... *almost.*

Jon whipped at the shoulders, suspending his movement as he poised and faced the direction where he last observed the tin-carvings of a levelled can of soda. The emptied can – having apparently accelerated its way through its artificial life cycle – was nowhere to be found.

We live. We die.

Jon snorted beneath his breath, his attention now firmly re-screwed on the automated teller machine on 17th Street, Allentown.

His intentions were steadfast, clearer than a cut of fine crystal. Jon demanded an explanation, a reason to dissolve the tennis ball of numbness lodged in his throat. And so it became his obligatory duty to re-enact the experience verbatim, hankering for a godly sign that could suggest that a singular, unrepeatable phenomenon had occurred at the ATM on 17th Street, twenty-four hours earlier.

WHAT DO YOU WANT TO DO? the machine asked as Jon's legs rocked from a chilling breeze and the distant cry of a howling wolf.

Well, we've certainly done this before.

Like a *Playstation* racer thirsting to conquer a personal best, Jon mimicked a ghosting that emanated from his very recent past as he slapped the transfer button on his *MasterCard* account. He pushed the corresponding buttons on the machine's hard-pad that would direct one-hundred-dollars – this time, a more sizable value of currency for good measure – into his savings account.

The ATM's internal computer murmured in a familiar grumble. It seemed belligerent – well, about as belligerent as any automated machine could be – as it processed the request in umbrage.

And then, just as it had done before, the machine's cryptoprocessor reached yet another gavel-toting verdict.

TRANSACTION CANCELLED.

The message flashed in a large, bold, bright red font as it spat out Jon's plastic card in antipathy.

Wow. Here we go again.

This time, Jon was not nearly as surprised as he was overwrought by the concordant result. It was time to play a game of red-faced charades. He ejected the plastic from the loosened grip of the magnetic card reader and brushed its jagged edges with the inline of his fingers, using his mouth to blow a current of air – *Nintendo*-style, once again – onto its surface before reinserting it.

So what did I do next, then?

He only needed a moment to muse before visions of a bold and bright white text flashing on an illuminated display screen lit up like a slot machine reel in his cerebral cortex.

While the faulty nearby streetlight provided a temporary fluorescence that only narrowly intersected his eye-line, murky splotches of shadowing and blackness suggested that Jon was in the thick of a crime thriller without a safeguard.

WHAT DO YOU WANT TO DO? The machine asked again with the kind of repeatable persistence that personified the smugness of a taunting schoolyard bully.

With little equivocation, Jon thumped the buttons on the ATM's control pad that would instruct the machine to deliver an account balance reading on his savings account.

BALANCE UNAVAILABLE AT THIS TIME.

Jon gasped. It was no longer the sleepy hours of a dark and icy Sunday morning and yet still, there existed no divergence by way of interaction with the baffling 17th Street ATM. The machine behaved homogenously – just as it had during each of his previous visits – and as such, Jon now stood face-to-face with a lucky dip of unanswerable questions.

A light funnel of rainfall began its nosedive from the clouds above as drops of precipitation – like falling bullets in a battlefield – gently struck Jon's shoulder blades before trickling down to his pants and onwards towards the street's drainage system creating a narrow rivulet.

Jon had committed to a strict step-by-step program without deviation but the variables had flipped on him once again. He *needed* answers and a 'play-by-the-rules' approach wasn't going to cut it. In order to appraise the machine's volatile and abnormal operations, the stakes would need to be raised.

Jon forcefully repeated the process not once, but five times over as he attempted to transfer a pentad of one-hundred-digital-dollars from his credit card to his savings account. With each transfer command, the computer's internal processor offered a mundane murmur – an audible signal that appeared to act as a precursory cue – before presenting a *TRANSACTION CANCELLED* message in bright red.

Okay, so if I've done this correctly, my savings account is going to be six hundred dollars in credit. Either that, or I've just given myself a pretty hefty credit bill

Jon suspected that if he were to truly decipher the ATM's constant foray of curveballs, he had to reconstruct his approach. On this, his fourth visit in less than a day – a computation that had him feeling a little like God in Genesis – Jon Jinks elected *not* to withdraw any of his vanishing cash transfer. Instead, he opted for a more tangible solution.

He churned at the uvula, battling to swallow through a drop of semi-dried saliva as he tightened the scarf around his goose pimpled neck and ejected the card from the insert slot.

As he made for the driver's side of his burgundy four-door station wagon – parked solitarily, as if it were a getaway vehicle, along the adjacent curb – he halted and performed a swinging one-hundred-and-eighty degree turn to stare down the temptation of the machine's cash dispenser.

Should I just do it? he pondered as his mind messed with its orchestration.

Jon had spent a lifetime repudiating the devil of temptation and true to his Jinks ancestry, he'd built a reputation on the very values of integrity and virtuousness.

Jon's father – the venerable Gordon Jinks – had once preached that the Bible itself had foiled with the idea that 'temptation was the work of the Devil, in his attempts to drag one to Hell.' Jon figured that the man above had been weaving his web, pulling his strings to create a catalytic domino of opportunities for him to fortify his faith.

This was not an inclination to sin. This was a test.

And Jon was certain he could pass.

Besides, Jon had very little desire to visit the netherworld; he was more than congenial tucked away in his two-bedroom Tudor-style home in Pennsylvanian suburbia.

9

THE PENNSYLVANIA PAINT CO.

Historically, the painter was responsible for the mixing of paints, keeping a ready supply of pigments, oils, thinners and driers for the privileged one-per cent of medieval society. The painter would use his expertise to determine a suitable mixture, ultimately dictated by the autocratic head of a *Westeros*-styled throne.

The evolution of the painter was sluggish, barely outracing the likes of political correctness and flippant racism. And while the demands of qualified craftsmen *had* eventually mushroomed into a functional, everyday profession, one variable remained unchanged: one-way or another, everything was *always* dictated by a modern-day Joffrey Baratheon.

"So let me pose this question to you," Chief Executive Officer Gerry McDaniels hollered as he leered at the Monday-morning faces drooped around the wood grained, Laminex-shielded table. "How do *we*, as a cooperative team of labourers and painters, prevent the ship from sinking and ensure that we acquire a list of contracts that can keep *us* profitable and *you* employed?"

McDaniels' self-penned 'Motivation 101' chapter opened the door for a thought-provoking pause as he granted his squadron a second for deliberation. A business once galvanised by its empirical goodwill was now in jeopardy, its commercial vitality seemingly as decrepit as the brittle, grey hairs on the scalp of its founder.

McDaniels dangled the daunting prospect of a unified severance by a threatening thread, pooling together his team of finger-painters-by-birth in a motivational attempt to brainstorm a last-ditch marketing strategy. What he had asked of his subordinates was not written under their contractual obligations, but it appeared that an ultimatum of this severity was the only hand he had left to play.

"Well," he interrupted. "Anyone aware of any opportunities out there at the moment? C'mon, y'all, we're talking about six degrees of separation here; there's got to be something big out there for us to catch?"

The boss did all he could to convey his closing remarks with more conviction than Steve Jobs at an *Apple* event. McDaniels waved towards a company history and portfolio slideshow that beamed against a white projection screen as Jonathan Jinks – seated silently alongside over twenty of his peers – studied the information on display like a *Harvard* student.

Jon belonged to the very rudimentary foundation of the business' hierarchy, predominately having executed the labour-intensive tasks of scraping, sanding, patching holes in drywall, masking preventative surfaces and applying paint coats.

But unbeknownst to him, he was about to be handed the most seminal task of his career. He was about to reach the precipice of transformation, the stepping-stone of graduation with a master's degree in 'single-handed fortification of a spiralling business'.

"I want everyone to head back to the office," commanded the moustached McDaniels, ordering his team to return to their superfluous working quarters that only compounded their growing expenses. "…And make some phone calls, do some research online; do whatever you have to do to get your foot and your goddam paint brush in the door somewhere!"

The team of twenty-plus – dripping from head-to-toe in sweat, paint and handyman work-wear – relieved their posts as they scurried like mice to a cheese trap for the meeting room's timber-framed doorway.

"Jinks," McDaniels signalled beneath his breath – and his food-catching moustache – as he waited for the room to vacate. "Stick around for a second, son."

McDaniels' directive was nurturing and tender, a certain shift in tonal expression from that of his presentation.

"Everything going okay, kid?" the boss encouraged, sensing a change in the status quo.

"Better than my old man at this point in his career, I guess."

"Listen... How's your dad going, anyway? I haven't spoken to him for a few months now."

"You and me both," he divulged, seizing the transmission of a hundred inner-demons. "From what my sister tells me, he's doing okay. Apparently mum's got him doing grocery shopping every three days."

"He hates that, I bet?"

"Well, what can I say... karma, even in its most minor of forms, is a son of a bitch."

Gerry and Jon snickered in unison as they basked in Gordon's vapid retirement.

Gerry McDaniels and Gordon Jinks shook hands for the first time in Harry Weinstein's recruitment factory, the dynamic duo primed to be a couple of consequential cogs in Weinstein's amusement park machine from the very outset. But just over a decade later, McDaniels' disbandment and subsequent exile from *Dunney's* senior development team had distanced their bond, limiting Gordon and McDaniels to a seldom, biannual phone call at best.

"Listen, Jon," McDaniels drifted as a twang of professional linguistics returned. "There's no denying it; I can't sustain the business at this rate any longer. We're struggling to maintain a consistent workload and if it persists, I'm going to have no choice but to shutdown our operations."

The Morning Call newspaper could not have reported it any better. Jon's ears ballooned and reddened as he listened on to McDaniels' inevitable verification.

"I understand, Gerry. I'll head back and get to making some calls – I'm sure there are some tenders out there that we're missing."

As Jon treaded on a backwards treadmill, it appeared as if McDaniels had a divergent solution in mind.

"Hold on, Jon," he buzzed, his moustache invading the roof of his top lip.

Gerry McDaniels reached for a leathered document wallet, unclipping the cold clasp as he plucked at a printed airline ticket.

American Airlines flight 781.

"I don't want you to think that I've sent the boys on a wild goose chase; I haven't," he vindicated, having never chased a goose before. "I've got a contact in Los Angeles – a woman from a construction company – they're demolishing a vacated aged-care facility and turning it upside-down and into prime Californian housing real estate. Of course, as part of the project, they're seeking quotes for paintwork from a couple of companies across the country. Now it's a long shot – and that's why I've got the guys looking for more opportunities – but they've got offices and developments ongoing across the entire West Coast and if we can somehow secure this one, it'll go a long way to re-establishing some security for us."

Jon's nose shrivelled like a foreskin in the winter, his eyebrows flipping direction.

"I know what you're thinking; this is my responsibility. But if I go ahead and do this myself I think they might be more likely to throw me *in* that damn aged-care facility instead. I'm getting old, Jon, and I can't relate to the customer like I used to. I need somebody adroit. I need somebody with enough balls to bring this Californian pot of gold back home to Allentown."

McDaniels flashed the airline ticket like Richard Branson in a cordial television commercial as he slapped it against the inside of his palm.

"Me?" Jon pointed to his chest, not in an 'I'm the M-V-P' kind-of way but more like an ignorant high school student with an underestimated perception of his own reading and writing abilities. "I think you've got the wrong guy."

"I couldn't think of anyone more pertinent."

"But what about the work we have outstanding?" Jon panicked, hastily squabbling for any kind of roadblock.

"What work?"

Ouch.

"If you can do this for me, Jon, I can guarantee that it'll be *well* worth your while as we look to move the company forward."

Jon hushed, twitching at the nose as his *Inside Out* minions activated their mayday mode.

I can't leave Maya right now; I've never been away from her before. With everything that's happening – the bills, the ATM – the timing couldn't be any worse.

His inner sentiments notwithstanding, Jon truly saw no alternative. The request was a metaphorical proviso, an imperative stipulation that had to be reached in order to attain a sustainable lifestyle.

Money? Check.

Employment? Check.

Maya? Check.

Happiness? ...

With reluctance, he reached forward and plucked the airline ticket from the hairy hands of Mr. McDaniels.

"So... You want me to send you a postcard?"

* * *

On a good day, gainful house painters were relieved from their daily duties by no later than three-thirty in the afternoon. But for the Pennsylvania Paint Co., a premature midday dismissal was becoming the regrettable norm.

McDaniels' demand had expedited this timeline for his vocational guineapig, allowing Jon just enough on the clock to prepare for his imminent departure.

The burn of diesel beckoned, Jon yanking the airline ticket from his back pocket as he peddled across the pavement of a parking garage and towards his burgundy station wagon.

Wow, I leave in seven days.

Seven days was barely enough time for God to create the Earth. And yet Jon – the proud owner of nothing even remotely celestial – *needed* to flush his conscience with ATM-answers and carbon-copy commitments within that very same interval.

Not a second could be wasted, not a breath taken for granted.

His mind addled and preoccupied, Jon steered out the parking garage, omitting his indicator as a shrieking car-horn sounded to the tune of an irascible driver with a Texas-sized chip on his shoulder.

"My bad!" he apologised, waving for forgiveness as he stiffened his hands in the ten-and-two position, turning left on Liberty Street before jetting down 17th and towards Sumner Avenue.

A prototypical mid-Winter's Allentown afternoon greeted him at the curb, the belligerent breeze blowing a hurricane of wind that almost unfastened his side door from its hinge.

This was getting repetitive – monotonous, even – in the most mundane way that a confusing adventure could be.

He stepped from the curb and tiptoed towards the hole in the wall, greeting the computer as if it were the Joey to his Chandler. Jon followed protocol, twisting at the neckline to identify the translucent shadow of a non-existent soda can, the manifestation of a chronological alteration in momentum.

INSERT YOUR CARD.

ENTER YOUR PIN.

The machine's demands had been memorised like a pestiferous song lyric and this time, Jon hardly needed a second to deliberate over his next move.

It had been a smidgen over twelve hours since his last visit to the automated teller machine on 17th Street. Having attempted to transfer a game show total of five hundred dollars in one hundred dollar intervals from his credit card to his savings account on a frigid Sunday evening, Jon was ready for 'Operation 2.0'. He warmed his scalp with an unseeable deerstalker and begun in a *Sherlock Holmes*-inspired inquisition into his very fickle banking history.

6174.

WHAT DO YOU WANT TO DO?

Jon tapped at the buttons on the ATM's control pad, instructing the machine to deliver an account balance reading on his savings account. Its cryptoprocessor boiled into gear as Jon tapped the edges of his fingernails in an anxious rhythm.

An earworm invaded his mind like a skull-sucking intergalactic alien as an involuntary drum roll thumped in an ascending crescendo against the inside of his cranium.

ACCOUNT BALANCE: $538.

Holy shit.

Jon gasped in disbelief, the single-patron audience of his very own magic show. It was as if his brain had short-circuited and required an emergency reboot. Around him, everything was in fast-forward while he remained motionless in the middle of a twirling and encircling hurricane of perplexity.

The Dr. Watson to his Holmes disposed Jon to survey one final clue. Gently, he pressed the button on the ATM's control pad that commanded a balance request on his linked credit account. He had to inspect the account's recorded activities to be absolutely certain.

The cashpoint processed Jon's request, displaying its indexed list of deposit and withdrawal transactions on screen. He scanned the information for the most recent date, navigating his fingers through a series of transaction statements like a librarian in front of a book registry.

And in that moment – a moment that would last an ageless eternity – Jon suffocated, his heart stopping its techno-tempo as he gasped for air through the knife-thin chill of a Pennsylvanian gust. The automated teller machine on 17th Street listed not a single transaction activity over the preceding forty-eight hours.

He browsed the transaction statements for his savings account, expecting to uncover some kind of correlation error.

But there was nothing.

Jon's savings account had reset and according to the information on screen, his experiment had summoned the magic Einstein-forces of success. He was now over five hundred dollars in credit with a band of waving leprechauns in his ATM-windowed reflection.

And he hadn't ever invested a single cent.

10

A ONE-WAY TICKET TO CALI FOR CASPER

Herbal tea brewed, steaming uncontrollably in the kitchen as Jon dropped the disheartening bombshell on Maya's fragile lap.

"So... When do you leave?"

Her intonation suggested a thousand displeasures. Her despondency was vivid and tangible, her eyes drooping as her lips dried and sagged.

"I'm still ovulating, Jon," she divulged, reaching for an empty excuse. "I don't know about you, but that's a really big deal to me."

Jon resented the implication, attributing her impulsive remark to the discharge of benevolent solicitude.

"And it's a *really* big deal to me, too," he replied, dodging her irrationality. "But honey, we can try again when I get back. I'm not going anywhere."

Maya twitched at the fingertip, wiping the excess liquids from her rosy fine bone China with a clean sponge as she soured at the mouth.

"Jon, We've been trying *so* hard for over two years now; I just don't want to miss out on another opportunity to conceive after we've been told that this may not ever happen for us."

Maya's trepidation was arguably warranted. Negative pregnancy tests had plagued the couple for over eight months before a fertility specialist diagnosed Maya with endometriosis. While a contingent of specialists had made appropriate recommendations to ameliorate their trying circumstance, the couple did their best to avoid the notion that gestation was improbable.

"In between that and this ridiculous hill of bills that keep piling up, I just feel like the timing couldn't be any worse."

You're telling me...

Maya continued to plead her case as Jon felt a suppressing pressure to waver.

He agreed; the timing could not have been any worse. He was still perturbed by an overbearing experience with a highly suspicious ATM. And this lingering uncertainty only compounded these entanglements.

"So what do you want me to do, then?"

Maya's eyes melted, her vague resolve forcing a dull response.

"I... I don't know," she stumbled.

"Well what do you want, Maya? C'mon. Do you want me to quit my job? Is that what I should do, then?"

Jon's genial tone now mutated into something far more confrontational.

"Because the last time I checked, we can't even afford fucking batteries for the TV remote."

Maya shrugged as a bubble of coal-fuelled steam began to funnel from her ears.

"This isn't about batteries, Jon," she emphasised. "This is about you and me, walking through the fire together when things start to burn."

The analogy was ironic, given the would-be balmy conditions of a Californian sun.

The verbal skirmish was getting them nowhere. Jon brushed off his thorns before identifying that the argument's context called for a far more supportive approach.

"Listen, Maya," he whispered as he exhaled and grabbed Maya by her trembling hand. "We've been through the fire and I know it's only getting harder; but right now, me doing this... me going to Los Angeles could mean the difference between being employed and being out of a job."

Jon stroked Maya's hand as he fluttered in her reflective, hazel eyes.

"And that could mean big things for us; it's going to give us the best possible opportunity to get back on track if everything goes well."

As the storm began to weather, Jon surmised that Maya was finally meeting him halfway.

"All you have to do is *trust me*," he implored. "We'll get through this together and once we're at the other end of the tunnel, we'll have everything we ever dreamed of... and more."

Jon placed his left palm atop her belly, Maya reciprocating his tender affection as she clasped her hand atop of his.

"I'm sorry," she whispered in irrational regret as her tear ducts began to swell. "You're right; go and make me proud."

Verbal four-play, timely distractions and earnest fornication could only mask their pain for so long. Jonathan Jinks and Maya Ververs were in the midst of momentously adverse hardship, individually and in unison.

In the presence of one another, they were united allies, prepared to sacrifice almost anything on a daring crusade to the realms of perpetual happiness. Privately however, they coveted something far different.

An escape.

* * *

A childhood was defined in a palette of artistic strokes, drowned across the criss-crossed textures of a blank canvas. In graphite, then in crayon – both prototypal tools of the imaginative child – swirls and expressions were imprinted on the surface, a blood-orange crayon scraped in a vertically escalated pain like a chimney full of toxic smoke. Each stroke held its own as they conjoined to produce a distinctly abstract and highly mysterious composition. Observing from afar, silhouettes of spectres, both dismayed and in fear, clouded the canvas' background while up close, spirals of graphite formed the contours of ambiguous shapes injected with crayon overlays. The imagery, though bright and apparently delightful, was hardly that of an amusing carnival.

The imagery was dark.

The imagery was painful.

Jon stepped backwards, admiring his latest creation like a mad scientist. His art smock was covered in a rainbow of stains, both wet and dry as he peered out the window of his makeshift art studio and stared at the moon.

After finalising the non-porous, protective layer of varnish, Jon unclothed himself, dishing his war-torn smock in an adjacent laundry basket, the evidence of another painted bloodbath on the front lines.

The closet-wide space – formerly that of a walk-in wardrobe – was still lined with metal-wire clothes hangers and worn shelving. Jon made for the main quarters of the bedroom where, as expected, Maya laid motionless, cloaked by nothing more than a sheet cover.

Jon reached for the cerulean blue acrylic paint tube in the top drawer of the dresser, squeezing out just the amount he required. Pacing quickly as not to spoil the paint dry, he collected the pointed-round paintbrush, lifting it by its ferrule as he dipped its bristles in a splotch of acrylic and prepared his paper notepad.

His deliberation was intense, critically sorting through an

agglomeration of phrases and similes before selecting the most applicable for Maya to discover.

The villain of a twinkling light wears green horns on its crown, he inscribed with fine brush strokes before cloaking himself in a dark coat and leaving the bedroom.

Jon was truly charmed by his equivoque at times.

I wonder if she'll ever figure it out...

A matter of silent moments later, he tiptoed out the front door like an unarmed cat burglar and ignited the burgundy station wagon. Like a camper by a baron lake, he rubbed his hands together for warmth and blew a passage of condensed fog in the air before releasing the wagon's brake pedal. As the vehicle rolled in reverse down the driveway and towards downtown Allentown, Jon bathed his conscience in prolonged periods of shuteye for as long as the sparse traffic would allow.

In a kind of rehearsed repetition that now came more naturally to him than the exercise of a lavatory visit, Jonathan Jinks had been systematically, yet secretly visiting the automated teller machine on 17th Street at a little after midnight, each night, like a haunting ghost with unfinished business. Replicating his actions and movements for five consecutive days, Jon had withdrawn and transferred a grand total of five thousand dollars in both cash and credit. And while each wintery night brought upon the practical withdrawal and subsequent transfer of one thousand make-believe dollars, by the following morning Jonathan Jinks' bank statements would report no such activities.

There existed no evidence.

There existed no misconduct.

Jon Jinks was indeed ghost-like. But even the friendliest of ghosts were demanded to expiate their sins before their souls were deemed worthy of marching through the Pearly Gates.

And if such conditions were not abided by, they were doomed to rot and wither away in an eternal purgatory.

11

THE MARQUESS OF QUEENSBERRY RULES

Thwack! Oomph!

"Oh, he almost knocked his fucking block off!" came a pitched-cry from the red corner of the lager-fumigated sports bar on Minx's ground floor. The retro sports bar harboured what seemed like a thousand gigantic, four-dimensional television screens, simultaneously broadcasting billions of endless testosterone-charged battles. The venue's primary demographic was about as patent as the target market for an electronic sex toy: Minx's sports bar was Allentown's unofficial home for rowdy, thunderous frat-like bros loaded on light Pennsylvanian beer. And although every international competition from *Major League Baseball* to godforsaken Canadian croquet was being streamed in high definition, Jon was anxiously poised, his eyes fixated and concerned with only one, very particular television screen.

Smack! Crash!

Yogi Beach III was articulate, technical and precise and his deadly left jab, right cross, left hook combination pressured his opponent into a hypoxic mini-cube. Yogi's *Wikipedia* page was brief, vague and imageless and while little was known about the fighter in mainstream broadcast media, Jon had hedged his bets on an anonymous online tip from a trusted world-boxing forum.

After a cagey, tactical opening, Yogi found range consistently with stinging right-hand leads. Even as his opponent fought industriously to cut off the ring, Yogi countered adroitly off his twinkle-toed back foot, landing a thudding left hook as the bell sounded for the third round's conclusion.

"He got him again!" cried a gasping voice from the rear as he burped his way through a mouthful of expletives.

Okay, so far so good, Jon thought, his spine tightening with the kind of tension that would perturb a physicist during a game of tug-of-war.

Jon had always found humour in the criticism of pugilism given that the very same instinctive nature of physical belligerence and formative combat was ingrained in basic human DNA. Children from all walks of life frolicked along the wafer-thin lines of play fighting and mischievous rage while adults demonstrated their primitive desires for fury-induced warfare. And while only a shallow minority of the Earth's alpha species had a tendency to employ a fist-first approach, the concepts of defence and mental fortification were deeply-rooted in the genetic makeup of the human race.

If the average human being had learnt anything at all from its centuries of evolution, it was that sometimes, in the most solitary of circumstances, a self-serving safeguard was vital in order to survive.

Jon was raised on the relentless right-hand of Smokin' Joe Frazier and the masterful defence of 'The Executioner,' Bernard Hopkins. It wasn't in the too distant past that Jon looked on from the stands at the *D.C. Armory* as an ageless B-Hop defied nature and logic by reducing Beibut Shumenov to a plodding, predictable foil, scoring an eleventh-round knockdown to become the oldest world champion in sports history. Jon was enamoured by the deft footwork, pivots, trap-sets, counterpunches and superior timing as he watched his heroes calculate battle strategies on their prey like lions in the savannah, controlling contests with stealth, speed and surprise.

In many ways, Jon interpreted boxing as a kind of formulate science; a science that compared its procedural planning and unwilling consequences to that of Earthly inhabitancy.

Yogi's offense only emboldened as the rounds progressed, showing off his hand speed as he wounded his opponent with vicious left-right combinations.

"So far, so good hey, Jon?" Zeke encouraged, slurping on a frosted *Yuengling,* his eyes never wavering from the television screen.

Jon approached the question with trepidation, hesitant to commit to the majestic performance on display by an extrinsic force that bore more control than he did over his own fate.

"He's doing okay," Jon subdued, suppressing an instinctive desire to rally in support of the fighter.

Levi and Marcus waffled beside them, apparently impassive to the low profile matchup as they sculled bottles of lager and trivialised over whose weekend escapade was more promiscuous.

The bantamweight boxers clocked up eight one-sided rounds – Yogi at the complacent helm of the judges' scorecard – before, a vicious, unanticipated and completely maverick counterpunch threatened to catalyse an improbable comeback.

"Holy shit!" Zeke cursed, almost regurgitating his drink. "How in the shit did he even get a fist in?"

Jon remained motionless, his skin tightening with fear as he compressed his lips together.

The blow caught Yogi unawares, *his* forehead now dense with perspiration as he heaved and laboured to replenish his pulmonary organs.

A voodoo-doll-like thunder strike channelled across Jon's body as he shared in the synchronised sweats of his prized fighter.

"Man, you good?" Zeke probed, Jon's taxing cement-face not going unnoticed. "He's got this bro, don't you worry 'bout a thing."

Yogi lifted at the neck and twisted his upper-shoulders perpendicular to his opponent in the far corner. The intensity of a rowdy live crowd seemed to raise the stakes, if only they could get any higher. Their rumbles and shouts were muffled while somewhere, deep in the acoustic crevices of the LED display's fifteen-watt in-built speakers, a hushed but reverberated a cappella rendition of Survivor's *Eye of the Tiger* could *almost* be discerned.

Blow for blow, the fighters continued to clash in a physical and mental skirmish that made David and Goliath look like *Starsky and Hutch.*

Thwart!

Crash!

Snap!

"Oh, you've got to be fucking kidding me!" came a non-rhotic cockney bellow by a British enthusiast standing by Jon's wayside. "He's about to lose his mouthguard if he ain't careful!"

A murmured grumble vibrated around the bar while glasses of lager spilled to the floor creating a sticky canvas. Jon shuffled his shoes around as if he were suctioned in quicksand while he played devil's advocate on his own destiny.

Don't panic, it's not even your money. He's not going to lose, anyway.

The opponent bounced forwards and backwards, suddenly filled with a spirited burst of energy. Yogi – tense and alert – swang from the corner as he flew a left hook that barely shaved the sweat beads off his opponent's brittle facial hair. The opponent countered with a jab of his own as he connected with Yogi's bright-blue gloves, forcing him to slip, parry and cover-up.

"Watch this Jon, I'm telling you, man," Zeke professed. "Anyone who slips like that knows how to throw the meanest counter-punch that you'll ever see. This one's about to be over."

The opponent, his prospects of success now suddenly revived, had little desire to face defeat after such a menacing resurgence. In an instant quicker than a well-trained reflex, he pounced on his groggy prey and fired an overhand that detonated on Yogi's jaw and sent him crashing to the canvas.

The live audience, both in attendance and on the sticky tiling of Minx's sports bar gasped in a collective awe.

"Well, I bloody well didn't see that coming!" the cockney Brit trumpeted, parroting the thoughts of hundreds of American boxing fans.

Jon's dejection was palpable as he froze and stared blankly at the screen while Yogi's opponent was declared the winner, his arm raised high up towards the heavens.

"Don't worry about it, man," Zeke consoled, dropping his hand on Jon's right shoulder as Levi and Marcus caught the changing tenor. "So he didn't win and you have to forfeit your condom budget for this week; it's not all bad, right?"

That's an expensive packet of condoms.

Jon stared towards his feet as the metaphorical quicksand below engulfed him in a swallowing sandstorm. A bilious pain struck his nervous system as he wrestled to recover from the unrecoverable.

"I... can't believe that he lost," Jon stumbled. "But... they said he was supposed to be a sure thing."

"Nothing's a sure thing, buddy," Zeke alleged with the faintest smirk. "Except for taxes and really good lesbian porn, of course. But hey, this is boxing; this kind of shit happens sometimes, man."

Marcus and Levi approached the leaders of their wolf-pack with apprehension.

"Yeah, Jon," Levi chirped. "Don't worry about it, man. And speaking of good lesbian porn, who's up for some milkshakes? My shout."

Jon gave him no attention – while pure with naivety, now was not the time for mindless foolishness.

The Internet, Yogi Beach III and his own estimable decision-making had failed him. And in much the same way as the beaten boxer, Jon's assertiveness had neglected to prepare him for a sturdy defensive strategy once the unparalleled novelty had worn off.

"Hey, man," Marcus whispered with caution as he spied the semblances of regret and trepidation across Jon's washed out skin. "I know this is a *weird* question, given after all these years, I've never actually known you to be much of a gambler, but how much did you lose on this fight exactly?"

Jon, disoriented, calculated the sum in his head, computing each visit to the cash machine by an average withdrawal figure. Panoramic visions of indistinctly blurry ATMs overlapped in his subconscious as an ejecting dollar bill haunted his manifestations like a contrite apparition.

"*Everything.*"

12

PASS GO, COLLECT $200

A dramatized re-enactment might have suggested that Jon was about as poverty-stricken as a Liberian immigrant on welfare. He had lost the wager, but that wager appeared to be nothing more than an allegorical time machine, resetting the parameters to the outset of his escapade like a 'Restore from Backup' function on a *Windows 10* machine.

Jon had lost nothing. Because Jon had *gained* nothing.

At least that was what the paperwork containing his banking history would reveal.

For the first time in his life, Jon had been bullish in his attempt to seize the day. He had acquiesced when the automated teller machine on 17th Street handed him the Holy Grail. But the entire adventure was conducted against his better judgment, disfavouring his acumen as it plunged him into a private pitfall of unsuspecting dangers and peccadilloes.

But for a virtuous – and perhaps, a little sanctimonious at the worst of times – Pennsylvanian, being cognizant of this transgression should have hardly taken the forfeiture of five-thousand-uncorrelated-dollars.

What the hell have I done?

Jon's actions were still buried in a hidden, mind-controlled journal, and his 'make-amends' shot clock was quickly approaching zero.

The short route from Minx's sports bar to Jon and Maya's Tudor-style home offered him just enough time to confess his sins to an automotive, pagan priest: the steering wheel on his burgundy station wagon.

"My last confession was... A really long time ago," Jon admitted with contrition as if he were darkened in a confessional at the *Cathedral Church St Catharine of Siena*. "And honestly, I stopped doing this because I've not felt it necessary for the longest time. But lately... I've done some really, *really* stupid shit."

Jon purged to mitigate his sin, knowing all too well that the admission of a misdemeanour to a vinyl car-wheel was hardly as permissible as a face-to-face Sacrament of Penance with a certified priest of the Catholic Church.

"It hasn't all been my fault, though," he claimed as he flung the steering wheel clockwise at a street corner. "I didn't seek to act with such malpractice... It was kind of, just... handed to me that way, you know?"

Jon was not far from the snow-ploughed bay of his compact driveway.

"I got my hands on something that didn't belong to me; unintentionally, of course," he mumbled through his teeth, avoiding eye contact with pedestrians on the sidewalk who might have otherwise deemed him rather certifiable. "And now I'm witnessing the consequences of my mistake."

He pulled into the driveway, the snow covering everything in his front yard except for the concrete. As he stepped towards the decked porch, a polar wind tilted the deciduous trees on the street's pathway on a sixty-degree angle, snapping wildly at the brittle branches of the lifeless foliage.

"Honey, I'm home," Jon trumpeted, bursting through the front door as if he were featuring in a prehistoric *Hanna-Barbera* animation.

Jon dropped his keys and threw off his coat as he thawed his body thanks to the home's automated heating system.

"There you are; I was wondering when you'd be home," Maya jumped as she plodded heavily through the hallway as if it, too, were layered in frosted snow. "It's freezing out there today."

Their recent squabbles had been forgotten, or, at the very least, had been conveniently swept under the rug until spoken of otherwise. They had hiked to the apex of an unimaginable summit but if their lingering dissention was to be left untreated, an inconceivable avalanche was surely destined to follow.

"How was the game?" Maya asked, botching the terminology.

"Normally we'd call it a fight," he teased innocuously, concealing any convulsive tic that could expose his discomfort. "But it wasn't too bad; Zeke had been drinking since before breakfast again."

A deflection of attention seemed to be his best move and Jon batted it away like a baseball player in the *World Series*.

"Isn't that the reason you stopped hanging out with those guys in the first place?" Maya asked, straining a pugnacious remark against a tensioned thin-fibre string. "Because all they do is drink and waste time?"

It was neither the time nor place to scramble to the defence of his fair-weather friends, especially given that Jon had repeatedly confided in Maya over what he considered to be banishment from his collegiate fraternity.

"I know, I know, you're right," he agreed, shimmying away from another potential hazard. "Today was an exception though; I was going to watch the fight either way, but the guys were shouting me chicken wings so I guess I didn't really have a choice in the end."

Like a cunning politician at a public debate, Jon was impressed with his performance. He hadn't let anything more than a fart slip between

Maya's ears about his journey from ATM-pseudo-thief to high rolling, squandering gambler. And for a moment or two, he could have easily induced himself into believing that the entire charade was nothing more than a nightmarish hallucination.

"You know what I thought about today while you were away?" Maya whispered as she sponged the stains of grime that lined the steel-coated kitchen sink.

"What's that?"

"That I had completely forgotten to even ask you – with everything that we've had going on – what actually happened to that thing with the ATM from last weekend that had you acting all funny?"

Jon's senseless mirage that suggested his pig-flying timeline was nothing more than a dream-world fantasy was debunked quicker than Kurt Cobain's suicide as Maya's ingenuous interrogation demonstrated that there was no escaping his high-stakes predicament.

"Nothing," he barked like a gentle puppy, the question penetrating a crack in his rugged shell as it forced a lapse in his otherwise unfaltering narrative.

Alarmed by the sudden tone, Maya twitched as an incongruous stare followed.

"I mean, *nothing,*" he diluted, shaking off the tone as if he were a testifying stand-witness who did not quite understand the gravity of an ongoing trial. "To be perfectly honest with you, I went by the ATM on 17th a couple of days after we talked about it. I checked my balance but everything had reset to normal. I guess there must've been some kind of glitch in the system or something."

Jonny's credibility was being tested as he padlocked his eyelids and warned them not to blink. The cadence of his explanation was both monotonous and crippled, his voice-box crackling like a busted AM radio player as he cleared his throat between takes.

"You mean your balance was no longer in the red?" Maya probed as she dangled a glass from an indestructible height and sent it crashing without a helmet to the casket of the kitchen sink.

"Nope," Jonny lied, straight-faced and all. "Everything was as it should've been; which I thought was really weird, actually. And since then, it's all been working fine – all my transactions were restored. I kind of forgot about it but like I said, I guess it was all some sort of mistake in the end."

At least on some paradoxical plain, Jonny had appeared to be speaking in half-truths; half-truths that – should Maya ever had decided to play plaintiff in a court of law – might very well have proven his acquittal on a prosecution of deceptive conduct.

There *was* a glitch in the system.

He *did* re-visit the ATM on 17th Street.

It *was* all some sort of mistake in the end.

But everything else was a noose of carefully harnessed manipulations that would dissimulate the truth and release his neck from a suffocating stranglehold.

13

WIDE OPEN OLD KENT ROAD (PACK YOUR BAGS & PULL OUT THIS EVENIN')

"Maya," Jon summoned, hollering from the bedroom as he turned his third of the chest-of-drawers upside-down. "Have you seen that tee I like with the astronauts that says 'CMYK?' on it?"

"It's not in your t-shirt drawer?" she shouted, eliminating the obvious as her voice echoed and bounced through the maze of an L-shaped corridor.

"No."

Duh.

"Well try my bottom drawer," Maya suggested. "I might've mixed it up with some of my stuff."

Jon drooped, bending his knees and balancing on his tiptoes as he grabbed and pulled at the rounded handles of the light oak-finished bottom drawer.

The fourth and lowest drawer was Jon's personal favourite. It was a Pandora's box of ravishing delight, a titillating thunderbolt of the finest lace lingerie and sleepwear found anywhere outside of a *Victoria's Secret* catwalk.

Maya glowed in class but her elegance did not hinder her desire to embrace her womanhood.

Jon rummaged through her collection like a vagrant in a dirty garbage disposal as he navigated the finely manufactured lace in search of his special t-shirt.

It's not here, either.

Before surrendering the search of Maya's magnificent fourth drawer, Jon plunged his hand in the lucky dip, pulling out a black pair of silk-laced panties with a rose-red lining trim.

As he ran his fingers through the gauzy fabric – delicate like a glistening and forbidden pearl – Jon determined that he could not return them back to their rightful habitat. He lifted the translucent fabric up to the tips of his nasal and inhaled like a critical asthma patient.

"Jon?" came the sweet-sounding voice from afar. "Did you find it?"

Startled, Jon bounced at the knees and shot upright, almost sling-shooting Maya's panties over his shoulder before the velocity fixed his internal compass on a beige armchair by way of the couple's bed. The armchair, flaunting designer elegance and French boudoir style, offered the perfect resting place for any neglected garment.

Including black spacemen printed t-shirts with bolded titles that read 'CMYK?'

"Got it!" he shouted as he collected his favourite short-sleeve and bundled it in his suitcase together with Maya's black and rose-red silk-laced panties.

The psychedelic shirt was Jonny's most emboldened expression of individualism; a design predicated on the setting of eight duplicated astronauts – seven of which were outlined in a holy conforming white while a solitary spaceman, second from the left, was printed in the colour palette of cyan, magenta, yellow and key. The design represented freedom, idiosyncrasy and everything that Jonny was not.

And for that very reason, it had become his prized wardrobe possession.

Jon gauged his mental checklist, ticking every stowed travel item from underwear to cologne before a reflective glare of sunlight beamed through the Tudor-window and against a sheet of contoured plastic, cueing a fortuitous aide-memoire.

He stretched towards the side table and lifted the white mask in slow motion as if it possessed the almighty powers of a magic lamp. It didn't, but Jon knew it would at least prove itself in good time.

Got to pack this.

He zipped the suitcase at its centre-point before unwrapping a TSA approved combination luggage lock from its plastic packaging.

So what do I make the combination? he contemplated, fidgeting through a range of options on the four-dial device.

My ATM access code: 6174…

It seemed the obvious of choices.

Jon verified the combination and locked his luggage as he dragged the cement-weighted goods and chattels across the floor and towards the gaping doorway.

But before he could leave the room – a room that incubated a collection of art and beauty in a plethora of dynamic forms – Jon had one final appointment with a pointed-round paintbrush and a palette of acrylics.

Deep in the pocket of a space now emptier than it had ever seemed before, a blank matte-white paper notepad rested beside a craftsman's tool on a side table, the symbol of a vacant canvas poised and prepared for a refined expression. A million ideas raced through his mind, passages and fragmented allusions that were part-academically acquired and part-intuition and instinct.

Let it come naturally.

Jon dipped the brush's point to the bottom of the painted lagoon as he filtered its head and began to scribble against the dense paper sheeting. Each stroke, delivered with the poise and grace of Leonard Bernstein before a symphonic orchestra, was inexorable and meticulous in motion.

Cry tears of pearls into a magic cup while I'm away and a mountain of richness awaits.

This time, the inscription was solely attributed to an implicit memory recall, a novella passage once perused so methodically in a high school assessment that it had stamped an unconscious imprint somewhere in the dark tunnels of his cerebrum.

'The Kite Runner'.

14

LAX, MORTGAGE VALUE: $1M

"This is the final boarding call for passengers flying on *American Airlines* flight 781 to Philadelphia..." the announcement fizzled through a thickness of airport static as Jon clenched his boarding ticket in one hand and Maya's soft, starless palm in the other.

A stopover was unavoidable, a forty-nine minute rendezvous with Pennsylvania's major international airport before the final slog to *LAX* could commence.

Jon detested stopovers in much the same way as he detested acts of wickedness and malfunctioning automated bank systems and yet ironically, none of these events were even remotely mutually exclusive. Rather, they were both holistically inescapable.

"I can't believe it's going to take me eight hours to get there," Jon moaned, disheartened.

The *Lehigh Valley International Airport* had been categorised as a 'nonhub' by the *FAA* on account of its rapidly declining air traffic but for local residents not eager to take the seventy-five mile-long drive from Allentown to *Philadelphia International Airport*, this was their *London Heathrow*.

"It'll be over before you know it," Maya encouraged, her soft fingers fidgeting inside Jon's hand-cave in a nervous rhythm. "Just close your eyes, fall asleep, and when you wake up you'll feel brand new."

In front of them and about to pass through the security portal like a space shuttle through a never-ending black hole, a husband, his wife and their two children embraced in a cuddled bubble as they bid each other a soul-stirring farewell.

"Did I ever tell you that I never really liked airports?" Jon divulged as he siphoned away the tears. "I mean, if we're going away on a vacation together it's obviously great. But it's like any other time I come here it feels more like a palliative care ward."

"It's only a week," Maya consoled in a needed role-reversal as she caressed his arm and kissed his cheek. "You can *FaceTime* me whenever you want and I'll be standing right here holding a box of goodies from *Victoria Secret*, waiting for you to land next week."

It was Mozart music to his ears, even *if* there was a chance that it was nothing more than an empty gesture.

"I better go quickly, Maya," he whispered, crestfallen, as if there existed not even the most infinitesimal desire to bask in the unpredictable thrills of interstate adventure.

"You better come back quickly, Jonathan Jinks," Maya joked in a waggish retort, her smile breaking the concrete in Jon's face as she made him feel warm in the Pennsylvanian freeze.

The airport at 3311 Airport Road was, by dimension, one of the smallest international airports in the world. But as Maya and Jon stood hand-in-hand inside the near-empty *American Airlines* terminal, between the two, the world itself could not have possibly appeared any smaller around them.

'Jonscha' – as any celebrity gossip magazine would likely have dubbed them – embraced, their lips suctioning together for the last time for at least a week as they captured the moment for bedtime playback on their cerebral camcorders.

Jon's smartphone was brimful of reverse-camera 'selfie' snaps of his beloved, but this waned in comparison to the real thing. He would have to learn to survive without her laugh, without her smile, without her galaxy-painted palm.

Alone.

As a tiny and brittle forty-five seat *American Airlines de Havilland Dash 8* waited on the tarmac for him beneath a gloomy Pennsylvanian downpour, Jon fumbled to articulate through his final words.

"I'll call you when I land. I love you."

Jon would only be gone for a week.

Except that really, he wouldn't.

15

CHUCKIE'S DINER

Steam sizzled and heat perspired from the circular heating elements of a range of flattop grills. Damp layers of forehead moisture were dried up by a ketchup-stained cloth as a crowd of cooks paced around the kitchen, rigorously surveying a scope of incoming order dockets. The grill's steel cook surface seasoned like cast iron cookware, providing a natural non-stick surface for an assembly of beef patties and fried chicken breast.

"Order's up!" the head chef shouted as a pair of waitresses in pigtails and yellow cotton-dresses retrieved the plastic cafeteria trays from the service counter. The trays were lined with a chequered paper padding while traditional red diner baskets provided the housing for stacked burgers, golden fries, sliced gherkin and any other delicacy that could be dependably deep-fried.

Thirty-five metres away, an awestruck Jon Jinks peddled his pedestrian feet along the sidewalk, flummoxed by the enormity of his surroundings and the grand scale repertoire promoted by a city that was far bigger than expected. His eyes dangled from their sockets as he head-checked left and right, absorbing each iconic landmark in Sunset Boulevard's glorious catalogue of modern-day tourism. Jon checked by everything from *The Comedy Store* to the renowned *Whisky a Go Go* as he trekked from *The Chinese Theatre* all the way out to West Hollywood in the midst of an archetypal Californian sunset.

As he turned at the corner of Sunset and San Vicente Boulevard, a stumbling human directional that was labouring to wrestle his mobile advertising board from the clutches of a narrow draught intersected his vision. The sign twirler – who was planted beneath a traditional eight-and-a-half metre high roadside sign that read 'Chuckie's Diner – West Coast Cookin' Done Right' – was being eaten by his own inflatable cheeseburger costume, exposing only his red-framed *Ray-Ban*s, his tinted and dried candy red faux hawk with darkly shaved sides and his tattoo-sleeved arms from the narrow inlets of the costume's neckpiece and arm slot. The cheeseburger outfit was stamped with the 'Chuckie's Diner' brand-mark as the logo protruded from the stems of the bun, forming an artificial flag at the costume's head.

"Chuckie's Diner, where your West Coast cooking is done just right," yawped the human directional in a broken chirp, his puberty failing him as he finally controlled the flabby, horizontal promotional sign with a Jedi-like mind trick. "Dine in today for a burger and meal deal – only twelve-ninety-nine!"

The timing was impeccable. Jon's stomach roar could be discerned over the sign waver's piercing spiel, a clear indication that his airsickness had subdued and his stomach clock was suddenly aware of its neglect.

"You guys do cheesesteak sandwiches and scrapple?" Jon asked, yearning for the home cooking that was a staple menu item at any Pennsylvanian diner.

"Scrapple?" the directional replied with an edge of flamboyance as he sifted his congealed hair in the breeze. "What happened, bro? Did a typhoon pull you in? I think you've drifted to the wrong side of the country, holmes!"

Jon shrugged, dismayed.

"But why don't you try one of our delectable, elongated slithers of deep fried, breaded mozzarella instead?" the directional suggested, gesticulating at the crotch as he extended his closed fists forwards and upwards to perform a visual, indiscrete and utterly inappropriate enactment of masturbation. "Here, it's on the house."

The directional slipped Jon a chequered coupon, the consolation prize for a homesick traveller.

"Thanks," he sighed.

"Don't mention it, holmes!"

Jon paced for the metallic double diner door and pushed at the handle, prompting a timely bell ring from the venue's sensory system.

Chuckie's Diner was a weight loss therapist's worst nightmare, sizzling some of the finest fried and unostentatious dishes this side of the Mississippi River. Its menu rarely wavered from 'good-ol'-fashioned' American classics while its patriotic cuisine and cultural appeal suggested that it could very well have been the younger, better-looking cousin of a *Denny's* franchise.

Jon tiptoed across the chequered flooring and towards a synthetic, burgundy, retro diner booth with a silver inverted triangular print smothered across its centre pane. Adjacent to him, an elderly man sat solitarily, gaping out the window as he cumulated the number of passing luxury cars while waiting to be served. Towards the restaurant's far side, a yokel family combined their collective brainpowers like a doltish version of *Captain Planet*'s 'Planeteers' as they sought to command the coin-operated *Wurlitzer* jukebox to spin anything other than the *Backstreet Boys*' 'Millennium' album.

"What'll it be, sir?" asked the pigtailed waitress as she removed a graphite pencil from behind her earflap and waited with order pad in hand.

Jon, having hardly studied the double-sided menu replied in a hastened locution.

"Ugh," he stumbled. "I think I'll get the Chuckie burger with curly fries – and a vanilla shake for the drink."

"Great choice," the waitress commended, popping a dollop of pink bubble-gum as she removed the sticky and stained laminated menu from Jon's sweaty palms.

"Oh," he halted as the waitress wiggled her way towards kitchen. "Get me some of those mozzarella sticks as well, if you can."

Jon flashed the 'free cheese sticks' voucher like an LAPD officer with an authority complex as he reached forward to redeem the coupon.

"You got it, sir, but you can pay with that at the counter once you're done."

Of course I can – idiot.

Jon's leg caught itself on a metaphorical hurdle as he continued his unchaperoned course of the Los Angeles wilderness.

Across the wayside, he watched like a spy as the red-haired burger mascot nonchalantly twirled his advertising board towards the oncoming traffic. A sports car – bright red with a recessed roof and loaded with underage passengers – dashed by the directional as if it were Michael Schumacher himself at the wheel. The driver squeezed at a novelty musical air horn – a noise so piercing that Jon could hear it almost absolutely through the deaden of the diner's window pane – sounding a flourishing fanfare sound bite at the costumed cheeseburger.

"Yeah, yeah; fuck you too, holmes!" cried the sign waver as he threw his body weight wildly towards the curb. "Suck on these gherkins!"

The faux hawked human billboard offered a ribald gesture, grabbing at the circular branches of his anatomy by way of his crotch as he swayed his fists in an urban uproar before charging for the diner's entry doors.

"Dad!" he clamoured as he burst into the restaurant's foyer. "I'm *so* sick of this shit; getting fucking harassed out there every day like I'm fucking Caitlyn Jenner in a bisexual brothel."

The directional brandished a lexicon of vocal hysterics as he discommoded the diner's entire occupancy.

"Jesus, settle down," placated a tall, curious and cautious man, cloaked in the finest *Armani* suit this side of Rodeo Drive.

The tall man made prudent attempts to pacify his disgruntled offspring, dragging him by the ear and away from the store's clientele.

"Nothing to see here, folks, now let's get back to that West Coast dining!" the suited gentleman assuaged, his face flushing a radish red as he shuffled his feet and bobbled over his polished dress shoes.

Jon was markedly flabbergasted.

But there was something peculiarly delightful about the skit that mirrored the happenings of an episode of Mark Wahlberg's *Wahlburgers* – the kind of episode that made him feel like a principal reality television show extra on the precipice of a starring promotion.

16
CHUCKIE JNR.

"Hey, attaboy – you ordered the mozzarella sticks."

The faux hawked redhead – now without his glistening red *Ray-Ban*s – marched towards a sated Jon Jinks who had just finished jiggling the contents of a saltshaker atop his curly fries. As the directional approached the leather diner booth, Jon perceived that sans the suffocation of a heavy cheeseburger body suit, he was not as slender as initially surmised.

"Mind if I sit?"

If I say no, is it really going to make a difference?

"Why not," Jon complied as he wiped away the food stains from his lips with a paper napkin.

"Name's Chuckie," the redhead trumpeted, offering an unwaveringly amiable right hand.

Wait a minute… Chuckie? As in 'Chuckie's Diner,' Chuckie?

"Jon," he reciprocated.

"Jon. Right, alright; pleasure to meet you then, hombre," said Chuckie who, in no way, shape or form, resembled anything close to a Hispanic.

"Listen, sorry about that scene before, bro; my dad's asked me apologise to the customers. He can't deal with what he defines as 'harmful goodwill' right now."

Jon's magic mojo compelled him to remain receptive but

unbothered.

"It's not a problem," he assured impassively as he crunched on a golden curly fry.

"Right, right, I appreciate that but listen, Jonny; mind if I call you Jonny?"

Jon's eyeballed expression offered a thousand alternatives.

"Okay, I'm going to run with Jonny; so Jonny," he forced like a nagging toddler in a toy aisle. "Listen, my dad is going to kill me – I mean, literally kill me; like 'slaughter me with a butcher's knife while I'm sleeping in my underpants' kind of kill me – if I don't convince him that my little *outburst* didn't force all these people in here into never coming back again."

Chuckie delivered the plea with minimal conviction and a puerile disregard for his father's wishes.

"Listen... I don't know you, but I like you; I get the feeling that you're the kind of guy who could sell an *Oculus Rift* to Stevie Wonder, am I right?"

Jon offered an ambivalent smirk, refraining from admission as he attended to a final handful of curly fries instead.

"Any chance you could put in a good word for me on your way out?" Chuckie supplicated with a feeble grin as he pulled his best Puss in Boots from *Shrek* impression. "You know, from one hombre to another?"

Jon dangled the directional's petition by a spaghetti thread as he mulled over the 'what's-in-it-for-me?' prospects.

"That your dad right over there?" Jon questioned, pointing towards the tall man in the dark suit who was pacing in and out of the facility's restricted kitchen area.

"Yeah, that's my dad, Chuckie Hooper Senior, or as I like to call him, 'Chuckie *Señor*," Chuckie divulged in an offensive and unconvincing Spanish matador accent. "And I'm Chuckie Hooper Junior; dad started the diner back in '92 in San Diego – now we own almost eighty locations across the West Coast."

Jon was surprised – especially given the meme-crazy reach of the Internet – that he had not heard of the restaurant before.

"So basically, we're pretty much at the top of the food chain, baby!"

"And yet somehow you're still outside in that ridiculous burger suit?" Jon quipped, lifting and shaking his eyebrows as he digested the last of his fried platter for one.

"Ouch! C'mon, man, that's a low blow – dad's just having me pay my dues is all it is before I take over his empire."

Chuckie's credulous presumption was far from incontrovertible. And although Jon was foreign to the ways of the capitalistic West Coast world, he certainly was *not* foreign to the browbeat pressures and uncertainties that polluted business models marred by nepotism.

"Anyways," Chuckie resumed. "You from around here? I haven't seen you come in before."

But apparently, if not anything else, he's perceptive.

"I'm from Pennsylvania – Allentown, actually," Jon disclosed.

Chuckie placed his left finger atop his dried lip as he widened his eyelids.

"Well what in the hell are you doing all the way out here?" he wondered. "I was only kidding about that whole typhoon thing, you know!"

"I'm here on business – work," Jon explained, keeping his exposition to a minimum.

"Right on, man, so what is it that you do, exactly?"

Jon hesitated before blurting out something impetuous like 'you mean other than stealing money from the Nations of Jefferson

American Bank?'

"I'm an artist," he replied.

"What do you mean 'an artist'? Like, what? You rap or something?"

Chuckie's benighted stupidity could not have been anymore apparent.

"No," Jon shunned. "I paint; I'm a painter. A painter artist."

"Well right on then, holmes, that's what the fuck I'm talking about!" Chuckie erupted as he mentally tug-of-wared with his father's perfectly defensible request. "Very cool – maybe we can get you to paint something on one of the walls of our restaurant then, what do you say?"

"Maybe," Jon lied with a glaring smile.

"So if you're obviously not sticking around, where do they have you shacked up while you're here?"

"Just this little place on Franklin Avenue, right by Hollywood Boulevard."

"Ouch," Chuckie bewailed. "That must be rough; there's a ton of shit-holes out that way. Plus, it always smells like barf and Chinese cat-piss."

Jon wondered what basis the animated redhead had to accurately describe the effluvia spawned by the urine of a Chinese cat.

"Not really," he gainsaid, his face paralysed in a 'why-are-you-wasting-my-time' naturalistic Emoji. "I'm only here for a week before I head back home."

A waitress roller-skated by in her classic *Converse* sneakers to scoop away the remains of Jon's fried platter.

"Well, Chuckie, it's been... a *pleasure*," Jon white-lied. "Thanks for the mozzarella sticks."

Jon permitted his fingers a final wipe down, soaking up the cooking oils that saturated his pores before dropping the napkin in a sudden evacuation.

"Hey Jonny," Chuckie chimed. "Don't you got a business card or something? Something I can pass on to my dad; I'm pretty sure once I tell him what you do for a living, he'd be interested in having a chat with you while you're down here to talk business... only if you have some extra time, of course."

"Sure," he begrudged, betting that the scarcity of time would prohibit any such interaction from ever occurring.

Jon reached for the pocket at the rear of his denim jeans and flipped open his trifold wallet, sliding out a vertically styled business card with the Pennsylvania Paint Co. logo emblazoned on its top left corner. He clutched the card with his index and middle fingers before flinging it in Chuckie's direction.

"Thanks man, I'll definitely give this to the head honcho over there," he assured as if Jon's life or death depended on it.

Chuckie, examining the card like a sleuth, deduced a discrepancy that even he could not miss.

"The Pennsylvania Paint Co. – domestic and commercial painters?"

Although Chuckie was cognizant of the contrariety between the logo on Jon's business card and his self-proclaimed profession, Jon was certain that he was dealing with the kind of character that could be easily fooled twice.

"Legal loopholes," he tricked him with a wink. "For tax reasons."

Jon hardly stepped away before a mumbled inflection of blabber returned from directly behind him.

"Oh, I feel that!" he chirped, slipping the card into his back pocket as he unclipped a ballpoint pen from his shirt and reached across the table to collect an unused 'Chuckie's Diner'-branded napkin. "I don't really *have* an *official* business card myself as of *right now*, but what I'm going to do is just drop my digits on this here napkin right here – you see, it's got the logo and everything on it so we're good and official – if you need anything at all while you're here, all you gotta do is call me."

Chuckie formed the shaka sign, raising his thumb to his ear while his little finger aimed towards his mouth as Jon accepted the napkin like a vegetarian to a porterhouse steak.

"All I gotta do is call?" he echoed as he surveyed the napkin, Chuckie's chorography closely resembling that of a kindergarten student with a learning disability.

"Yes, sir! Oh, and Jonny – don't forget," Chuckie reminded him as if Jon had already forgotten. "If you just so happen to inadvertently sing my praises to my boss over there on your way out that'd be super cool and I would totally be like, forever indebted to you."

"I'll see what I can do," Jon offered lukewarmly.

Jonathan Jinks had dabbled in the bucket of Californian living for only a handful of hours, but he was already dazzled by both its exuberance and its obnoxiousness. As he approached the metallic double door, he paused, rotated his gears clockwise and swung his body to divert his attention to the *real* Chuckie in charge.

"Excuse me, sir," Jon murmured to the dapper gentleman who was coaching a waitress-in-training on the particulars of the milkshake machine. "Your son over there..."

Jon pointed towards the diner booth now wholly occupied by the manager's porky son.

Dorney Park. Those Goddamn cotton candy sprinkled keys.

"A word of warning," he prefaced, grappling the burger magnate's eardrum like a noisy one-man-band. "Don't slaughter your business by passing it down to your kid. Nepotism never ends well; trust me."

Jon offered a frolicsome thumbs-up as he smiled back at a beholden Chuckie Junior.

The crass redhead grinned at him with gratitude, none the wiser.

17

REGRUB MOON HILLS

It was more like a decrepit abandoned prison than a once glamorous retirement village. Standing like a crumbling fortress atop a hill of lifeless soil and tumbleweeds, the dilapidated single-storey building massed the entirety of a land-field, its remaining structure occupying the bulk of a Southern Californian village.

Cranes, excavators, skid steer loaders and heavy-duty concrete trucks lined a makeshift driveway as the decommissioning of two-thirds of the vacated facility had already reached its demolition phase.

The area's garden beds were dug away and its fencing removed, making room for construction offices and portable lavatories.

Jon, having thanked his *Uber* driver for a sound voyage, paced his way through the mud, his shoes miring in the sticky soil beneath him.

"Hi there," Jon croaked, kicking the remains of slushy dirt from his heels as he approached the site foreman's office. "I'm looking for Felecia Randolph?"

An assembly of unhelpful labourers who were using the foreman's office as a lunchroom turned to one another, biting into their jelly sandwiches like a zoo of flummoxed meerkats.

"Anybody?" Jon asked for a second time.

"Hold on, that's me!" came a brawny, female voice from behind, prompting Jon to return back to the unflattering soils of the building site's very own yellow brick road.

The plump African-American woman – carrying a foam-plated clipboard and dressed in a dark pantsuit with second-hand heels – struggled to trudge her way through the swamp as she swang her arms to improve her aerodynamics.

"Not a good day to be wearing heels, hey?" Felecia admitted as she reached the promised land of dry loam and grassy terrain.

"I'm not wearing any heels?" Jon quipped as he forced a convincing smile from his prospective customer. "I'm Jon Jinks from the Pennsylvania Paint Company."

As Jon identified himself he offered his forearm to the unsteady facility manager, providing a human platform to escape the melting pothole of quicksand soil and cement.

"Pleasure to meet you Jon," she expressed, offering a firm and harmonious handshake. "Thanks so much for coming out all this way. Was the flight okay?"

"I'm not much of a flyer," he admitted as they ambled towards the open-framed building, conscious of each and every footstep. "But I've learnt that closing my eyes and asking 'what would Superman do?' often helps to kill the nerves a little."

If that's true, then it feels like my life right now is a never-ending aeroplane flight to Planet Krypton.

"Gerry mentioned on the phone that things were a little slow for you guys back in PA?"

Jon was torn between candour and safeguarding the prospects of an impending deal.

How much has Gerry told her?

"I wouldn't say 'slow' per say," he mitigated as they passed through a curved opening before stepping upwards onto a solid concrete slab. "We're mulling over a couple of contracts at the moment but we must have enough going on to comfortably send me on a working vacation to California so all can't be *that* bad."

Felecia saluted Jon's precautionary answer as she ushered him towards a bench top textured with architectural drawings.

"So to provide some clarity," Felecia began, carefully shuffling through a pile of ARCH C-sized sheets as if she were handling the Declaration of Independence in the Arctic. "There are two phases to this project; the first phase involves the renovation and refurbishment of the pre-existing two-storey south wing – that's where we are now – as we transform it into a operational centre for a number of small businesses and a local grocery store. This space is going to act as the central communal hub of the new district."

Jon's mind-alarm knocked between his ears, his eyes reflecting the detailed drawings like tiny mirrors as his nervous system steam train reloaded on a fresh shovel of coal.

Shit. Gerry didn't mention anything about this part of the project. I'm not prepared for this.

"Phase two," Felecia continued, sorting through the remaining diagrams. "Obviously involves the construction of two-hundred dwellings with all interior facades to be coated in cool white based on the global requirements of the estate."

White.

Jon loathed the drab and nondescript simplicity of white painted walls. In fact, he loathed the simplicity of a white painted anything. White, when associated and defined by its presence in light and psychology commonly indicated innocence, wholeness purity, virginity and safety. But for Jon, when associated with a tin of water-based paint, it represented nothing more than mechanical, mind-numbing soullessness.

"All roads are in place and building works have already begun on the first one-hundred townhouses," Felecia informed, pointing outwards towards the rear wall where a window frame had been replaced by a thickened sheet of protective, weather-resistant plastic.

"So what are they calling it, the estate? 'Felecia-ville'?" Jon queried as he sought to generate some bonus brownie points.

"I wish," Felecia responded in kind. "They're provisionally calling it 'Regrub Moon Hills' at this point."

"Regrub?"

Felecia sighed and dropped at her shoulders.

"Don't ask, no idea. 'The Chuckie Group' and their marketing department have a weird fetish when it comes to birthing names of any kind; we normally just go with it."

The Chuckie Group? It couldn't be... Could it?

Felecia chuckled in a deep and uncomfortable below, cueing like an orchestra conductor for the conjoining of a choir of laughter as Jon, his flute tucked between his moistened thighs, merrily obliged.

"I'm so sorry, Felecia, but 'The Chuckie Group'?" Jon probed, momentarily interrupting his feigned convulsions as he squeezed the question through his gritted teeth.

"Oh, I'm sorry, it was remiss of me to not explain given that you're from the other side of the country," Felecia apologised, still glowing from their ice-breaking encounter. "The Chuckie Group are the financial conglomerate behind the project — you ever heard of Chuckie's Diner? Let me tell you if you haven't, you *need* to visit and try their Mac N' *Cheetos* — it's a seriously salivation-inducing concoction that fries together mac and cheese with a crispy *Cheetos*-flavoured coating!"

Felecia's plump belly jiggled in a finger-licking jubilation as she vomited the sales pitch from the television advertisement almost verbatim.

Jon, however, was not nearly as exuberant.

You've got to be kidding me.

"You know, I think I actually drove by one on the way to my hotel," he dissembled for no apparent reason.

Felecia's concentration drifted, her professionalism withering as four *Cheetos*-coated circling birds pivoted on a gyrating spindle around her bushy dark hair.

"Listen, Felecia, do you mind if I have a couple of minutes just to take some rough measurements and to examine the building's wall textures and any peripheral fixtures I may have missed?"

"Sure," Felecia permitted, making notes on her bounded paper pad. "I'll also e-mail you the building's schematics for exact dimensions of each space."

"That'd be great," Jon answered cordially.

As Felecia made for the construction offices – her ballooned backside voluptuously swinging like two tennis rackets on a porous and clay court – Jon began his examination of the empty labyrinth, patrolling through its open archways as he carefully avoided a band of building hazards dumped on the cracked floor beneath him.

Resting flat atop a temporary steel workstation, a bright blue indelible marker lured Jon on a fishing rod, its toxic open-capped scent of xylene and toluene reeling him in like freshwater fish to illicit bait. He rolled the cap off the steel table, hitting the concrete as he lifted the marker close to his nose before marching solitarily towards a peeled sheet of drywall.

Jon examined the plastered canvas, a reference book of dimensions and calculations made by previous inspectors as he prepared to estimate the per-litre paint cost for a building of this scale.

Okay, so I'll calculate the area of the space, subtract 20 square feet for the door and 60 square feet for the four windows and then divide this by two gallons of paint at 800 square feet...

As the marker's tip kissed the wall's gypsum and left a speck of dotted ink on the surface, Jon pulled away, deducing that a slightly alternated course of action might have been more pertinent.

He pivoted off his back foot, pirouetting in an unsuspecting slow motion like a dancing cat burglar as he scanned the surrounding areas.

All alone, he deemed.

On an external wall to his side, fragments of drywall had been gashed in multiple locations, exposing the dark red brick behind it, the fallen plaster resting at his feet like uncleaned evidence from a vicious crime scene. Jon wrapped both hands around the edges, decapitating a chunk of drywall in one mouse-like show of testosterone as its remnants crashed to the concrete and a cloud of white powder stained his sneakers.

Jon perused his red-bricked canvas, a welcomed change from the white of fabricated linen, and shook the bright blue marker in a gesture of readiness.

PA–, he begun to stroke in capitals, outlining the spur of the 'a' several times before proceeding to the subsequent letter.

Well look at that – Pennsylvania.

Forty-seven seconds later, Jon retreated in a two-step motion and popped the cap on the marker before stuffing it in his back pocket – a symbol of his timely consummation. Each letter was drawn punctiliously in the kind of charming typography that would have taken a digital artist weeks to draft.

He bent at the hip and collected a handful of solid plaster fragments that had fallen from his earlier demolition, fitting them back in their unstable position like cracked jigsaw pieces against a bricked backdrop.

Jon huffed, his hand curled beneath his chin as his straight-faced demeanour dripped at its points.

PAIN, the engraving read, the remainder of its lettering hidden like buried treasure beneath a deep sea of reassembled drywall pieces.

He dusted off his hands, patting them against his trousers as he tittered at the unintended double entendre that his glorious art had created.

As Jon turned away and made for the exit – his inspection only moderately complete – an earthquake tremor from the rumble of a thunderous outdoor excavator forced the plastered jigsaw into a booming collapse, revealing in its process, the remainder of Jon's artistic Morse code.

PAINT THE STORM FOR ITS DARKNESS PAINTS THE BRIGHTEST RAINBOW.

18

CROSSROADS & BLACK DOGS

"So... how did you go?"

Maya's approach was tentative and reserved, her question carrying a thousand dependencies as she grappled with the consequential significance of Jon's meeting.

"I left no stone unturned," he replied candidly, recalling the slushy dirt and pebble-mulch that stuck to the back of his heels. "The client was friendly – a little spirited – but nice enough; I feel like I won her over. I guess it all comes down to price now."

Jon Jinks tucked the smartphone between his neck and shoulder as he brushed his fingertips against a landscaped garden bed, rich with the scent of lavender, rosemary and incense.

A tourist detour ushered him through the historic Venice Canals Walkway at the intersection of Washington Boulevard and Pacific Avenue. Rich, European architecture adorned every route as rowboats, kayaks and canoes were moored in front of a line of quaint bungalows.

Jon rested his burning toes by the flora and fauna of a mighty duck pond, his legs stretching as he whispered into the smartphone's microphone.

"The weather? It's phenomenal. The closest thing to a snowball out here is the top of a vanilla ice-cream cone," he juxtaposed to Maya's silent resentment.

"And how are you feeling? You know, is everything going okay?"

The question was an unanswerable one, particularly in the haze of the moment. She had cornered him – benevolently, of course – but Jon discerned a palpable threat, a disruption to his very fluency. He could not afford any distractions.

"I'm fine," he advised as the fluttering sing-a-long by a twosome of spotted dove's tranquilised him. "Just ready to start this next chapter, you know?"

Maya exhaled heavily, the fog against her frozen Allentown window dispersing through Jon's smartphone loudspeaker.

"You and me both, baby," she empathised in a fatalistic sigh. "But don't worry, it won't be long until you're back home with that contract in hand; I can just feel it."

Jon felt something too, something entirely different. He was the protagonist of the novel, but the successive chapters remained unwritten.

He was at a crossroads between nobility and a myth, an alternate lie that was beginning to tell its hidden truth. Faced with a decision that bore the potential of an unpalatable consequence, Jon sought to freeze the timer on his metaphorical stopwatch.

In British folklore, crossroads were considered the intersection for first-person encounters with hideously fiendish black dogs, ready to devour their vulnerable prey as they deliberated over a left or right turn.

Jon was hardly easy quarry in this game of survival but if he was to endure, to emerge outstandingly triumphant, a reprehensible commitment – a deal with the black dog-like devil, if you will – was called for.

"Listen, I've got to book an *Uber*," he mumbled, choking on a bowling ball of saliva in his throat. "But I'll call you later, okay?"

But he knew that he would not.

It was yet another lie from a man who had never really lied before.

19

CALIFORNIA DREAMIN'

Between the alpine mountains, the foggy coastline, the hot deserts and the fertile central valley, California was a rich and diverse contiguous state. But when standing at the foot of the double-jointed pier off Colorado Avenue, all Jon could spy was a collective of free spirited, nonconformist lazing by the beach in the midst a crisp, Californian afternoon.

As he journeyed down Santa Monica Pier and towards *Pacific Park,* he gaped at the Pacific Ocean and towards Catalina Island as his record-playing subconscious hummed a string of melodies from The Mamas & the Papas' classic *California Dreamin.'*

Jon bounced downhill where, to his left, a career costume-busker was slipping into a claustrophobic Elmo-suit while to his right, a family of Chinese tourists snapped candid photographs of semi-naked beachgoers as they giggled like a gleeful assembly of schoolgirls staring at condoms in the pharmaceuticals aisle of a grocery store.

The pier's wooden structure was supported by separated pillars and with each step, the friction produced a memorable clunking sound as Jon's feet floated on the surface. Pleasure piers were first built in Great Britain during the early nineteenth century to combat the capitalist-conflict of large tidal ranges for seaside resort consortiums. The pleasure pier was the resorts' answer, permitting holidaymakers to promenade over and alongside the ocean like awestruck swans in a wet lagoon.

Santa Monica Pier's *Pacific Park* boasted twenty-five fabulous attractions – including amusement rides, carnival games and souvenir stalls – and was visited annually by millions of locals, tourists… and a Pennsylvanian painter with a portfolio of problems.

Jon planted his derriere by a seaside park bench as a radiant sunray struck the rear of his sunblock-less scalp. His eyes fastened shut, spreading his arms like a lounging seagull as he basked in an impromptu one-man sunbake. The sun's beam was savage; so savage, in fact, that it grilled the bench's wooden surface into a charcoaled cauldron, leaving Jon in a torch of flames as if he were meta-morphing into *DC's* 'Firestorm'.

An assembly of teenagers gathered at the shore-side of the Pacific, wedging a red and white beach umbrella into the coarse, yellow sand as the boys took turns launching tennis balls into the ocean. The girls lazed along a body of beach towels, exposing their generous curves while they laboured in sweat on a nine-to-five quest to darken their skin.

Jon had taken a particular liking to a brunette whose tanned, leather exterior was spotlighted by a glowing black, halter cut-out waist bikini. And although Jon could not dissect the nuances of the woman's features, he was certain that if Los Angeles had anything at all to offer in abundance, it was an unequivocally irresistible contingent of mortal West Coast goddesses.

After a moment's reverie, Jon's mind snapped back to his partner in Pennsylvania as he admonished his cerebrum for flirting with a guilty pleasure.

"Jonny?" came an idiomatic voice from behind the anti-glare lenses of a pair of red-rimmed *Ray-Ban* sunglasses.

Startled, Jon sprung up to a standstill, his face slowly swelling to a peach-like tint as if he had been caught out masturbating to pornography at the back of a *Pizza Hut.*

"Hey," he erred with caution, bulleting his body into a state of pliability as he tried to shake off a budding erection. "Thanks for meeting me."

"I must admit, I know we hit it off really well and all when you came into the diner but I was still *pretty* surprised to see a text on my phone from 'Jonny – The Scrapple Guy'," Chuckie professed, flexing at the finger joints as he gestured in inverted commas.

You aren't the only one.

"Well, you did say that if I needed anything at all to just let you know, right?"

"Actually, what I *did* say was that if you needed anything at all to just give me a *call*," Chuckie trivialised in a belly full of chuckles as he slapped his arm against Jon's muscle-tensed shoulder like a wooden *Louisville Slugger* to a baseball. "But enough beating around a hairy feminist's bush, what can I do for you, holmes?"

Jon was suddenly swelling in a well of regret as he deliberated over the vapidity-versus-reward ratio his text message had created.

"How much do you know about your dad's holding company, 'The Chuckie Group'?" Jon questioned as he surveyed Chuckie's eyes for an unexplainable insight.

"How much do I know? Well, considering I basically run the company when he's on leave, I'd have to say a fair flipping bit," Chuckie embellished as he relieved his arm from Jon's shoulder and hopscotched down the boardwalk. "Let's take a walk, holmes."

Jon struggled to decipher between Chuckie making a preposterous proclamation and being indirectly deceived by his own preconceptions.

Chuckie played a round of 'follow-the-leader' as he navigated Jon through the iconic Californian boardwalk and into the playful thickness of *Pacific Park*.

"But you're just a sign twirler?" Jon eluded, prompting Chuckie to anchor his footbrake as he parked his *Nike*'s by the Pacific Wheel.

"Excuse me, but the correct terminology is a 'human directional,' thank you very motherfucking much," Chuckie corrected as they passed by an ice-cream parlour and *The Coffee Bean & Tea Leaf* store. "There's no need to be an asshole, now, holmes."

Jon was struck by a thunderbolt of unforseen self-reproach as he quickly apologised for his indiscretion.

"What I meant was that I didn't realise you had such a hierarchical role is all," he rectified in a donkey-like grin that could have won *Shrek* himself over. "So in that case, you're obviously across the Regrub Moon Hills project, then?"

Jon ascribed to his superiority complex as he offered him a handful of artificial credit.

"Across it? I named it!" Chuckie chuffed superciliously.

Figures.

"Hold that shit up to a mirror and you'll see why!" Chuckie broadcasted, revealing the company's naming policy like a puerile tattletale as Jon began to spell backwards in a quest to decode the semordnilap.

"*Burger* Moon Hills?"

"Ding, ding, ding!" Chuckie buzzed as he wiggled his index finger around like Dikembe Mutombo after a blocked shot.

"I need to know what I have to do to secure this contract?" Jon begged as a flurry of squeals bounced around from passengers riding the *West Coaster* fifty-five feet in the sky above.

Chuckie's eyebrows pricked and sprung in a gravitational whip. Chuckie could be duped twice, but three times? That was optimistic, as even *he* could no longer ignore the inconsistency in Jon's narrative.

"Contract?" Chuckie echoed like a pet parrot. "I thought you were an *artist?*"

Chuckie reached for his back pocket as he sorted through his everyday essentials: car keys, a lighter and Jon's Pennsylvania Paint Co. business card.

Jon's dry mouth opened wide but the words betrayed him.

"Jon?" Chuckie cued, fishing for an answer.

"By night," Jon declared, grasping at straws as he attempted to galvanise his position.

"Right, right, I get it now!" Chuckie replied, bopping his head like a nineties rap star. "Kinda like a superhero, right? Yeah! I feel what you're saying."

Chuckie's credulousness did not fall on deaf ears as Jon, conscious of every movement and nuance around him, looked to seize a competitive advantage.

"Well, what can I say? I work a nine-to-five during the day back in P.A. and when the sun goes down I put on my cape and paint."

Chuckie was impressionably stunned, beaming from ear to ear over something relatively inconsequential.

"Holmes!" he shrieked over a wave of rollercoaster squeals. "You *are* an artist! You paint *and* you can rap – that was one of the dopest lyrics I've ever heard!"

It took a moment, but Jon connected the dots.

Day. P.A. Cape. Paint.

Wait... does that even rhyme?

"So listen," Jon recommenced while Chuckie pranced in a fitted frenzy of rousing glee. "How do I secure this contract? I know there's an enormous scope for future developmental works and I know that we want to be apart of it."

Chuckie stiffened his arms as he sculpted a still grin and wrapped his grubby hands around Jon's shoulder.

"Jonny, my man," Chuckie whispered, his index finger pointing out towards the golden, celestial globe above them. "You see that over there?"

Jon gazed to the heavens above, trying to find something out of the ordinary.

"The sun?"

"No, the *sun*," Chuckie mimicked like a stoned seventies hippie, spreading out his eagled arms as Jon turned inwards to face him in a countenance of perplexity. "In California, this motherfucker is bright enough to light up the colour of pale champagne. And you know what else? In California, the sun *never* sets."

What in the hell…

Jon was convinced that the heir to the Chuckie's Diner throne was about as anecdotally insane as they came.

"I want to tell you that I know what you're talking about but you're making no fucking sense right now."

Chuckie flailed his arms, thumping Jon against his upper back with an open fist.

"Listen to me, holmes. That fucker up there is always shining – no matter what. Whatever happens down here, that thing up there is always lit, it always shines."

Jon stared back towards the luminous glow of the sun, squinting as he used his hand as a stopgap sunhat.

"You want to shine too, right, Jonny?"

Do I want to shine? Okay. I'll play along.

The question seemed rhetorical, though Jon had an answer prepared for this kind of question since the days of petunia planting and paint touch-ups at *Dorney Park*.

"I want this contract," he replied, driving along the same highway but in a different lane.

"Well, if you *want* this contract then you gotta prove to me that you *need* to shine like a star," Chuckie advocated, offering counterintuitive council that disregarded every psychology textbook ever written. "And if you *need* to shine like a star then you have to be where it shines brightest."

"In space?" Jon twitted in a dry sarcasm as he gestured towards the ball of fire above him.

"No," Chuckie huffed. "You have to *live* where the stars live – you have to live like a winner before you get to be one. *That's* how you'll secure this contract."

Jon failed to identify the absurd interrelationship between lifestyle and workmanship. Nevertheless, he understood that his requirement was to continue to play along.

"The *Chateau Marmont…*" Chuckie whispered, butchering the pronunciation as he donned a terrible French accent. "…Where a lot of people go to do things that they aren't supposed to do."

Jon pinched at the chin and tuned his ears to 'Radio Redhead' as he mulled the budding proposition.

"… Like winning a big-budget painting contract at a booming and expansive housing estate," Chuckie evinced, finishing the puzzle on Jon's behalf. "I'm gonna book you a room!"

Chuckie chirped, slapping Jon on the back once again as he saluted his nutty idea.

"Then – and only then – after you figure out what it means to be a winner, can I favour *you* for this contract."

Was this dim-witted simpleton really the judge-and-jury, the all-powerful tender-awarding deity that would determine Jon's fate?

There was only one way to find out.

"Alright, Jonny, that's what I'm talking about, holmes!" Chuckie bellowed between acidulous burps, his motives still roundly questionable. "Let's get you out of this fucking peasant, horse-shit-stable of a hotel you're staying in and into something fancy, fancy!"

As the pair tiptoed along the boardwalk – by the lime-green soaked *The Coffee Bean* store and adjacent to a cluster of red and white heavy-duty vinyl umbrellas wedged between metallic benches – Jon's wandering eye caught sight of a marvellous monument so frighteningly familiar that he tumbled over his own feet like Jennifer Lawrence at the 2013 *Academy Awards* ceremony.

"What's the problem, holmes? Slip on some wet paint?" Chuckie chuckled as if he were a front-row audience member at his own stand-up comedy show. "You gotta watch where you step – most people take the stairs at the *Chateau* and the last thing you're gonna want in a fucking place like that is to make a scene."

As far as Jon was concerned, it was the 'scene' itself that followed him like a translucent ghost desperate to eject the shackles of purgatory.

Fixed on a mobile enclosure in the centre of the boardwalk stood a Nations of Jefferson American Bank ATM, gazing at him with its filthy keypad, taunting him as only it knew how.

Two answers offered themselves to Jon's mental multiple-choice quiz: run away, or run towards it.

Let destiny decide.

The correct answer, though, was as clear as the reflections off the blues of the Pacific Ocean.

"Oh, and also, listen up…" Chuckie bumped into his side, his swivelling head not partial to a moment's concentration. "…From now on, it's 'Jonny'. Not 'Jon'. Not 'Jo–'. Not 'Joe-Blow-The-Homo who stuck his ass in an oboe'…"

This is… surreal.

"Just 'Jonny.'"

... Just Jonny.

20
PINNED 5.0

INSERT YOUR CARD.

ENTER YOUR PIN.

It had become a sieging computerised command, an incontrovertible indication of the thrall the machine had over Jonny.

If the innumerable visits to the automated teller machine on the frosted pavements of 17th Street in Allentown had been his college, this was well and truly his first employment, his opportunity for rectification.

"I'm gonna hit you back later, holmes," Chuckie announced, leaving Jonny alone on a deserted, Californian islet swarmed by nothing but a cool breeze, trivial teenage chatter and the devilish demands of an ATM. "Make sure you check into the *Chateau* A-S-A-P! They ain't gonna hold your booking forever!"

Jonny's hotel arrangements were now far from the priority as a whistling soda can came screaming down the boardwalk, knocking into his *Nike*'s like a thunderous bowling ball striking out ten pins in an explosive collision.

You've got to be kidding me, Jonny ticked, unable to escape the inauspicious foreshadowing.

Sans the soda can, the dispositions of each scene – the ATM on 17th Street in Pennsylvania and the ATM on the *Pacific Pier* boardwalk in California – were markedly divergent. On the darkness of 17th Street,

Jonny was a frigid unenlightened, doused by the unsuspecting confusions caused by the cold, the liquor and the cryptoprocessor. The ATM on 17th Street was congruent to chaos, a malfunctioning malpractice of a machine that offered its users a repeatable chance to offend when triggered after dark. There was an unavoidable consistency in its fortuity that forged a bubble-wrap around its opportunist, fostering the dangerous development of an illicit addiction. It was the kind of addiction that made a polar opposite of its addict and possessed an ability to second-guess anyone with a shrewd and incorruptible moral grounding.

Anyone just like Jonny.

But on *Pacific Pier*, that status quo had shifted. The daytime sunshine burnt red holes through his shoulders as it thawed the frosty ghost of his Pennsylvanian past. Jonny's momentary lapse had been washed away by a wave of karmic comeuppance. It was the kind of indiscretion that offered a menacing reminder of how unpredictably simple it was to make the involuntary transition from Anakin Skywalker to Darth Vader; the kind of indiscretion that, for a guy like Jonny Jinks, would only happen once.

Or so he thought.

ENTER YOUR PIN.

The machine insisted, flashing like a police siren as it sought the attention of its user.

Jonny followed protocol, thumping four digits on the number-pad as the ATM churned and croaked to search through its system files.

6174.

WHAT DO YOU WANT TO DO?

The question was a real humdinger. What *did* Jonny want to do? He had about as much of an idea as Paris Hilton in a spelling bee. An eighth of his soul, the only fragment that had remained uncleansed, whispered locutions of Lucifer that exhorted temptation, a spiralling urge to play 'spot-the-difference' with the *Pacific Pier*-based automated teller machine.

But Jonny was uneasy. The machine had become a thieving nemesis, re-robbing every last cent Jonny had withdrawn as it funnelled back into the banking system via deposits from a sports betting firm.

Yes, the setting had changed. Jonny was in a whole other state, a whole different time zone at a whole new time of the day.

But this *was* a Nations of Jefferson American Bank ATM.

And Jonny's wallet was empty, save for a notorious library card.

Jonny surveyed the options presented by the machine, mentally cross-referencing every parameter with the memorised framework of the ATM on 17th Street as he sought for any considerable differences.

Wait a minute...

After a string of instinctive key hits, Jonny's arrival at the machine's 'Transfer' screen pricked his 'spot-the-difference' senses like a *Ninja Turtle* beneath a New York City sewer.

Jonny had indeed found a variation.

The automated teller machine now provided five choices as opposed to the familiarly fantastic four. But just like a trivia question on *Who Wants to Be a Millionaire?*, only one answer would prove to be remunerative.

Savings. Cheque. MasterCard. Visa. Credit Card.

Jonny swiped sideways using the machine's arrow keys, hitting the right-directional arrow four times before hovering over a button that read 'Credit Card.'

Jonny was the proud owner of a magic *MasterCard* credit card, this much had been confirmed by his frequent visits to the mystical ATM on 17th Street in Allentown. But was a 'credit card' not the same thing? Where existed the differentiation between the machine's terminology and usage of the words '*MasterCard*' and 'credit card'?

Jonny could not figure out why, but he knew he had to find out.

His finger lifted and trembled as he progressed towards the 'ENTER' button in a cheesy eighties slow motion sequence, *Chariots of Fire* theme song and all.

Wait...

Had Jonny overlooked something? Had the circumstantial configurations been underemphasised? Were there significant correlations surrounding timely junctures and the behaviour of the machine?

Jonny twirled in a whirlpool of questions where he only needed answers.

And one way or another, he was going to get them.

Click.

The rickety 'ENTER' button jammed in a fixed position before releasing itself along with a build-up of dust particles and nitrogen.

... And then, as if Jonny hadn't already been apart of something so uncannily unplanned, a truly extraordinary event took place.

ENTER TRANSFER AMOUNT.

A clear instruction was delivered, a text-based command that was hardly as ambiguous as its bipolar operations.

The Californian sun radiated in a burning fireball as a bead of sweat dripped down Jonny's neck.

What's the worst that could happen?

Jonny had absolutely been here before.

He pressed on the number pad, first hitting the five key before following with two zeros and the 'ENTER' button.

SELECT TRANSFER TO ACCOUNT.

It was as if they were playing a remarkable mind-game, the ATM sending guileless commands as it teased the latency of yet another banking malfunction.

Loophole 2.0. There's no way this works... Is there?

Presented with the same five options as before, Jonny manoeuvred the ATM's controls like an arcade claw crane operator as he skipped to the *MasterCard* option and smacked the 'ENTER' key.

The machine's cryptoprocessor grumbled and groaned as it grinded on a goldmining quest to complete its operation.

Ahem!

To Jonny's oblivion, a line – longer than the queue for the *West Coaster* – had begun to form behind him as its front-row leader coughed and choked at something between a throat clear and a hustle play.

"So sorry, guys," Jonny apologised, red-faced. "Won't be much longer."

The pressure was trivial, virtually non-existent save for a handful of querulous Californian locals, and yet it hardly felt so. Jonny's conscience was in a race against an apparition of itself – an apparition feverishly clenching the fuse of a ticking time bomb.

Had Jonny exposed yet another fracture in the machine's flawed system?

TRANSACTION CANCELLED.

The message flashed in a familiar bold, red font as it spat out his card like a toddler to a bowl of broccoli.

Jonny's mind was strapped in a bunker at Area 51 as it sank into a fortress of the unknown.

Perhaps, he wondered, the location of the ATM truly *did* matter. Perhaps the time of day mattered much the same. Or perhaps the 'TRANSACTION CANCELLED' message was yet another variable error, and he was once again, five hundred dollars richer.

WHAT DO YOU WANT TO DO?

Jonny commanded the keypad, sliding across the selection panel as he instructed the machine to deliver on an account balance request.

If his memory was to be trusted his *MasterCard* had been reimbursed, resetting to a zero balance, an account that was no longer in credit or debit.

ACCOUNT BALANCE: $500.

The typography flashed on the machine's screen in a vivid green.

Jonny fell victim to Mr. Freeze's cryogenic 'Ice Gun,' triggering his body to immobilise as the gravity of his ATM wielding exercise became apparent.

It... worked. Wow.

Jonny almost refused to believe it; it had all seemed too simple, too straightforward.

How has nobody figured this out yet? Does the bank really not know that their entire system is corruptible?

He sought for an excuse, any reason to turn a blind eye to this fortuitous gift that had seemingly risen by the will of Plutus, the ancient Greek God of Wealth.

But it was about as easy to disregard as a hippopotamus in a college dorm room orgy; lightning had struck twice, Jonny the victim – or benefactor – of not one, but *two* seemingly illogical exploits.

Divine destiny appeared unbreakable, his fate preordained as with each passing moment, all signs pointed to a Pennsylvanian painter who – contrary to his devotion to probity – should not incriminate himself but rather thrive on Schadenfreude.

The tug-of-war prolonged in his mind... until only one side emerged victorious.

21

THE CHATEAU

i had no choice.

I was destined to surrender to the grandiloquence of the *Chateau* – the infamous hideaway where the extravagant luxuries of new could be desensitised. It's like when you first stay here, they give you this whole entire reason to *want* to educate yourself on the history, the spellbinding aura of the place. Modelled after a royal residence in France's Loire Valley, the *Chateau Marmont* was this fantastical folly in the land of make believe; the perfect setting for my soon-to-be-realised fantasy.

The *Chateau* was the ideal co-conspirator, its eccentric and rich history and its tarnished patina promoted the kind of charm that persuaded its residents to become whoever the hell they truly wanted to be.

And for me, whenever the dusk of evening would settle, I'd spin the needle on a collection of smoky jazz on this vintage record-player stashed in the hotel room closet and sink into the aphrodisiac that was the *Chateau*'s teal-coloured couches. The *Chateau Marmont* was the pageant and the parade, and it lured in all its guests in search for martinis and sex appeal. At the *Chateau,* I was on liberty, sabbatical, furlough from a once familiar life, as the manor acted as a truly humanised base-of-operations for the late night lust of Los Angeles living.

This was the place that I could be my new self.

this was the place my new self could call home.

* * *

"I'd like to check-in, please," Jonny uttered to the twinkling hotel clerk as he fidgeted with his wallet in hand.

The lobby at the *Chateau Marmont* oozed with five-star royalty, its delightfully mismatched vintage chic interior styling itself as the perfect imperfection. Beamed ceilings, gothic arches, wooden finishings and specks of red damask and velvet tailored the immortal hotel in gothic glamour while dimly lit indoor lamps illuminated its hallways in a 1940s-inspired backdrop.

"Certainly, sir," the clerk confirmed, her face frozen in a permanent smile as if she'd been violated and mutilated by The Joker. "Did you have the booking information with you or perhaps I could look up your surname?"

Jonny's instructions were limited. In fact, he had hardly a reason to believe that his proposed benefactor had even made such a reservation for his sojourn in paradise.

"Ugh," he fumbled, stalling to deliberate over the correct booking credentials. "Yes, my surname is Jinks, J-I-N-K-S."

The hotel clerk typed on the keys of her furbished computer, searching for the day's reservations as Jonny's neck panned horizontally in an attempt to scope out a more favourable vantage point of the computer's screen.

"Okay, I have a booking for a Mr. Jonny Jinks in a single queen-size bedroom with a garden view for a seven-day stay?" the clerk enumerated, seeking a verification of the booking items on her display screen.

Jonny. Of course.

A mind-knocking rhythm of germane George Strait lyrics vibrated like a drum-crashing troop of monkeys across Jonny's cranium as he mulled over the clerk's booking details.

I ain't here for a long time/
I'm here for a good time/
So bring on the sunshine, to hell with the red wine, pour me some moon shine/

Jonny Jinks had just stepped foot in Los Angeles' most notorious accommodation establishment; a hotel submerged in rich Hollywood history and majesty where even the city's most reticent could escape their otherwise peculiar inhibitions.

Consequently, Jonny Jinks was not partial to a rudimentary three hundred square foot one-bedroom apartment. At the *Chateau Marmont* it was either 'live like a king,' or 'die with the peasants.'

"I believe that's right," Jonny affirmed. "But I'm sorry ma'am, may I ask: did you have a penthouse apartment suite available instead?"

Jonny swung for the Babe Ruth homerun as he petitioned for a seldom but nonetheless necessary upgrade.

"Let me just check for you, sir," the clerk mumbled, hesitating before keying in a room availability search. "Okay, it looks like we do have our premier penthouse suite available on the sixth floor for two-thousand-seven-hundred a night – would you like me to update your booking?"

It was not the exorbitant evening rate that compelled Jonny into a mild trepidation – the price may as well have quadrupled – but the immeasurable repercussions of such a blithe commitment. Jonny was about to cross the rainbow of no return with nothing but dancing leprechauns, golden cauldrons and impossible fantasies ahead of him.

This was his stepping stone – a leap to a coloured dark side.

"If you could, that would be great," Jonny accepted with aplomb as he offered a subtly suave head bow. "But could you please do me a favour? The credit card that was provided and filed upon placing the booking, could we replace that with a different card for this transaction?"

Chuckie can't know.

"Certainly, sir."

No questions asked.

Jonny swept the pavement of evidence with a credit card-shaped broom, inadvertently refusing Chuckie's generous offer as he safeguarded his adventure against any corroborating records.

Chuckie will never check his credit card statement to know I never used it, anyway.

"Okay, sir, I now have a booking for yourself in a one-bedroom penthouse apartment suite on the sixth floor for an indefinite stay?" the clerk repeated once again.

"Yes, that is now correct."

"Excellent, Mr. Jinks, we'll get someone to help you with your luggage."

The receptionist snapped her fingers as a big burly man approached like a manifested genie summoned out of thin-air.

"Andre, please take Mr. Jinks' bags to apartment number 64," she commanded as the mystical bellboy granted her wish.

"Now, may I please have the appropriate credit card to process the bond, sir?"

My MasterCard.

Jonny was eased by the receptionist's request as he reached for his wallet and removed his plastic-laminated goldmine.

"Thank you, Mr. Jinks," the clerk expressed with a counterfeit smile as she returned the credit card and handed him a collection of apartment peripherals that included a bronzed key tagged onto a green-plated keychain. "Please make your way down this corridor to your right where you'll find the elevator lobby that will take you to your floor."

The convivial receptionist gesticulated like an airline attendant during a pre-flight safety demonstration as Jonny followed her instructions explicitly. He paced along a carpeted brick-road and towards the gothic wizardry of the hotel's gold-encrusted elevator lobby.

The shaft-housed compartment was glossed in gold while aureate directional plaques stationed between each elevator blurred and bounced incoming light signals across surrounding reflective surfaces.

Ding! The elevator rang as its automatic doors stretched open to greet its ground-floor passenger.

As Jonny crossed the unofficial equator between loiterer and official *Chateau* guest, he wondered if he had just stepped foot in the same elevator that ruffled the libido and ignited an unsanitary tryst between Scarlett Johansson and Benicio Del Toro after a particularly fabled *Oscars* ceremony.

As the *Chateau* elevator graunched and grinded in a reverberated cable churn, Jonny paused to admire the elegant and enduring cubicle of vertical transportation before involuntarily manifesting a transparent and nearly headless bellhop from *Disney's The Tower of Terror.*

Should've taken the stairs he lamented, recalling the royally red-carpeted stairway and sturdy balustrade.

As the elevator doors slid open – this time, apparently a far more arduous and persistent exercise than before – Jonny sprung out into the sixth-floor corridor, passing rooms 61, 62 and 63 in sequential order as he engrossed in the uniform fabric and colour patterns of the manor.

Here it is: Penthouse apartment suite 64.

Jonny numbed his movements as he pricked his earlobes and tuned his eardrum to the sonic signals of *Live: Chateau Marmont 60.4FM,* intending to overhear any kind of explicit celebrity chatter vibrating through the indistinct passageway of the exclusive sixth floor.

After a string of silence, Jonny removed the bronze-plated apartment key from his pocket. He ran his fingers over the roughened identification engraving before inserting the key and twisting the door's lock free.

As the door creaked open and Jonny caught his first glimpse of the penthouse apartment's splendour, he was certain he had just unlocked his soul to a majestic portal of indescribable phenomena.

The unassuming hallway was not to be misjudged. The penthouse suite's entrance flooring was surfaced with chequered black and white chessboard tiling. But unlike that of the strategy game, this chessboard represented a sequence of events that were entirely stochastic in nature.

A pair of gold compact chandeliers hung from the ceiling while a trident of framed portraits adorned the walls of the main hall.

Jonny crept through the walkway like an elusive investigator, his eyes jackpotting in dollar signs as he ranked each extravagant article in the penthouse suite from expensive to exorbitant. Wall-mounted candles, gold-plaque mirrors, charming lounge suites and meticulously crafted lamp fittings all made up a minor portion of the apartment's valuables as Jonny instantly recognised the individual opulence in each.

And although the suite's interior contained a plenitude of useful household treasures, the pinnacle of the room's magnificence existed not beneath its white ceilings but on the outskirts of its rounded walls.

Jonny, wonderstruck by this latest revelation, marched through the main living quarters, passing a teal leather sofa as he stepped through a gaping passageway and into an open-aired haven.

As his feet pressed firmly down on the paved balcony of the idyllic penthouse terrace, he hid his eyes from the glaring Californian sunshine and allowed his mind to dream. He dreamt of the utility this extravagant stomping ground provided to those that came before him. He dreamt of some of cinema's most famous conquistadors, cohabiting on the moulded plastic beach chairs under the cloak of the terrace's protective awning. He dreamt of the sirens of the silver screen that might have made the legendary outdoor hangout the primal and secluded setting for their scandalous liaisons. But mostly, he dreamt about what it would have been like, had he not been there alone.

The higher altitude offered a cleansing breeze as Jonny's thick hair rode the gentle current like a wave-rider at Huntington Beach.

The view was nothing short of breathtaking.

The Californian adventure was nothing short of surreal.

And it was only just the beginning.

* * *

An afternoon's four-wheeled adventure around 'The Golden State' often took its passengers into the high mountains, where eagles circled above naked forests and cold blue lakes. Explorers from all over the globe would journey over the depths of the Mojave Desert, blissfully photographing its unearthly vegetation and immense vistas before detouring towards Death Valley, Yosemite National Park and the Sequoia Forest to bask in the ageless glory of its immortal trees.

And while any traveller to the city could be excused for being blind-sighted by the glamor of its metropolis, not to visit such places would be regarded as a globetrotter's sin.

This was the unfeigned nature of California.

This was the secret behind its fascination.

This was the untamed, the undomesticated, the aloof, the prehistoric, the candid panorama that relentlessly reminded the traveller of his mortality and the circumstances of his tenure on the dusted soils of the living planet.

But Jonny Jinks was no ordinary traveller.

As he rested his legs atop the plush teal sofa and stretched at the shoulders so that his fingers clasped to form a humanised pillow, he softened his eyelids and began in an illusory conversation with the gatekeeper of the city of Los Angeles.

"You are perfectly welcome," it whispered as Jonny dazed off into a subconsciously erected labyrinth. "During your short visit here, consider everything I have to offer you at your disposal."

Jonny's obstructed airways pressured his nasal into an indolent snore as if he were some kind of reincarnated Darth Vadar.

"Only, I must warn you, if things do go wrong, do not blame me," the voiceless gatekeeper cautioned. "I accept no responsibility. I am not part of your neurosis. Do not cry to me for safety. There is no home here. There is no security in your mansion or your fortress, your family vault or your bank account or your king-size bed."

Jonny twitched in a mindless dreamscape as the air's humidity squeezed at his sweat glands and showered him in a still perspiration.

"Understand this fact, and you will be free. Accept it, and you will be happy."

22
PRETTY WOMEN & PINS

The next victim had been determined, the laboratory rodent that would play the role of 'Test Subject #2' on Jonny's newly-discovered *Monopoly*-squared hopscotch.

A driver in tinted sunglasses – disguised as if he were a senior executive of the *Men in Black* – pulled to the curb outside the *Chateau Marmont* in a gloss-black 'Power California Chauffeur Service' number-plated *Rolls-Royce Ghost*.

"Booking for 'Jonny'?" the chauffeur queried in New York City English as he whistled through his wounded window.

I guess that's me.

"Pleased to meet you, sir," Jonny saluted, untucking the rear of his sleeve-rolled midnight blue sweater from his stone-coloured chino shorts as he tugged at the doorhandle and slid into the back seat.

"Name's Santino," the chauffeur said as he realigned his rear-view mirror, his plump cheeks reflecting off the prismatic anti-glare glass. "Santino Barsotti, but you can call me Sonny."

Sonny Barsotti.

"Got it," Jonny acknowledged, the *Ghost*'s creamed interior camouflaging with the colour of his shorts.

"Where we heading, sir?" Sant–... Sonny asked as he tightened his black necktie and twirled at his grey goatee before releasing the handbrake.

"Rodeo Drive."

Jonny avoided eye contact as he fidgeted with the polyester webbing of the seat belt.

"Well, well, you certainly picked the right car for that!"

Alive with cutting-edge technology, the *Rolls-Royce Ghost* was one of the most advanced luxury saloons ever built. The essence of simplicity combined with signature levels of luxury, the *Ghost* forged a silent path with effortless power, its exterior design offering poise and verve while its luxurious interior – with soft, supple leather and indulgent lambs-wool floor mats – cosseted its passengers from the outside world.

And it was for this very particular reason that the *Ghost* was unquestionably the ultimate experimental vehicle for Jonny Jinks.

"So not from this town, hey, sir?" Sonny barked, grinning in the rear-view, his innocent Italian glow radiating with the geniality of a costumed dinosaur at a *Wiggles* concert.

"What gave it away?"

"Well, you know," Sonny continued innocuously, spinning the steering wheel right from Marmont Lane onto Sunset Boulevard. "Chauffeur call, room at the *Chateau Marmont*; you know, that kind of stuff."

Sonny was the quintessential stereotype for a middle-aged chauffeur. Cloaked in a black suit with gold buttons and buckled by a platinum tie bar above his double-breasted blazer overlap, Sonny's ensemble was completed by a pair of silk white gloves and a gold-embroidered poly wool chauffeurs hat with a high crown and low brim that flaunted a wave of royalty and excellence to his clientele.

"I'm not from here either, you know?" the driver hinted. "I'm from New York; Queens, actually. Moved over here in my late twenties to open a pizza place with my wife."

Jonny's expression suggested curiosity but his mind yearned for silence. After all, what was he paying for?

"What happened?" Jonny asked.

We're only fifteen minutes away, anyway. I can deal with it.

"Building fire; took the whole place down in one hit. Luckily we were covered by insurance, but after the incident the wife and I didn't feel much like rebuilding the place."

Sonny changed lanes as Jonny ticked off a contingent of timed landmarks along the boulevard – *Sunset Plaza, The Viper Room, The Roxy Theatre* – before the *Ghost* turned and zoomed along Sierra Drive and onto Santa Monica Boulevard as if it were featuring in a product-placement advertisement.

"Anyway, she decided to stay home with the kids and I picked up this gig where I get to service some awesome folks like yourself."

Jonny admired Sonny's persistence; sure, there existed the possibility that an unexpected building fire at a depreciating property owned by a cunningly well-dressed, middle-aged Italian migrant could have been self-induced, but what did that matter? Jonny was grasping at straws and even if he were wrong, he preferred his own version of the narrative far more.

Sonny's commitment to the survival of his family was laudable and this was a sterling quality that Jonny was beginning to relate to.

"Alright, sir, here we are, just up ahead," Sonny indicated, turning left as he broke before the traffic lights at the road's northern terminus and in front of the *Yves Saint Laurent* store, the unofficial beginning – or ending – of the sumptuous motif that decorated the heralded Rodeo Drive.

For generations, the three blocks of Rodeo Drive had been home to the epicentre of luxury, fashion and entertainment. But Jonny hardly recognised the strip before him as the world-renowned thoroughfare of splendour and charm.

This was *the* Rodeo Drive, the cultural setting of a 1990's rom-com classic.

"Hey, Sonny," Jonny commanded, reaching forward as he loosened the stranglehold of the *Ghost*'s seatbelt. "Think you could start me off on the other end of the strip? The side closest to Wilshire Boulevard?"

"Sure thing, sir," Sonny obliged as he winked in the rear-view. "For an out-of-towner you seem to know your L.A. quite well?"

He didn't. But it wasn't Los Angeles, the city, that Jonny felt a close familiarity with.

"I watch a lot of TV."

Two minutes, forty-three seconds, a horn honk and a window wind-down later, the *Ghost* arrived at the foot of a landmark Jonny had seen so many times before on DVD, Blu-Ray and satellite television.

The Beverly Wilshire.

Constructed in 1928, the *Beverly Wilshire* – squared at the intersection of Wilshire Boulevard and the famed Rodeo Drive – was a varnished expression of Italian Renaissance excellence. Its 395 rooms and suites, wall-graced frescos and elevator-adorned velvet settees had played host and hostess to countless presidents, foreign dignitaries and Hollywood elitists that included the likes of Warren Beatty, John Lennon and Elvis Presley. But today, the ornamental *Beverly Wilshire* was affectionately fabled for a far different reason... for acting as the backdrop in a cult-classic starring Richard Gere and Julia Roberts.

"Hey baby, what's your name?"

"What do you want it to be?"

"You know, sir, they actually filmed the movie *Pretty Woman* here," Sonny revealed like a local tour guide, apparently unawares that his client's Pennsylvanian girlfriend routinely screened the film in

Allentown suburbia.

Jonny scanned the hotel's façade as a Canadian and United States flag stood waving in an almost still breeze, its unmistakable flagpoles nationalising the otherwise international building.

"Actually, they used the outside of the hotel for exterior shots and built sets to mimic the hotel's *actual* guestrooms," Sonny continued, his memory loaded with *Google*-generated information.

"I've never seen it," Jonny dissimulated, unbuckling his seatbelt as he inhaled the *Ghost's* fine leather and prepared to vacate the vehicle.

"That's too bad," Sonny sympathised. "A gentleman like yourself roaming solo around L.A. could really benefit from some of the... *ideas* in that film."

Jonny did not disagree as he recalled some of the finest scripting he had ever seen on film: *"You and I are such similar creatures, Vivian. We both screw people for money."*

"So, Sonny, do I pay up-front or do you follow me around Beverly Hills until I'm out of dollars and then charge me interest until I'm back on my feet?"

Sonny loosened the grip of his seatbelt before re-adjusting his rear-view mirror.

"Sir, from where I'm sitting, your feet rarely ever leave the ground," Sonny lionised, incognizant of Jonny's unexplainable conundrum. "And for whatever reason, if they do, we take in-vehicle credit card."

Sonny disconnected a wireless POS-integrated credit card terminal from its holding bay as he reached back and presented the unit to his passenger.

Here we go again.

The process ran like clockwork, Jonny relieving his *MasterCard* from its in-wallet pouch before inserting the plastic in the card reader and entering a four-digit PIN code that was becoming as naturally recallable as a '911' call.

6174.

The four-digit PIN code as provided to him by the Nations of Jefferson American Bank was settled by an unsystematic lotto spin, a random generation of numbers that, only by chance, suggested a peculiar prophecy between its digits.

Kaprekar's Constant was a fascinating mathematical theorem that explored the almost impossible relationship between four-digit integers and the number '6174.' By arranging the digits in descending and ascending order and deducting the difference between these figures, the resulting numeral would eventuate into the number combination of '6174.' On its surface, this appeared meaningless, a quantifiable principle to which Jonny was utterly oblivious to.

But upon deeper analysis, a far clearer and prognosticated kismet would reveal itself, a layman's alternative to the mathematical principles as proposed by Kaprekar: that no matter where one was to begin, the ending had already been determined.

23

DROP IT LOW & RODEO

rodeo drive.

It's a mammoth of a fucking cliché, I know. But where the hell else do you go to cure the world? People used to say that money wouldn't solve a man's problems; that problems were central only to behaviour, habits, and mindset. The only problem with that? It *was* my behaviour, habits and mindset that had me deep in a hole, buried alongside the cow shit in the first place.

Speaking of problems, what're the chances of uncovering not one, but *two* fucking loopholes in a national banking system? I mean, it's like someone screwed a GPS to the collar of a sniffer dog and screamed the words "go find a tennis ball" in the middle of a *Wimbledon* practice court.

It was too obvious, too convenient.

I needed to equip my Dr. Emmett Brown costume and play mad scientist.

this bullshit would require some serious experimentation.

* * *

The sun sizzled and sparkled, glistening the gold plaques of the Rodeo Drive Walk of Style as Jonny trekked from Wilshire Boulevard,

South Santa Monica Boulevard and back again.

Tourists snapped photos at Bijan Pakzad's custom mustard-coloured *Rolls-Royce Phantom Drophead Coupé* while others basked in the fifteen-seconds of faux-celebrity at the red carpet entrance of *The Beverly Hills Hotel*. Jonny – in a quiet solitude that might have mistook him for a perverted prowler – gazed and people-watched, dissecting the movements and smiles of each of the strip's pedestrians.

"Welcome, sir," the doorman greeted as he held open the supersized entranceway for his customer, his lavish suit the most inexpensive off-the-shelf item in the entire fashion house.

It only took a moment before Jonny knew he was being hawked... for all the wrong reasons. The triple-storey flagship *Louis Vuitton* store at the corner of 295 North Rodeo Drive and Dayton Way was the paragon of luxury fashion and splendour. On the outside, the three-layered facade was a shower of modern-day opulence, its face clothed in louver-like stainless steel ribbons over squares of white fabric while on the inside, the house was reversed, gasconaded in a slice of the brand's historic mid-nineteenth-century roots. Blond wood floors, brown, geometric-patterned carpets, a long, linear staircase – wrapped entirely in *Vuitton*'s super-soft leather – that ran in a straight line along the boutique's north wall from the first to third floor and its fitting room walls lined in honest-to-goodness woven leather projected a grandiose aesthetic, a palette that demanded the presence of only the city's most elitist aristocrats.

Jonny – poised by the front door and beside a three-metre tall, bright pink mixed-media sculpture – locked eyes with a haughty saleswoman who offered the kind of supercilious stare that suggested he was as unbefitting as Julia Roberts in scruffy hand-me-downs.

I don't think we have anything for you here. You're obviously in the wrong place.

It wasn't that Jonny was inappropriately dressed; after all, his cuff-rolled sweater and chinos were ubiquitous across the front page of almost every mass-production department store catalogue across the country. But what Jonny lacked was an empowering and magnetic deportment, a self-possessing charisma that screamed swagger and confidence.

Without that, he was nothing more than a handsome window-shopper, a time-wasting tourist who did not belong.

Jonny severed the Superman-like laser-beam cord that bridged him with the *Vuitton* saleswoman as he paced to the right, lifting his chin towards a suspended stainless steel and aluminium tangle reminiscent of a Santa Ana tossed palm tree.

"*Ghostwriter*," came a soft but stern voice from behind, startling him with the fear of a thousand poltergeists. "It's by Peter Rogiers – we wanted something that could honour Southern California, something that could steal the breath of our clientele... and by the look on your face, it appears that it has served its purpose."

That it has.

The saleswoman's disparaging stare flipped one-hundred-and-eighty degrees as Jonny realised that close up, she was actually rather attractive. Not the kind of attractive one would see under almost every umbrella at the Santa Monica State Beach but instead, an elegant, nubile kind of attraction that made teenage students fall in a spiralling, taboo lust for their high school temp teacher.

"I love the way he's used the negative space around the piece," Jonny critiqued as if the *Vuitton* saleswoman were a recent alumnus of the *California Institute of the Arts*.

"So how can I help you today, sir?" she hunted, "Are you shopping for yourself, or perhaps a spouse?"

Maya.

The next step of her sales process triggered a subconscious reverie, a mental musing of the whereabouts and activities of his unconditional lover.

"Just for me," Jonny replied, unsure if even that were true.

"Certainly – in that case, our second floor is home to the men's offerings. If you'd kindly like to head upstairs, Alastair can help you to a glass of lemon water and will assist you with your selection."

Jonny thanked the saleswoman before her accommodating smile expired, reverting itself to a bipolar leer of unpleasant superiority.

The second floor was explicitly merchandised to showcase the latest in the *Louis Vuitton* range of men's timepieces, made-to-order shoes and belts and a selection of writing implements, notebooks, inkwells and stationary.

After surveying a handful of price tags, Jonny ambled towards a vacant seating area that was appointed in vintage mid-century modern furniture and artwork before a dapper gentleman who appeared befitting of an aristocratic appellation such as 'Alastair' appeared from behind a velvet curtain.

"Good afternoon, sir," Alastair chirped, his long, blonde locks and feminine features resembling a gay doppelganger of Chris Hemsworth. "My name is Alastair and I will be your sales assistant this afternoon. So how can I be of assistance?"

A slice of Jonny understood, yet detested such conventional, white-collar lingo as Alastair played the role of in-house butler meets at-your-service sales clerk with honourable conviction. And yet there existed a subsidiary slice in his soul, a slice that was festering with every passing moment, appealing to an almost hidden ego that was never there before.

What the hell do I buy in here that isn't going to raise too many alarm bells?

"Let's start off with the wallets," Jonny suggested, curious as to why beginning his sentence with the phrase 'let's start off' was a clever idea.

"A fine choice, sir," Alastair indulged, escorting Jonny to a glassed cabinet that appeared as reinforced as the president's White House bedroom. "Here is our most recent collection for your perusal."

Alistair gestured forwards as Jonny browsed the wallets in the window like a man who was unsure if he could afford them.

"I see you've taken a particular liking to our 'Brazza wallet,'" Alistair shadowed, unlocking the security glass with a lanyard key as he showcased the leather between his palms.

The *Louis Vuitton* Brazza wallet, crafted in an iconic 'LV' monogram canvas and decorated with a three-tone, hand drawn giraffe illustration exuded playful sophistication. Woven in a textile lining with a cowhide leather trim and silver coloured metallic pieces, the Brazza wallet came equipped with a seven-hundred dollar price tag and a sixteen-slot storage surplus for just what Jonny was after: his bank cards.

Jonny recognised the significance of the decision he was poised to make. The experiment would go on, Jonny willingly testing the credit card's limits as he stretched its wings and forced it to fly. But it was time for *Jonny* to play the hamster in the spinning wheel; it was time for *Jonny* to masquerade in a smoke-screened guise, an unrecognisable illusion that would aggrandize his artificial dynasty and give further credence to the symbolic transformation of 'Jon' to 'Jonny.'

"I'll take one of those," he ordered nonchalantly as if he were shopping for seasonal fruits at a grocery store. "And let's take a look at the watches next?"

In his three years spent occupying *Louis Vuitton*'s men's quarters, Alistair had never seen a purchase-decision made with such expediency and disregard for dissonance.

"We can certainly do that, sir," Alistair served, smelling the budding fumes of a transaction terminal overload. "May I ask your name, sir?"

If the saleswoman on *Louis Vuitton*'s ground floor took him for nothing more than an aficionado of fine Californian art, a frivolous traveller without a spendable dollar, then Alistair's preconceptions juxtaposed that in a glorious antithesis. To the sales clerk, his client was an affluent juggernaut, a compulsive spender who embodied the metaphorical phrase of 'do not judge a book by its cover.'

"Jon Ji–," he stuttered, slamming the brakes as he composed himself and tried to remember who he really was. "*Jonny* Jinks."

Alistair did not know the difference – after all, 'Jonny' was nothing more than a diminutive suffix, a hypocorism of his given name.

But there *was* a difference. And Jonny was beginning to see it.

24

MY CARD SAYS' FILLE DE JOIE'

An emotional imbalance swarmed him as he weighed his adversaries on a scale and swallowed them whole like sleeping pills in a gushing waterfall of *Ketel One Vodka*.

His mind was riddled – an unsolvable conundrum without a clue from Edward Nygma to show the way.

Jonny was two-and-a-half-thousand miles away from the love of his life with a giraffe-plated wallet full of digital dollars that were seemingly never to run out.

And perhaps it was the vodka that was to be blamed, but Jonny wasn't sure that Allentown and all its tribulations were deserving of his new-found fortune.

Jonathan Jinks and Maya Ververs had been sharing in the heartache of infertility and financial and occupational insecurity for months on end, a fate that now appeared solvable by the swift swipe of Jonny's standard-issue *MasterCard*.

But the heralded son from Allentown was ultimately undecided on his next dice-roll.

Was he already in too deep? Had a commitment to splurge at *Louis Vuitton* unlocked a portal of no return, an automatic incrimination that, even if Jonny were to confess to the events of this accidental escape, would render him liable to a charge of 'theft by finding'?

His conscience battled with a shadow of himself as he wrestled with three options:

- Option A - seize all spending on his credit card, fulfil his occupational duties and report the loophole – otherwise recognised as a minor misdemeanour – to Maya and the Nations of Jefferson American Bank, integrity in tact.

- Option B – repeat steps as above with the exclusion of a confession to authorities, forge a two-way secret between he and Maya and utilise the pot of gold for the 'greater good,' clearing the couple's debts as they position themselves for the future.

- Option C – do not fulfil occupational duties, do not confess to the Nations of Jefferson American Bank, do not confess to Maya… and bleed money in Los Angeles like a desolate oil magnate at a porn-star gangbang.

It seemed clear that 'Option A' was a no-brainer, a mechanical decision made unconsciously as a result of years of righteousness, altruism and gospel.

Except that the decision was *not* mechanical and Jonny's instinctive gears seemed jammed and unresponsive, frozen like a broken grandfather clock.

Nothing was quite as it had once seemed.

"This seat taken?" a woman asked, approaching an unoccupied barstool to Jonny's left as she swayed ever-so elegantly in a knee-high baby blue dress.

Jonny opened his palm, sliding his barstool across as he gestured in consent for the women to be seated.

The woman in baby blue was something out of a Japanese erotic anime, a thin stripe of blue hair dye in her ponytail rendering her the perfect illustration subject for any caricaturist.

"Can I get a fresh fruit cocktail?" she ordered, the bartender making a move for the pureed fruit on the rear shelf as Jonny caught a mischievous second glimpse at the woman in baby blue. "I prefer to *eat* my calories rather than *drink* them."

Jonny could tell. The woman was a fresh, tropical mixture of curves and skeleton, her legs longer than an exotic outback spider that possessed the power to turn men into mulch and saints into sinners.

Jonny fidgeted with his vodka before being given a reason to stop.

"I'm Yasmine," she introduced herself, holding out her hair-stripe-matching baby-blue-painted nails like Daenerys Targaryen to an unworthy unsullied.

"Jon... -ny. Jonny," he stumbled as he cupped her fingers, still not quite assimilated to the change.

"So, Jon-ny," she chaffed, breaking his new name down into fragmented syllables as she imitated his stutter. "What's a guy like you doing at a bar like this in the middle of the day?"

Jonny did not understand – what was so unusual about these variables?

"Drinking."

"Well *that* I can see," she slithered, not unnerved by his bashfulness as she thanked and compensated the bartender for his addictive services. "You know normally that seat is reserved for the forty-to-fifty something year old businessman with a stiff headache and a wife who doesn't love him..."

Jonny shuffled his backside like a royal houseguest seated on a throne not befitting of him as he puzzle-pieced the clues together.

"... And something tells me you don't *quite* fit that description," Yasmine suggested, somewhere between a compliment and a criticism.

"I didn't see the 'reserved' sign," he joked, searching for a metal table-top as if he were seated at an exclusive, reservation-only Beverly

Hills restaurant.

"Honey, there's a lot you don't see," she confessed mystically, her eyebrows jiggling like bouncing breasts in a 'no sports-bra' marathon as she sipped her fruit-based concoction and lifted the ends of her baby blue skirt up her thigh.

In the background, the bar's ceiling-mounted sound-system transitioned its playlist from up-tempo rock and roll to Elton John's '*Goodbye Yellow Brick Road*' classic, '*Sweet Painted Lady*' as Jonny signalled for another *Ketel One* refill.

"So... you're... an... *escort*, then?" Jonny surmised as he speculated that the very barstool beneath him was in fact, her base of operations, her 'batcave' of a sexual prison where interested adulterers could discretely make themselves known.

"My card says 'fille de joie," she corrected in an elegant euphemism as she elevated her own societal position.

"I don't speak French."

Jonny was determined to avoid her entangling web of carnage as he employed any conversational method that would redeem him from her toxic temptation.

Maya. Maya. Maya.

"Do you *kiss* French?"

So... that backfired.

* * *

Given the circumstances – two hours of uninterrupted banter and conversation with a Californian prostitute he would never pay for – he felt compelled, his inebriated shoulder-demons suggesting that a precise enactment of an iconic rom-com scene was absolutely necessary.

After all, Jonny was in the home of Hollywood. And when in

Rome...

"You know, you and I, we're pretty similar creatures," Jonny confessed, his muddled mind numb at the force of a memory recall. "You screw people and I screw banks for money."

Jonny was drunk enough to realise that he had butchered the line as a mirage of Richard Gere appeared before him to gesticulate a dispirited finger-wag of disapproval.

Oh shit. Wait. What did I just say?

"Metaphorically, of course," Jonny bubbled as he scribbled a line through his incidental comment and sipped at his glass of vodka.

"How do you metaphorically rob a bank?" the courtesan asked, tugging at his collar as Jonny's face bled in a light red.

Great fucking question.

"You ever played *Monopoly* before?"

"I make money every time I make a man 'pass go' if that's what you're asking."

Such witty innuendo drew parallels to Jonathan Jinks and Maya Ververs in a verbal tug-of-war by an Allentown-manufactured kitchen counter.

"Have another drink with me?" Jonny insisted, signalling for the waiter as Yasmine collected her *Yves Saint Laurent* handbag, no doubt purchased at the company's flagship American store on Rodeo Drive.

"Do you try to fill all the women you meet with alcohol before asking them home with you?" she purred, apparently unbothered by the forthcoming answer.

Jonny blushed, uncertain of the boundaries as another sip of *Ketel One Vodka* spun him around like a faulty washing machine.

"I don't have any money," he lied sheepishly.

"Who said anything about money?"

Yasmine's eyebrows danced once again as the diamond on her

finger reflected off the glass of her fresh fruit cocktail.

"You know, if you're not open to change, you're going to be like this forever," she teased innocuously. "Now is that *good* news?"

Jonny sunk into a social limbo. The woman was a working prostitute, a glamour who recruited her clientele from the very barstool Jonny was occupying... and yet, she appeared prepared to voluntarily forfeit compensation.

Something... doesn't... I... feel...

"Just give me a quick second," Jonny blurted, thudding the glass of vodka on the bar bench as he sprinted for the men's lavatory like a preschooler with cooties.

"Well... that was new," Yasmine whispered to the bartender, the man snickering like a witness-turned-pimp who had apparently been privy to these first-hand pre-copulation exchanges more than once before.

Jonny rushed through the lavatory door, knocking the gentlemen's restroom sign like an All-Pro linebacker to a rookie halfback as he peddled for the sink.

The restroom – complete with chequered tiling, fire engine red cubicles, arguably artistic 'latrinalia' and a vile and unmistakable stench – squeezed Jonny inwards as he made for the cast iron sink.

He rotated the tap handles before a waterfall of cold water came pouring through his palms and downwards into the spiralling sink. Jonny splashed a lagoon of cold water against his face as he tried to regain consciousness, his mind swimming in the suffocating blur of a drowning fisherman stranded in the middle of the ocean.

He checked his reflection in the dirty mirror, panting heavily before gently waving his right hand up and down, his mirrored likeness mimicking the gesture verbatim.

I'm still me. This is still me.

Jonny's reflection, while virtually identical, was quickly becoming unrecognisable.

What am I doing. This isn't me... is it?

Jonny ran the tap, its splatter and spray hitting everything from the chequered tiling to the off-white, graffiti-scribbled walls around him.

Communal and public toilets had long been associated with lowbrow street art – a far more flattering alternative to the term – of a transgressive or lowbrow nature. But for Jonny, art was art – in any kind – and was worth his extra heeding.

At first, the messages of vandalism appeared hackneyed – everything from 'What Would Jesus Do' tags to bulletins of social disapproval, scrawled doodles and derogatory accusations of horse fornication.

But as he surveyed the chequered area cubicle by cubicle, something strange became abundantly clear: it seemed that a forthcoming bowel movement possessed the wildly unorthodox ability to foster insightful declarations and potty propaganda.

Two inscriptions stood out from the herd. The first:

Since writing on bathroom stalls is done neither for wealth nor critical acclaim, it is, in fact, the purest form of art. Discuss.

Jonny knew he wasn't seated in a lecture theatre at *The Baum School of Art* on Linden Street, but the impetus of the topic sure made it feel that way.

Is this for real?

He needed a disconnect and such trivial subject matter – trivial, of course, to any layman not aroused by the nuances of art – offered a debatable relief.

For Jonny, the truest of art was one in which existed for little to no purpose, outside of itself. Under this sentiment, elements like cars and buildings were *artful* – embodying many of the attributes revelled by art lovers – but their primary purpose was something other than existing for the sake of art itself, a perspective he knew would turn Antoni Gaudi in his grave.

And while this belief formed the rudimentary fragments of his very philosophy on the arts, it was a belief of arrogance, a bias and unfair assessment of an ever-evolving dexterity that Jonny would soon be re-evaluating.

He reached towards his derrière, not in a self-gratifying, squeezing one's own ass kind-of-way but rather to pat down his pockets like an airport security guard inspecting for dangerous or sharp objects.

My back pocket.

Jonny reached deep into the cookie jar before relieving the bright blue indelible marker pilfered from the south wing of the under-construction communal hub at Regrub Moon Hills. He popped the cap, waving the marker as its toxic odour filtered the restroom from the stench of faeces and bad breath.

Discuss? That, I can do.

He shook the marker up and down, touching its inked head against the wall's plastered surface before a second dribble of latrinalia forced a sudden halt in handwriting. The graffiti was a kind of edification, a rare glimpse into the conflicting intellect of a cubicle artist that offered an enlightenment, far more purposeful than a pun about toilets and human shit.

If no one comes from the future to stop you from doing it, then how bad of a decision can it really be?

The quotation was hand-printed in black ink, somewhere between a messy first-grader's cursive calligraphy and the lettering of an adult who had long forgotten his pen-etiquette.

Jonny wondered if a toilet god – a God of Excrement – had ever existed in any culture or spiritual belief and if so, what business had it with him? For not the first time, it appeared that he was being dictated by divine intervention, by an all-seeing, all-forgiving *Big Brother* determined to manipulate his every move for his own pleasures... or television ratings.

Another crossroads manifested – to stay or to go, that would be the question.

Be good. Be bad. Be good. Be bad. Be good.

Jonny dried his face with the back of his hand, absorbing the liquids like a sponge before re-reading the passage on the wall beside the furthest cubicle.

If no one comes from the future to stop you from doing it, then how bad of a decision can it really be?

Jonny was ready to deliver an answer.

He pressed the marker's tip against the wall as he began to carve a response to a very pertinent question.

That'll do, he decided, standing with his hands rope-tied behind his back as he re-read both the question and response like transcripts from a court hearing.

It was time for Jonny to execute his order, to face fate head on without a helmet. He switched his footing, slapping the hand dryer's activation button as he parched the remains of any liquid on his hair-pricked skin before rushing for the restroom's exit.

Left for Yasmine, right for the rear emergency exit...

Jonny stopped, head-checking both ways before angling his ankles in the direction he determined was *right*.

As he scurried down the corridor and towards the green glow of a hard-nosed plastic wall sign, he heaved a sigh of principled relief at the bright blue marker-dictated response he had given the arbitrating God of Excrement.

What if the decision is so bad that there is no future?

25

RETURN OF THE CHUCKIE MONSTER

"So…" the redhead beamed, his ruby-rose *Ray-Ban* sunglasses indicating a clear penchant for fitting in with a crowd that ultimately – minus the bulge in his wallet – he did not belong to. "How's it hanging at the *Chateau Marmont* – everything you could've ever dreamed of, right?"

Sure. I bet the single queen-size bedroom with a garden view was going to kick ass.

"You're right," Jonny admitted as the background noise in the hotel's lobby increased by a decibel or two. "It definitely *is* a dream."

The duo occupied a floral-patterned sofa, their polished shoes resting against the lobby's unmistakable red carpet as a scallop bell-shaped lampshade illuminated the space like a lit wick in a gothic dungeon.

"Hey let me ask you something man," Chuckie prefaced in a whisper as a wash of mischief poured over him. "What's your guiltiest pleasure?"

"Excuse me?"

"You know," Chuckie pressed. "A guilty pleasure; c'mon, holmes, I don't believe that you don't have one. There's got to be something you want that you can't have?"

That appeared a different question entirely. Jonny Jinks had already bitten into the golden apple – and, spat out a mouthful of a baby blue one – and it came in the form of a plastic bankcard and an automated teller machine. And while it was not the kind of guilty pleasure Jonny had ever coveted, it was, without a shadow of a doubt, the kind that could not be ignored.

Something I want that I can't have? I want to pay my bills. I want to keep my job. I want to sell my paintings. I want to have a baby.

There aren't enough lines for this kind of list…

"Okay, okay," Chuckie said, clearly more intent on answering his own question. "Let me help you out, alright? So, my guilty pleasure…"

Chuckie leant forward in a boyish zest before a smartphone ringer interrupted his big reveal in a surrogate interpretation of conversational 'blue balls'.

"Hold on," Jonny instructed, reaching for his pocket to retrieve his humming smartphone.

The screen's brightness had been dimmed, but *this* caller ID could not be shadowed.

Maya.

The generic ringer on his device chimed to a hidden rhythm of regretful betrayal as Jonny tapped the locked button a single time to activate its 'silent mode.'

"You don't want to get that?" Chuckie asked, his legs crossed like a mafia boss at a family meeting. "What if it's Felecia calling with an update about Regrub Moon Hills?"

Chuckie's eyebrows wiggled as if he had a scoop that Jonny hadn't yet heard about.

"It isn't."

For how long he would continue to obstruct Maya's line of communication was a question with innumerable answers. After all, to ostracise his lover was nothing short of callous, senseless, and curiously abnormal.

Was he doing this for her? Perhaps. Was he testing the waters, biding his time uninhibitedly before calling for a secondary life raft? Perhaps again.

Or perhaps he had decided on a solo voyage into the open seas without an on-board life jacket.

Whatever the case, this was a Jonathan Jinks that was becoming unequivocally alien to anyone that knew him.

"Anyway, anyway, as I was sayin'," Chuckie burped as Jonny slid the smartphone back into the desolate wasteland of his pants pocket. "My guilty pleasure..."

Chuckie manoeuvred his hands as if they were lifting some sort of theatre curtain.

"... Picture this scene: there's me and then there's this Mia Khalifa look-alike, right?" Chuckie painted the landscape as Jonny agreed that he *did* in fact, appear to be a Mia Khalifa kind-of guy. "Not *actually* Mia Khalifa herself, no, no; just like a stand-in, like a stunt-double, right? Anyway, we meet under this daredevil of a circumstance; I save her from starvation or some shit like a superhero flying into *The Hunger Games* before she takes me back to her apartment for a little one-on-one time."

Chuckie's deepest desires appeared moderately perverted for a man of his physical appearance, a microcosmic exemplar of a captor's necessity to connect sentimentally with his captive in spite of his inadequacies.

"Anyway, I introduce her to a little friend of mine I keep hidden away for a rainy day that needs some sunshine," he continued mysteriously, perturbing Jonny on account of how well planned Chuckie's ad-hoc exposition was. "Before she gets fully naked... and I just start ramming her like a horse outta some kind of bestiality fantasy wearing nothing but a facemask!"

Chuckie's primitive fetish – announced with an exuberant gusto – was the kind of forbidden wish that would have been prohibited along with the age-old 'you cannot wish for more wishes' adage under a genie's 'supernatural secrecy pact.'

"A facemask?"

"Yeah, you know? A facemask; that's where it all starts to get a little interesting," he repeated, his hands illustrating the way like a descriptive Italian as if Jonny had not ever heard of the article before. "Like in those masked sex orgies that they dub as 'rituals' to add some bullshit layer of ceremonial mystique or something, you know? Kind of like the Illuminati, right, holmes? You've heard of them fools, right?"

Jonny had. Just like anybody with access to the Internet in the twenty-first century.

"Of course."

"Well… I once watched that movie *Eyes Wide Shut* – you know that erotic drama they made while Nicole Kidman and Tom Cruise were still doing it?"

Jonny offered a blank stare as his mind narrowed in on its surroundings.

"Anyway, so there's a scene in the movie where this guy, he walks into this Vatican-looking cathedral and the dude at the door asks him for an entry password. He drops the password and then walks into this big-ass open space where a bunch of dudes in red cloaks surrounded by bitches wearing nothing but facemasks like they're at a Venetian Carnival in the middle of a Catholic church are fucking each others' brains to pieces."

Jonny knew the scene – it was as controversially uncomfortable as it was unforgettable. But its graphic nature could only be recalled in small and inaccurate mind clips.

"*Your* guilty pleasure sounds tasteful in comparison," Jonny quipped as a group of middle-aged glamour-models waltzed through the doors of the *Chateau*.

"Hey, don't get me wrong, if I could I'd go all out – I love all this secret society shit, 'novus ordo seclorum' and all that, holmes, you feel me?" he chanted, dictating the backside of an American dollar bill. "But they wouldn't let a hermano like me into a room like that – no way, that kind of shit is only reserved for Hollywood's privileged elite."

It appeared remiss of Chuckie not to acknowledge the obvious irony behind his proclamation, multi-million dollar fast-food empire and all.

"So I guess I'd just like to... *simplify* that arrangement; take a couple of its best bits and let it ride."

Let it ride, he could. And while Jonny was largely horrified, he did know one thing with a paramount of certainty: Jonathan Jinks possessed the very rare means to grant the faux hawked, tattooed redhead's fantasy and this, in itself, was an advantage that he could leverage.

"Listen, Chuckie," Jonny said as he bent at the knee and stood upright, relieving his backside from the congeniality of the floral-patterned sofa. "I'm going to head back up to my room for a little while – I've got a couple of figures to work through for Regrub Moon Hills so why don't you give me a call a little later and we can meet up?"

With each passing moment, Jonny's unnatural ability to falsify the truth was progressing in its development.

"Okay, holmes, yeah, let's do that," he agreed, searching for a pseudo fist-bump-meets-corporate-hand-shake routine. "You do your thing, I'll go and see what's what at the diner and we'll be in touch."

Jonny had to work against the clock. Chuckie Hooper Junior was perennially zealous in his promises and for this, Jonny expected no difference.

It came at a cost, but he knew what he had to do: buried inside a zip-locked pocket of his suitcase, a matte-white PVC mask with a moulded moustache and a white elastic band hid away from plain sight.

And all he needed was a four-digit code and a paintbrush to unlock this Pandora's box.

26

"WE ALL WEAR MASKS, MR. IPKISS"

The similitude between he and Jim Carrey was unmistakable as he lodged the mask between his hands like a heavy jar of face cream before application. Jonny made acquaintances with the mask's moulded shape, his fingers fidgeting at its contours as he slowly lifted the plastic towards his face and suctioned it against his skin.

The only thing missing was a computer animated tornado and a latex-layer of bright-green face paint; otherwise, it seemed likely that Jonny was on the cusp of pulverising a ringing alarm clock with a cartoonish, supersized mallet.

Alright, then. Let's do this.

The clock was indeed ticking and *without* a mallet in hand, he knew he had no choice but to get to work. Jonny suited up like a superhero in a cheesy nineties popcorn flick, cloaking himself in an art smock as he reached deep inside his suitcase of tricks to retrieve his palette and acrylics.

On the chequered tiling he laid out a drop cloth made from the open spread of a handful of large newspapers before laying the PVC mask upright and in its centre, the sole focal point of his imagination.

Chuckie's guilty pleasure would be his muse while the mask would be his canvas, its clear white backdrop offering just enough of a clean slate as to not be deterred by its moustached ends.

Jonny needed to achieve something pragmatic, abstract and apposite, a creative detonation of both inward and outward emotions. He searched the banks of his memory for an eidetic recollection of *Monopoly*'s indubitable Rich Uncle Pennybags as he dipped his paintbrush in acrylic.

Jonny swirled and sliced, detailing the canvas in an irregularly variegated likeness of the top-hatted character as he made sure that a perceptible dissimilarity existed between his creation and its source material.

As he released the brush from the surface of the PVC, a black and white headline adorning the top of a newspaper spread behind the mask screamed for his unbendable attention.

PLiNKER CEO JACKPOTS IN STOCK-FOR-STOCK EXCHANGE WITH JELLITECH INTERNATIONAL.

Jonny balked at the headline, repudiating the notion that such a vile and unethical technology – its Machiavellian features tutorially introduced to him on a frigid, Allentown evening at Minx – could carry such an exorbitant price tag.

They'll pay anything for everything these days.

They can afford it.

Jonny Jinks scrutinized the early elements of his composition, eliciting self-praise for his use of definition, line-work and spacing as he admired his impressionistic interpretation of the fabled *Monopoly* man.

But something dramatic was still missing. The piece lacked emphasis and uncontrollable vulnerability. It seemed too predictable, too structured in its intricate layers.

The piece lacked rage.

The piece lacked mysterious deception.

Jonny cross-contaminated the acrylics, blending colours to form a carefully selected amalgam of paint on the tip of his brush as he stood back and let his wrist flick like *Indiana Jones* with a bullwhip in hand.

Jonny splattered the rainbow-wash of colour across the mask, the black and white newspaper behind it changing like a 1960s colour broadcast transmission on a new television set as he unclenched his muscle tension and engaged in the 'action painting' style.

A demented rainbow appeared from the blank nothingness of a plastic backdrop. Was it the *Monopoly* man? Was it the *Mad Hatter*? Or was it a cataclysmic cross between the two? The interpretation did not matter; after all, that was the beauty behind the madness.

What *did* matter was that the modified article represented unconscious freedom; freedom to espouse who he really was. The mask could trade his reality for a role, just like in the movies.

After all, man was least himself when confessing in his own person. But give man a mask? Give man a mask and he will surely spill the beans… and *all* the alcohol.

27

PHONE-A-DECEPTICON

His cell rang.

And rang.

And rang again.

Day's without a text – let alone a phone call – stockpiled like a swarming of stamp-less envelopes at a post office. The *Uber* tour from the Venice Canals Walkway to beyond had awoken an unspoken consciousness, an inhibited need suppressed *only* in his Allentown habitat.

But this wasn't Allentown anymore. This was Los Angeles; and he was *Jonny*.

Maya waited days for a returning phone call that never manufactured as Jonathan Jinks exchanged the cost of sacrifice for what he deemed to be a conditional greater good.

This was for her own protection after all, he was certain of it. This was her plausible deniability, her 'Get-Out-Of-Jail-Free Card,' her painfully unenlightened freedom. She needed it too, Jonny surmised; the freedom, even just temporarily.

The I-40 west linked their two plains across the country but Jonny was building a bridge that was everything the Mexican border wall wouldn't be. He didn't want to keep her out; he *had* to let her In eventually.

He had slipped up, sliding on a banana peel before crashing

through a hundred glassed windows at Chuckie's Diner. The mistakes he'd made were reprehensible lapses of intoxicated judgment, his polluted morality compass leaking at the tap of every taboo adventure.

None of this would be for nought, every error a clogging putty that could eventually seal each and every broken window. It had to be this way; Jonny had no choice.

Except that he did.

This was *all* his choice.

This was all a choice that activated a defence mechanism, a churning of the gears that transformed him from a cunning Optimus Prime into a pathological Decepticon.

28

FOOD TRUCK FIASCO

"Welcome to the Chuckie's Diner official food truck – where your favourite West Coast cookin' is done so right that you'll never want to fuck a vegetarian again!"

The announcement – pledged in Southern Californian vernacular across the PA intercom of the mobile food truck – collided with a blur of static white noise, mortifying its swarm of onlookers.

"Hey, yo, Jonny!" came a cry from the driver's side window as the truck's hydraulics system suspended, its driver piercing the rim against the curb before pulling in to park. "Oops! Anyway... I told you I'd pick you up in style, didn't I? Let's get going, holmes!"

Jonny was torn somewhere between amusement and confusion. Parked in front of the elegant and sophisticated entrance of the *Chateau Marmont* was a four-wheeled pop-up restaurant, a mobile diner on triple-treaded tyres, fresh out of a Jon Favreau feature film.

"You have got to be kidding me," Jonny scorned as he sauntered towards the passenger side, surveying the truck in all its fast-food glory.

The near twenty-foot long food truck mimicked in colour and décor to that of its four-walled counterpart as splashes of vibrant reds, yellows and pinks dominated the vehicle's glossy lacquer-based paint palette. It's exterior was enveloped in a cluster of diner decals, the truck's outer chassis providing the ideal canvas for a clipart graphic re-

render of the internal elements of an archetypal Chuckie's Diner restaurant.

In modern-day America – where personal finances were as insecure as social-media sleuthing ex-lovers and even the most modest of inner-city dining outfits necessitated multimillion-dollar renovations for social and economical survival – consumers had begun to grow stale of the deep-fried condescension by large chain consortiums. But the consumers of corporate America still demanded – with a table-bashing, cutlery-clasping set of flabby double-clenched fists – a quality food alternative that was not only novel, but inexpensive *and* expeditious.

Enter, the food truck: the new incubator of a wildly expanding culinary innovation.

The explosion of the food-truck phenomenon was largely credited to celebrity chef Roy Choi and his independently retrofitted, Korean short-rib taco selling *Kogi* empire. *Kogi* offered edible symbols of Los Angeles' famous cross-cultural inclusiveness, dripping portable takeout plates of food drawn straight from the city's recombinant DNA. But it was the pre-established franchises like Chuckie's Diner, not the audacious and dare-devilish start-up small businesses like *Kogi* that sought a widened gulf of opportunity through grassroots vending in multifarious territories.

And as the vogue culinary culture of food-truck-mania continued to spread its artificial sauces across the gridded borders of North America, in L.A. – where on some afternoons a moving plantation of food vendors were as thick and as frequent on the city's freeways as impatient taxicab drivers on New York City's Sixth Avenue – they had quickly begun to redefine the metropolitan's interchanging conditional landscape.

"I'm not a kidder, Jonny, you know that," Chuckie affirmed as he corralled the public address microphone and abused it like an insolent child to a plasticised walkie-talkie. "C'mon, man, just get in the truck; Roger... *Ugh*, I mean, over... I think."

Chuckie's ignorance delighted Jonny as his attempt to mimic the dialect of a radiotelephone operator floundered in a miserable muddle.

Jonny swung his foot atop the steel truck steps, boosting himself through the passenger door and onto the sterility of a fleecy seat cover.

"What you got in that backpack, Jonny Cash?" Chuckie queried as Jonny relieved the compression straps from his shoulders and planted the bag at his feet.

Jonny Cash. That's... a new one.

"Ugh, the human remains of an occult secret society leader and a plastic bag full of extra-large *Cheetos*," he joked. "So what? You deep-fry while I take cash over the counter, then? Is that what the plan is?"

Operating deep fryers, sandwich presses, cold storage facilities and portable power generators was hardly Jonny's idea of the sacrificial West Coast escapade he was promised. But from the little he had already come to understand of the idiosyncratic redhead, this appeared to be nothing short of a working pretence for a far more exhilarating adventure.

"You see that steel fridge back there?" Chuckie pointed as he span the steering wheel, brushing the edges of the gutter once more. "Open it up and bring back whatever you find inside."

Jonny refrained from securing the seatbelt clasp as he peeved through the narrow walkway of the truck's chassis and spotted the two-door bottom mount reach-in refrigerator.

"What? Now? While we're moving?"

The request seemed to startle him.

"Don't be a pussy," Chuckie taunted, neglecting the road and its oncoming traffic. "We're going like five miles an hour on a road straighter than my penis during an interracial porno. You'll be fine."

Jonny huffed, retracting his seatbelt to its holder before balancing himself as the star in a steady highwire act at Chuckie's Circus of Fuckery. Using his hands to maintain his equilibrium, Jonny stumbled through the truck's walkway as he waged war with the unforgiving Gods of gravity.

The food truck, extensive in all of its mobile culinary frameworks, was fitted with combinations of almost every kind of restaurant apparatus that could squeeze into the vehicle's limited real estate. Radiant char-broilers and grills, floor model fryers with stainless steel pots, hot food tables, electric steamers, compartment sinks with touch-free faucets, merchandising cabinets and countertop food warmers formed the basis of the portable facility's high-octane infrastructure while steel work tables and benches provided level surfaces for plastic oval food baskets and boxes of takeaway packaging.

As Jonny crept awkwardly around his backpack and towards his target, an abrupt change in gravitational pull forced him into an obstructive tumble, his outstretched arms desperately reaching for a nearby safety net that could secure his landing. But unfortunately for Jonny Jinks, the only tangible article within arms length came by way of an unscrewed tomato sauce squeeze bottle.

Splat!

"What the fuck happened?" Chuckie yelped as he balanced his focus between switching road signals and back-seat shenanigans.

"You hit the curb when you pulled around that bend, moron," Jonny berated, his fingers dripping in a rufous spillage as he barked on hands and knees.

Chuckie replayed the scene in his mind like a post-production movie editor, cutting moving fragments and pasting them back in places they did not belong.

"What bend?"

There was no use in quarrelling. The damage had been done.

Jonny resumed his expedition, approaching the refrigerator with an existential angst as if the cooling appliance were some kind of demonically forbidden but mystically gratifying temple from an *Indiana Jones* instalment.

He yanked at the handle, staining the steel door with the blood of an artificial tomato paste before a vibrant aura emitted from a cluster of beer bottles resting on the fridge's internal shelving.

"What's this for?" Jonny asked, removing an icy, green-tinted bottle from the refrigerator as the lager's condensation moisture coalesced with the tomato sauce to produce droplets of reddish rain.

"You said you were from Pennsylvania, right?" Chuckie called over the clatter of car engines and civilian hubbub. "Just thought I'd get us a little something to make you feel more at *home*, vato, you know what I'm saying?"

Yeah... I know what you're saying.

Jonny removed a couple of *Yuengling*'s and carried them to the front seat, popping the bottle cap on one before refastening his seatbelt.

"What the hell are you doing?" Chuckie clucked, one hand on the wheel as he navigated the Californian roadway like a Mexican gangbanger on a cartel drive-by.

"What?"

"You ain't planning on offering me my drink yet?"

"You're driving, Chuckie."

"So what? Don't let my balls mislead you; I *can* multitask. Pop the cap, man."

Over the course of two hours, Chuckie had navigated San Vicente through the bi-directional roads of West Hollywood, merged with the crowded traffic on Sunset Boulevard in Silver Lake before traversing through Downtown Los Angeles' exasperating one-way streets, crossed towards the city's north by way of the International Airport, Culver City and Santa Monica and zipped across its northwest to southeast street grid that flaunted its luminous coastline.

"Now this is the life, isn't it?" Chuckie applauded as he kicked his feet up on the truck's vinyl dashboard and interlocked his fingers behind his head like an arrested felon.

The food truck's handbrake pedal was locked and fastened as the lengthy vehicle stationed itself in the parking lot by Colorado Avenue, overlooking the Santa Monica sunset.

"Hey, hey, Jonny," Chuckie nudged, rocketing for his attention as he gestured towards a set of winsome women exiting their two-door ultra-compact hatchback. "A couple of cuties that could suck a tennis ball through a garden hose, ten o'clock."

Jonny shot upwards and like any warm-blooded male would, refocused his gaze like a waterlogged camera lens as he located the targets with his cognitive scouter.

"Well," Jonny groaned with guilt as his mouth moistened. "So *this* is California, then?"

"What? You thought this was only in the movies? This is real life, holmes," Chuckie asserted as he banged his hands against his knees. "But you got to be *real* careful when you spot 'em. Fine Californian women are like condoms; if they're not *on* your dick, then they're *in* your wallet."

Their lecherous ogling might have fogged the truck's windows into a portable sauna had it not been for a heckling knock at Chuckie's driver-side door.

"Excuse me," the old man slurred, pounding his cane against the doorframe as he tugged on his scruffy beard. "Can I get a cheeseburger? Please, I don't have any money and I just want something to eat."

It was written in local lore that the enveloping lands of Palisades Park and Santa Monica Beach were considered a categorical hub for the homeless, its beach community providing access to public restrooms and showers for those without permanent shelter. And as such, it was hardly unconventional to find vagrants seeking out soup kitchens on Fifth Street and leftovers in Santa Monica trashcans.

"Get the fuck out of here, old man!" Chuckie howled erratically. "Can't you see that we're closed, holmes? Nada. Finito. Caput."

Chuckie's vile denial shooed the homeless man away as he shrugged in exasperation.

"You realise that he was homeless, right?" Jonny queried as an invisible effluvia evaporated from the pores of his torn pant-pocket and into a cloud of unbearable stink.

"Homeless?" Chuckie rebuffed in an insensitive sarcasm. "Oh, I'm sorry, I didn't realise that my truck had the words 'SHOW US YOUR FOOD STAMPS AND DIRTY BALL SACKS FOR FREE FUCKING FOOD' labelled across it in bold, fat, capital letters."

Chuckie's outburst expressed a clear lack of compassion and a deliberate disassociation for both the underprivileged and the socially deprived as he nailed Jonny in an unforgiving silence.

"Now if there's no more interruptions, let's get back to the task at hand, what do you say?" Chuckie said as he bent his fingers and arched them around his eyelids as if they were magnifying binoculars.

"You know it's not polite to stare?" Jonny apprised even as the pulchritude before him made it all the more difficult to adhere to his own advice.

"Says who? Maybe out east, holmes. But over here, staring is like a moth to a flame," Chuckie alluded in what could only be described as something close to a regional Welsh accent. "The longer the stare, the luckier the chance."

Jonny huffed, unconvinced. Besides, a valve deep inside of his nervous system urged him to sabotage Chuckie's full proof experiment and board the closest transportation bus en route back to the *Chateau.*

There was still time to turn back. He hadn't reached the game's conclusion yet and at any moment, could downgrade his componentry from *Jonny* back to *Jon* again.

"Holy shit, they're walking right this way Jonny; look, look!" Chuckie buzzed, squirming in his seat as he regained a more astute posture. "I didn't actually think that was going to work!"

The beauties tiptoed like lightweight feathers on a bed of clouds as their lengthy, shiny hair blew in the Californian current like swimsuit models at a seaside photo-shoot.

Just relax; you've done nothing wrong, Jonny's mind oscillated as a fuel of bothersome regret gobbled him whole.

"Hey there," the brunette and tallest of the brazen twosome whispered in a sultry Valley Girl cadence as her magnificent twin stood beside her. "I didn't know that Chuckie's Diner went mobile? Are you guys open for business?"

For Chuckie, the query was as transparent as the mindless small talk he would endure before engaging in copulation with a prepaid prostitute.

"For you two, honey, we're always open," he crowed in a rare succession of sweet talk. "Now why don't you gals walk around to the passenger side and my buddy here'll let you in."

Jonny wrestled his head side-to-side as he stared at the plump redhead, his eyebrows turned inwards while his toes clenched the backpack between his feet.

"C'mon, Jonny," Chuckie nudged. "Be a gentleman, why don't you?"

Jonny swung open the passenger door, the cool Californian breeze carrying it like a leave in autumn as he offered a helping hand to the duo that were evidently challenged by the high footstep.

"Not a good day to forget my panties," the taller woman teased in an angelic giggle as she latched onto her frilled, turquoise and higher-than-knee-high mini skirt.

"Holy shi– let us help you out of your troubles," Chuckie offered as chivalrously as he could. "Jonny, fire up the grill and the fryers; we're gonna cook these ladies a feast!"

"What? Are you serious?" Jonny blurted. "Do you know even what you're doing?"

The beauties stopped in motion as they awaited a succeeding instruction.

"Pa-lease!" Chuckie spat, rolling his eyes as he attempted to convey a telepathic hush. "I'm Chuckie Junior, son of Chuckie Senõr and heir to the food diner throne; I can do anything, especially with these lovely ladies by my side."

The winsome twosome tittered at Chuckie's Joffrey Baratheon impression as the faux hawked redhead galvanised them into action.

"And speaking of you lovely ladies, I don't think we caught your names before you boarded my mobile diner of love?" Chuckie fawned, his eyes never wavering from his delectable guests.

Both women were equally impressed. Not so much by Chuckie's cursory flirtation but by the presence and chary of a bashful but handsome man, hiding inside the security of his favourite CMYK t-shirt.

"I'm Sasha," the brunette chirped. "And this is Madison."

"Well, it's a pleasure to meet you ladies," Chuckie chimed, his eyes blinking erratically in Jonny's direction in an attempt to encourage a two-folded expression of engrossment. "... isn't it, Jonny?"

Jonny shuffled at the feet, tipping over the backpack as his sprouting uneasiness showed no signs of purging.

"Yes, it's nice to meet you both," he indulged, shaking at the nervous cobwebs as he offered a hand in a moratorium on guilt and consternation. "And if you guys couldn't tell by the sign on the truck, this right here is Chuckie."

Jonny offered his first lick of banter, his witticism coming at the expense of his sycophantic partner as the blonde-haired Madison simpered delightfully.

"I was just getting to that part," Chuckie replied, wholly unimpressed at Jonny's lunch-cutting intrusion. "Anyway, fuck it, let's get to cooking!"

Jonny had said enough, embellishing a little before turning in to sous-chef burger flipping duties.

Chuckie barraged through the messy walkway to ignite a selection of necessary kitchen appliances while Jonny, at Chuckie's command, pulled a plastic bag full of frozen potato fries and tasty brioche buns from the portable freezer.

"Hey, Sasha," Chuckie bellowed over the sizzling splatters of the deep fryer. "Can you turn the truck radio on? Hit that green button up top over there."

Sasha served her cook, attenuating the volume dial as the truck's retrofitted sound system blared the harmonic chorus from Dr. Dre's hypnotic West Coast record *Xxplosive*.

"When I met ya last night, baby… before I blew your mind," Chuckie crooned, pounding his pipes in his best Nate Dogg impression as he waved an oil-dripping spatula in the air and pointed in Sasha's direction.

Sasha and Madison crept forward, swaying their hips to the bugged-out weed jam as they began a bewitching girl-on-girl dance sequence to the track's hip-hop rhythm.

Oh... my...

Jonny, his back nestled against the truck's double-pivot rear door, could do nothing but stare and swallow in compunction. Two girls, strangers for all but ten minutes, were gyrating to the smoky samples of a rap song while a pomade-styled, redheaded wannabe pimp flipped beef patties and tossed a fryer load of French fries beside them.

* * *

"Yo, Jonny," Chuckie whistled, his arms wrapped around the hips of the second-most attractive women inside the food truck. "You said you were like a painter or something, right?"

Jonny was not totally partial to the term. According to his interpretation, a painter was rewarded for his labour while the artist for his creativity. And Jonny was certainly done cashing paycheques for blue-collar drudgery.

"Yes, an *artist*," he corrected, his fingers moist with tension as he kept his distance.

"What'd I say? And girls, I know you like to party, right?" Chuckie probed, tickling the underside of Sasha's nose.

Sasha and Madison giggled in a twin-like telepathy as they nodded their heads and pushed up against their voluptuous curves.

"Alright, alright, you guys get comfortable, dim the lights and I'll be right back," he promised as he wriggled his way to the rear of the truck.

Melted American cheddar oozed from the retrofitted bench tops to the laminated flooring as the scent of freshly grilled beef patties blended with the scent of a designer label perfume to create a hybrid fragrance of melted cheese and erotica.

Sasha, acknowledging the nonexistence of a dim knob, unplugged the mains power from the generator leaving only the reflective glow of a nearby streetlight as a means of illumination.

What are we doing now? Why do I feel like I'm in a portable-brothel?

"Okay, okay, here we go," Chuckie croaked, his hands preoccupied as he bent at the knees and navigated the darkness like a wild hunter sleuthing for psilocybin mushrooms. "Ten points and a blow job goes to anyone who can tell me what this little baby right here is?"

Chuckie sat, legs crossed, his laces sticking to the filthy floor as he held a thin sheet of blotting paper atop a rectangular fast food takeaway box in-between his fingers.

"And that goes for you too, Jonny," Chuckie quipped as he activated the spotlight on his smartphone and aimed it towards the paper sheeting.

Jonny could identify the artwork, but the suggestions of its canvas were still a mystery.

The fine sheet of blotting paper looked more like an enormous, dissolvable *Listerine Strip* with a perforated, advent calendar-like grid. And ironically, it was this kind of illegally distributed solution that had even the starkest of non-believers rousing like uncontrollable children on Christmas morning.

"That's blotter," Sasha answered, giddy at the prospect of her probable reward.

Blotter?

Jonny recognised its material state but the illustration puzzled him. The paper was psychedelically decorated, adorned with the printed digital drawing of the head of an abstract, cartoon teddy bear in the foreground. Sunflowers made up the composite of the bear's eyes while a contingent of retro, free-spirited drawings filled the bear's facial details. The teddy, duplicated in the background in a repeated tiling, was glowing in a mixture of golden yellows and tree leaf greens, adding an explosion of multi-coloured smoke at its core for additional emphasis.

"Also known as?" Chuckie quizzed, empowering himself with more game show swag than Bob Barker.

"Windowpane?" Sasha guessed.

"*Also* known as?"

Sasha dithered, straining her mind to release the fabrics of the answer Chuckie sought.

"Microdot? Cid? Acid?" Sasha shouted as if Chuckie's trivia night had transformed into some kind of hybrid game of *Wheel of Fortune* and charades. "Can I buy a vowel?"

The girls gushed as Chuckie's lips pressed together and his throat vibrated to emanate a sound that suggested the guess was incorrect.

"Oh, I do apologise Sasha but it appears that we are all out of vowels — we've only got three consonants left, in fact!" Chuckie revealed, his voice bordering between on-air-personality and British royal. "L-S-D."

The broads thumped their palms together like crash cymbals in a marching band as they threw their hands to the sky and squealed in uncontrollable delight.

"And you know," Chuckie continued, separating the perforated grid into an edible entrée for four. "I hear that this brand right here is supposed to be the best on the entire West Coast."

"Where'd you get it from?" Sasha asked, her tongue moistening at the very notion of an unadulterated state of mind.

"Just this Asian motherfucker who has lunch at the diner like *every single day*," he replied, placing a piece of blotter paper in Sasha's cupped hands as if he were an iniquitous priest at a holy communion.

"Orders the same shit, day in day out: the chicken and waffles with a glass of fresh grape juice. And on some days as I'm taking his empty tray back to the kitchen, he slips me something a little more serviceable than a tip if you know what I'm saying!"

Grape juice.

Jonny was undeniably fixated. Voluntarily trapped in an enclosed cave, he was a first-hand-witness to something both forbidden and suggestively amoral. And yet even so, his eyes could not withdraw from the pulchritude, the magnificent peccadillo of an art style so unfamiliar yet so perfect.

"Batter up," Chuckie signalled as Sasha and Madison nudged one another in a playful curtain raiser.

The girls administered the blotters sublingually so as to counter any appreciable loss of potency before closing their eyes in anticipation of its intoxicating effects.

"My man," Chuckie beamed, offering the third piece of blotter paper to his Pennsylvanian recruit. "You're up next."

Jonny arched his back and squiggled to the rear of the truck, crossing his arms, fingers and toes in the process.

"What's the problem, bro?" Chuckie blasted. "You said you were an artist right?"

"So...?" Jonny rebuffed, obtuse to its significance.

"What do you mean, 'so'? All the greats owe their inspiration to drugs, don't you know that? van Gogh? Absinthe alcoholic. Basquiat? *Cocaine, cocaine, cocaine.* Picasso? Psychotropic drug addict. And the list goes on."

"What kind of shit do you know?" Jonny asked, relatively stunned.

In a very strange and historically veritable way, Chuckie's argument held validity. Picasso's influential visual art style of 'Cubism' was born from the artist's penchant for the illicit while the effects of the green, hallucinogenic liquor known as Absinthe was the elixir that drove van Gogh to the realms of both the ingenious and the insane.

"Hey, man, when you're in the business of entertainment and hospitality, you gotta know stuff, right ladies?" Chuckie bumped his waist against Sasha's hip as he slithered his arms up and down her torso. "Madison, baby, why don't you spoon-feed my boy over there?"

Madison had been pining for such an actionable assist and Chuckie delivered like Steve Nash in the fourth quarter of a basketball final.

Maya.

The blonde-haired beauty crept towards her quarry on hands and knees, the blotter paper clenched between her thumb and index finger as Jonny's skin and soul – forged like a repellent nylon – could no longer muster the logistical navigation of an escape route.

"CMYK," Madison tantalised, her soft and velvety whisper melting between the porcelain cracks of Jonny's repellent spray as she tugged on the collar of his t-shirt and pointed at each letter of its print-design with a single finger. "You want to tell me what that stands for?"

Jonny's back arched as if he were preparing to strengthen his chest muscles on an inclined bench press.

"Ugh, umm," he fumbled as if he had misplaced the square-shaped key to his rounded voice box. "It's an acronym that refers to the four inks they use – you know? Cyan and... and... magenta and all that. For coloured printing. For printing art and designs and for printing... Stuff that needs to be printed."

What... in the the hell am I saying?

"Oops!" she jumped, tapping against the tip of his nose. "That's my bad; I thought it stood for 'C'mon Madison, I know You're Kinky'? I was going to ask you how you already knew so much about me!"

Madison's demeanour oscillated between the counterpoising peaks and troughs of virginity and promiscuity as she traced the letters on

Jonny's CMYK t-shirt, curling the tip of her finger around its cotton fabric upon reaching the tail of each letter.

Jonny fumbled and stuttered, his brain ricocheting and thumping from the forces of a thousand conflicting and irrational deliberations.

"What does it taste like?" Jonny questioned in a quest for more time.

"Taste?" Chuckie interjected, squishing his fingers into his forearm flab. "Well it's suppose to be tasteless but this shit right here has a little bitter kick to it – it's kind-of like when people eat newspaper but with flakes of dark chocolate sprinkled on top."

Delectable.

"But if you swallow it this way, it'll just taste like me," Madison pledged, sending the magnets of his moral compass on an uncontrollable whirlwind.

The dashing blonde peeled off a blotter tab, wedging it between her index finger and thumb before diagonally descending towards Jonny's tongue.

It seemed coercive.

Except that it wasn't.

In almost every facet, Jonny felt like a hostage of an unrighteousness law, a victim of a wicked and dastardly ring of immoral criminals, indoctrinating him like a Donald Trump presidential campaign.

Maya. The ATM. Debt. Infertility. Allentown.

Until it became discernible that a microscopic fragment of Jonny's soul coveted the title of existential ringleader and this very compulsion granted an improbable opportunity to explore a curiosity, a temptation prohibited but without repercussion.

This was Jonny's forbidden fruit and, secretly he had been longing for a bite.

Jonny dropped his neck, squeezed his eyelids together and opened at the mouth as Madison released the blotter paper in front of his uvula and beneath his saliva-drenched tongue.

Close your eyes. You'll be fine.

After the first swallow, Jonny began to see things as he wished they were – Maya pushing their unborn offspring on a swing-set by a bed of sunflowers and candid smiles. After the second, he began to see things as they were not – a dazzling, luxuriated lifestyle from the ocean-view balcony of a cliff-faced apartment on the Amalfi Coast where he and Maya could bask in the simultaneous glows of fire and rain without a distraction, without a presumption. Finally, with nothing more than the remnants of leaking ink between waves of his saliva, he saw things as they really were and that became the most ominous and inescapable sight conceivable.

"It looks like all you've got left are consonants, too," Madison beguiled, her focus shifting from Jonny's squid-squirted tongue back to the four capital letters on his t-shirt as she piggybacked off of Chuckie's game show host narrative to deliver her own impression of Chuck Woolery and Vanna White's hypothetical lovechild.

Jonny's eyes rolled backwards, Madison's slinky movements appearing as nothing more than an intense *Photoshop* motion blur.

Maya. Love. Commitment. What am I doi–

Madison prepped her lips, licking at the outlines of her lipstick as she leant inwards.

"I'm thinking that right about now, you deserve a *vowel*," she titillated, her hands wedged against Jonny's chest as an aura of impenetrable energy began to encompass them.

At first, Jonny did not quite understand.

But in a matter of moments, all would be far clearer.

As Madison suctioned his neck with her preternatural fangs, Jonny let off an uncontrollable moan in the kind of cadence that sounded a lot like the letter 'A.'

29

LUCY IN THE SKY WITH DEMONS

Darkness. Total darkness.

It was yet another sequel to *Alice's Adventures in Wonderland* – but this time, Jonny was the star; the star of his own fantasy that only served to perpetuate the realities of an undiagnosed psychosis.

In this world, Jonny was distorted, non-existent. All sense of objective reality was lost as his mind juggled the balance between consciousness and unbridled imagination.

In this world, the hallucinations were as frighteningly vivid as the dream itself. Jonny's feet dangled off the edge of a cliff face, his wavy hair gliding in the cool breeze as he watched a flock of ruffed crows swooping between fluffs of salmon clouds as if they were Bludgers on a Quidditch pitch.

As the birds soared, the clouds fashioned themselves in a heavenly topiary, moulding their cushiony surfaces into silhouettes of giraffes, trees and oil-painted portraits of Rich Uncle Pennybags and John Lennon and Yoko Ono.

"Well, you're not just going to sit around here all day, are you?" reverberated a gentle voice from behind him as instinct commanded him to turn at the neck. "Come on, grab my hand."

The request spawned a silent acquiescence in Jonny, her luring invitation as irresistibly unimpeachable as a wolf in a bloodied nightcap.

The woman was a nebulous silhouette, an indistinct figment of an undefined and unbounded imagination. The woman could not be seen by Jonny's subconscious, only felt.

He squeezed her hand as she giggled and offered a frivolous smile, yanking Jonny into a meadow of greenery and sunflowers.

"C'mon!" she squealed as she swung herself under Jonny's arms. "You know you want to dance, so just dance!"

Jonny was torn, his dancing styles ranging between contemporary sway and the electric boogaloo. He swung his partner in the air, her fingers tightly squeezing his forearms as she shrieked like an electric guitar.

As the dancing duo spun and twirled to the organic sounds of an artificial wilderness, clusters of clouds gravitated towards one other in the sky above, darkening the atmosphere in a purple haze.

Jonny tilted his neck and stared towards the materialising tempest before feeling the soft press of an even fingertip against his gawking lip.

"Don't worry about it, its just a little storm," his partner conveyed, flicking her sultry index finger against Jonny's moistened lip as she tilted his head downward in an attempt to recapture his attention.

The vibrant but toxic storm cloud seemed to be on the precipice of destruction as a gushing wind rocked their dancing cradle and threatened to topple their balance.

An unearthly sound filled the air as the wind began to whip into an outrageous frenzy. Before Jonny could surrender, a thunderous bellow emerged from the unconventional clouds above as they crashed and struck like a collegiate marching band. Not even the nearest tree could provide him with the necessary shelter. Not even his mind could conjure up an umbrella of safety.

"What are you *so* afraid of?" the woman taunted, her eyes now wide open in an irregular bloodshot. "Whatever happens here doesn't matter; you're free, Jon!"

The unknowable girl chortled in a semi-sadistic mercilessness as Jonny gasped, desperately searching for the glowing exit sign like Macaulay Culkin's animated protagonist in *The Pagemaster*.

"We have to run!" he beseeched as a palette of multi-coloured paint splotches fell from the sky and trickled across the meadow in a liquid rainbow.

These were hardly ordinary raindrops. These were wild, colourful and indiscriminate; a plethora of plump missiles of mass destruction that splattered viciously onto the softened soil of the meadow.

The paint splatter teemed down in a biblical deluge, flooding the meadow and drowning its every inhabitant. It was a Noah's Ark-cataclysm of rain, an unending cataract of water sluicing from the sky.

"Run? You know, you're not suppose to run if you're afraid," she preached. "We are afraid because we run."

Jonny's avatar had little time for philosophy, especially with the doom of an apocalyptic cloudburst looming.

"How do you not see how dangerous this is right now? We've *got* to run!"

"You're crazy!" she giggled, covering her glistening teeth with the palm of her hand as she ignored the obvious hazard on the horizon. "Look, whatever you want to run from, you can stop. *We'll* run together. I'll run through the fire with you and if things start to burn, then we'll incinerate. But until then, let's just be *free!*"

Jonny Jinks' doppelganger felt about as free as O. J. Simpson during the trial of the century: a foot from imminent danger, and half a foot from being swallowed whole by contrition.

"Where are you going?" Jonny cried, his fingers unlocking from the soft embrace of the woman's as she sprinted like a lioness and danced to the splattering sounds of rainbow paint drops.

"Come on, this way!" she instructed as the core of the multi-coloured climate began to freeze over, causing the hued raindrops to vaporise into lethally pelting darts of pigmented snow balls.

Jonny's breath rose in the cold, his exhale condensing the water vapour in his breath into a mystic fog.

The meadow had frozen over as a thick blanket of frost turned blooming petals and grass compounds into a lifeless ice rink.

"Stop!" he roared, slipping and sliding like a wannabe prom queen in a pair of cramped heels as he tried to reduce the distance between him and the impalpable vixen.

As if the field of vision was not already blurry enough, the woman's calculated prance coupled with a perennial downpour of what could only be described as a blizzard of *Teletubbie* faeces made it almost impossible to detect her through the storm.

"I'm going!" came a hidden voice from somewhere inside the woven fog. "Are you coming with me? Or are you staying?"

"Who are you?" Jonny begged, his eyes squinting in pain as the smoky mist thickened. "Do I know you? What's your name?"

Jonny raised his forearms and criss-crossed them in a protective shield as his face bruised in splatters of multi-coloured sleet. The turbulent tornado sizzled in a raging tempest as Jonny laboured his drowning legs forward in a tenacious perseverance.

A mass of snow had begun to build, an icy fortress that rivalled the fortitude of the Berlin Wall as Jonny, enfiladed by snow grenades, channelled his inner army tank and ploughed forward to reach the obscured woman on the other side.

"Hey!" he bawled, afraid that she could no longer hear him as the budding snow wall continued to mound. "Can you hear me? I said 'what's your name,' goddammit!?"

Jonny's body froze quicker than the water droplets above him as a savage vortex of wind bowled him over like an indefensible tenpin. His ears boomed in a sonorous numbing and in that moment, all that could be heard was the still haunting of a very familiar voice in his head.

" *What do you want it to be?* "

The answer parted the fog as if the woman were Moses at the Red Sea, as – for only the most microscopic of moments – an irresistibly sultry gaze could be seen across the seductive lips of a woman who looked nothing at all like Julia Roberts.

30

REVENGE OF THE SUCCUBUS

His eyes flung open, his chest suffocating from the tight cloaking of the bed sheets. A pool of vaginal fluid moistened the fabric, perpetuating a perceptible discomfort. In the dark stillness, Jonny could not see much, but the dim glow of a bedside alarm clock and the indistinct shadow of a lava lamp beside it.

What time is it? What happened last night? I remember the food truck but... ugh...

He fumbled with the bed linen before stumbling towards the cream-tiled bathroom, slogging with one foot behind the other as he dragged himself through the hotel slush.

After a nimble rendezvous with the flashiest toilet he had ever seen, Jon scrubbed the bacteria from his hands and checked his reflection in the mirror. His eyes and the inky circles that drowned beneath them made his drawn-in face almost unrecognisable. He waved his right hand up and then down again, his reflection duplicating the gesture verbatim.

No scars, no bruises; eyes are a little murky but I seem to be ok.

A dozen needles danced across his forehead, the pain penetrating his cranium in an uncomfortable agony.

The aroma of stale bourbon and tobacco flooded the atmosphere as he redirected his focus to the naked woman nestled atop a hotel mattress, cloaked only by a thin bed sheet that barely covered her backside.

Television static flashed in bright lights across his cortex as the visual before him appeared eerily similar to paintings and artefacts featured on a daytime television special on the *History Channel*.

"Holy fuck! Succubus! It's a succubus!" he squealed, his voice dry, hoarse and barely audible.

In his condition, a beauty of such exotic magnificence, cloaked in cloth and resting on a cushioned mattress before him had to have been the work of a seductive, supernatural demon, entering his nightmares to beguile him.

Any other possible explanation did not make sense.

Jonny would not have consented to it.

"Be gone, demon!" he whispered as he swung his arms from side to side like a broken pendulum.

A mixture of confusion and discomfort burdened him, Jonny now ever hesitant to refrain from a return to the occupied bedspread.

Breath. Compose yourself.

"Hey," he whispered as he nudged the woman before rolling her on her back to reveal her plainly exposed breasts. The woman's bosom had been peculiarly annotated, circled and arrowed in bright blue marker like an indigenous native at a tribal ceremony.

"Yoo-hoo, Madison, is that you?" he yodelled.

Madison – blonde haired and as fit as a butcher's vegetarian dog – was unresponsive. A palette of blues and purples smothered her cheeks and forehead, smudging from her features in a dusty paint-mixing lagoon.

Jonny inspected her body like a pathologist in an autonomous autopsy. Scribbled in a permanent blue marker – the kind of marker found beside a Regrub Moon Hills blueprint – were two proper nouns, swirled, outlined and tattooed in a sophisticated graffiti.

Jonny Cash.

"What… the…fuck?" Jonny gasped before flexing his underpants and reaching for an uncorked bottle of distilled wine. "I'm not thinking straight right now. I'm still tripping. I have to be. Quick, distract yourself."

An almost empty glass with a single drop of Brandy – suggestively the remains of an evening spent splurging in fine Cognac – was within arms length, nestled on the bedside table beside him.

"The origins of brandy," he read out aloud, mimicking an eighteenth century theatre performer as he scanned the stickered label on the reverse-side before tipping the bottle's contents in the glass. "Brandy comes from the term brandywine, derived from the Dutch word 'brandewijn' which loosely translates to burned wine."

The Dutch word, 'brandewijn.' Dutch.

The sentence resonated almost instantaneously; a glimmer of a life neglected penetrated at his burning throat as he poured and sculled an overfilled glass of Cognac to numb the pain.

Maya!

"It's just a dream, it's just a dream," he whispered, brainwashing his psyche in a repetitive chant.

Jonny scanned the bottle for anything that could provide an engaging diversion.

"So how do we make it?" he continued. "Brandy is produced by fermentation and distillation of the grape skins, seeds, and stems that remain after grapes have been pressed to extract their juice for making wine."

Fucking grape juice. Are you kidding me?

Jonny released the bottle from the clenches of his fingers as he shelved it on the bedside table and extended his legs, his back grinding against the hard wood of the headboard.

What the hell is that smell? Jonny pondered, twitching and wiggling his nose like a hairier, two-thousand-year-old version of Barbara Eden. His snout traced the scent, steering his eyes towards a precarious creature shadowed behind the curvatures of a narrow hallway.

"Psst," he whistled, arresting the attention of the malodorous animal. "Don't be scared little buddy, come on over here."

Jonny double-tapped against the mattress and softened his bark as he lured the creature closer. And in a clear moment of dog-to-man deliberation, a brown and black Yorkshire terrier appeared from behind the shadows, taking four steps at a time in his direction.

"Well aren't you just the... *hairiest* little thing I've ever seen."

Jonny tickled at his fuzzy chest hair before curling a strand above his abdomen.

"You know..." he whispered to the terrier as if it possessed *Scooby-Doo*-like communication powers. "... I hope this isn't one of those 'may karma never *bite* you in the ass' kind of scenarios."

Jonny checked the canine's collar for a nametag as he braced for a worst-case scenario tetanus shot.

"So he's yours then, I assume?" he muttered as he leant forward and stared into Madison's closed eyes.

If Jonny hadn't known better, he might have presumed that his one-night-stand had pulled a Brittany Murphy. But given the evidence within the ambient hotel suite, even the most novice detective would have rolled the dice on unconscious intoxication instead.

"Oh, what's that, Spike?" he whispered as he brushed his soapy fingers through the canine's grubby fur. "You want to try some of this?"

Jonny baited the terrier towards the bottle of Cognac as he maintained a steady stroke through the critter's furry cloak.

"You know what's ironic?" he huffed, the animal's tongue leaking and dripping with saliva. "After you take a sip, we're *both* going to be in real need of a '*hair of the dog*' remedy tomorrow."

Jonny was citing the colloquial expression used to refer to the consumption of alcohol that was often imbibed as a way to cure the ailments of a painful hangover.

"The only real difference," he continued as he pounced off the mattress to collect a single-compartment dog feeder from the far corner of the suite. "Is that you grow it on your back and I have to pay eleven fucking dollars from a hipster bar in California."

Jonny raised the stainless steel container from the carpeted floor and returned to the filthy canine.

"You thirsty? *Well*, if you're anything like your old lady…"

Jonny sloped the bottle of Cognac on a sliding diagonal and watched as the brandy funnelled and splashed its way into the bowl. The liquid hit the bowl's surface with such velocity that drops of excess brandy splattered in every direction, blotching the grubby bed sheets.

The parched terrier slurped at the vermillion-coloured substance like a stranded traveller in the Sahara as it imbibed the bowl's entire contents in a regurgitating barf.

"I'm guessing *she* taught you how to use your tongue, right?" Jonny theorised as a ghostly silhouette emerged from Madison's nakedness, reincarnating her spiritual rendezvous with a slice of blotter paper.

Minutes later, Jonny – with both hands wedged down his underpants – diagnosed something alarmingly anomalous in Madison's furry companion. The terrier – who had already swallowed a surfeit of the thick liquid – was marred by a surfacing diagnosis of very pronounced symptoms. The dog was disorientated and drowsy, his motor functions regressing to that of a demented newborn puppy.

Rumbles of a digestive catastrophe murmured in the terrier's abdomen as it struggled to swallow its own saliva.

"Hey, Spike, you okay, buddy?"

The terrier wasn't.

He choked and expectorated a mucus and vomit-based concoction before sedating into a quiet drowse.

What Jonny had so foolishly failed to consider was that while his late-night cough syrup drowned *his* soul in an unbalanced and unwavering guilt, for the average *canine*, grape-fermented alcohol was a dangerous catalyst for ethanol toxicoses.

"Holy shit!" Jonny cursed and kicked in a panicked uproar. "I've killed the dog! I've killed the dog!"

In a reflexive moment, Jonny hastily clothed himself and rushed for the apartment's exit door, knocking the timber frame against its hinge as he darted for the building's stairwell.

"Sorry about your dog – I'll... *buy* you a better one!" Jonny burst from a distance, Madison none the wiser as he draped his CMYK t-shirt over his shoulders.

As he yanked the handbrake at the central corridor, Jonny Jinks descried an extraordinary scene that forced him to anchor at the foot pedal.

"Chuckie!?" he blurted, stunned, as he stared through an open doorway and looked on at his redheaded associate. To Jonny's astonishment, there stood Chuckie in a *Crouching Tiger, Hidden Dragon* combat stance, actively pile driving a blindfolded beauty from behind... in a Jonny Jinks-painted, Rich Uncle Pennybags PVC mask.

"Hey, Jonny!" he panted, snapping at the neck as he squealed in disjointed sentences. "Oh, sorry man, I went snooping around your backpack when you fell asleep and I just couldn't help myself; you remember Sasha, though, right?"

Plant the seed and watch it prosper.

Jonny feigned a reaction of bewilderment while deep within the fibres of his intoxicated bloodstream, he rejoiced knowing that Chuckie had taken the bait.

The sightless brunette waved in a direction away from the doorway as a rhythmic thrust caused her to moan and stumble to her knees.

"Man, what the fuck are you doing? We've got to get out of here! And bring that goddamn mask with you!"

Chuckie exchanged a series of irate expressions before collecting his trousers off the leg of the footboard. He bounced off the box spring below the mattress and defied the Earth's gravitational pull as he pounced for the doorway.

"Ugh, Sasha, baby," he whispered as he tightened his belt buckle. "I'm sorry; listen, I've got to get going but we'll finish this off next time, I promise."

"But what about my money!?" Sasha cursed, waving her arms around in exasperation.

"You said you'd pay her to fuck you!?" Jonny blurted in repulsion.

And just like that, Jonny Jinks and Chuckie Hooper vanished from the dim hallways of a highly questionable hotel, leaving more than one blindfolded, vulnerable, and intoxicated beauty alone in the middle of a damp mattress.

31

MEATLOAF MANOEUVRE

Disorientation was an utter understatement. It was as if he were channelling the unfortunate malady of Madison's poisoned canine, the sympathy pains slicing at him in sharp and unrelenting intervals.

What have I done? What happened? Maya. Oh shit.

Jonny had crossed a line, a threshold of no return, even. This was *not* part of the plan and yet it happened, anyway.

The omnipresent Californian sun was on the rise as a futile racket thumping from a reverberated microphone made Jonny feel like a gospel singer at a Meat Loaf concert.

"I'm that Chuckie mother-fuckie…" came the chorused chant from the stage of an empty karaoke bar. "That'll slap your mama in her *ass*."

A delirious Chuckie Hooper, still juiced with gusto, slurred through an impudent hip-hop verse that bordered along the lines of sexual abuse before hurling an empty soda can at an idled vacuum.

"*Tickle* on her *pickle* while she screams to make it *last!*"

Jonny curled his limbs above his shoulders in an awkward disguise as he thumped his head on a wooden table and pressed his eyes shut. Chuckie's voice was numbing but Jonny had not the vigour nor bounce to encourage him to swallow the microphone.

"I'm a *pimp*, your dad's *limp*, your grandma's a *hag*, and your mum's up in your bedroom stroking my dick with her *hand!*"

Chuckie's intimate performance was highlighted by a lumbering dance manoeuvre that seemed to unify Michael Jackson's 'moonwalk' with Migos' 'dab.'

To Jonny's fortune – an arguable adjective at this point of the adventure – the makeshift concert hall was relatively barren, save for a pair of hummingbirds perched by the branch of an artificial palm tree.

Nobody would be close enough to heed any attention to the foolishness of his redheaded companion.

Just ignore him. Block him out. Let him do what he wants – he gets away with it anyway, right?

A placid breeze offered an offsetting serenity to an otherwise incoherent morning as Jonny counterbalanced the need for remembrance with rest and recovery.

"Oh, c'mon, man," came a malcontent grunt, Chuckie's voice clamouring with each syllable. "There's no way you could *possibly* be tired; haven't you ever heard of adrenaline?"

"Not now, Chuckie," Jonny dismissed, his head walloping with the force of a thousand orbital explosions. "Give me a second to recover, will you?"

He took the bait. He wore the mask.

Jonny had earned his brownie points, that much he was sure. But it was his total point tally in a game of Morality Pursuit that had him bleeding through the heart.

"You've got six-and-a-half-minutes," Chuckie barked. "Then we're back on the road; so little time and so much to do!"

The hotel's karaoke stage assumed its position to the far rear of the heated swimming pool, separated only by an adjoining bar and a stock hold. To its side, twin tennis courts occupied the outskirts of the facility, jointly owned by the building's body corporate and a local Los Angeles tennis association.

"You want to have a swing?" Chuckie proposed, gesturing towards the court's clubhouse where a stack of tennis rackets lined a wooden open casing. "Watch me go Maria Sharapova on your ass, horse-grunts, fake orgasms and all!"

Jonny lifted his head and widened his eyes, terminating the dilation of his pupils for the first time in what seemed like hours as the abrupt change in light created an agonising flash blindness.

"Uh, I think you have to be staying *in* the hotel to use their shit, Chuckie," Jonny speculated, rebuffing the redhead's request as he rubbed on his eyelids with the cushioned-ends of his knuckles.

"Sure, sure, that's no problem. My dad's got a bunch of shares in the management firm here so as far as I can tell, I just about own at least seven or eight of those rackets anyway."

Chuckie was either the world's most assertive bullshit-artist or The Chuckie Group were, in fact, one of the shrewdest acquisition and investment firms on the West Coast.

Jonny shrugged his shoulders, stretching his arms as he gesticulated a 'whatever' kind of assent.

As he slid his legs out from beneath the wooden table, an instinctive Spidey-sense locked on a pair of burly men clothed in matching navy uniforms, accented by the shine of a chest-plated metallic badge.

The men emanated an aura of authority as they marched around with valiant demeanour.

Oh shit! This can't be happening! They've found me!

Murmurs of sirens and flashing lights encircled his psyche like an out-of-order wooden horse on a carnival merry-go-round.

How had they found him so soon? It seemed like an unfeasible episode of *CSI: Crime Scene Investigation*. He hadn't even the time to devise a lawyer-less defence strategy — could they really have executed an investigation with such expediency?

Jonny banished his paranoia as he instilled a calm and hunted for the nearest exit sign.

Holy shit, think of something quick, you're running out of time.

To Jonny's left, a service attendee – clocking on for her mid-morning shift – now manned the bar counter, wiping at dirty glassware as she prepared for the hotel's bikini-wearing patrons. To his far right, the custodian of an unclaimed vacuum twirled at his South American moustache as he returned to his polishing and disinfecting equipment.

Shit, I'm cornered! Stay calm.

Jonny blinked heavily, bracing for judgment as his hands penetrated with the pain of a hammering needle on a crucifix.

"Chuckie Hooper!" signalled the officer in the most gravelly voice that Jonny had ever heard.

Chuckie, having already attempted a sly evacuation of his own, halted and snapped at his flabby, sugary hips.

"Who's asking?" he answered both unwarily and superciliously.

The police officer flashed his badge with vigour, conjecturing that his suspect may have either been colour-blind, witlessly disobedient or a combination of the two.

"We'd like a word with you," the officer commanded.

Jesus, it's not me they want, Jonny pacified, quelling his burdening sense of contrition as a slither of sweat streamed down his cheekbone.

Jonny's relief was patent, his shoulder's releasing from a rigid, physical tangle with its conjoining nerves. He watched on with vigilance as the officers began their approach, modelling their path by way of Chuckie's footprints.

They hadn't come for him. For all Jonny knew, the authorities hadn't identified any irregularities in his spending charade.

They hadn't come for *him.*

Not yet, at least.

32

COMMANDER BURRITO

"So, we meet again, Commander Burrito," Chuckie huffed as if he were challenging Emperor Zurg in the combat crescendo of *Toy Story.* "For the last time!"

"Stop being a fucking moron," the commander shunned in disdain, his identification tag beside a single silver star suggesting that Chuckie had a problem with pronunciation.

Commander Clayton… Bommarito?

Maybe it was because Jonny was still descending down the snail-paced escalator of his unnatural high, but the provocative nickname seemed hilarious. That Chuckie was apparently not only familiar with the commander, but could circumvent the kind of dialogue that might have landed a hoodlum from South Central Los Angeles with a bullet in his chest somehow made it all the more amusing.

"What are you doing out here?" Bommarito inquired, his thickened eyebrows and thinning hairline providing much of a distraction.

Bommarito's ripening wrinkles implied that he was the kind of police commander who had paid his dues, bearing witness to everything from petty thefts to celebrity homicides. They also suggested an irritated contempt for the spoilt, entitled and privileged son of a fortuitous Californian fast-food magnate.

"Why we're just out here playing some tennis on this grand and glorious day."

"You're trespassing."

"Well *excuse* me! I've never heard such bollocks in my lifetime!" Chuckie discredited, his accent switching from British to American to Spanish to American and back to British again. "Prove it!"

"What'd I just tell you about being a fucking moron, kid?" Bommarito scolded, clearly exhausted by Chuckie's childish ring-around-a-rosie shenanigan. "Now tie up your shoelaces, we're going for a walk."

Chuckie looked down at his feet like a giant to the foot of a beanstalk.

"But I'm not wearing any laces?"

Three pigeons, two delinquents, one commander, an officer and a partridge in a pear tree trooped away from the private property in single file, Chuckie and his accomplice leading the way as the commander and his subordinate maintained order from a distance.

"Chuckie," Jonny whispered, avoiding eye contact and lip movements like a blind ventriloquist. "Do you... *know* this cop?"

"Shit, I know everyone, holmes, this is L.A.," he replied, his voice box requiring the attachment of a firearm suppressor to maintain its silent undertone. "He knows my dad and my dad knows me. You know what it's like with this chain of command bullshit."

"What the fuck are you talking about?" Jonny murmured, their conflicting verbalisations mirroring that of a *Tom and Jerry* chase sequence. "Are they going to drug test us?"

With the dawn of reality upon him, the tortilla-teasing surname quip was no longer quite as mirthful as Jonny's heartbeat began to race faster than his feet could peddle.

"Fuck no, man," Chuckie assured him with the kind of credence offered by a dentist to his patient moments before a dental filling. "He probably just wants to ask me a couple of questions like he *always* does. He pulls me up like once a fortnight anyway."

Once a fortnight? What the hell for?

"No, no, hold up," Chuckie halted, his pace decreasing as he slowed down his physical being to match the speed — or lack thereof — of his spinning brain. "How long is twelve days? Maybe more like once a week, now that I think about it. That's only seven days, right?"

Jesus.

"I know I'm going to regret asking… but why?"

"Oh, you know… just because, mostly."

Of course. Why did I ever both to ask?

"Well you know how it is, Jonny," Chuckie continued, his faux hawk stealing all the attention as he fumbled through an idiomatic explanation. "One minute you're flipping beef patties and the next you're buried eighty fucking inches deep in a sandpit filled with cocaine while a dwarf dressed in a knights costume takes off with your underpants."

"Seriously?"

"No! Well, kind of — he was working at some role-playing card tournament or something — but that's beside the point. Basically, what I'm trying to say is that when I'm not putting out fires at the diner, sometimes things can get a little out of hand and I… occasionally *become* the fire."

Chuckie whipped at the shoulder as he cross-eyed his eyes and winked in Jonny's direction behind the cloak of his candy red *Ray-Ban* sunglasses.

"Bommarito behind us is my watering can."

Jonny was beginning to understand just how exactly this Californian thing worked.

"The kind of watering can you have lying around your garage or the kind you pay for from a gardening store in a newspaper ad?"

"The kind that *others* have to pay for, but *I* just happen to have lying around on a rainy day."

Jonny was impressed. For all his flaws, Chuckie *could* speak his language when called into action.

"If it's raining, what'd you need a watering can for?"

"You *always* need a watering can."

"Alright you two," Bommarito interjected, sensing that an unsettling grin shared between his prisoners undermined his sovereignty. "So tell me something that'll make me laugh."

Chuckie and Jonny glanced at one another, their grins flipping to an expression of thoughtful brainstorming.

"Ugh... two Jews walk into a bar..." Chuckie began, confident that he had found a throat-tickling winner.

"Let me be more specific," Bommarito buzzed, vexed by the beginnings of Chuckie's wisecrack as he tightened his vocal cords and thundered in a heavy baritone. "Tell me something you two did *last night* that'll make me laugh."

Chuckie wedged his glasses inwards, tucking the temple tips behind his ears with adhesive earwax as a line of high-performance sports cars zoomed by.

"Don't look at *them*, I asked *you* a question," the commander roared, he and his subordinate paying the noisy vehicles no notice.

"Well, personally," Chuckie confessed, his chest buffing as he whistled with aplomb. "I actually picked up a part-time job driving around L.A. and switching on all the faulty street lamps with a remote control. Then I made a pit-stop at a retirement village before heading home to read *American Psycho* for the third time – *damn*, I love that book. What about you, Jonny?"

"If you want to act like a fucking monkey I have no problems with throwing you in a cage right now," the commander threatened, his booming warning drawing the attention of nearby pedestrians who were almost too ruffled to look away. "It seems like you may be experiencing a mild fucking case of amnesia so give me a moment to jog your memory."

The officer handed his commander a tablet device, Bommarito swiping through its properties as Jonny's legs began to tremble.

"Seen this before?"

The commander stretched the digital tablet in front of the twosome in a single-handed grip like Jim Carrey on the DVD cover of *Ace Ventura: Pet Detective*.

"Ugh, sure, that's our van, a mobile Chuckie's Diner food truck," Chuckie Hooper Junior hypothesised as the colour from Jonny's face drained down into his abdomen.

"And can you tell me what's *wrong* with your Chuckie's Diner food truck?"

"Well, when we bought it," Chuckie stuttered, wishing he was standing in the presence of the Hooper family lawyer. "I *definitely* don't remember it coming with that picket fence attached to the hood."

Jonny face-palmed like a moving translation of an Internet meme as he felt his web of lies unravel before him.

Jesus, is that what happened? Holy shit. They're going to charge me for this. Then find out where I'm from. Then find out what I did. I'm so... totally... fucked.

Gleaming on the tablet in front of them was not a 'game over' screen capture from the mobile video game *Reckless Racing* but a night-time photograph of a Chuckie's Diner food truck. Its hood was cloaked in the debris of a townhouse picket fence while its front bumper hung loose, its headlights shattered on the dark lawn in subdued particles of glass. The image appeared to have captured the moment the townhouse's horrified residents grappled with the gravity of the attack on their front yard, their hands cupping their wide-open mouths like eyewitnesses of a fleeting hate crime.

"What about you, kid? What's your name?" Bommarito interrogated, Jonny feeling about as paralysed as a Nigerian immigrant at a Ku Klux Klan gathering.

"Jon..." he replied, deliberately shortening his adopted appellation.

"And what did *you* do last night?" the commander probed. "This time, *don't* make me laugh."

"I was with *him*," Jonny blurted, incriminating himself in the process.

Shit. Why did I say that for?

"So I guess *you* can corroborate his story, then? Go on, what retirement village did you visit? They got any vacancies? Because let me assure you, the way this little bastard has pushed me over the years, I'm seven-eighths of the way to unlocking my motherfucking 4-0-1-K plan."

Jonny's throat tightened, his mind spinning like a bingo rotary machine full of Ping-Pong ball-inscribed alibis, none of which seemed tenable.

"I was with him *after* he visited the retirement village," he falsified, filling in the gaps as best he could.

"And was that *before* or *after* he read *American Psycho* for the third time?"

Jonny looked in Chuckie's direction, the tattooed troublemaker appearing unbothered, unperturbed.

"During."

"Well isn't that a pretty picture?" Bommarito jabbed, seething at the trail of obvious lies. "Well let me tell you what's going to happen from here."

Bommarito swiped at the tablet as he began to scribble on the screen with an LAPD-marked stylus.

"Mrs. Picking is now out of pocket by approximately fifty-two-hundred-dollars. Now she's already filed an insurance claim but you know what you're gonna do Mr. Hooper?"

"Give her fifty-two-hundred-dollars?"

"Wrong!" the commander buzzed. "You're going to give her *seventy*-two-hundred-dollars – an extra thousand because you're a fucking moron and an extra thousand on top of that for wasting my time and forcing me to clean up your mess again."

While the commander – like a powerful magistrate deity – demanded an additional two-thousand-dollars in compensation, the general consensus was that poor Mrs. Picking would see nothing more than the fifty-two-hundred-dollars she needed to repair her property damage.

"And what about the truck?" Chuckie burped, estimating that a considerable repair fee was incoming.

Instantly, Jonny understood that his trepidation was all for naught. He was no expert in civil *or* criminal law – and as far as he was concerned, this palm-greasing prearrangement was common in corrupt police force practice. In a way, it explained Chuckie's nonchalant perspective, his blasé approach to anything impermissible and illicit. But for Jonny, his curiosity sauntered into the realms of actionable kinetics. Chuckie's Diner appeared to be the redhead's birthright, a patrimony of perpetual capitalism. But was that *really* all it took to bankroll a personal LAPD-inspired version of *Ray Donovan*?

"Buy a new one," Bommarito proposed.

"Oh man, dad's gonna be *so* fucking pissed."

33

PLEASE LEAVE A MESSAGE AFTER THE TONE

"You want to know when it was... those moments I knew you were the one?" she quivered, tightening her tear ducts as her voice broke like bent bamboo. "It was in those moments that you saw the darkest part of me and, instead of running away, you took my hand and painted me the stars."

A monochromatic montage played from a cognitive movie reel as Jonny's mind dramatised the moments like an out-of-body poltergeist unable to touch but more than able to feel.

Whenever sadness pays a visit, he paints galaxies on the back of her hands.

"... Please, Jon, just tell me how you're feeling," she pleaded. "Tell me where you are and what you're doing; I'm *so* worried about you. Please, just call me back, that's all I ask. I just want to hear your voice. I just want to know that you're okay. I love you, Jonathan Jinks."

The tear-jerking sound of a dejected sniffle followed by an 'end of recorded message' automated prompt was enough to blow a seven-hundred-pound statue over a ledge. Maya had tried, unsuccessfully grasping at Jonny-coloured straws as she willed him to return to her.

For Maya Ververs, none of this computed. Sure, Jonny's anomalous behaviour was alarming and perhaps suggested a more prescient issue. But like John Lennon and Yoko Ono, there was nothing that the two could not conquer together and a pile of never-ending bills, endometriosis, unemployment or a working vacation to California was *not* supposed to change that.

But Jonny had broken his vow of fidelity. The guilt consumed him and mixed in a paint bucket of actionable, vicarious desire. Jonny had to deem it a sacrifice; a sacrifice of the life he lived for the one he never thought he could.

If I could say it in words, then there'd be no reason for me to paint.

34

OFF TO SEE THE WIZARD

Jukebox music blared throughout the diner as Chuckie Hooper Junior crunched a French fry to the bouncing rhythm of a rock and roll break beat.

Birds chirped, their sonic signals fighting over the pre-recorded melodies of an automated door opening as the Californian sunshine concocted an involuntary sweat-based sauce in the restaurant's steaming kitchen.

"So tell me, Jonny Cash," Chuckie sputtered as chunks of potato cannonballed towards the chequered tile, Jonny suddenly noticing an uncanny similarity between the flooring at both Chuckie's Diner and his hotel suit at the *Chateau Marmont.* "Would you say that you've figured out what it *means* to be a winner yet?"

* * *

hold it right there for a quick second.

You see, this question got me really thinking which was a huge fucking surprise given that almost *nothing* Chuckie says ever obliges anyone to descend down a sinkhole of deep thought. This world, virtually characterised by one-upmanship and competition, is painfully obvious to anyone not sharing a rock-hammock with a lost tribe.

Outside of stuff like *The Biggest Loser* – where the biggest *loser* actually becomes the biggest *winner* – people rarely volunteer to lose. This need, this desire to win is baked into our DNA on account of our earliest ancestors, the earliest survivors, who prevailed in the face of certain defeat.

Fortunately, our new generation, the humans of today, came fully-equipped with the brainpower to *invent* our own way to victory, even if we didn't *really*, actually win. That age-old paradigm of 'I win, you lose' – the kind of thing you'd taunt your siblings over as a child – is no longer sustainable. Nobody has to lose anymore for someone else to win.

And that's why I had to wonder: did me winning – and in turn, a victory for The Pennsylvania Paint Co. – really mean that anyone else came off second best? Did my triumph really obstruct another's road to glory? And if so, how exactly could I have suggested that I won?

Did I win because I uncovered a loophole in the ATM system at the Nations of Jefferson American Bank? Did I win because I upgraded my suite at the *Chateau Marmont*? Did I win because I denied the intoxicating pleasures of a prostitute? Did I win because I could now pay my way through expensive shopping districts? Did I win because I painted Chuckie a sadistically erotic, Rich Uncle Pennybags-inspired ceremonial sex mask? Did I win because I did LSD with a woman whose name I'll never again remember? Did I win because I played involuntary accomplice to Chuckie's life of juvenile petty crimes? Or did I win because I continued to neglect the love of my life, the centre of my world, for an intergalactic sideshow that was about as real as the money in my bank account?

now thats how you get someone thinking. lets get back to it.

* * *

"I'd say I'm *winning*," Jonny replied, borrowing an article from the Charlie Sheen starter kit. "I mean I'm in the lead, that much I think I know. But I haven't crossed the finish line – not yet at least, anyway."

"Smart," Chuckie commended, slurping through the straw of a Chuckie's Diner-branded strawberry thick shake. "So let's have it then; what do you need to do to spray champagne on the podium?"

Jonny mulled, his attention drifting out the glass window that separated his retro diner booth with the tyre-burning Californian asphalt.

"Besides buying more champagne, of course," the redhead added as he rubbed the flab on his arms that acted as a skin-based canvas for his tattooed sleeve.

"I guess I need to show you that I can paint," Jonny proposed. "But to do that, I'm going to need some help."

Chuckie was hardly allergic to the concept of aid, having offered a helping hand to Jonny on more than one occasion. But this felt different; this called for a higher kind of power and Chuckie was growing more giant-like by the millisecond.

"Tell me what you need and I'll make it happen," Chuckie assured, clicking his fingers like an unruffled Mafia don.

There was an unspoken undertone, a ruling that both understood but did not dare to say. The ruling was taboo and utterly irrelevant to both Regrub Moon Hills and the Pennsylvania Paint Co.

Indeed, Jonny needed to prove his worth as an artist, a painter on a grander scale. But not to Chuckie; no, Chuckie's adjudication, the labouring contract and the entire impetus behind the Jinks boy's visit was becoming extraneous.

Jonny – the Allentown native, once without a self-centred,

acquisitive or mercenary bone in his body – had to prove it to *himself.*

* * *

The Nations of Jefferson American Bank stood for absolute patriotism but in a parallel universe, it may as well have typified the unscrupulous descent towards an American dream instead.

An ATM was omnipresent, his credit card a free-spirited eagle as Jonny spread its wings and watched it fly, time and time again. Every dollar spent was erased, evaporating into thin air like a steamy card trick with the swift electronic funds transfer from a non-existent credit card.

Cordon bleu cuisines, upmarket clothing, lavish utilities, exorbitant champagne; the merchandise itself mattered little. They were all financial pawns in his sandbox game of *Monopoly.*

Jonny was the commander, the puppet-master, the Rothschild to his very own federal reserve. He was the printing press, the credit creator and the sovereign figurehead of Chartalism by which the chain of his money supply would originate with the spontaneity of direct economic activity – or, with a bad new penchant for reckless spending.

But that very penchant was beginning to sound wailing alarms, emitting a warning that Jonny Jinks *had* to heed. His vocation for achieving the astronomical, for breaking the barriers and for flipping dimes into dollars was meritorious, even if it all appeared to be the result of an elaborately programmed confidence game.

Jonny had become a glorified *cheat*; a swindler of sorts, robbing his inanimate victim before appropriating funds for an egocentric endeavour. His access to a hidden loophole was monopolistic, his decision-making slightly diabolical. But *eBay* demanded his soul and if the painter from Pennsylvania desired any kind of longeval self-preservation and protection – despite it causing a crippling affliction to all that adored him – he had to be provident.

35

HOW THEY LIVE IN TOKYO
東京

The whole thing was like a wild incarnation of *Michael Jackson's* 'Neverland Ranch.' The estate and its associated courtyards and gardens were comparable to that of the late King of Pop's fantasy-inspired Santa Barbara home. With its savannah-like grasslands bordering its inclined fencing, the land was largely gated, accented by a spring of flowerbeds and moulded shrubs while an infinity edge pool overlooked the Californian horizon. The courtyard was encircled in a kaleidoscope of roses, peonies, carnations and chrysanthemums while each meticulously crafted garden feature showcased a geometric topiary with clippings of foliage trimmed into gloriously grassed statues of an African safari. A pebbled pathway steered visitors towards an octagonal gazebo while a tiered, cascading fountain stood at centre-point, pissing a funnel-spray of water in every direction.

But perhaps the most astonishing feat of all was the dreamlike existence of a thunder-striking mammal that had no business yanking leaves from a tree in Pacific Palisades. Amidst the commotion of a playboy Fun Park, the tallest animal on Earth sauntered in a nonchalant free roam, its poking neck sticking out like a mole in an *Austin Powers* feature. The creature – coated by a light tan and covered in splotches of brown – could have peered into a second-story window without ever having to lean on its tiptoes.

He's got... a pet giraffe?

Jonny's hand reached for his pocket as he traced his *Louis Vuitton* giraffe-decorated Brazza wallet with the tips of his fingers like a blind man to a sheet of braille.

"Jonny," Chuckie introduced, escorting his meal ticket up a flight of small concrete steps as the dark tint from his red *Ray-Bans* hid his eyes from the giraffe. "I'd like you to meet my *very* good friend, Tokyo van Wolfswinkel."

Jonny jarred his teeth to his tongue to keep from laughter as he leant forward and extended a sign of 'I-come-in-peace'. The hackneyed J-pop chorus from the Teriyaki Boyz's *Tokyo Drift* looped inside his mind as he hummed and swayed to the melodious tune.

I wonder if you know/

How they live in Tokyo/

If you've seen it then you mean it, then you know you have to go/

"Tokyo... van Wolfswinkel?" Jonny echoed. "That's a... *different* kind of name."

Tokyo – his hand stroking the silky textures of his pet giraffe like an evil emperor to a minion – grunted his chagrin, having no doubt exchanged in this very conversation a gazillion times before.

"I'm adopted," Tokyo clarified in an elocution that consolidated the pronunciations of a Japanese pitch accent with local Californian surfer slang. "My father is a Dutch migrant and my mother is Japanese."

"What a coincidence!" Jonny chirped as if his underpants had wedged uncomfortably between his crotch and backside. "Me too!"

Tokyo's eyebrows arched as his eyes snapped towards Chuckie.

"I mean, my mum's not *Japanese*," he corrected nervously, careful to avoid a feast-frenzy for the looming giraffe as if he were composed of compound leaves and not human flesh. "My dad's ancestors, they came here to the United States from Holland..."

Tokyo blinked. Then blinked again.

"So, I mean, you and I, we've got something in common is all I'm trying to say."

Jonny's words were in haste as Chuckie shook the locks of his candy faux hawk, the corners of his mouth tipping upwards as his eyebrows sank into a rueful gaze.

This... isn't going so well.

There was no question; Jonny had already thought he had seen it all. But an affluent half-caste with a Californian harboured giraffe forced him to reconsider.

"What can I do for you?" Tokyo prompted sternly and without patience.

Chuckie proffered Jonny a seldom seen nod of approval, endorsing his Allentown buddy like a financial backer on *Dragon's Den*.

"Ugh, I'm new in town and..."

"Do I look like a local to you?" Tokyo barked.

Silence.

Jonny was totally vulnerable and exposed, his bones quivering in a J-pop chorused jitter.

"No," he admitted sheepishly as his eyes drooped and sloped off his face.

"Well don't start your bullshit with that because I have little sympathy for foreigners; have you not seen this estate that I live on?"

Jonny surveyed the multi-level manor – its doorways engulfed in a natural kingdom of boulders, foliage, flowers and handcrafted demigod sculptures – as if he were a real estate agent conducting a property valuation. The self-contained jewel box was an architectural masterpiece, a cinematic dreamscape that overlooked the entirety of

Downtown Los Angeles, Catalina, and the coastline of California in a single, unobstructed, sweeping view. The house was encased in reflective glass, an ethos that guided the thematic of the estate as a glimpse at its transparent panelling revealed the interior perspectives of each of its six bedroom and ten bathrooms from the gardens.

"Start again; I'm going to give you one more attempt," he threatened.

This really was a *Dragon's Den*-styled pressure-cooker, Jonny fighting for survival as he grasped at an impressive band of straws.

Maya. She would know what to say.

"I'm an artist – a painter – and from what I can tell when I look around here, you seem to have a unique appreciation for fine craftsmanship," he said, gauging Tokyo's steadfast leer as he pointed towards the topiaries and statues outside the eccentric manor.

"And just like I believe *you* did, I also came from a place of unjust oppression where no matter how good you were at something or how great an opportunity you believed you had to do something extraordinary, the very fabric of the community you're supposed to be about didn't want to know you."

He wasn't lying. Jonny had once submitted a collection of work to the *Allentown Art Museum*, Lehigh Valley's finest exhibition of creative crafts. And while the organisation's mission claimed to enrich the lives of its visitors with its displays, not even Jonny's conducive ancestry could convince the museum to showcase the artist's oeuvre.

"You're playing the foreigner card again," Tokyo warned.

Jonny shook his head as he raised his hands in a visual stop sign, pleading for the venture capitalist to wait until his spiel was over before delivering on a final verdict.

"They've always told us that America was 'the land of opportunity' – I say that *Los Angeles* is the real American Dream, the land of the second chance; a place where even the craziest of dreams can come true."

Jonny was close to quoting a passage of the Declaration of Independence, revising the proclamations of an equal right to life, liberty and the pursuit of happiness. He gazed upwards and grinned at the abnormal presence of a pet giraffe as he tensed at the bicep, sensitive to the pulsating energies of an escalating momentum.

"I came here, just like you, because Los Angeles is the kind of place where everybody here was once from someplace else. Because Los Angeles is the kind of place that desperate people run to; desperate people who are drawn in on a fishing line by the dream, but dive back into the water, trying to escape a chasing nightmare. I came here because Los Angeles is the home to twelve million aspiring celebrities, playboys and tech-head entrepreneurs, squashed together in a transient city, all of them ready to make a run for it the moment things don't work out the way they'd planned."

Chuckie's jaw dipped as he gawked at Jonny's adroit salesmanship.

"And I came here to this very estate, Mr. van Wolfswinkel, because I believe that you're the one-in-twelve-million who *doesn't* run."

Jonny's tremors ceased, his nerves vanishing with the terminating expeditiousness of a cyborg assassin as a toxic tension released from his pores.

He's not saying anything...

Tokyo stood faceless, impassive and stiller than one of his stone sculptures in a Californian gale.

Silence.

Nothing.

Why is he just staring at me?

"I fucking like you a lot, my ninja!" Tokyo bellowed as he smacked his hands together in jubilation and pounced from the cushion of his royal throne. "I know what you're thinking; what kind of a businessman keeps a giraffe as a pet but takes life so seriously, right?"

Evidently, Tokyo van Wolfswinkel was more than conscious of his Bohemian behaviour.

"You've been standing there lecturing me for ten minutes like a motivational speaker at a motherfucking, goddamn AA meeting," Tokyo chortled as his sidekick giraffe stared blankly at a patch of green grass.

Chuckie bathed along in a union of uncontrollable laughter as if he were at a comedy show, awkwardly applauding to limit the discomfiture of a novice stand-up comedian.

"I don't understand?" Jonny replied.

"Listen to me, Jonny boy," Tokyo clucked as he stepped forward towards the priming artist. "Lay it to me straight; what is it that you'd like from me, exactly?"

Although the circumstances were highly unorthodox to say the least, the obvious aperture had presented itself.

"Patronage," he solicited as a wary hesitation returned.

From the ancient world onwards, patronage of the arts had become as important to art historians as any palette of work. And although the concept was explored in its greatest detail during medieval and Renaissance Europe, patronage was heavily prominent in feudal Japan and the traditional Southeast Asian kingdoms.

The kind of Asian kingdom that Tokyo van Wolfswinkel had erected in the opulent real estate mountains of California's Pacific Palisades.

Every illustrious artist in mankind's history – from Leondardo da Vinci to Michelangelo through to Mozart, Beethoven and William Shakespeare – sought and prospered from the support of a noble patron. And by accommodating for modern society's capitalist social reform, Jonny too pursued the benefits of such a credible advocacy.

"I need a vouching endorsement from someone who means something to the people of Los Angeles; and I'd also like for you to host an art exhibit to showcase my work. Chuckie tells me that you've got a network that'd rival *Verizon*."

Jonny paced himself, taking a moment to self-applaud his use of metaphor.

"I *know* you've got the kind of drawing power that can turn the dreamers of this city upside-down at the click of your fingers. I'm confident in my product; all I need is a little... *support*."

Jonny's implication seemed to galvanise Tokyo as a mythical being capable of both Dumbledore-calibre wizardry and Killgrave-powered mind-control.

"Okay, okay," Tokyo nodded. "And what's in it for me?"

Everything. You'll see.

"A wild fucking ride," Jonny proposed, planting the seeds. "Chuckie tells me you recently sold off your PLiNKER platform? You allow me to use your real estate, your network and your capital and I'll give you a new kind of revenue stream that'll guarantee that you can turn that one giraffe beside you into a *Central Park*-sized petting zoo."

Jonny was not sure what merit he had to pledge such a guarantee. But he *was* certain of one thing: he possessed the ultimate contingency, granting him the kind of riskless freedom that was considered the Holy Grail to every high rolling gambler from the riverboats of Louisiana to the jackpot-capital of Nevada. Even if he weren't able to vend any of his paintings, Jonny had the luxury of instantaneous access to an inexhaustible cash fund should any kind of deal-breaking ransom require compensation.

"I knew I liked you, Jonny Jinks," Tokyo emboldened.

Chuckie beamed, his eyes widening as he sensed that a favourable result was imminent.

"I can't tell if you're about to hit the panic button," Tokyo admitted, voicing his ambivalence. "Or if you're so genuinely over-confident that you're either on the verge of breaking from the shackles or you're about to become another endangered fucking mammal in a long line of 'would-be somebodies'."

There's only one way to find out, though, right?

"Look around; you know I'm *obviously* not a man short of wealth, although my ears are always in the streets searching for opportunities. But I'm sensing you've got some other kind of elbow grease up that fucking sleeve of yours," he continued, snapping in his patented semi-oriental twang. "Don't worry; I don't need to know. Whatever it is, either way, I'm *very* intrigued."

Jonny's lashes fluttered and his insides clenched in the presence of an intimated consent.

"So we have a deal, then?"

Jonny offered forward his right hand as he stared wishfully into the eyes of the bright-teethed half-caste before him.

"My ninja… Like I'm fucking Howie Mandel, you bet your ass we have a deal!"

Jonny pumped his fist as his brain exploded in a thousand firecrackers and party poppers.

"But!" Tokyo interjected, ensuring that Jonny's solemn celebration was only shortly lived. "I do have just *one* condition."

Chuckie had almost engineered the perfect escape, the introduction of a mastermind to manipulate a coequal genius into the ultimate outcome.

But there was one problem: Chuckie himself was far from an alpha-ninja polymath. In fact, he was its polar opposite.

Tokyo's command came with rapid, unwavering injection.

"You *must* do something for me in return."

36

MONEY GROWS IN ATMS

His giraffe-decorated Brazza wallet spread open like an enchanted cauldron of gold. Bulging and expanding the coarse leather, classified duplicates of hundred-dollar bills were amassed together with rubber elastic, sprouting like paper money leaves off a credit card tree trunk, the perfect summer feast for a hand drawn giraffe on a wallet canvas.

"Looks like we've already got *two* things in common – we're both trying to turn hundred dollar bills into mammals from the savannah," Tokyo suggested, inspecting the *LV* wallet before counting each green note as if he were a sceptical bank teller. "And they tried to tell me when my ship docked all those years ago that money *didn't* grow on trees in this country."

"ATMs," Jonny corrected, revealing his trump card before closing his wallet. "It grows *in* ATMs."

Jonny and Tokyo sat head-to-head in the kitchen of Tokyo's Pacific Palisades palace like chess players in a globally televised tournament. Between glances and unmistakable tics, their wax-headed mutual friend – who remained in the gardens circling Tokyo's pet giraffe as he provoked the mammal with an elongated stick – intermittently distracted their negotiations.

"It was all a total accident," Jonny avowed, as if he were making a fanciful plea to a ruling jury. "I thought it was only going to work in Pennsylvania and was ready to notify the bank; then I discovered the credit card loophole here in Los Angeles and realised that every single fucking machine could be used as a goddamn unlimited *and* unquestioning cash dispenser."

Tokyo was no foreigner to the farcical. Ludicrous declarations had been heard and shunned on countless occasions before. Yet there was something empathetically rare and plausible, something that appeared vulnerable to a fluid manipulation that disposed Tokyo to yield to Jonny Jinks' guilt-riddled narrative.

"So tell me this, Jonny Jinks," Tokyo began, moving his pawn forward a space. "If you can piss out mechanical money whenever you want, then what in the fuck do you need a ninja like me for?"

Jonny inhaled heavily as he weighed the pros and cons of transparency on a balancing scale.

"Plausible deniability," Jonny revealed as the drowning Californian sun began to droop, shadowing his eyes behind the moving silhouette of a shaking palm tree. "And, of course, your crazy, vast network. For one, how would I ever get my art to appear in front of the eyes of the people who need to see it? And for two, how does a guy who could barely afford to pay his fucking rent on the basic salary of a housepainter fund a trip to L.A. to showcase his paintings in front of the city's elite?"

Jonny imitated the screeching wail of a police siren as he motioned his index finger around in a miniature whirlwind.

"You see what I'm saying here?"

Tokyo formed an L-shape with his right hand as he squished it against his cheek and leant forward.

"So let me get this straight," Tokyo probed. "You want *me* to fund an elaborate showcase of your work with my own money and in my *own* name and then you want to reimburse me with interest for everything I've spent in cold, hard cash?"

"It's that simple," Jonny persisted as he poured from a bottle of alcohol and into a uniquely stylised whisky glass that featured – in a miniature re-rendering – the Swiss Matterhorn from finely crafted crystal at the base of its bowl.

The constructs of the proposal were as intriguing as they were uncompromising. And while the risk-return trade-off seemed significant, the fortuitous timing for an ambitious immigrant with damaging secrets was unmistakable.

"So let me paint a little picture for you then, *Mr. Artiste*," Tokyo patronised as he tapped his uncut fingernail against the chime of the stylised whisky glass. "Let's say that one day, them motherfuckers sitting in a sweaty corporate boardroom at the Nations of Jefferson American Bank work out this little loophole you uncovered here and back trace the leak of its flaw directly to you – then what?"

It was an apposite question, and one in which Jonny still had no answer for. As far as he was concerned, Tokyo's prospective involvement could void him of any budding suspicion and offer a virtual escape rope, a complicit incrimination that would keep Jonny from incarceration should the circumstances ever exacerbate.

"It's the twelfth round and you've got sweat dripping from your forehead," Jonny narrated, his voice itself a smooth metaphor for something sedating and glorious. "Your lip's busted and you can hardly see straight anymore. Your opponent, a big, bad son-of-a-bitch, has been chasing you around for forty-eight minutes straight, swinging and missing and swinging and missing but he's always *only* been that half a step behind you, waiting for you to falter, waiting for you to slip up."

Tokyo's fingers wagged back and forth as he continued to scrape his fingernail against the quarter-filled glass of whisky.

"The bell rings and you know that you've only got three minutes left – three minutes to get enough clean punches in that'll hand you the ultimate victory."

Jonny's heart began to pound, tearing at the seams of his chest as his anecdote, divergent to the calm of his delivery, caused for an abrupt and bubbling nauseousness.

"But if you don't," he continued, his forehead reflecting the glare of the Californian sun against the Matterhorn whisky glass. "That big, bad son-of-a-bitch I told you about earlier? He's made up the difference and now he's half a step *ahead* of you... and he *will* knock you the fuck out if you don't get to him first."

The barely audible sound of Chuckie scolding Tokyo's ginormous giraffe for its indecent behaviour broke a long, drawn-out silence.

"That's a huge, fucking risk that you're asking me to take here, you know that?"

"I guess that's why you mentioned you had something for me to do in return, then?" Jonny said, rekindling his relationship with the Matterhorn glass as a peering at its blurry reflection provided a brief moment of respite between reality and fiction.

"You're a man of unrivalled transparency, you know that?" Tokyo commended, pleased by his intuition.

Every sentence split back-and-forth like a jousting contest as each competitor fought for the ultimate edge.

"Of course you understand that I am a man of business – I built this whole fucking PLiNKER empire with these ten, tiny-ass fingers," Tokyo boasted, wiggling his disjointed hands in front of Jonny's face. "But see these fingers here? They can't offer the same kind of magic that *yours* can."

You scratch my back and I'll scratch yours. An ultimatum.

"My magic expires but yours," Tokyo suggested, staring at Jonny's fingers as he pictured them smothered and dipped in a variegated inkwell. "Yours are injected with enough preservatives to keep them safe and serviceable for a fucking lifetime."

"So what do you need me to do then?" Jonny asked, searching for a modicum of humour to break the tension. "And just to let you know in advance, I only have nine fingers available for hire. The tenth is reserved for Chuckie's sister this weekend."

"Very good," Tokyo smirked, indulged. "But what I need from you is no different to what you need from me, my ninja."

Jonny loosened the muscles in front of his vertebrae as his eyebrows bent inwards.

"I need you to paint, Jonny."

"You need me to paint?" Jonny reiterated nebulously.

"No, I need you to act like a fucking sterile parrot; *yes*, I need you to paint."

Jonny's brain was addled, unable to fit the uneven pieces of Tokyo's request together.

"Paint what?"

"Paint the whole fucking town! Paint it hypnotic, paint it mesmerizing, paint in a way that's so fucking mind-boggling-ly irresistible that it bares the kind of power that could sell a ketchup popsicle to a lady wearing white fucking gloves in the middle of July."

Jonny's knowledge of Hollywood blockbusters allowed him to make the instant connection.

Tommy Boy.

Jonny Boy.

"Well, you really narrowed it down for me, Tokyo," Jonny chirped, his hands rubbing against the Matterhorn glass as if he were peeling the skin off pork salami. "Forgive me if I'm sounding ignorant, but…"

Jonny paused, the Californian breeze filtering through the glassed doorway and throughout the hall as his brain churned to dissect

Tokyo's demand.

"What the *fuck* are you talking about?" Jonny questioned, the rumbles of his voice box a hair above a mouse whisper as he juxtaposed his choice of words with a tendency for punctiliousness.

Tokyo's lip twitched, his brain clicking over into a hidden gear.

"There was this robbery once in Nagoya; this city in Japan that they call the 'home of the pachinko parlours' – consider it the Las Vegas of the oriental, right? Anyway, so the robbers, they shout at everybody inside of this bank: 'don't you fucking move, money belongs to the state, life belongs only to you.' Everyone in the bank – I'm talking mum's with newborns and pussy-whipped, dishonest bankers in cheap, hand-me-down suits – they lay down on the ground and they aren't whispering a single word."

Jonny stared deep into the eyes of his prospective patron, clinging onto every syllable as if each word, each breath, was brimful of both potential wisdom and brewing cynicism.

"One lady in particular – who looked like a girl you'd find at a rub-and-tug – she spreads herself provocatively on a table before the robbers burst: 'be civilized, bitch, this is a robbery not a fucking rape!' So the robbers, they load up their trash bags with bucket loads of cash and make their getaway without a police siren in sight. When they return to their hideout, the young robber says to the older robber: '*anikibun* – big brother – let's count up our score!' before the older brother replies: 'do not be a fool, this is too much money to count. Tonight on TV they'll tell *us* how much we stole!'"

Jonny's mindfulness maintained, but a part of him wondered about the incipient symbolism behind the anecdote.

"After the thieves make their grand escape, the bank manager instructs his supervisor to phone the police. The supervisor turns back at him and in a whisper, he says: 'wait, wait, wait; let's mark that money we embezzled into the sum that was stolen.' The bank manager turns to him and replies: 'wouldn't it be great if there was a robbery *every* month?'"

Tokyo chuckled, wiping the remnants of sweat and liquor from the clean-shaven skin beneath his nose.

"The next day, TV news reports that fifty-million yen was taken from the bank. The robbers count and count and count for days but can only account for *ten-million* yen. The robbers, rightly pissed the fuck off, scream at one another: 'we risked our lives and only took ten-million while the bank's managers pocketed forty without breaking a sweat!'"

Tokyo wiggled his eyebrows, the forthcoming climax already producing a galaxy of goose bumps on his forearms.

"'Looks like it's better to be educated than to be a thief!' he says."

Jonny knew where he was heading.

"*I* have the knowledge," Tokyo gloated in conceit. "And now *you* have the bank."

Jonny's limbs numbed and his veins froze over.

Now what?

"You know what, Jonny?" Tokyo interjected. "Time and the world, they don't stand still. They don't wait for you at the station, they don't give you a chance to pick up your things after you've dropped them. Change is the law of life, my ninja, and those who look only to the past or the present are going to miss the future."

Okay… and so what about now… now what?

"You're right, I *do* need something from you Jonny Jinks," Tokyo admitted guiltlessly, his left eye twitching as he steadily imbibed the remaining drops of liquor from his glass.

Tokyo called for a toast like a sinful and nefarious disciple at The Last Supper, raising his empty glass as it clinked against Jonny's Swiss

Matterhorn.

"I need you to make me rich *again*; salut."

37
COPS & DONUTS

"I know, I know; it's a stupid fucking cliché, but somebody *please* tell me they bought me some chocolate-iced donuts today?" Bommarito barked, his beer-gutted belly doing most of the talking.

Commander Clayton Bommarito's years of investigative fieldwork underscored a stunningly self-legitimising resume. Touted as one of the 'top dogs' in all of American law enforcement, Bommarito's resilience, superlative organisational skills and conflict management excellence – or, as he preferred, 'bully ball 'til the bastard breaks' – indicated an aptitude for outclassing the gruelling demands of the Los Angeles Police Department.

"On your birthday? How could we forget, boss?" came an uppity chirp from a subordinate, her fingers tucking from the cuffs of her navy blue long-sleeve as she held a pair of sparkling candles – wedged in the centre of two large and freshly baked donuts – in an upright position.

"Why, thank you, darlin'," Bommarito replied, thrusting his index finger between the circular air hole of a smaller donut as his squad performed a pitchy and disjointed rendition of the *Happy Birthday Song*.

The scene was something out of a *Twin Peaks* sheriff's department, a pop-cultured painting of police officers and donuts in a hand-in-hand proviso.

"Speech! Speech!" the department staff urged in a chanting choir as they took full advantage of their break in duty.

Bommarito cleared his throat, his scruffy facial trim hiding away the blush from his filling cheeks.

"I might be getting older and my tolerance for patience might be getting thinner," Bommarito declared, bemoaning the onset of senility. "But there's one thing that'll never change with age: my love for the good people standing around me here today... and my love for extra-large, chocolate-iced donuts!"

The men and women in navy blue guffawed in unison as they fed in to their commander's humour and humility.

"Now everyone, take a quarter of a ring each and let's get back to work," the commander jested in a 'I'll-share-anything-but-my-donuts' kind-of-way.

The team followed their commander's orders in a playful conga-line before remanning their posts.

"Commander," a detective by way of the 'Bat phone' signalled. "I've got a woman on the line from out of state who says her spouse is missing in L.A. I'm thinking that it might be the kind of call you're going to want to take today."

"Donuts and mysterious missing persons? This is my kind of birthday," the commander chuckled, snatching the phone from his detective.

"This is Commander Bommarito speaking," he roared in the phone's receiver.

"Yes, um, hi," spoke a soft, trepidatious but candy-cane-sweet voice on the line's other end. "My name is Maya Ververs and I'm calling from Allentown in Pennsylvania."

The commander sensed the agony that would follow, the woman's voice breaking in fragile fits of dread as she sniffed and stuttered through her delineation.

'My partner, Jonathan Jinks, is missing in your city. I haven't heard from him, I haven't been able to contact him and I'm scared that something might have happened to him."

"Why couldn't baby Jesus have been born in Pennsylvania?" Bommarito whispered to the detective beside him, covering the telephone's transmitter with the cup of his palm as Maya Ververs continued her elucidation on the line's other end. "'Cause they couldn't find three wise men or a virgin!"

The joke brought the house down, his team of officer's biting their collective tongues to keep from causing a sonic distraction.

"I'm sorry, ma'am, slow down, slow down," he implored as if he had been listening intently all along. "What did you say your partner's name was again?"

Bommarito reached for a pencil and a large yellow pad as if he were in an episode of *Blue's Clue's*, a slave to his handy dandy notebook.

"Jonathan Jinks," Maya repeated in slow-motioned syllables, her patience growing thinner than that of an aging police commander celebrating a birthday with a chocolate-iced donut. "He took a flight out of *ABE* almost two weeks ago... or was it three? I can't remember. But I haven't been able to reach him since."

Bommarito took notes on his pad, certain that the name of his 10-57 rang a familiar bell.

"And you mentioned that he was missing here in Los Angeles, is that correct?" the commander verified, the telephone wedging between his right shoulder and earlobe as he balanced the device in a multitasking circus act.

"Yes," Maya stuttered. "He left on a business trip but nobody from his office has heard from him. I've talk to everyone, I mean *literally everyone*: his friends, his family, his colleagues. Nobody can reach him."

"And when was the last time you spoke to him?"

"Day three of his trip," she documented. "He didn't sound himself at all, like he was a hostage of his own thoughts or something crazy."

On average and at any given time, over ninety-thousand people were filed as missing in the United States of America. Whether by misadventure or dysfunctional anxiety, the draw to unnatural and involuntary escapism had fascinated Clayton Bommarito since his very induction into the police academy. But – aside from the Pennsylvania pillory – this case in particular, offered something uniquely stimulating; something less sinister than an abduction or a homicide but yet something far more labyrinthine than a victim of mental health pursuing the tangled wonders of an atypical disappearing act.

"Ma'am, has your husband ever–"

"My partner," she corrected. "We're not married."

"I'm sorry ma'am, your partner," Bommarito checked. "Has your partner every exhibited this kind of behaviour in the past?"

It was a question that caught Maya off-guard. Jon *had* been acting suspicious, uncharacteristically extrinsic in his conduct particularly after a rare night out in Allentown's social circuit.

"Only once before," she sighed, sinking into a disheartening ocean. "Right before he left. He went to a bar with a couple of friends and when he woke up the next morning he was a train wreck. He ran out of the house talking about malfunctioning ATMs and art supplies like he was possessed."

Maya's palpitating heartbeat was almost discernible through the bass tones of the telephone speaker.

"He left me and didn't say a thing. I didn't even get a chance to ask."

"But he came back, Miss Ververs?" Bommarito asked.

"He did. A couple of hours later."

"And did he say where he went?"

"He was vague. First he said he needed paint. He's a painter, an artist, you know? That's what he was doing heading out west – to provide a proposal on a new estate complex. Did I say that already? Then he said he thought that the ATM he had visited that night had been playing up and overdrew his own bank account by mistake. But he said that everything was fine and back to normal before he left for Los Angeles."

Maya was messy, her mind jumping from one chapter to another as she flipped the pages back and forth in an attempt to be concise.

Bommarito and Maya continued to exchange information, the commander inquiring about everything from birth date, physical description and cell phone number to social network information, last known location and medical history.

"Okay Miss Ververs, I think I have everything I need for now," Bommarito advised, licking the chocolate icing off his fingertips as he signed off on his notepad. "Normally about seventy-per cent of all reported missing persons are found or voluntarily returned within forty-eight to seventy-two hours of report. I will keep you apprised over the next day or two."

Bommarito revealed a statistic that only existed in a perfect world.

But this was far from a utopia. In this very existential *dystopia*, it would become far more exigent to find the unaccounted thirty-per cent...

... the final thirty-per cent that did not *want* to be found.

* * *

The portable whiteboard was filled with interconnecting marker lines and computer printouts, a connect-the-dots mind-map puzzle brimful of clues and estimations. Illustrations of GUIs linked in chains while full-colour photos and broadsheet clippings – from both local and international newspapers – nested by the uppermost branches of the diagram. The map was comprehensive; annotated in timestamps and evidence props, it was a real Hollywood movie-like investigation board with some serious legs and only a single suspect.

Bommarito and his team had been probing for months, collating together a litigious case full of everything but giraffe DNA. The accused was running on a burning fuse, a fuse that was only a week away from detonation.

"Alright you donut-stealing bastards," Bommarito bellowed, his attention now fixated on the investigation board before him as he stood like a rigid timber plank and crossed his arms. "Let's go get this motherfucking money-hungry 'little ninja'."

38
ARTS DISTRICT

On the eastern edge of Downtown Los Angeles, an unlikely triad sauntered through the gritty streets of the Los Angeles Arts District. Lined by silhouettes of decrepit industrial buildings reinvigorated by the fresh strokes of a wet paintbrush, the corner of Mateo and Willow Street in the Downtown Arts District bore an ironic similitude to the common architectural renderings of a picturesque neighbourhood. Couples of all sexual orientations – males, females, others, purple penguins – sketched in notebooks while poodles and Labradors snoozed at the tips of their owners' *Converses*. Townsmen waved at one another in the streets as they crossed paths on pushbike while a delectable *Egg Slut* truck and a taco stand – that looked a little like an incubator for a paedophile fun house – offered gourmet delicacies to the district's sun-soaking civilians.

"Hey, look over there," Chuckie waved. "It's Little Tokyo!"

The boundary of Alameda Street, west of the Arts District, served as the transit station interconnecting the rest of Los Angeles with both downtown districts.

"You get it?" Chuckie poked. "*Little...* Tokyo! Because you've got a *little* you know what!"

Tokyo sharpened his fingers before ricocheting the backside of his palm against Chuckie's unsuspecting neck.

"Ouch," Chuckie flinched. "What the fuck was that for?"

"For being as fucking useless as a condom machine at the Vatican," Tokyo said as the trio surveyed the area like sleuths at a paint-balling massacre. "You know, if you ran the way your mouth does, you'd be in pretty good shape so do me a favour and either pipe down or take a long run-up and work on your hundred-metre sprint. There's a lot of rich, cultural history in this area and I'm sure your boy over here would prefer some silence from you right now."

In the early 1970s, local artists braved hazardous conditions as they began to colonise the area's dilapidated buildings, converting former industrial and commercial spaces into fully operational art studios. The resulting surge of activity stimulated the development of stylish art galleries, handsome coffee shops, socially conscious boutiques and the most marvellous, burgeoning hub of contemporary art that Jonny had ever seen.

Jonny, Chuckie and Tokyo continued along the stretch of early twentieth-century warehouses. With its exposed brick faces – coated in spills of surface-planted artistic raindrops and glorious floor-to-ceiling windows – an insatiable creative energy and unstoppable trendiness emanated from every repurposed warehouse and industrial-inspired artist loft. The neighbourhood's candour was plainly outspoken but *never* plain as fine, coloured craftsmanship gloated over every brick façade and loading-dock doorway that could be mistaken for a painter's canvas.

The Arts District was a bona fide, unmistakably painted bastion for incoming artists, fresh-faced visionaries and occupational painters from Pennsylvania with guilt-riddled secrets and dreams.

"So what time's Boo-Boo supposed to be here?" Chuckie pried, confounding the athlete with the close companion of his native Jellystone Park namesake.

Tokyo hit the home button on his smartphone, compelling the

screen to awaken from its pocketed siesta.

"Right now," Tokyo responded as he commanded the device to open the composition screen for a new text message. "And his name's Yogi, you redheaded stepchild."

The incessant name-calling had become a fundamental fragment to Tokyo and Chuckie's relationship, the pair relating to each other mostly by the virtues of money and mockery.

"Wait," Jonny interjected as his stomach whistled in an uncomfortable uproar. "Yogi?"

On a bar graph of given name frequencies, 'Yogi' was at the very bottom of the baby-naming barometer and as such, Jonny was certain he'd already connected the dots.

"Yeah," Tokyo confirmed, hustling him onwards. "You wanted my network, right? Well, who better to show out for than the future bantamweight champ himself?"

Jonny's eyes flashed as pay-per-view visions of a red-gloved boxer pouncing on his groggy prey came roaring back to him.

Minx. Allentown. The boys. Maya.

"Where's he meeting us?" Jonny stuttered, navigating the scene like a fish out of water.

"Just over there, my ninja," Tokyo pointed, his finger wagging towards a mural that could have been mistaken for gang-related graffiti had it been painted on a bricked-canvas anywhere other than Los Angeles' multi-coloured outdoor museum.

The prismatic and abstract design appeared influenced by the motley attire of a medieval harlequin and court jester as Jonny carefully scrutinised its repetitive brushstrokes.

"There that fucker is!" Tokyo cursed as he dashed towards a piece of furniture beneath the graffiti wall.

Occupying a four-seated patio table, four young African-American men – each with the kind of muscle definition that could make Arnold Schwarzenegger appear scrawny – sat two in a row, nibbling at three bowls of French fries and Buffalo wings.

"Yogi, my *motherfucking* man!" Tokyo burst, separating the adjective for emphasis as he prepared his body for a daft, combination-based handshake.

"What's good, man?" Yogi greeted, the warmth in his bass-heavy voice suggesting their relationship extended well beyond the jurisdiction of eastern Los Angeles.

"Man, we're just out here chilling on this beautiful day – it's lively, right?" Tokyo suggested, panning from side to side at the vibrant mixture of personalities that inhabited the district.

"Bet," Yogi agreed, his pearly whites bursting through his gums as he stopped to scan Tokyo's associates. "This your boy right here?"

Jonny blushed, unsure of the proper etiquette.

"This is Jonny Jinks," Tokyo presented, stepping backwards as he ushered Jonny through an invisible tunnel of air. "Jonny, meet Yogi Beach III."

"I caught your fight last month," Jonny admitted, careful not to come off as commiserating and plaintive. "That was a tough way to go down."

Jonny engaged in an entrepreneurial right-handed handshake with the man he'd last seen on a television screen in Pennsylvania.

"Well, you win some, you lose some, right?" he rationalised, concealing the numbness of failure. "Have a seat, young blood – you want some fries?"

Jonny and Tokyo dragged two patio chairs from an adjacent table as they formed a seated circle with Yogi and his crew, combining in a configuration that seemed to emulate a medieval scene by King Arthur and his knights.

"Hey there, Mr. Beach Three," Chuckie slipped, extending a fraternal forearm as his inability to properly translate roman numerals became awkwardly apparent. "Good to see you again, man."

Chuckie blinked twice like an anthropomorphic cartoon as an impermanent pocket of silence was only interrupted by the sound of a teeth-crushing French fry.

"Who the fuck are you?" he disparaged, certain he had never laid eyes on the redhead standing before him.

"It's all good Yogi, this fucking buffoon is with me," Tokyo assured him with a smirk.

"So, let's get down to business?" Yogi hustled, a firm believer in the age-old 'time is money' idiom. "Tell me about this proposition you mentioned on the phone earlier."

For the half-Dutch, half-Japanese migrant, his experience at PLiNKER had long prepared him for the informalities of an on-the-spot sales pitch. And while the circumstances were not the same, this was the kind of the setting where Tokyo van Wolfswinkel excelled.

"So listen," Tokyo began, showcasing his sparkling molars as he interlocked his fingers together. "I'm not going to beat around the bush – you're the future, right?"

"Yeah, I'm the future," Yogi responded with a flavour of confidence as his entourage exchanged fist-bumps in affirmation.

"In twelve months, you're going to be unstoppable," Tokyo apple-polished, rubbing against his proverbial ego as he began to manipulate the forthcoming events. "Every promoter in this town from Bob Arum to Don King is gonna want to book you."

The fist-bumps continued as Yogi and his crew revelled in the daydream of ubiquitous wealth.

"If..." Tokyo burst, slicing their wishful bubble of fiction. "We can put you on the map in a way that'll ignite a fucking Kim

Kardashian-level of hype all the way to your first cash-in."

Yogi mulled over the equivocal suggestion as Jonny and Chuckie sat silent around the circular patio table.

"What, you want me to release a sex-tape or something?" he jested, his entourage interchanging fist-bumps for high-fives like sarcastic hyenas in a zoo exhibit. "Because, I mean, I wouldn't even have to do any work; I've already got a library full of that shit back in my apartment, you know what I'm saying?"

Tokyo's face cemented as he micked the stubborn expression Jonny first encountered at his Palisades mansion.

"Laugh all you want," Tokyo chirped. "But that collection of yours? You can keep it in a pissy, hand-me-down bookcase in your one-bedroom apartment, or you can move it into a grand fucking library in a mansion on a Beverly Hills boulevard; the choice is all yours."

Tokyo's analogy seemed to reign supreme as Yogi pondered at the intimation with greater gravitas.

"What did you have in mind?" Yogi probed with an extra ketchup drop of professionalism as he leant forward to pluck a handful of fries from the table bowl. "Something to do with your boy, I'd imagine?"

Yogi's eyes pivoted in Jonny's direction in a kind of unpredictable stare that bordered between the equivocally fine lines of indisposition and zing.

Tokyo's senses pricked at the notion of a closing deal as he slung his arm around Jonny's shoulder and pulled him inwards.

"You ever heard of body paint?"

39

BULLETS & BODY PAINT

"… And once it's complete, I'm gonna upload this motherfucker to PLiNKER and reach one-hundred-and-fifty million users at the tap of a button."

Jonny was glued as he analysed each drop of Tokyo's quick spitting sales-pitch in adoration.

The proposal would've been a favourable nominee at any advertising award convention across the globe: Jonny – a skilled and dedicated artist from the Northeast – would create the illusion of a dimensional universe where 2D and 3D would become one. It was perception-bending art, an alternate reality by which a mask of paint would mimic its subject beneath to create a painted replica of the real-world as it commonly stood. Jonny would use a selection of latex layers and body paints to transform Yogi and the bulky contours of his boxing body into an acrylic-coated living painting of himself. Using Tokyo's infinite supply of connections, a supply of boxing props and other inanimate objects would be coated in an artistic style, collapsing depth and appearing two-dimensional when photographed.

Jonny had adapted the classical French art form of trompe l'oeil – the art of making a two-dimensional representational painting appear as if it were a real three-dimension space – and turned it on its head by doing its exact opposite; making real life appear as if it were nothing more than a wall-hung painting.

The upshot of such an extravagant undertaking? A mutual legion of new fans, followers and unstable stalkers lurking behind their every next move, the ultimate payoff for fifteen minutes of viral fame.

"Fuck that whack-ass bullshit," Yogi repudiated, dropping a half-chewed French fry onto the patio table. "Man, I ain't no fucking painting; I'm Yogi Beach III and I'm my *own* man."

Tokyo did not take kindly to such an unsavoury rebuttal as the team of 'Yogi and Friends' snickered amongst one another.

Thankfully, though, the PLiNKER kingpin had come prepared.

"You're gonna be less than half your own man if you don't shut the fuck up and listen to what I'm trying to tell you," Tokyo said as he lifted at the lining of his striped shirt and revealed a barrelled object that glared with the sun's piercing reflection.

Inaudible alarm bells rang in perpetual motion as Jonny gasped before turning by his wayside to create a physical separation between he and his patron.

Yogi caught sight of an instant glimmer of chrome, thudding the caps of his knees against the patio table in an attempt to hurl his crew and vamoose.

"Nuh, uh, uh," Tokyo said as he flicked his fingers. "Take it easy, my ninja; what, you think I'm gonna use this shit? Get the fuck out of here."

Tokyo dropped his striped shirt back down to his knees as Yogi's posse of counterfeit-gangsters wiped beads of jittery sweat off their foreheads and reconnected with the metal of the patio chairs.

"Are you fucking crazy, Tokyo?" Yogi tensed through his teeth.

"Yeah, even for me, now I'm also convinced he's fucking nuts," Chuckie confessed with the kind of poise not often seen by a spoilt brat who'd just laid eyes on his first firearm.

Jonny sat silent, still and stupefied. The juxtaposition between both teams was adventitiously counterintuitive and yet somehow, nobody but Jonny had seemed to notice.

Did he just threaten to shoot him? Why the fuck are Chuckie and Tokyo so calm?

"What's wrong with you, man?" Yogi begged to know. "Do you pull a gun on all your fucking friends?"

"Friends don't scorn at the motherfucking counsel given by other friends who have made more money and eaten more pussy than they have," Tokyo pounced. "Now listen to me; I wasn't fucking with you when I told you that you were the future. You've got a choice: you can be the *future* Mike Tyson and announce that shit to the world in a way that'll grant you more hype than a Cassius Clay promo or you can be the *future* Sonny Liston with your tail between your legs on the inside of a casket ... *Metaphorically*, of course."

Tokyo knew he hadn't really given the rising boxer the freedom of choice as much as he had provided an uncompromising ultimatum: follow his orders or meet the wrath of a bipolar tech guru and borderline unofficial yakuza.

"Whatever, man, just take it easy and put that shit away," Yogi served in spite of Tokyo's hostile methods of persuasion. "You made your money so if you're telling me that doing this'll make me king, then let's do it."

Yogi locked eyes with the man who would soon use his chiselled body as a portrait canvas and shared in a harmonious twinkle of trust.

"Listen," Jonny said, disrupting the tension between the African American boxer and his psychological captor. "I know this is going to work out; I've been painting for a long time and I've never had an opportunity like the one Tokyo's about to give us. This is *that* stepping-stone... for all of us; I know it."

Like a goddamn ATM wasn't a stepping-stone in itself.

Yogi's muscles tensed, his crew remaining as hushed as a congregation during silent worship as he nodded and slid the patio chair from underneath him.

"Well… What are we waiting for?" he uttered as he stood upright, his henchmen mimicking him in an animated shadow. "Let's get this shit moving while the sun's out."

As the men in Yogi's ringside corner prepared for the unknown, Chuckie slid his backside to the edge of the seat, forcing a bend in the chair's frame as he leant atop of Jonny's shoulder.

"Did I bring you the holy grail or what?" he whispered inside his earlobe like a string of wax, proud of his matchmaking efforts.

"Yeah," Jonny replied, hiding his lips from everyone's eye-line. "Like the fucking Last Supper."

"What's Leonardo Da Vinci got to do with Tokyo?" Chuckie buzzed, his foolish ignorance never more than a necessary breath mint away. "You painters just crack me up."

Jonny's history of the grail of Christ suggested a conceivable foreshowing that he definitely did not want bestowed upon him: that a cataclysm of lies, deception, betrayal and death were surely destined to follow.

40

BOXING BRUSH STROKES

An audience swarmed, a painted whitewash of faces from every race and social caste marshalled by the scrumdiddlyumptious presence of a Chuckie's Diner food truck. Every man, woman, animal and child gravitated towards the prismatic mural and the sphere of non-traditional art that was crystallising beneath it.

Jonny's latest work was not an art form of defined discipline, but rather a cultural strategy, an experimental process that might otherwise have been excluded from established curatorial and critical frameworks. It was a framing device and involved a catalogue of approaches by a promising painter who was choosing – at the guidance of his tech-crunched patron and an all-seeing ATM – to warp the edges of artistic tradition and identity.

"That's right, folks," Chuckie chimed, Tokyo's smartphone wedged in between his soggy fingers as he framed in a three-hundred-and-sixty degree twirl. "Move in a little closer if you want to make the director's cut. This thing is about to stream live to the world any minute now!"

Yogi's sour stare was slowly swallowed by a pigmented combination of latex, body paint and non-toxic face crayons as he surveyed unfalteringly below Tokyo's waistline like a vulnerable deer to its carnivorous hunter.

"Keep still, Yogi, your head keeps drooping," Jonny directed as he outlined a detail across Yogi's jagged jawline.

The process was punctilious and precise: first came the painted mural using the only blank-bricked façade that wasn't already cloaked in a pre-existing brush stroke. Jonny used *Google's* potent image search engine to uncover a graphic from Floyd Mayweather Jr and Manny Pacquiao's 'Fight of the Century' at the *MGM Grand Garden Arena* as a reference shot to illustrate the abstruse background – concentrated beams of bright blue spotlights in two separate triads, black-shirted photographers with interchanging lens flashes and a wash of hypnotised fans illuminated by the ultraviolet blue and red laser light gobos that rained down from above.

Next, painted veils of two-dimensional interpretations were brushed atop each inanimate object, reimagining the tangible boxing ring's four parallel rows of rope, turnbuckle and light-blue canvas into two-dimensional, spaceless portraits.

The penultimate step involved the painting of a cast mould that was to act as Yogi's immovable opponent. One of Tokyo's slippery contacts had delivered the light-weighted sculpture from the cargo bed of a pickup truck whose guerrilla branding seemed to suggest that it was... 'conveniently borrowed' in the fairest of senses.

"Oh my God! It's Michael Strahan!" Chuckie whooped at the sight of what he believed to be a manufactured forge of one of his footballing heroes.

"It's not Michael Strahan, you idiot," Tokyo lambasted, thumping him across the head with a vicious right-hand. "It's supposed to be Mike Tyson – now quit making a fucking moron of yourself."

"Looks like Michael Strahan to me," Chuckie muttered beneath his breath.

Jonny re-illustrated Tyson's iconic parted fade in a multi-tone –

tribal face tattoo and all – while Tyson's black trunks and red gloves were given a watercoloured varnish to solidify the ensemble. The ballooning crowd rallied before wiping spillages of American mustard from their mouths with a Chuckie's Diner-branded napkin.

The concluding task involved the scrupulous body-painting of an African-American man who had gone from being the subject of gunpoint low-scale terrorism to the subject of artistic expressionism. Yogi – dressed in his boxing battle attire that included his boots, trunks, mouth guard and gloves – had been reborn. His skin dripped with the excess of paint splotches while his entire body – every manageable fragment but the crystallised reflection of his pointed irises – was cocooned from head-to-toe with an artificial overlay of its subject hiding beneath.

And eventually, what remained was a picture-perfect painting of a person, the real being beneath the colouring buried somewhere deep in concealment.

"Ladies and gentlemen," Tokyo addressed like a ring announcer at a boxing bout as he stepped into an organic spotlight of glimmering Californian sunshine. "What you are witnessing here today is a metamorphosis; a real-world transformation unlike anything you'll ever see again! May I proudly present to you, the magic… and the man behind it: Yogi Beach III and Jonny Cash!"

The audience applauded as the painter approached his half-Dutch, half-Japanese patron in the foreground. The pair engaged in a rehearsed handshake as a sparkle in Jonny's smile swept a handful of female onlookers off their feet and into a wet paint puddle.

"This kid right here is *the future*," Tokyo lauded, stroking his spine. "And the future is *now*. Now I know this whole thing right here behind me looks totally planned but what makes it even more special is that everything about it was completely and unequivocally spontaneous."

It was an inauguration of sorts, an unveiling of two up-and-coming talents who had fused their crafts to give birth to a wave of digital propaganda that could be leveraged for the longevity of their careers.

"Besides, we all know what 'The Baddest Man on the Planet' thinks about plans," Tokyo prefaced, clearing his throat as he prepared to activate the signature 'Iron Mike' lisp. 'Everyone has a plan until they get punched in the mouth,' am I right?"

Tokyo stared in Yogi's direction while the crowd cackled, a double entendre as transparent and as gnomic as a cartoon ghost.

"Oh, and speaking of being punched in the face, how about a round of applause for our main man, the subject of this kickass artistry: Yogi Beach III!" he crowed, Chuckie panning the recording smartphone as he captured the reaction in motion.

The onlookers swarmed like starving paparazzi, snapping happy photos on their twelve-megapixel cameras as their focus zigzagged between live art and an *Instagram* filter on their smartphones. Every angle was recorded, a digitally updated photo album of a ground-breaking innovation picking up steam under a trending hash tag.

Yogi was statuesque, only moving on Jonny's visual cue as he played his role with precision inside the kinetic portrait. As the cheers rained down from the mesmerised audience, a boom box – something out of a *Fresh Prince of Bel Air* episode – thundered with the audible sounds of a Kendrick Lamar mash-up. Yogi's tripping twitches were almost perfectly punctual, his shoulders warping as his hammer-hands swung in slow motion hooks and jabs. Each strike was choreographed in simplicity, Jonny composing the sequence in a repetitive combination, each thwack knocking in time to a thick snare drum crunch.

The congregation along Alameda Street were roused in a

wonderful veneration, their applause transcending into 'oohs and ahhs' and spirited double-fingered whistles.

"You see this boy right here behind me?" Tokyo huffed and puffed, the MC back in control. "You're looking at a future world champion! Give it up once again for my ninja, Yogi... Beach... III!"

Tokyo's firearm was concealed but it was all Yogi could see, his pupils swirling towards the corners of his eyes as the tech guru saturated his primary focus.

Together – and despite the artificial tension – they had achieved something conspicuous, something more noteworthy than an Internet fad.

And while no singular celebrity or notable socialite was present to document and share the phenomenon, the power of PLiNKER combined with the collective social media count of each eyewitness skyrocketed with the reach of a Hollywood superstar.

It was the kind of reach that could see its truth distorted by a digital Chinese whisper. But most pertinently, it was the kind of reach that could stretch *very* far... as far as the metropolitan of the Lehigh Valley, in fact.

41

A PAINTER, A BEAR & A HELICOPTER

a helicopter truly is a fine fucking way to travel.

But you know the thing about choppers is that they induce a view of the world that only God and corporate CEOs really ever get to see. And if you're circling above the city of Los Angeles at night in a helicopter, you're actually looking down at the most expensive and most controversial real estate on the planet.

three thousand feet beneath your toes lies the real world american monopoly board.

* * *

To call their social media experiment a rousing success would have been a gross understatement. Tokyo van Wolfswinkel's abstract mind and coding dexterity promulgated Jonny Cash and Yogi Beach III on an online hype-train that steamrolled quicker than *Gangnam Style* on *YouTube*.

As the view counter continued to tick at an unquantifiable rate, Chuckie, Tokyo, Yogi and his crew now had only one thing in mind; unleash in a wild jubilee.

After a rapid rendezvous with a nearby ATM – a financial stopgap that supplanted whatever notes and coins remained in his *Louis Vuitton*

Brazza wallet – Jonny and the rest of Team Tokyo were poised and primed for the celebration of the century.

"You said you wanted to see the city, right, Jonny?" Chuckie announced as the team and a row full of beddable females occupied the back seat of a Power California Chauffeur Service limousine with Sonny Barsotti behind the wheel. "Well why not see it like an eagle? Why not see it like *Superman*? Why not see it like the fucking supersized 'el capitano' that you're about to become with this tiny-ass, flaccid fucking world dangling beneath your feet?"

Jonny's blood-pumped as Sonny activated the backseat strobe lights, twinkling the limousine like a drug-overdosed disco.

"Sonny, we far away?" Chuckie questioned, roaring through Fat Joe's *All The Way Up* as the bass-heavy track thumped through the sound system.

"Just pulling in now, sir," Sonny replied, enraptured just to be on the Jonny Cash payroll.

"Men, women, boys and girls of all ages," Chuckie introduced as the limousine came to a halt. "Welcome to 'The LA Helicopter Tour'!"

The vehicle's occupants disembarked like celebrities on a red carpet as Yogi and his wannabe gangsters offered chivalrous hands to their exiting princesses.

Jonny signalled in an 'I'll-call-you-later' gesture beside Sonny's tinted window as the group giggled and stumbled towards a waiting *Robinson Raven II* and its ebullient pilot.

"Hello, hello!" the middle-aged captain fizzed, his entire physical appearance almost mimicking that of an aviation version of Sonny Barsotti. "Name's Eddie and I'm going to be your pilot this evening. Who's ready to have some fun?"

Chuckie, his arms wrapped around two coquettes like a strangling python at a zoo orgy, zipped his lips and pointed back and forth to the simpering women beside him.

"Alrightey, then! Let's get you guys high!" Eddie popped, his arms waving towards the stars as he ushered his passengers towards the chopper's landing skids.

"A little too late for that," Yogi quipped as he fidgeted with a cannabis cigarette in his back pocket.

Eddie began a game of 'follow-the-leader' as Chuckie, Jonny, Tokyo, Yogi – and friends – and their all-female entourage formed a two-filed conga line behind him.

"Hold up a second, Eddie," Jonny whispered as he raced forward, his arm wrapping the shoulders of the flamboyant pilot before pulling him to the side for a private interrogation.

The helicopter captain and his passenger exchanged glances that bordered between disbelief and comical understanding as they murmured in a secret to-and-fro.

"Consider it a handshake confidentiality agreement – I think they call it 'hush money' in these parts, right?" Jonny winked as he slipped a bundle of green-coloured bills in Eddie's pocket before returning to his posse. "Don't worry, it'll be fun. You'll see."

Jonny tapped the pilot on the back before backpedalling to re-join the group. He had become emboldened by the Jonny Cash sobriquet, taking the reins of extravagance and wastefulness as he rode his drunken horse like Captain Jack Sparrow on the Black Pearl.

Gallantry behaviour was in full effect, the 'gentlemen' escorting their female counterparts into the helicopter with a single hand like *Aladdin* on a magic carpet ride. As the party took to their unassigned seats, the helicopter's tail boom dropped and its rotor blades began to spin clockwise.

"We ready to rise?" Eddie shouted via the chopper's headphone intercom system, his hands gently resting against the collective and the throttle.

His passengers were passive, distracted at the very least. This was their *Air Force One*, their covert aviation experience where boundaries bore no existence and secrecy and security were explicit directives.

Eddie opened the throttle with caution, reaching the necessary operating RPM before pulling the collective up gradually. As the collective's pitch increased, Eddie slapped the left pedal like a rally car driver around a sharp bend as he continued to pull the collective and depress the pedal, adjusting the cyclic to level the aircraft for a smooth take-off.

"Woah, there, Eddie!" Chuckie said, spilling a puddle of champagne on the aircraft's flooring. "I can see it now! We're gonna turn this chopper into a sinking swamp of drink, sweat and semen!"

"Easy there, sir," Eddie buzzed through the intercom system. "This aircraft can only handle so much weight so you better try and drink as much of that as you can."

Chuckie sensed an opening for licentious banter.

"Did y'all hear that? That goes for you too, *ladies*," Chuckie burped before a slap across the cranium from Jonny's half-Asian, half-Dutch patron caused him to stumble. "What? I know I can drink all the liquor but who the hell did you expect to drink up all the... *bodily fluids?*"

The libidinous women – perhaps the antithesis of a traditional feminist rights group – welcomed the misogynistic remark as innocent and innocuous, an unvarnished icebreaker that cut to the chase without awkwardness as they simpered and giggled with impish glee.

The aircraft took flight, Eddie narrating like a well-paid pilot-slash-tour-guide as they circled the Californian skies.

But the passengers maintained an apathy towards their captain and his mission. Tokyo, Jonny, Chuckie, Yogi and the squadron of ravishing women were far more concerned with a different kind of objective: excessive and uncontrollable celebration and debauchery.

"Hey, check this out!" Chuckie yawped, flinging his phallus from his underpants as he rotated his hips clockwise and spun his crown jewels to the rhythm of the revolving propellers above him. I'm doing 'the helicopter'... on a helicopter!"

A sultry woman who looked a lot like Sasha with a slimmer figure reached out and squeezed Chuckie's weapon of mass destruction, tugging it to a standstill as the organ began to inflate like a balloon with a helium injection.

"Crash!" she seduced, pressing her breasts against Chuckie Hooper's as she clenched one hand around his penis while the other rubbed through his pomade.

"Boys and girls," Tokyo reported as the unofficial ringleader, a bottle of *Ketel One Vodka* wedged in his hand as he raised it towards the chopper's ceiling. "Tonight, y'all are about to join the 'mile high club' – so let's avoid the stranger shit and get it in!"

The crew erupted in a zealous hurrah.

"And just so it's clear, the cockpit is off limits!" Eddie disseminated to the dismay of his passengers.

"That's no problem, Eddie," Chuckie wagged, his tongue escaping the mouth of his escort for a brief millisecond. "All the 'cocks' will stay put back here!"

The space drowned in ebullience as the helicopter soared over California like a *Disney* theme park simulation ride.

Jonny, Tokyo, Chuckie, Yogi – and friends – and their contingent of volunteering mistresses unified as their clothes stripped off of their shoulders in a rousing bacchanal. Hands wandered and bodily fluids dropped like light rain as Team Yogi formed a coordinated faction and actively engaged in a crowded white-and-dark-chocolate-flavoured orgy.

"Sorry about before, my ninja," Tokyo chirped as a women without a face hid between his thighs. "You know, for being strapped and all – threatening to kill you etcetera, etcetera. I was just trying to make a point and I'm hoping *now* you can see why."

Yogi's eyes fastened and his head tilted back, his hands lifting and pushing on the head of a woman like a *Sale of the Century* contestant behind a buzzer.

"It's… all good, bro, considered it forgotten," he moaned, unbothered.

This was the definition of hedonism, three-thousand feet above and away from any hazardous consequence. The indulgence was excessive, the jollification arguably warranted, and yet still, a bothering Pennsylvanian reminder survived, an uncomfortable and guilty feeling that was entirely out of Jonny's control.

ATMs. Maya. Allentown. Money. My art. My life.

"You know something, Tokyo," Jonny stressed, his thighs being massaged by a petite brunette as Tokyo handed him a smoking Cuban cigar. "In this life and on this helicopter, you're either a pilot, or you're a passenger."

Tokyo's eyebrow winced as he begged to understand why, at three-thousand-feet above downtown Los Angeles and beside a bevy of flawless seductresses, philosophical navigation around a moral compass was truly necessary.

"But you can't be both. You can *never* be both."

42
ALLEN'S TOWN

In the beginning of the eighteenth century, the land now occupied by the City of Allentown and the entire Lehigh County was a vast wilderness of history, scrub oak and deciduous foliage. Neighbouring tribes of Native Americans fished for trout and hunted for deer and grouse, as their survival instincts quickly became the means for commonplace living. On one fall evening, twenty-three chiefs of five great Indian nations deeded the native tract to the business partners of William Allen in exchange for an outlay of precious goods that included shoes, hats, knives, needles, looking glasses, pipes, and rum.

Less than a century later, the town was crowned with a mark of perennial historical significance, occupying the land that acted as the successful hiding ground of the Liberty Bell in America's battle to keep the metallic icon of independence out of the hands of the British.

Yet now, more than three hundred years later, Pennsylvania's most riveting local narrative was becoming a matter of great debate.

The grapevine chatter was unavoidable as residence spanning from Philadelphia to Harrisburg could be heard conversing over servings of Lebanon bologna, scrapple and shoofly pie.

"Did you hear about the Jinks boy?" was the typical cry of the Lehigh County. "Gordon's son; he's fled the state on a cross-country binge! I could hardly believe my eyes when my little one showed me the video of him in California!"

It was a disbelief that resonated with every citizen familiar with Jinks family lore. Such an unimaginable calamity caused devastation across the community as families and friends of the Jinks' struggled to come to terms with the choices made by their beloved Pennsylvanian son.

"I hear that people out west are calling him 'Jonny Cash,'" was the chatter between clusters of Pennsylvanian middle-schoolers, bewitched by the audaciousness of his notoriety.

"What do you mean? Like that country music guitarist guy?"

"But I don't get it; they don't do country music out west? Do they?"

And while confusion clearly amassed among the young, in their very juvenile and never-so-passé eyes, this kind of scandalous rebellion was one in which fabled legends and local heroes were predicated on.

* * *

The ringer woke her from her nap, her eyes black with exhaustion as she plucked her smartphone from the top of a scribbled notepad on the bedside table.

"It's me," sounded a despondent voice through the phone's speaker.

"Zeke... what do you know? Please tell me everything is okay?" Maya replied in a rush, rubbing her eyes before shaking her head in an unmistakable reality.

"I just sent you a text with a video link," he said. "Just click it, watch it, and promise me not to freak out, okay?"

This was a promise she could not make. A lead had surfaced, Maya and Zeke playing out-of-state detectives as she clawed for a reason to hope.

Was it Jon?

Was he okay?

Where had he been hiding?

The video file played back via an application browser, Chuckie's unsteady home movie cinematography making the focus difficult to discern as she fingered her resting hand atop of Jon's untouched notepad.

The clip rolled and music blared through her smartphone speakers as Chuckie narrated the footage like a documenting protagonist in *Cloverfield*.

And then it happened.

Maya gasped, her hand with barely the strength to cover her mouth as suddenly, it was she that appeared more tremulous than the video clip's cameraman.

Jon. Oh my God.

"Did you see it?" Zeke questioned in a pure rhetoric.

"Jonny… Cash?" she stuttered in terror.

"That's what it says. He's still in L.A., Maya. Voluntarily, *apparently.*"

"I can't believe it," she said in a choking stranglehold, unsure of where to turn next.

The footage summoned sentiments of consternation as an invisible knife wedged in between her abdomen, her spleen spilling in wine-coloured blood.

This was worse than a kidnapping, worse than a ransom note that she could not fulfil. This was permissive desertion and betrayal, a crucifixion of the very worst kind.

Whatever pieces remained of her heart snapped with the impetus of a discharging grenade. And all she could do – with the falling fibres of her bloody soul – was to wonder why; why the quintessence of virtue and companionship would run from the life they had built together.

Why would he desert Allentown? Why would he desert her?

It made no sense.

And for some kind of unidentifiable reason, he did not even *look* the same.

This was *not* Jonathan Jinks as she knew him.

"So what do we do, then?" Zeke sought guidance, leaving the decision-making tennis ball on Maya's side of the clay court.

She croaked and rubbed her eyes as she rationalised.

Maya Ververs needed answers.

She needed answers immediately.

"We find him, and then we bring him home."

43

MR. VUITTON

Melodies of enchanting jazz music smoked the hotel room as the pickup cartridge rested over the groove, the stylus tracking it with the desired force to offer the optimal compromise between frequency control and minimal abrasion of the record groove.

Jonny's brain, hypnotised by the syncopation of a howling saxophone, lacked the potency to perform any cognitive assignment and his bones dripped in inertia.

While the magnetism of the brassed instrument was its 'sax-y' appeal, Jonny's fondness for the saxophone was predicated on another emotion altogether. Understanding the splendour of the saxophone was like trying to explain the allure of rock n' roll to a band member of The Jesus and Mary Chain. While it would often commence like a demure little lady seated by the exit doors of a night club, its powers would unknowingly insinuate itself into the pit of ones abdomen, sending bursts of shimmy-shakes down the spine before flowering like a bagpipe and into a cascading wail. The saxophone was a musical banshee shrieking its very soul over a hidden backbeat until the time came for it to sneak out of the way of the sunlight. In a silk dress running like a watercolour in the rain, the saxophone was both starry and magical, painting the sky with a thousand sonants as it mesmerised its awe-inspired listener.

But to Jonny, it was neither its opulence nor its charm that enticed him, but the familiarity of the instruments tonal vibrations that resonated far deeply within. To Jonny, the saxophone, for all its grace and glory, sounded just like a weeping man in unrepairable agony, begging for mercy and divine repentance as his tears waterlogged the instrument's harmonic valves and cried for absolution.

The generic ringer on his smartphone woke him from his mid-afternoon siesta, interrupting the tranquillity of Wayne Shorter's *'Teru'*.

Maya? Is it Maya?

The Pennsylvanian painter pounced like a panther, throwing a cashmere throw off his belly as he tightened the knot on his silk bathrobe before lifting the needle on the record player and accepting the call from an unidentified number.

"Hello?" he answered, holding back a yawn like a flatulence-plagued school student in a classroom of silence.

"Yes, hi, is this Mr. Jinks?" came the squeaky but courtly voice on the other line.

Jonny was perturbed by the formality of the dubious caller.

"Who's calling?" he responded apprehensively, his eyes locked in and focused on a singular direction of nothing in particular.

"Mr. Jinks this is Clio Mays from the Nations of Jefferson American Bank, how are you, sir?"

Alarm bells clanked together in his cranium like a midnight Orthodox gathering on the eve of Easter Sunday. Jonny's pupils dilated and his fingers battled to resist the smartphone from slipping through his sweaty claws.

"What can I do for you, Ms. Mays?" Jonny replied, as if the phone call were pleasantly unexpected.

"Sir, our records seem to indicate some abnormalities with your recent transaction history and as such, I'd just like to validate a number of payments on your credit card if I could?"

Jonny's instincts impelled him to act once again like the furred panther that rose from a faded slumber, this time imploring him to seek an excuse, disconnect the call, and sprint away as fast as he could. But he knew he could not run forever; he would eventually have to confront the unpleasant rebuke he was due.

"Certainly," he obliged, biting his tongue to the point of piercing.

"Now there seems to be a series of transactions that have occurred over the past three weeks away from your immediate place of residency," she authenticated as Jonny decoded her claims. "For example, I have up until as recently as Monday, a transaction on your *MasterCard* for the amount of thirteen-hundred-and-twelve dollars at *Louis Vuitton* on Rodeo Drive, California?"

Jonny exhaled, cogitated and moistened his lips. He deemed this a fortuitous opportunity for circumvention and it became apparent that he had a decision to make. The banking representative had handed Jon a "Get-Out-Of-Jail-Free Card," should he had elected to use it. He could continue along a deranged road of fantasy and serendipity, hanging by a thread from the edge of a cliff face as a ruthless herd of rabid wolves savagely plotted his demise.

Or, he could deny that the transaction had ever taken place, report the card as stolen, wipe his hands clean of toxicity and return to Pennsylvania to repair what had become a sorely damaged relationship with the people who cared for him most.

Silence.

Contemplation.

ATMs.

Maya.

Jonny had been given the golden goose... And although the swallowing guilt admonished him to restore his once-instinctive integrity, neither Slugworth nor Wonka would be getting it back anytime soon.

"Mr. Jinks?" Ms. Mays probed.

"Yes, ugh, that was me," Jonny confessed, resolving his moral quandary with a flicker of unredeemable regret.

The line ceased in a hush for a moment before Clio Mays continued the validation process.

"What about a nine-hundred-and-seventy-three dollar transaction at *Providence* on Melrose Avenue in Los Angeles, a two-and-half-thousand dollar transaction at the *Beverly Hills Hotel & Bungalows's Polo Lounge* and multiple transactions at the *Chateau Marmont* in West Hollywood?"

Jonny assumed Ms. Mays' supposition as he goggled around the sumptuous one-bedroom penthouse suite of the *Chateau Marmont*.

"Yes, they were all paid for by me on my credit card," he asserted as yet another string-thin silence broke. "I'm on vacation — you can't blame me for splurging a little, right?"

"That I can't, sir," Ms. Mays agreed. "Well, if there is anything at all that you need from our end, please don't hesitate to call our customer support line. Otherwise, enjoy the rest of your vacation, Mr. Jinks."

It was as if something did not quite compute; but then again, perhaps it did not need to. The Nations of Jefferson American Bank were indeed aware of Jonny's irregular spending but by all intimations, remained ignorant to the life-changing loophole he had been gifted.

Jonny hung up the phone and wiped a bead of sweat from his forehead with a chic, *Chateau* hotel throw. The pressure was mounting thick and fast. And yet Jonny could not determine whether the call suggested an imminent threat to his Californian adventure, or if it suggested nothing more than a due diligence from an institution that was for more apt at servicing the favourable needs of its more prestigious clients than it was at recognising detrimental systematic defects.

One thing was for certain. The bank had been right behind him one way or another; they had been following him all along, obligingly servicing the needs of its brand new, big-spending customer.

Jonny had to wonder: if time was money, was a Nations of Jefferson ATM his time machine?

44

A KALIKO ATTACK

Maya. Allentown. Art. Family. Love.

The Californian sun closed in on him and his skin loosened in a melting wax. He felt weightless, an astronaut spaced out in an unidentified nebula. Jonny knew he could offer more than a whisper but his voice strained, and the demonic asphyxiation warned him not to scream. His throat tightened, numbed, as if he had swallowed a bag of marshmallows as his heart forced his lungs to inhale in rapid, shallow breaths. He had fought the indecision of 'beer goggle' bewilderment countless times in recent weeks, but this was something utterly different. His vision blurred as dry tears formed at the eyelids, Jon clutching his fists onto any part of his body that he deemed sturdy and supportive.

What's happening to me?

Such a strange and unforseen panic seemed to fall right in line with his newly adopted string of anomalousness. This didn't make sense and Jonny's eyes wept in symbolic paint-strokes as he fought away the fear.

Allentown. Art. Family. Love. Maya.

The sky and the heavens were in flames as his deepest nightmares personified themselves in a burning and eternal combustion. Jonny was helpless, no longer in control of his own destiny as his heart rate beat incessantly. Inside him, a hundred miniature Mohamed Ali's punched him in the abdomen while a thousand bombs detonated in his soul; and for a short moment, he succumbed to the prospective arrival of the Grim Reaper.

Jonny nestled his backside slowly on the dark-tiled driveway of the *Chateau's* entranceway as he battled a cauldron of intense psychology and physical agonies.

A line of jet-black limousines pulled into the hotel's driveway as its anonymous occupants, hidden by the camouflage of a blackened window tint, occupied their *Armani* jeans and *Gucci* sweaters on the leather.

Love. Family. Art. Allentown. ATMs. Maya. Money.

"Sir," came a concerning mumble from behind. "Is everything alright?"

Jonny, dripping in perspiration, turned like a heavy semi-trailer as his obscured line-of-sight made a futile attempt to identify the Good Samaritan.

"I'm... fine," he groaned, hoping his aide would decode his bogus response.

"No, you're not, sir," the Samaritan insinuated, as he took a seat beside his patient. "Listen, could you tell me your name?"

My name? I really don't even know anymore.

"Jon," he said.

"Okay, Jon, can you hear me all okay?"

Jonny nodded.

"Okay. Listen Jon, my name is Sam and I'm a doctor, okay. Have you ever had a panic attack before? Are you on medication?"

Jonny wondered if illicit narcotics qualified as the answer the doctor was seeking.

He shook his head from side to side. His bones trembled and his stomach continued to ache in a perpetual cramp.

"Alright. Can I ask you to do me a really big favour, Jon?"

Jonny considered the timing of such a request to be rather odd – given the state of his ongoing panic attack and whatnot – yet nonetheless he maintained his attentiveness.

"I want you to stretch your arms out and then bring them back to your chest like this for me," Doctor Samaritan ordered as he gesticulated his instructions.

A crowd of solicitous onlookers had formed at the *Chateau*'s steps, numbed by their own collective silence as they whispered play-by-plays to one another like Kevin Harlan and Reggie Miller during the timeout of an NBA broadcast.

Jonny obliged with the doctors orders, feebly outstretching his arms as they almost unjoined from their sockets.

"Okay, Jon, that's real good," Doctor Sam encouraged, sensing no responsive shift in Jonny's breathing. "Alright, I'm going to get you to do one more thing for me, okay?"

Family. Art. Love. Allentown. Money. Maya. ATMs. Criminal.

Jonny gestured his consent once again.

"You over there," Doctor Sam signalled to a bystander. "Run into the bar and get me a wet washcloth."

The startled bystander processed the unrehearsed command before fulfilling his gallant destiny with heroism.

"I want you to try and breathe in and out on my count," Sam requested, reinstating his attention to his patient. "Just breathe in for two seconds and then out again for two seconds, do you think you can do that for me?"

Jonny shrugged at the shoulders, muted by the restless sensation as the super-bystander returned with a damp cloth.

"Okay, here we go, on my count," the doctor prepared, loosely wrapping the soaked washcloth against Jonny's spine. "One... two..."

Doctor Sam and Jonny Jinks parroted the process two and then three times over before incrementally raising the breathing count to four, then six, and until Jonny's heart rate had regulated.

"How are you feeling, Jon?" Doctor Sam probed, extending his examination.

"Better."

The crowd of over a dozen had dispersed on the orders of a *Chateau* security guard, leaving the doctor and his convalescent patient in isolation.

"Listen, Jon," the doctor added as the painter continued in an idled recuperation. "I'm going to write you a prescription for diazepam."

Doctor Sam unbuckled his leather finished messenger bag and removed a pre-printed notepad.

"Valium, Jon," he clarified as he scribbled with a fine line marker before handing the script over. "I'm going to prescribe you with a packet containing two-milligram tablets; depending on the severity of your symptoms, you can take up to six-milligrams, three times a day as a maximum."

"Is that really necessary?" Jon asked, considering the drug's side effects when consumed during any forthcoming debauchery-soaked encounter. "Doc, I'm on vacation at the *Chateau Marmont*; does that mean I can't even drink now?"

Jonny already knew the answer.

"Listen, Jon," the doctor warned. "It's never safe to drink while on Valium; the combination of alcohol and diazepam in the body has an additive effect and enhances the most dangerous characteristics of both drugs while potentially leading to overdose."

Jonny frowned in dismay, sensing yet another transparent obstruction in his quest for decadent transcendence.

"But with that said," Doctor Sam whispered like an international spy, leaning over to mould a secret palm-funnel with his right hand.

"While I certainly do not recommend it, my clinic is at least a thirty minute drive away from here. And today, maybe I never took a vacation day."

The doctor, who now seemed a little more like Satan masquerading as an angel of light, smiled and delivered a patriotic nod, a symbol of unquestionable 'freedom.'

"Thanks for everything, Doc," he whispered as he shook hands with his impromptu practitioner and pocketed a business card for safekeeping.

As the doctor and his patient parted ways – Doctor Sam heading to the elevator lobby while Jonny made for the concierge desk – Jonny Jinks stared upwards and towards the heavens of destiny.

He was not yet done obeying the signs; and as long as they continued to manifest, Jonny was a slave to a much more powerful and spearheaded deity.

"Excuse me," he interrupted the concierge, forcing her to disengage a phone call.

Money. Love. Art. Allentown. ATMs. Maya... Money.

"Please arrange to have a bottle of your finest French champagne sent to that gentleman's apartment on my behalf," Jonny instructed as he gestured towards to the doctor in the distance. "And don't worry about a thing; just charge it to my credit card."

45

WILDE & UNCLEAN

Jonny drifted towards the kitchen of apartment suite 64 and towards a double-door cupboard with metallic silver handles. He arched his body inwards before opening the cupboard door to remove a white prescription pack with bright-blue highlighted markings.

The packet's inverse revealed the following message: *NDC 0140-0004-01 Valium. Each tablet contains 2 mg diazepam. 100 tablets. Usual dosage: See package insert.*

Jonny had forgotten how to play by the rules, how to follow decorum and directive. His new mantra circled around the abuse of power and the negligence of responsibility, discarding almost every loose trace of beneficence that wasn't rope-knotted around his very DNA.

He peeled open the packet's contents as he popped out 8 mg – or, four tablets – and prepared a half-empty glass of ice-cold water.

As he loaded the tablets one by one on a conveyer belt of tongue-saliva, he tilted his head upright, forced his eyelids down and allowed the liquid to flush down his oesophagus like a rip current, clawing its tiny victims deep into the stomach of a dark ocean. He guzzled then gulped, slowly regaining possession of his internal organs before gently loosening the stranglehold around his rib cage.

Breathe in, breathe out.

His throat tightened and he coughed without restraint. Jonny held his breath in fragments of two to three seconds as he pressurised his internal oxygen tank to moderate his heartbeat.

Four minutes later, Jonny was back in control, gazing again at the very hand-painted piece of art that catalysed his anxiety attack in the first place.

What was once yet another blank canvas in his workshop of Frankenstein had quickly become a medium for the communication of a visual typography. Stacked and disposed by written typeface, point size, line length, line spacing and letter spacing, this was not a piece stylised by its artistic intricacies but rather, a piece glorified by both its aesthetic arrangement and its evocative script.

Jonny recalled a scene in *The Holiday* whereby Cameron Diaz's character Amanda Woods – a movie-trailer maker in Los Angeles – adjured her co-workers to develop the font for a movie header, guiding them with the following feedback: "make it twice as big, but try it in a red, like a happy red, not a Scorsese red."

This particular piece however – inspired by the wisdom of Irish playwright Oscar Wilde – was absolutely bloodied, machete-slashed to pieces in *Scorsese* red.

The truth behind its very letters terrorised Jonny in every way imaginable.

He had created a monster, in person and on paper.

And didn't he know it.

Vivid reds, whites, golds and pinks soaked the canvas before him as he leant forward to scrutinise the unconventionally drawn passage one final time.

If a work of art is rich and vital and complete, those who have artistic instincts will see its beauty, and those whom ethics appeal more strongly than aesthetics will see its moral lesson. It will fill the cowardly with terror, and the unclean will see in it their own shame.

Jonny sniffed and snorted, his nose leading him to a lining of silk with the pleasant scent of a purple and grape-like wisteria flower. Buried in the bottomless pit of his luggage, a black pair of silk-laced panties with a rose-red trim squished beneath a handful of acrylic tubes.

Jonny had been witness to a catalogue of L.A. lingerie but none compared to Maya's *Victoria's Secret* catalogue, snatched from the fourth drawer of their Tudor-style home. He lifted the soft silk and scrunched it like a stress-ball, resting it under his nose as if it were an exotic entrée of illicit medication.

Fumes of Maya's natural odour drifted with the force of a dangerous gas leak and suffocated him in a haze of guilt and agony. This whole ATM-thing was for her, he was *still* sure of it. She was the reason, the impetus behind every dice-roll. The money, this lifestyle, it would save her.

It would save them.

Or maybe it wouldn't. Objectively, how could it? Only Jonny knew.

The flat screen television – activated but muted for concentration – that rested beside him on an oak cabinet streamed monochromatic footage from a Martin Luther King Jr. documentary, persuading the painter to liberate the broadcast from its silent prison.

"Every man lives in two realms, the internal and the external. The internal is that realm of spiritual ends expressed in art, literature, morals, and religion. The external is that complex of devices, techniques, mechanisms, and instrumentalities by means of which we live. Our problem today is that we have allowed the internal to become lost in the external. We have allowed the means by which we live to outdistance the ends for which we live. This is the serious predicament, the deep and haunting problem confronting modern man. If we are to survive today, our moral and spiritual 'lag' must be eliminated.

Enlarged material powers spell enlarged peril if there is not proportionate growth of the soul. When the 'without' of man's nature subjugates the 'within', dark storm clouds begin to form in the world."

It's where you go when it thunderstorms and you're the only one left in the cold without an umbrella.

The storm cloud had already formed, its thunderous threat omnipresent as it necessitated Jonny to admit something he knew all along: after all this time, he was *still* without an umbrella.

46
STRIP CLUB SCHEMIN'

For those that fancied themselves as the irregular badass, too avant-garde to succumb to the wiles of the average bottle-blonde stripper, *Cheetahs* was the place to be.

The tattooed, punk rock, *Suicide Girls* vibe that had become synonymous with everything *Cheetas* offered patrons the sexual equivalence of an eco-conscious political party, demurring of the unwritten standards of stereotypical beauty.

Cheetahs was the undisputed gentlemen's Mecca of Los Angeles and a worthy pilgrimage from anywhere on the West Coast. Its skinny stage matched its performers' collective waistlines while its plentiful bar provided the perfect comrade for an evening of lascivious leering. On any given night, one was just as likely to be seated beside a midlife crisis-stricken author blabbering about how methamphetamines helped to conquer his writer's block as they would a hipster couple drenched in unimaginable irony.

And as it would so happen, on this given night, one was even *more* likely to be seated beside a Pennsylvanian house painter, gripping with the jaws of good and evil as he battled earnestly between crapulent desire and sober regret.

"What the fuck are you doing!?" the exotic dancer barked, her tattoos dripping down her shoulders as her zany dark hair flung around in Chuckie's face.

Chuckie had filled his wallet with white ones, yellow tens and blue fifties that ditched the traditional seal of the United States of America for a clipart train and a *Monopoly* logo.

"Well, if you're gonna throw fake titties at me, I'm gonna throw fake money at you!"

The remark was as facetious as it was misogynistic.

"Alright, alright, take it easy now, he's just had a little too much to drink is all it is, honey," Tokyo mitigated, splitting his attention between the disgruntled stripper and her hawking security team. "I'm really, *truly* sorry about that."

Tokyo yanked Chuckie away by the collar as he conjoined the tips of his thumb and index finger, offering the security guards the universal A-Okay sign.

"Hey, c'mon man, what the fuck are you doing?" Chuckie contested as the dancer retreated.

"You're going to get us kicked out, asshole," Tokyo insisted, mumbling beneath a bass-heavy hip-hop track. "There's only so much fucking privilege money can buy before you blow it. But of course you've never had to learn *that* lesson before."

Ouch, Jonny thought as his eyes followed a duet of dancers sliding up and down a chromed pole.

"The only lesson I've learnt is that there's only so much fucking blow money can buy *when* you're one of the privileged," Chuckie parried, warding off Tokyo in a clever verbal pun as he simulated the oral practice of an open-aired fellatio with his chubby hands.

The exotic dancers twirled and slid, offering a series of physically imposing pole tricks to the backing rhythm of an indie rock jam by *The Strokes*. The slim stage showcased more half-naked acrobats than the backroom of a circus but Jonny had his eye fixated on only *one* in particular.

"What's her name?" Jonny asked of the *Cheetahs* regular as if he had spotted her for the very first time.

"Which one? Her?" Tokyo clarified, his eyes drifting from the Ron Jeremy look-alike disc jockey to a fine, tattooed and petite dancer with a stripe of red in her straightened ponytail.

Jonny nodded, his eyes reflecting the gelatinous booties bouncing before him.

"Her name is irrelevant. All that matters is that *you* understand that she's crazy, my ninja," he delineated chauvinistically. "She paints her lips the same colour as the stripe in her hair and changes that shit weekly like she's the stripper-equivalent of fucking Dennis Rodman."

I always liked that she was a painter, Jonny recalled, the memory of his rendezvous with the part-stripper, part-hooker at a Los Angeles bar easily recoverable.

"*And* if she takes you out back, she lets you pull on her ponytail while she shoves all that ink in your face."

"I thought that the hookers at *Cheetahs* don't get naked, though?" Chuckie challenged, raising question marks over the club's most notoriously unpopular policy.

"Anyone gets naked for the right *person* and the right *price*. And they're strippers, Chuckie, not hookers. Where's your manners?"

That's what you think.

"Can you get me a lap dance with her?" Jonny requested, knowing fully that this was a task achievable on his own.

"My ninja I can get you a dance with a cavewoman virgin from Virginia if that's what you really want," he gloated, wielding his Californian-powered Excalibur.

The Virgin of the Rocks. Madonna. Maya

"I think just the dance from her will do for now."

"Hey, whatever you say, my ninja."

Jonny had to see her again. But more importantly, *she* had to see *him*. The direction of the pendulum had pulled a one-eighty, Jonny now boasting the kind of confidence exhibited by an obese indolent who had shed three-quarters of his weight and was suddenly the coolest cat in town.

And while an ever-present trepidation wasn't *entirely* avoidable, Jonny had developed a penchant for combatting his self-sabotage, his goody-two-shoes persona.

Jonny Cash.

He had a point to prove, a voluptuous mountain to conquer, and he was far too high to trek back down now.

"But listen, holmes," Chuckie bumped, his two cents on offer to anyone willing to rob him. "Whatever you do, keep your hands to yourself. These girls are crazy; not only will they call security on your ass, but security'll call the LAPD and then we're all fucked."

Jonny explored his mind-box before formulating a succinct and droll response.

"I'm good, Chuckie," he confessed with aplomb. "Where there's fire, there's gasoline. And besides, L, A, P and D are the first four letters in 'lap dance.' So if you *really* think about it, you can't have one without the other."

For the proceeding hour, the trouble-making trinity squabbled over which of the on-stage exotic dancers was the most nubile.

"Man, she's a straight ten," Chuckie nominated, allocating his ten-point ballot like a *Eurovision* voter. "I'd lay her like a turkey egg on Thanksgiving."

"C'mon, Chuckie, haven't you heard what they say?"

Chuckie offered a familiar shrug of cluelessness, the setting and its dialogue eerily similar to that of a late-night debate in an Allentown bar.

"You never wife up a ten, *especially* a ten that's a stripper," Jonny preached as he rehashed a batch of Pennsylvanian knowledge.

"Well I'm not gonna wife her, Jonny," he avowed as if the sentiment was unexpected. "I'm just gonna fuck her."

"You're not gonna do either, you quadriplegic ass-hat," Tokyo chaffed, shattering Chuckie's dreams like a window-bursting brick.

"Whatever, asshole."

The banter prolonged between drinks, disco balls and dainty light and smoke machines before finally, business made its way to the top of the agenda.

"Listen, Tokyo," Jonny said. "You got contacts at the *Bar Marmont*, right?"

"What about me, Jonny?" Chuckie interjected, piqued by his omission. "Don't you think *I'd* know someone there, seeing as I'm the one who booked you a banging suite at the hotel in the first place?"

You mean the room that I upgraded all by myself?

"You know, I was going to ask you but –"

"Okay, so do you know someone or not, Chuckie?" Tokyo asked monotonously.

Chuckie's eyes bent inwards as his nose shrivelled and his eyes tightened.

"No," Chuckie yielded in acquiescence.

Quietness rumbled behind the booming of a drum and bass beat as the exotic dancers rocked the stage as if performing a pornographic parody of *You Got Served*.

"Right, you were saying, Jonny?"

"Anyway, if you know someone there, can I get you to make a reservation for me?"

"Sure," he said. "So I'll just book a table then?"

Jonny smirked as he prepared to gauge the dumbfounded reactions of his Californian La Cosa Nostra.

"I need you to book the entire place," he requested inscrutably. "The *entire* place."

Jonny repeated the sentiment for good measure.

"You ain't serious are you? What in the fuck are you going to do with the whole bar? You know how expensive that shit's going to cost?" Tokyo replied as if a dollar would ever leak from his own pocket.

"Write it off as a philanthropic donation – an investment in a greater cause," Jonny proposed, wielding an unwarranted power that labelled him the aggressor. "You can just use it as a tax deductible, anyway."

Chuckie blinked uncontrollably as he leaned back and awaited an answer from the apprehensive Asian Dutchman.

"If I'm booking out the whole place for you, who are you inviting?"

Jonny paused, his mind wandering back to the X-rated entertainment on stage before him.

"Absolutely nobody."

The proclamation was smug yet nonchalant, Jonny grinning in budding confidence as he relaxed his shoulders and pressed his lips against a chilled glass of bourbon.

Focus. You can do this.

"Now, how about that lap dance?"

* * *

"It's... *wonderful* to see you again, Yasmine," he said, fixing his fingers around the curvatures of her waist.

"You're like a whole new person, Mr. Jinks," Yasmine evinced in a gleeful surprise, her red-bleached ponytail wagging atop his chest as she danced for him in a playful striptease. "Or so Tokyo tells me, we're meant to call you 'Jonny Cash' now, right?"

The whisper of his adopted appellation sent shivers down his already tickling scrotum. He had become unpredictable, a client without an indicative track record, rolling into the foreign vagina of a delighted fille de joie.

"Just 'Jonny' is good enough for me," he corrected as if the opulence of his nickname did not satisfy him even a little bit.

Yasmine undressed, slipping the straps of her bra as the scintillating scent of perfume and perspiration intoxicated him behind a private curtain.

Jonathan Jinks would have supplicated for a HAZMAT suit, for protection against the unprincipled.

But not Jonny Jinks – *not* Jonny *Cash*.

47

THE VIETNAM WAR

No one had ever booked out the *Bar Marmont* in its entirety. Perhaps it was because even the *Chateau*'s most ostentatious clientele lacked the daring audacity. Or maybe it was because L.A.'s untamed, its most animalistic socialites respected the boundaries of home-cooked hospitality.

Whatever the case, Jonny Jinks was not from *the* city. And the regular rules, the unwritten guidelines – the handbook of right and wrong – of Los Angeles living did not apply.

Classically posh and surprisingly accessible for the average-Joe not privy to aristocratic society, the ever-enchanting *Bar Marmont* had become as notorious as its hotel namesake amongst Hollywood natives.

As Jonny Jinks, Chuckie Hooper and Tokyo van Wolfswinkel wobbled towards the bar's French doors, a lounge area – with trussed ceilings, vibrant skylights and hanging greenery that amalgamated to produce a prototypical outdoor café – awestruck the trio in a regal welcoming. On an ordinary evening at the *Bar Marmont*, affluent entertainers and delirious musicians would lounge on leather ottomans to light tobacco and confabulate over their latest top-secret projects.

But on this evening – Jonny Cash's evening – the typically populated lounge bar was as desolate as a movie theatre on the opening night of Keanu Reeve's box office disaster *47 Ronin*.

"Good evening Mr. Jinks, Mr. Hooper, Mr. van Wolfswinkel," the pre-rehearsed waiter saluted as he ushered the triad through the Parisian doorway and onwards to a tiny Bohemian bar. "Right this way, gentlemen."

"Well gracias, amigo," Chuckie bowed, tipping his South American hat to the usher as he squeezed through a passageway, fruitlessly leaning on a paper bag that was tucked between his fingers as if it were a sturdy cane.

The bar was decorated in clads of floral wallpaper, a smattering of thematic tables and a Louvre-like hallway of Asian-inspired artwork that looked like the result of a Dr. Jinks and Dr. van Wolfswinkel mad science experiment gone wrong.

"Or perhaps you would prefer to begin with a meal?" the waiter suggested as Chuckie rubbed the fat in his belly like a malnourished weight-loss patient.

An open skylight cut into the dining room roof, stimulating a slippery breeze as a streak of silver fringed by dangling succulents cut through the *Marmont* air. Directly adjacent to the bar's lounge area, a series of steps proffered indulgences from the delectable *Marmont* menu in the facility's elegant dining room. The dining room – with its vintage Hollywood décor of plush red banquettes, lace draping, mirrors, and walls of ivory moulding – was presided by an oil painting of the watchful Vietnamese figurehead Ho Chi Minh.

"This fucking guy," Tokyo cursed, instantly identifying the Communist revolutionary leader as he scoured the portrait and prepared to preach. "You know what's crazy? In Vietnam, they love this guy like America loves George Washington."

Jonny was far more preoccupied with the artistic techniques explored in the portrayal than the disputation of a political figure he knew little about. Nonetheless, he now understood better than to totally dismiss a Tokyo van Wolfswinkel tangent.

"They teach their children his doctrine in their schools," Tokyo explained, holding out the five fingers on his right hand as he began to count. "Patriotism, hard work, cooperation, discipline, humbleness, integrity, bravery and hygiene – fucking hygiene, can you believe that? And they still all wreak like spicy noodle soup and contaminated seaweed."

Tokyo's immunity and exemption from a xenophobic reproval stemmed from the actualities of his own existential lineage.

"But really, the guy was a megalomaniac; this cunning dictator with a diabolic, fatherly smile who banged a bunch of women while married to his Chinese midwife."

Jonny was suddenly agog as the notice of Ho Chi Minh's infidelity propounded an instant curiosity.

"In one way, it's actually pretty fucking appropriate to this entire theme they've got going on over here," Tokyo said, flailing his arms around.

"Wait, I don't get it," Jonny confessed, the teachings of Tokyo whispering higgledy-piggledy in a mind-boggling confusion. "He sounds like such a bad guy. So if he's really as shitty as you say he is, why do the Vietnamese people worship him like some sort of enlightened demi-God?"

"Well don't *you* ask the right questions, Jonny Cash," Tokyo bubbled, driven by a new curiosity for a subject only *he* really understood. "That wasn't even his real name – his name was Nguyen something or other – I don't fucking know, Nguyen is like the Asian equivalent of fucking Smith or Mohammed but I'm pretty sure that's what it was. Anyway, he changed it 'cause 'Ho Chi Minh' directly translates to 'The Enlightener."

A change of name, whether uncertified in the elemental wilderness of a West Coast world or formally recognised on a passport was something Jon-*ny* Jinks could uncannily identify with.

"This was a guy that was said to have liberated the people he loved the most while he journeyed for prosperity and a better lifestyle. As the story goes, he was a patriot, sacrificing his own life and fighting for the good of his family and his community; and of course, he was a lovable little cunt-face for that. But while this little ninja was busy liberating and preaching and ass-kissing and pussy-licking and doing whatever the fuck else he wanted to do, in his spare time, he was free to swindle, deceive and fuck over the entire world – *including* his own people."

It took a moment, but Jonny quantified that this *was* a topic that carried a strangely appropriate significance. He fine-tuned his ears and mimicked Tokyo's lecture, disfiguring his physical self into a warped and talking oil painting.

"I mean Ho Chi Minh is looked upon like some sort of infallible saint," he continued, burying the Ho Chi Minh bequest beneath a pile of horse manure. "They chanted his name at soccer games to rally their teams for fuck's sake; soccer games! And while they were singing and moshing, Hitler Chow Bow was sending a team of his own to Vietnam's north to kill hundreds of thousands of these little Asian ninjas who opposed him and represented a threat to his own regime."

The impromptu history lesson was poised for a final examination as Jonny whipped out his invisible pencils and took cerebral notations on the topic.

"Take nothing away from that motherfucker," Tokyo commended, applauding the notion that the legacy of his stylised visage had become an ubiquitous countercultural symbol for rebellion and global insignia. "That ninja was a genius who fooled the world and whacked himself, smack, bang, on the top of the pyramid. But I guess that's the very reason that he's on the wall up here – for inspiration."

The bar waiter, detecting that the edifying had concluded, gathered the trio on a concentrated leash as he ushered them towards the *Marmont*'s secondary bar. Just like its main counterpart, the facility's secondary bar often boasted a stylish clientele of celebrities, hipsters, and international sybarites. Red silk lanterns cast a warm glow on the fandangle of stuffed peacocks and pinned butterflies across its ceiling as the bar oozed in royal beguile.

"Take a seat, gentlemen," the part-waiter-part-usher-part-tour-guide suggested as he passed along copies of the bar's drink menu in a grown-up game of pass-the-parcel. "What can I get for you?"

Jonny's mind zigzagged to an era of *Yuengling* lager and Pennsylvanian sports bars. That was a place he did not belong. Those were a people he did not belong to.

A quick survey of the menu indicated that the days of prosaic lager consumption were but a mere paint splatter in his rear-view mirror. An aristocratic proclivity for daily libations had now become the exceptional standard. The drinks menu at the *Bar Marmont* offered a breakdown of seven major brew categories: rum, whiskey and rye, tequila, rare breeds, gin, vodka and classic aperitifs. Each beverage bracket contained a list of sub-products exotically titled – with names like the Millionaire Cocktail, Diablo, Brass Flower, Gold Tooth, Pimm's Cup and the Havana Mojito – in a cleverly manipulated sales ploy to entice its vulnerable clientele.

"What do you think, fellas?" Chuckie interjected, dropping the paper bag to the floor and between his feet. "Should we kick it off with three of these Diablo thingies? I'm feeling a little tequila-ish tonight."

"Go hard or go home, right?" Tokyo advocated.

"Whatever you think, I'm down for," Jonny settled, unperturbed by the potential effects of the drink's heavy toxicity.

Tick tock. Tick tock.

"Three Diablos coming right up then, gentleman," the waiter

pencilled before collecting all three menus and making for the cash register.

Okay. It's go-time. Go hard or go home… right?

"Ugh, sorry," Jonny said, abruptly gyrating in his chair as he waved to steal the waiter's attention.

"Yes, sir?"

Jonny's eyes drifted towards an analogue bar clock hanging by the head of an alcoholic wonderland as he tracked the lively ticking of the seconds dial spinning around the chapter ring.

"I know this is a little strange considering we paid big money for exclusivity tonight," Jonny tittered. "But could you be kind enough to advise your manager that I'd like to open the bar back up to the public in around fifteen minutes?"

If Chuckie Hooper and Tokyo van Wolfswinkel had already been served their shots of double-glassed Diablos, they would likely have exploded in a shocking spit-take of the mouth.

"Sir?" the baffled waiter choked as Jonny grinned nonchalantly.

The *Bar Marmont* and its amiable wait staff had anticipated an evening of private hospitality but Jonny's untimely request had ricocheted the plan completely off course.

"Now fucking what?" Chuckie asked, perplexed, while Jonny Jinks locked horns with the unforgiving eyes of an oil painted Ho Chi Minh.

"Tokyo," Jonny instructed, swelling with the refined confidence of a marksmen from a flawless rooftop vantage point. "Could you do me a favour? Can you open a new room on PLiNKER and name it 'The Jonny Cash Invitational'?"

Tokyo wrestled with his mobile device before tapping on the application's loading icon.

"What are you planning on doing when they open those doors? An 'invitational'? We holding a fucking golf tournament with Tiger Woods' mistresses?" Tokyo quipped in bewilderment.

Jonny crossed his arms and leant forward, his fingers pressed against the table while his neck yanked his shoulders towards Tokyo like a cement ball on an incarceration chain.

"When the prison doors are opened," Jonny whispered, pointing in a whirlwind of directions as one eye locked onto the analogue clock's minute hand while the other never deviated from the scribbled fingers of an oil-painted Vietnamese communist. "The real dragons will fly out."

A silent calm ensued as Jonny slapped the skin of his knuckles against the table's surface in an escalating tension.

"What the fuck kind of crazy medieval talk is that?" Chuckie said, snapping the suspense.

Jonny winked, rolled his body weight backwards on the chair's rear legs and signalled towards the oil painting of Ho Chi Minh.

Beneath the frame that hung above the maître d's station, a golden plaque inscribed with that very passage in roman calligraphy rested against its black lacquered wall canvas.

"So what?" Chuckie pressed. "We're just quoting Chinese guys now and pretending like it has some kind of super-mystical meaning, are we? Is that what we're doing? And what the hell does that have to do with opening the bar back up again?"

"Vietnamese," Tokyo corrected him as he zoomed his senses into Jonny's soul to search for a more profound explanation.

"Take it easy, Chuckie," Jonny hushed, levelling his chair legs with the tiled *Marmont* surface. "That's not all we're doing."

"So then what in the fuck *are* we doing? And why in the fuck did you ask me to carry this Rebel Wilson-weighing paper bag in here? What's the plan?"

Jonny appealed for composure, flicking his focus between the oil painting, the analogue clock and the entranceway as if each component were a shifting Powerball in a Californian lottery.

"The plan?" Jonny asked rhetorically as he dragged the large paper bag across the sparkling floor and wedged it between his ankles. "Who ever said anything about a plan?"

48

BAR DRINKIN' & SALES PITCHIN'

The objective was clear: erect a free-for-all hedonistic play-palace, an intergalactic frat party on the Sunset Strip that could serve to fulfil Jonny's mission of self-aggrandizement.

The means? A highly popular mobile application. The method? Manipulation. The target? A mouth-watering dose of Jonny Cash's finest.

"Garson, what can we get for this lovely lady?" he queried the bartender as he gestured towards the shelving behind him.

Garson mulled, considering Jonny's earlier directive before offering a palatable suggestion.

"How about a 'Sun Goddess' for the radiant beauty?" he proposed with the kind of clever wit that even Jonny Jinks could applaud.

"Seems appropriate," Jonny blandished, flattering the beauty into a twitching blush.

"Sounds good to me, but what is it?" asked the blushing, twitching not-so-sleeping beauty.

"It's one of our signature concoctions: *Belvedere Vodka, Lillet,* lemon juice, simple syrup, mint and muddled grapes," Garson cited as he began mixing drinks with the swagger of a disc jockey mixing vinyl's at a nightclub in the seventies.

"So in other words, it's a pretty fucking great time," Jonny winked, the charm both palpable and endearing.

The not-so-sleeping beauty's first sip of the exotic potion took her to a hypnotic place, a place of sybaritic ecstasy as her vision blurred and her veins pulsated in a sassy rhythm.

"So listen, I'm hosting an arts exhibit out at Tokyo's property in Pacific Palisades," Jonny apprised as he swung his arm around her shoulder. "You know Tokyo van Wolfswinkel, the guy who created the PLiNKER mobile app, right? Anyway, it's called 'The P-art-Y!' – you know, as in 'the *art* party.' Cheesy, I know. But I'd love it if you could make it; there's going to be food, drinks and a lot of pretty cool shit going on. It'd be a shame if a woman as beautiful as you wasn't in attendance."

The slithery salesman cajoled his prospect, handing her a colourful advertising flyer with the aptly titled 'The P-art-Y!' inscribed on its header as she agreed to attend the decorative showcase.

"Oh," he blurted, as if he had almost forgotten. "Don't forget to check-in to 'The Jonny Cash Invitational' on PLiNKER. You'll be able to jump the line on the night if you show your proof of check-in to my man Chuckie at the door."

The woman had not a clue about fine craftsmanship or the arts. But she *was* primed in local geography and *fully* understood the perks associated with the not-so cryptic translation of an exclusive event on Los Angeles' affluent Westside.

* * *

"Here's a-hundred-bucks," Chuckie patronised, handing the bill to a tentative young woman who had been ambling by the front patio as a group of voluptuous middle-aged ladies ambushed Jonny and his advertising paraphernalia with their PLiNKER-installed mobile devices.

Chinese lanterns made of wire and rice paper hung across the entrance of the front patio bar where a congregation of social revellers puffed away on their tobacco wands like sailors on leave.

"Buy yourself some drinks on me until I'm really good looking, then come back and talk to me and I'll have a little surprise for you, you feel what I'm saying?"

The woman repelled his extended hand, rejecting the offer in repugnance.

"The amount of alcohol I'd need to fuck you would actually kill me, asshole," she rebuked as she flung her hair away and treaded off in disgust.

"Well," Tokyo intervened like an omnipresent *Big Brother* from behind the chaotic shadows, snatching the Benjamin Franklin greenback from Chuckie's flimsy clutches. "That could've gone better. Why don't you let me handle the financials from now on; that *is* my motherfucking job title in this charade after all, isn't it?"

* * *

"Alright, Garson," Jonny pumped as he leant forward and placed his elbows on the bar counter. "Let's get two Diablos, three Westsides, two of the Framboise Suavages and, ugh, I'll get another... *Millionaire* Cocktail while I'm here."

Jonny winked at the bartender as a wave of enlivened women formed a line like toddlers at a store-Santa exhibit waiting to place their order, gratis from Jonny Cash himself.

"And you know what? While we're at it, bring out a few three cheese boards with the buckwheat honey and that date and fig jam – these fine ladies need to eat something!"

"Certainly, sir," he obliged as Garson the *Marmont*-tender began mixing deadly drops of liquor like a nefarious scientist.

The bar was officially back open for business and yet, in an instant quicker than an adolescent orgasm, it became immediately apparent that the *Marmont*'s single-night GDP would still be generated mostly by a mysteriously beneficent Pennsylvanian pilgrim.

Jonny Jinks had indeed dedicated a great portion of his teenage years to academics, creativity and communal altruism. But even he could not have imagined that such typical tendencies could manifest once again in such an atypical moment.

* * *

Chuckie and Tokyo swam around the *Bar Marmont* like two intoxicated peas in a confined pod.

"So let me get this straight," Chuckie probed over the channel-breaking noise of hundreds of lively voices as he sought a clarification from the Jonny Cash financial secretary. "Jonny books out the entire *Bar Marmont* because he can, he prepares his own fucking simulated viral advertisement because he can, and then he gets the place re-opened for these muppet-Nazis so that he can capitalise on his; I'm sorry, *your* investment?"

Tokyo grinned as he distributed a handful of The P-art-Y! flyers to passers-by, most who recognised the social start-up businessman and thanked him by name before posing for a impromptu *iPhone* selfie.

"You got it straighter than Donald Trump at a gay-rights convention, my intuitive little ninja," Tokyo corroborated using a dictionary that only he and Chuckie owned.

"So... is this guy a fucking mad money moron or is he really just some kind-of genius?"

"I don't know about whatever the fuck he is to everyone else, but I know exactly what he is to me."

Chuckie scrunched at the eyebrow, his body language begging for a more concise elaboration.

Chuckie Hooper was along for the thrills of the real-life rollercoaster and for an overindulged, mollycoddled son of a local diner magnate, that more than sufficed. But Tokyo's patronage necessitated something far more substantial. Tokyo van Wolfswinkel was in dire need of a rewarding return on his investment.

"Chuckie, I'm a magnate that owns a mine. And like any other businessman, my mine can only yield so much of its own gold for so long, especially after I sold PLiNKER last year," he admitted as he gazed towards Jonny, the bar counter and an endless line of desperate women thirsting for a complimentary beverage. "But this ninja Jonny; shit, Jonny is a motherfucking two-legged walking goldmine with an endless supply of hammer-toting leprechauns on his payroll."

* * *

The dawning of a newfangled and mischievous era cried for a final crescendo. Like Michael Jackson's balcony dangling of his blanketed offspring or Miley Cyrus' provocative booty shaking twerk dance, Jonny needed a notorious exclamation point, an indelible publicity stunt that possessed the kind of pixie dust that could catapult him into perpetual relevance.

For his master plan to truly triumph, the name Jonny Jinks – or, at the very least, the sobriquet of Jonny Cash – would need to be emblazoned across the numbing brains of every A-list wannabe at the *Bar Marmont.*

Over time, Jonny's social media networks were ablaze with tourism adverts promoting a different kind of party across the Mediterranean for would-be travellers. These European parties were more-like wild psychedelic rave festivals, dance parties predicated on the concepts of polychromatic rapture intertwined in the escape of a foreign jamboree.

And while they were often inclusive of elements and attractions commonplace at any typical rave across the globe – food, merchandise vending, performances and social activities – each of them were founded on a constant theme, a nuance that divided them from the orthodox: *Paint.*

'Paint Parties' boasted the leading disc jockeys from across the world as they endeavoured to unite their audiences through the spreading of universal love and neon paint. And while they were often messy affairs, by combining the mortal elements of colour, sound, light and love, an ineffable euphoria would engulf its revellers as they coalesced to fight for a common purpose.

"Listen up, everyone, can I have your attention, please," Jonny beamed in a pseudo-dictatorial commandment as he climbed atop a table and planted his imprint like a hypnotic Neil Armstrong on a bleeding Hollywood moon. "Are we having a great fucking time, or what?"

The crowd roared, slicing their arms in the air as if they were in the mosh pit of a rock concert at *Madison Square Garden.* Behind the turntable, the in-house DJ released the digital needle on a remix that fused the tranquil euphony of *Bakermat*'s *'One Day'* with the vicious saw-synth hook of *Martin Garrix & Firebeatz*'s *'Helicopter.'*

The ravishing melodies of an echoed saxophone squiggled atop a minimal pad section before pacing towards a drum break as the bar's guests swayed and bopped to the compulsive rhythm.

"Let me tell y'all something: A lot of shit gets said about people who like to drink. But you know what I think? I think, contrary to a very popular public opinion, that alcohol doesn't turn people into somebody they're not," he preached as he shifted the mood into something more relatable. "It just makes them forget to hide *that* part of themselves to the rest of the world. So allow *me* to free your inhibitions; tonight, you can be whoever the fuck you want to be!"

Another roar ensued, this time, in a side-chained tempo to match the particular cadence of the thumping remix as a smattering of revellers began to pound their hands in a drumming pattern.

"So on that note, here's a toast," Jonny proposed as he raised a translucent glass bottle, brimful of the premium Dutch export *Ketel One Vodka*. "To a night we won't remember... With a bunch of people we'll never fucking forget!"

Jonny's speech was delivered with the enigmatical vigour of a Vietnamese revolutionary leader as he commanded his socialite army to revel and rebel.

As if on cue, the gritty portamento-lead saw-synth hook composed by the Dutch trio reached its crescendo, underscoring Jonny's monologue in a quintessential moment of magnificence.

The apogee had arrived, erupting implacably as a spiralling spray of non-stainable neon paint rained down on Jonny's adopted disciples, enveloping them in a camouflage of colour. Splashes of vibrant hues produced a tangible rainbow inside the *Bar Marmont* as Chuckie and Tokyo squeezed their hands together around a carton supply of bottles of blue, green, yellow and red pigmented neon paint tubes, squirting them into the sky like kaleidoscopic cannonballs.

The *Bar Marmont*'s service crew countered in a panicked frenzy, the wait staff scurrying for cover under the shield of a table while a pair of security guards battled the uproar on a mission to retain order.

Amidst the chaos, Chuckie had climbed the *Marmont* mountain as he too, stood atop a wooden dining table, kicking away the cutlery in a quest to improve his paint-squirting vantage point. As the bar's patrons sculled shots of tequila and cases of mixed drinks, Chuckie split a batch of The P-art-Y! flyers in two, distributing copies in each hand as he channelled LeBron James' patented talcum powder toss and released the photocopied documents into the air's gravitational pull.

As the flyers slip-slid from the ceiling of the *Bar Marmont* – a whirlwind funnel of falling advertising and charity – the venue's ravenous guests collided shoulders and knocked drinking glasses, slipping over plops of neon paint as they fought for sole ownership of just one leaflet.

"Hold on!" Jonny howled, suddenly reappearing like a biblical deity, this time with a paper bag wrapped around his palm. "We've got more to give 'em!"

Jonny folded and twisted at the bag's handle as if he were serving takeout at a drive through-window.

"Chuckie, blow this fucking shit up!" he commanded, launching the brown paper bag in the sky as Chuckie gobbled it in one hand.

Had anyone else filled the roster at wide receiver, one peek inside the contents of the bag and a contingent of unanswerable questions were surely destined to follow.

But not for Chuckie.

Chuckie was a foot solder; a cotton-candy-covered foot solder with an insatiable appetite for unrealistic theatrics. There was only a single decision he knew to make – follow orders and never beg to understand why.

Chuckie Hooper reached deep into the crevice of the brown paper bag and begun propelling the contents in a boomerang-styled hurl – one at a time – high into the air.

Jonny tilted his neck backwards, worshiping his plastic-painted creations as they fell in slow motion like enchanting snowflakes in a dry desert. His minions were ostensibly torn between two golden tickets as they raced to grip a flyer in one hand and a Rich Uncle Pennybags mask – the *very same* mask Chuckie assumed while fornicating in a questionable Californian hotel room on a drug-infested splurge – in the other.

"You see, Tokyo," Jonny said, resting his hand on the shoulder of his patron as his voice became barely audible over the beautiful chaos below. "That's the thing about *Monopoly*. Nobody ever reads the fucking rules until an argument breaks out."

Jonny snickered as he observed two bare-skinned women, seemingly in a vortex-like vacuum as they wrestled one another over a fallen mask.

The rules did not apply any longer. In fact, the rules never existed. This was Jonny's board game and he owned every property from Old Kent Road to Mayfair.

"Or in this case, a paint-mud-wrestling bout!"

Tokyo gawked in awe, mesmerised by the developing scene before him as Jonny swallowed a chunk of saliva before injecting himself with a metaphorical serum of courage and control.

"Remember, y'all," Chuckie reminded the unbidden scavengers below him as he discovered a pleasure for the abusive capacity of a commanding power. "Not only do you gotta check in to 'The Jonny Cash Invitational' on PLiNKER, but you *gotta* bring either a flyer or a mask with you if you want in – this is for exclusive motherfuckers *only!*"

Chuckie's disclaimer only furthered the vulture-like convulsion as a The P-art-Y! flyer snapped in half, courtesy of a pair of cat-fighting women who craved the demonic indulgence of social notability.

The *Bar Marmont* was alive with colour and craziness. Everything from its red silk lanterns, its yellow-painted tile flooring, its curvy black chairs and its plush banquettes were stained in a myriad of brushless paint splatter. Even the room's ceiling-glued insect habitat of butterflies, moths and dragonflies were dripping with the remnants of an obstreperous paintball battle zone.

White bottle caps scattered across a minefield of crushed paint bottles as residue of the concentrated neon paint stuck to the floors and twirled across the room from the propelling of a carousel of dancing women. Everybody inside the *Bar Marmont* was shrouded from head to toe in a euphoric mixture of pigmented paint paste.

Had evidence of two sets of easels and a vacillating judge been found at the scene, one might have been excused for thinking they had entered the aftermath of an erratic courtroom paint-it-out-bout between Amy Adams' and Christoph Waltz's feuding characters in Tim Burton's *Big Eyes.*

"You!" came the bellow from a roaring security guard beneath Chuckie's feet as he rubbed his eyelids with the tip of his knuckles, removing a chunk of paint in the process. "Get your fat fucking ass down from that table before I pull you down."

The security guard's ultimatum intensified as he stretched his claws forward.

"Hey, take it easy, holmes," Chuckie placated as he slithered backwards. "If that's how it's going to be, then I'm out-ie!"

Chuckie extended his feet, skidding backwards like a hapless *Looney Toons* animation as he tumbled and crashed in a puddle of particoloured paint on the floor below.

"Get your ugly ass up, kid, we gotta rumble!" Tokyo bawled, appearing from an apparent black hole as he jerked Chuckie's limb, almost snapping it away from its socket.

"Y'all know what to do!" Chuckie cried like a satanic dictator with a legion of staunch foot soldiers as he skidded through patches of paint.

"Pick up all the fucking flyers and masks you can find, bring your iPhone's or Android phones or whatever the fuck phones you have with PLiNKER on 'em and we're gonna rock the panties off at the party of the century! Oh yeah! And fuck the police – they can suck my fat, ketchup and mustard-stained dick!"

Chuckie's thunderous cue reverberated across the bar as Tokyo hauled him through a slippery maze of falling drunkards.

The bar was nothing short of disorderly as the overlapping sounds of hard-core dance music, feet scuffling and exhortations by the *Marmont*'s security personnel submerged the lounge in a drowning disarray.

"Where the fuck has Jonny gone?" Tokyo asked as he swerved through the rainbow-coated stampede, his right hand still firmly clasped around Chuckie's wrist as he towed him like a shopping trolley in a busy supermarket.

Chuckie and Tokyo were lined in a back-to-back old western gunfight position, Chuckie effectively acting as Tokyo's backpack-attached rear-view mirror as he bounced side-to-side, dragging his feet beneath him.

"He's right behind us, son!" he slurred, pointing his index finger forward as Jonny, followed by an outfit of semi-clothed – semi-naked in a world where the glass was always half-full – women, darted through the slipstream behind them.

"Let's go!" Jonny squealed as he peddled his feet only a handful of strides behind them. "We did what we came here to do – now let's get the fuck out of here!"

The threesome dashed for the exit door leaving a triad of multi-coloured footprints, a single Rich Uncle Pennybags mask and a room full of anarchy behind them.

There was no doubt about it: Jonny Jinks had succeeded in his strategic pursuit for instant notoriety. But such a controversy would never lend itself attachment to the name on Jonny's birth certificate. No, 'Jonathan Jinks' was void of significance and impressionable resonance.

But 'Jonny Cash' – now that was an appellation worthy of historical eminence.

49
COPS & 720P WEB STREAMS

"I'm looking at it right now, ma'am," the commander qualified, his eyeballs super-glued to the 720p resolution video playback displayed on a miniature computing tablet.

"So you know where he is, then?" Maya anticipated, her vocal chords skipping a semi-tone as she sought for more answers.

Clayton Bommarito knew. He knew exactly what the footage indicated. His missing suspect was hardly missing at all; it appeared as if he was more like a harboured fugitive slipping and sliding beneath a hidden radar, up to no-good alongside a brotherhood of contemptible super-villains.

"I believe I may know how to locate him," the commander intimated, considering the GPS-tracking dog leash planted around Chuckie's chubby neckline.

Bommarito fiddled with a box of *Krispy Kreme*'s – six perfectly glazed donuts lined up in two rows of three – as the sweet treat became a necessary fuel, a sugary stimulant towards the finish line.

"And from the evidence on display in this video, I'd say your man has been up to no good, Miss Ververs."

"What do you mean?"

"You see that overweight redhead and that almost-Asian looking fella standing on either side of him at the thirty-six second mark?"

Maya used her finger to drag the dial on the digital timeline to Bommarito's suggested timestamp.

"I see them?"

"Let's just say that our man Jon *probably* should've found himself better company during his stay."

Maya didn't understand, nor did she care. She just wanted to find him.

Bommarito offered a vague explanation as he rummaged through a garbage can of paperwork and documentation. Amidst the *Excel* spread sheets and insipid *Word* documents, it was an *Adobe Photoshop* printout that emerged as the unmistakable rainbow in an otherwise black and white skyline.

This was a detective's dream, the 'aha moment' he had long been waiting for. Everything now made sense; each name had a face and each puzzle piece perfectly aligned with the next as the finished jigsaw began to blossom in both his mind and on his evidence corkboard.

All that was left was for Clayton Bommarito and his squadron of LAPD officers to accept an invitation to what was certain to be the wildest party in all of California.

50
THREE GRACES

The perfect work of art was considered a subjective interpretation of a body of cultivated and poetic expression. But Jonny's definition for fine exemplariness was far broader.

The only thing that makes it possible to regard this world we live in without disgust is the beauty that now and then, men create out of the chaos. And the pictures they paint as they rise from the burning flames are the richest kind of beauty.

The perfect kind of art.

The preparation and execution was always the same: wooden triangles were pegged in the corners so the picture could be tapped tighter when the canvas loosened its grip. Next, a canvas – linen, muslin and even sometimes a panel – occupied its space where the gesso – a primary white coat – was applied. And finally, a layer of under paint in a pastel was dabbed to build a rudimentary foundation before the secrets could be unleashed.

The paint.

Swished around, roughly, gently, layer on layer, thick or thin and not more than a quarter of an inch – ever. An overshooting of the allotted quarter of an inch threshold left open a damaging door of unpredictability and risk. A brush hair could be left embedded, colours had a tendency to mix over one another, tones could filter through and weaves of linen could expose.

Upon completion, varnish would swab over the entire illustration, galvanising the piece in a glitter of artistic perfection before being left to set.

Jonny repeated the strict formula – supplemented by the looping, smoky tones of an enchanting jazz record on his *Chateau*-supplied record player – over and over until a cohesive, thematic and expansive core of wondrous colour and expression was achieved.

On and on his fingers stroked as they continued over a countryside coloured out in greens and browns and over roads and rivers, winding through an eccentric landscape like a curled and reflective ribbon wrapped around a forbidden birthday present. Jonny's paintings offered a little mystery, a drop of imprecision and a splotch of wild fantasy. The ambiguity of his works would ensure that no admirer, young or old, would ever bore when in its presence.

Jonny swiped his smartphone from a nearby dresser and dialled a number under the 'recently called' listing.

"Hey, Chuckie, can you hear me?" he prompted, responding to a hazy mumble ruffling on the line's opposite end. "I'm done, man, everything's complete."

The line dripped in static as Chuckie fought over the background noise of his demanding fast food customers.

"Alright, holmes, I heard you already, you don't want no mustard on your hotdog, I get it, you don't have to tell me three times," Chuckie – the paradigm of customer service excellence – murmured to a disgruntled diner, his mouth an arm's length away from the phone's microphone. "Sorry Jonny, what kind of cock-juggling thunder-cunt doesn't want mustard on his hotdog? Fucking foreigners... No offense."

None taken, my fellow American.

"I take it you're at work then?"

"Nah, I'm volunteering at a fucking hotdog stand at a local youth softball tournament," he scorned "Of course I'm at work."

With each brush stroke, Jonny's art had offered a sedating effect that would last for hours – and not even Chuckie's insolence could distract him from his mediative state.

"Anyway, listen man, I finished my batch for Tokyo's exhibition – can you give him a call and let him know that I'm ready to set up everything at his place?"

"What do they look like?" Chuckie pestered, avoiding the question in its entirety. "I hope you haven't just dumped a bucket of paint on a big-ass piece of paper and called it 'art' 'cause I've seen someone try and pull that off on this TV show called *Work of Art* on *Bravo* and that boy got booed off the whole damn set."

"When in the hell did you ever watch *Work of Art*?" Jonny asked, certain there was another explanation in waiting.

"Man, I don't fucking know," he scoffed. "So I changed the channel when Chuckie Señor walked in on me watching porn one day… whatever, man, I still saw it, okay."

Now that sounds more like it.

51

LOVE & THE UNIVERSAL ATM

i couldnt stop. i really couldnt.

It had become an addiction; like I was a fucking heroin addict and my vein was a coveting paint bucket of blood and boil.

I kept doing it, time and time again. I'd spend a dollar, I'd withdraw two. I'd splurge three and then transfer four. I know I told you before, but it really had become a never-ending Groundhog Day and I relished rolling in the money-covered mud.

The Nations of Jefferson American Bank had made it feel so easy, so accessible. And at times, I grappled with the idea that this was all a twisted episode of *Prank'd* and at any moment, Ashton Kutcher would pounce from behind a bush and squirt me with a *Super Soaker*.

God only knows how much I would have spent. Well, God and, eventually, the bank. But aren't they the same thing half the time?

If money is the root of all evil, then why do they ask for it in church?

If capitalism is religion, then are banks churches? If bankers are priests, is wealth heaven? If rich people are saints, poor people sinners and commodities a blessing, is God just another term for money?

There's no way to deny it; I was a sinner. But I was a *wealthy* sinner in a present heaven whose fetish for the boundless wings of an ATM and a credit card warped me into a man I never thought I could become.

A man my woman could *never* love.

I loved Maya with every inch of my soul; I still do. The thing about love is that at times, it's a universal fucking migraine, a bright stain on a painted vision, blotting out all rhyme and reason. Love is something we have and forget, something we cherish and then discard like a movie ticket or a childhood trophy.

And that's the problem.

the language of love may be universal, but its not one of the options on an automated teller machine.

52
THE P-ART-Y!

"Step right up, don't be shy, and come inside for the wildest ride!"

It was as if Chuckie Hooper Junior – the son of a burger magnate whose very name resembled in irony, that of a *Burger King* 'Whopper Junior' – had been rehearsing for an acrobatic circus carnival, his work experience as a human billboard at Chuckie's Diner paying dividends in a forum that emboldened him as a grand commander and not a spoilt punk.

"Thank you ladies, and now can you show me your PLiNKER geo-check-in?" Chuckie asked as he swiped a printed flyer from the broads and tipped his index finger atop a sprinkle of dried neon paint.

The beguiling blonde and her buddy – reminiscent of a pair of exuberant *Playboy* bunnies found on the DVR of a Hugh Hefner home video – flashed their illuminated smartphone screens at the tattooed redhead, blinding his eyes with the floodlighted radiance of a Gotham City Police Department bat-signal.

"Shit, ladies, turn your damn brightness down before you head in – didn't you get the memo that this is a *private* party? Keep it *dark* and *seductive*, alright!" he said, his reflexes forcing him to blink his eyes in a forceful twitch.

"You girls got a mask each from the other night, right?" Chuckie asked.

"Isn't the flyer enough?" the bunny replied, tickling the saliva below her tongue.

"Why, of course it's enough, honey," Chuckie professed, a dumb lab-rat vulnerable to any suggestive discourse. "I just want to make sure you gals have everything you need to enjoy the night like the rest of us is all."

Chuckie reached for a pair of Rich Uncle Pennybags-inspired PVC masks from a storage display case and tucked them neatly within the woman's cleavage.

"But hold up for a quick minute," he uttered, his right arm outstretched. "Since you flashed your phones and damn near burnt my eyes out, if you guys still want to get in, I'll need you to flash something else for me. You know, as a very spiritual gesture of healing."

Chuckie rubbed his eyelids with the ends of his knuckles, only aggravating the damage further.

The *Playboy* impersonators stared at one another in a moment of telepathic cognizance before synchronously dropping at the cleavage of their low-cut garments to expose their perfectly annular breasts.

"Was that good enough for you?" whispered the little minx, her wing-woman squeezing her behind in a moment of provocative commendation.

Chuckie – still stupefied by the frequency of female genitalia he had been privy to in recent weeks – rubbed at the eyeballs in a 'real-or-make-believe' moment of magnificence.

"*Now* it's becoming a party," he shouted as he ushered them through a walkway enclosed by a red velvet rope.

Chuckie – standing at a fourteen-foot wide pivot door and flanked by glass on either of its sides – was guarded by a contingent of security personnel whose selective work attire disguised them amongst the palace's colosseum of handcrafted demi-god sculptures.

Tokyo's glass house in Palisades – the kind that rapper Childish Gambino dreamt about in his record *Sweatpants* – was a practical hub for misbehaviour and *Mad Hatter* madness. Even with the van Wolfswinkel pet giraffe safely behind its fencing, a palatial property filled with party people made for an unforgettable evening.

"Chuckie!" came a cry inside the velvet rope. "Get in here, I need your help for a second."

Chuckie – having collated an assembly of invitational flyers like a movie theatre ticket taker – delegated his duties to a Tokyo-recruited assistant before heading inside the palace.

"Listen," Jonny began, tugging Chuckie on the shoulder as they passed by a descending wine cellar and wet bar. "I need you to do me a favour."

Chuckie's eyes widened.

"Anything, holmes, what's up?"

"I need you to go to the third bedroom on the right at the end of this hall down here," he conveyed, gesturing directions like a traffic controller on Hollywood Boulevard. "Under the bed you'll find a big blue box with a paint palette inside. It's not very heavy so grab it and bring it out back for me."

Chuckie stared down the hallway as if it were an infinite abyss of no return, a sponging black-holed labyrinth of hidden secrets and mystical games that only Jonny knew how to play.

"Seriously? And what do you want me to do with it? Walking around like I'm a fucking Scandinavian *Smurf* isn't really going to bode well for my prospects of getting laid tonight, you know?"

Not that Chuckie knew it, but his choice of simile hinted at a prophetic and pretty pertinent double entendre. Besides being the name for a colony of blue-coloured, mushroom-inhabiting creatures, a 'smurf' was *also* known colloquially as both a money launderer and an evasive criminal that deposited, transferred and spent illegally acquired money.

"I can assure you, Chuckie, if, by some miraculous injustice of humanity you *don't* get laid, that box is *not* going to be the reason why," he taunted. "Listen, I promise it won't be long; and when the time is right, open the fucking thing like a jack-in-the-box and make sure *everyone* can see the palette inside."

"And how, monsieur, will I know when the time is right?"

"Just watch for my cue."

Jonny knocked Chuckie across his backbone as he paced through Tokyo's palace and towards the opaqued doors of the outdoor garden.

An island of glass, water, fire and light floating against the Californian sky, the spectacularly luxurious eleven-thousand square foot mansion made for the quintessential blend of romance, sophistication and mischief. Each room was a jewel box, an individually conceived, precisely functional and dramatic sensory experience with its own depth of architecture.

The scene had been purposefully arranged, the aftermath of a *Marmont* massacre with a deliberate instruction. Every third or fourth guest strapped the infamous *Monopoly* man mask around his or her gloating cranium, a picturesque paradigm of social and financial control softened by its carnival-like setting.

"How's everyone doing tonight?" Jonny asked a group of strangers standing by a marbled counter as he tugged on his chequered navy bow tie and slipped his hand into the right pocket of his chino pants.

"We're doing good, Jonny, how about you, baby?" came the answer from the first respondent, a woman in a Rich Uncle Pennybags mask and a stripe of pink in her silky ponytail.

That voice. I know her.

The woman dripped the PVC from her face to reveal her behind-the-mask identity.

"I was wondering if you were coming, Yasmine," Jonny smirked like a lustful ex-lover.

"You know I wasn't going to miss this, honey. We can't wait to see what you've got to show us."

Just like I couldn't wait to see what you had to show me.

Yasmine guided her index finger as she pointed to a cluster of meticulously aligned easels concealed by drips of black cloth.

"What can I say? Expect surprises," he winked.

The platonic twosome had forged a raggedy history as the painter from Pennsylvania went from dodging wanton bullets to succumbing to succubus-camouflaged lap dances.

Jonny sauntered through the open-plan living area, stepping into the state-of-the-art kitchen with its Italian lacquered cabinetry and integrated *Miele* appliances.

"Can we get some cheese platters brought out to the guests outside?" Jonny asked the chef, staring intensely at his *Ratatouille* French moustache.

"Certainly, sir."

Jonny was in control. It was not his house, but it certainly felt like his home.

His night.

His audience.

From the main foyer, Jonny jumped left and climbed a hidden chain of cantilevered floating steps that lead to the building's third floor. With each stride, the aperture between each step offered a gravity-defying sense of 'walking on air', only validating Jonny's newfound immortality.

Tokyo's third floor was occupied almost entirely by the master bedroom while a glassed fireplace encircled a stunning six-person hot tub on the balcony.

"I need another drink!" came the cry from a splashing young female, gyrating in the hot water as she tugged on the bathers of her soon-to-be one-night stand.

"C'mon, baby, I got all the stiff juice you need way down here," her not-so-perfect-match cajoled, his swimming trunks nothing more than a throwaway pair of in-ring boxers.

"You having a good time, Yogi, right?" Jonny chuffed as the boxer's squad engaged in an underwater re-enactment of their aviation adventure.

"Jonny, you are the motherfucking man!" he lauded, the woman's hands now acting as an electric centrifugal juicer beneath the blurry veil of the dark Jacuzzi water. "Hey ladies, listen up: this cat right here is the only light-skinned nigga I know who can rock this game *like* a black man, without the *oppression* of a black man!"

Oppression; now there's a subjective term.

Pacific Palisades, with Brentwood to its east and Malibu and Topanga to its west was the home of a cohort of celebrities from Ben Affleck and Arnold Schwarzenegger to Kobe Bryant and Kate Hudson. And while for most residents, neighbourhood privacy was often paramount, the configuration of the cliff faces meant that from Tokyo's third floor, sandy bunkers and perfectly mowed fairways could be seen of Sugar Ray Leonard's backyard golf course.

"No way!" Jonny shrieked as Tokyo – his thigh leaning against the hot tub as he gossiped and grinded with Team Yogi and his posse of pussy – briefed him on the who's-who of the neighbourhood. "Sugar Ray Leonard! Sugar Ray Leonard! I used to watch him and the rest of 'The Fabulous Four' beat the living shit out of each other on old videotapes when I was growing up!"

"So what you thinking then, my ninja? You want me to invite him over to see your stuff then?"

Jonny's nerves tightened at the thought of one of his idols relishing in *his* body of work.

"Maybe at the next one," he said sharply, his eyelid turning lazier with each shrewd wink.

The school of hot tub fish roared in endorsement, clinking their crystal with the clanking of a falling chandelier.

Jonny's rendezvous' with the guests of Tokyo's mansion continued as he scurried back down the stairs of heaven and towards the outdoor gardens.

The gardens boasted a jaw-dropping moat water feature that flowed like silk lace from the pool and encircled the palace in a curvy horseshoe. A lining of glass-encased fire pits criss-crossed the boundaries of the water feature, culminating in an exotic and Godly storm of fire and water.

Jonny lifted a glass of champagne from the silver tray of a passing waiter as he stretched his eyes and panned from side to side at the beautiful madness he had created.

"Hell of a fucking party, Jonny Cash," saluted a guest with a perfectly styled pomade and a twinset of licentious females wrapped around each arm.

Jonny raised his glass and lifted his head as a funnel of champagne burnt the inside of his throat. As he sponged his lip, a couple embracing beneath one of Tokyo's stone statues stole his undivided attention. The hazel-eyed girl in red fidgeted with her white gold necklace as her lover worshiped both her and her jewellery in all their sparkling wonderment.

Jonny, observing intensely from the steps of the patio, stumbled with disquietude as echoes of a Saturday night in Allentown ping-ponged around his aching heart.

And then, he began to hear voices.

"If I don't get to tell you later, I had a really good time tonight."

The moment and the memory – the nuances of her voice, the polish of her touch – were unmistakable. He saw it so vividly, as if his head had jarred and unlocked like a Jedi droid and began to project home-video visuals in a candid hologram. He watched as he clasped the ends of a sparkling jewel around her neck in an extravagant *Pretty Woman*-inspired role-play.

Then he watched as she smiled and melted the ice in his heart.

Snap the fuck out of it.

Jonny rushed his head back, watching as a tiny drop swam from the bottom of the glass and towards his tongue in an action-sequence-like slow motion.

I need another drink.

"Tokyo!" he cried, funnelling his hand in a human loudspeaker as his patron ditched the convivial hot tub and made his way to the ground floor.

"What's up, my ninja?" he barked, tiptoeing down the divine royalty of the palace's floating steps as he gripped a half-empty bottle of *Ketel One Vodka* in his right hand. "You ready to do this now?"

Jonny peered through the transparency of the manor's frame, counting each cloth-cloaked easel in ascending order.

"Yeah," he affirmed, channelling the energies of a Vietnamese marvel. "Let's do this; round up the troops and get everybody inside."

Jonny idled by the pit flames as he heaved, the signs of bashful butterflies and sheepish stage fright consuming him before the official curtain raise. He had been feigning a counterfeit persona for so long that he had almost entirely forgotten about the timorous house painter from Pennsylvania.

He had become the antithesis of the Jonathan Jinks his *Facebook* page demonstrated.

He had become *Jonny.*

He had become *Jonny Cash.*

The living area slowly began to fill like a raging colony of ants in a congested pavement cavity. The in-house DJ lifted the needle on a scorching trap-step break beat as Tokyo stretched towards a wireless microphone.

"Yo! For those that didn't hear me, let's move you party animals inside – it's time for the viewing!"

Had it not been for Tokyo's ebullient elocution, he might as well have been a funeral director at a visitation service, ushering family members of the deceased into a room full of something morose.

Most of the event's invitees knew not what the 'art' in 'P-art-Y!' constituted while the rest perceived Jonny Cash's showcase as a necessary evil on the path of party-crazy enlightenment.

"Silence!" Chuckie roared, his belly flopping around as he secured Jonny's blue box beneath his armpits.

The audience shuffled in a squishy shoulder-to-shoulder as a handful of lubricious male guests seized the opportunity to massage their groins against a group of booties. The sexual tension conjoined as a sea of horny DNA filled the glass cube with the scent of sweat and sperm.

Jonny, stagnating at the rear of the room, discerned that the growing libido might have materialised in an indiscriminate orgy if not for the untimely disruption of his display.

Tokyo and Chuckie stood like the Queen's Guard at an embryonic easel marker as ribaldry chatter kept the not-so patient audience occupied.

"Yo!" Tokyo bellowed. "Didn't y'all hear the man? Let's go people, it's time to celebrate what we all came here for."

Tokyo's entitled guests had overlooked the legislative as the effects of a night of substance abuse caused a collective amnesia over who was actually in command.

A hush arose, the swarming body of invitees blinking at the Oriental half-caste and his redheaded buddy like a crowd of Minions in *Despicable Me.*

"Alright," he praised, content. "First of all, I want to thank everyone for coming out to my Palisades palace tonight to party with me and my crew!"

The crowd roared in delight, applauding in a stormy thunderclap.

"But you know, for the first time in a long time, tonight isn't about *me,* and it's not about PLiNKER," he declared hollowly. "See, y'all have been with me since you linked up with your first chick or your first man."

The capabilities of Tokyo's PLiNKER mobile app were blatantly defined, albeit, misunderstood by most of the world's media and social justice groups: it was an online dating platform on cocaine in the back bathroom of a taboo swingers club. Its operation, however, was far more orthodox: A 'PLiNKER Room' was created for every nightclub and every localised party on the planet. And once joined to, the app's users were at liberty to browse, evaluate and communicate with one another through the emboldening luxury of their smartphone. A 'PLiNKed' couple might have only been standing feet apart, but the risk of a humiliating abash was abolished as the application offered even the most timid the freedom to escape their inhibitions.

"*Or* your first chick *and* your first man... at the same time; am I right, ladies?"

Howls of wolf-whistles invaded the room offering a two-toned 'whip-woo' as the women giggled and the men salivated at the discovery of an ancillary usage.

"But listen, y'all, in all seriousness, tonight is about a dude with a big dream and an even bigger talent," Tokyo introduced, galvanising Jonny and his unexceptional resume. "It's about a dude who was born and raised in the Chocolate Capital of the United States but ditched the cold for the bright lights of Cali' to create his own marvellous motherfucking factory of colour."

Jonny squeezed his ears, marking his own juxtapositions as Tokyo painted an exaggerated synopsis of his very own episode of *This Is Your Life*. And while the outcomes were homogenous, Jonny's version of the narrative was tainted with enough guilt and dishonesty that would have made a Lance Armstrong documentary appear meritorious.

"It's about a ninja who ditched cheesesteaks and scrapple for champagne and caviar; who ditched the monotony of the Amish for the luxury of naked women, bottles of vodka and a handful of hundred-dollar bills!"

The audience exploded as if they too, were entirely empathic to Jonny's sacrificial change of scenery.

If only they knew what I had to do to get here.

What I've lost for what I've gained.

What I've had to trade.

"So ladies, gentlemen, and fuckers of all ages," Tokyo harped as he spread his wings and magnetised the crowd. "Without further adieu, I present to you..."

The suspense bubbled with the rumble of a silent drumroll, Jonny's heart providing the speedy rhythm as he shook his fingers and wiped a bead of sweat from his forehead.

This was the inorganic birth of everything Jonny had ever dreamed of: the attention, the affection, the gusto, the fortune, the art. And although his creative appetite was whet with delight, this synthesis was the unmediated by-product of a greater sacrifice.

The sacrifice of a divine obligation.

The sacrifice of wicked sins.

You see, that's thing about dishonesty and bullshit; when you've mastered the art of feeling lonely in a room full of people who fucking adore you, that's when you know...

"My ninja: Jonny... Mother... Fucking... Cash!"

53

CHOCOLATE RIVER OF CHAOS

The glassed cube vibrated with the thunder of a thousand handclaps as Jonny peddled his weighty legs towards the improvised stage. Unfamiliar faces beamed at him with intoxicated glee while his shoulders tensed, bracing the penetration of a band of incoming backwhacks.

"Fuck yeah, Jonny!"

"We love you, Jonny!"

Screams of approbation were cannonballing from every direction as Jonny slithered his way through the human maze.

"I'll show you my art if you show me yours," a blonde vixen proposed as she dropped the top of her dress, revealing nothing more than a quarter-inch of her nipple.

The moment was hypnotic and engulfing. Jonny was the star of the show; a show he never would have watched in his Tudor-style Pennsylvanian home.

It was a show about a man suffering from emotional oppression. A man whose very existence hinged on the precipice of his next unfulfilling pay check. It was about a man who had hit the jackpot, battled relentlessly with a changing morality and exchanged his devilish dollars in an ungodly sacrifice.

It was about a man whose story, picturesque as it was agog, was still very much untold.

This was the story of Jonny Cash: the unvirtuous virtuoso.

"Come on Jonny, let's get it boy!" Chuckie animated from beside the first easel as he reached out to drag him through the crowd like a security guard to an ambushed rock star.

"Alright, alright," he tittered, twinkling through a two-shade lens of both discomfiture and gratification. "Thanks everyone."

A verbal rumbling began to build, relatively inaudible in the beginning until a clear syllabic diction could be discerned.

"Jonny! Jonny! Jonny! Jonny!"

The united chant felt more like an unorthodox incantation, although it was the chanters and not Jonny himself who had become spellbound.

"Jonny! Jonny! Jonny! Jonny!"

The rallying continued as Tokyo's palace transformed into the bleachers of Old Trafford.

"Thank you, thank you," he quavered, wiping his red face.

What is going on? Why the hell am I feeling numb?

"First of all," Jonny began. "I have to reiterate what Tokyo said: I want to thank you all for coming out to The P-art-Y! and for rocking with me tonight. And thank *you*, Tokyo, for this glassed paradise that I'm sure I *still* wouldn't have been able to afford even if I owned the fucking stock exchange."

Jonny reached out and shook Tokyo's microscopic hands.

"You know, my namesake – the Jonny Cash most of the world had already heard of – he once said that success is having to worry about every damn thing in the world... except for money," he continued, his palm practically suctioning in moisture against the microphone's canister. "So you've got no worries then, right, you successful son-of-a-bitch?"

The crowd recharged before splattering another round of bulleting cheers.

"No, but seriously, I've been dreaming about a day just like this my whole life."

Jonny's brain ricocheted in a rewound flashback, summarising his timeline from Pennsylvania to California in a clouded nanosecond.

"And let me tell y'all, it's been a long road. You see, a long time ago I was handed the keys to a castle I never wanted to live in so that I could do a job that I never wanted to do. And ever since that day, I've tried to do things the way *I've* wanted to do them."

Jonny sensed a growing preoccupation as he realised it was time to cut the ethical connotations from his speech.

"And believe me when I tell y'all that I've had my fair share of luck along the way – I mean, you don't end up *here* with all these great fucking people around you because you're some wannabe painter from Pennsylvania."

Jonny's unlikely destiny, whether serendipitous or misfortunate, was still a matter of great debate. He had become a confidential tycoon, a fortuitous modern-day pirate, amassing all the luxuries and professional accolades that everyone from Silicon Valley's finest tech-gurus to Hollywood's most glamorous elite would have envied.

And yet he was hidden, protecting a secret nearly three-thousand miles west of those who deserved to share in his harrowing truth.

"You end up here with a lot of fortune," Jonny revealed as he seesawed his selective wording in a double entendre. "And a fuck-load of help so again, I want to thank these two dudes to the right of me – Tokyo van Wolfswinkel and Chuckie Hooper Junior – for giving me the golden paintbrush that has allowed me to paint my perfect masterpiece here with you all tonight."

The crowd clamoured in slurs of approval for the raging half-blood and his red-bellied buddy.

Chuckie played 'little drummer boy' on the blue box gripped between his murky hands as he gestured a cue in Jonny's direction.

"You know when I was a kid I didn't have a plan. All I had was art. Art and no end game. And usually when you start out like that, it really means you have no fucking idea what you are doing. And really, you know what? None of us still have any fucking idea what we're doing to this day – we're all just winging it," Jonny implied, his voice bouncing in a dynamic of bass and treble tones. "I mean, you think Obama had a plan when he shoved his boxers in the bottom drawer of the President's Bedroom for the first time? No fucking way! And that's the beauty of it. People who know what they're doing, they understand the rules. They're aware of the boundaries. They know what's possible, what's impossible. They don't follow the adventure because their reality is less precarious."

Jonny's monologue resonated deeply with his legion of minions. Jonny, Tokyo, Chuckie and the hundreds of debauchees occupying Tokyo's glassed mansion shared in a homogenous commonality; they were victims of vapid, social oppression, carrying out lives that were as foreign to them as the floorboards beneath their *Loubotin*'s.

They were stripped, robbed of their First Amendment rights and enslaved in a world of plight and textbook routine. And while their flair and zeal eclipsed that of the others around them, the lay of the land pillaged them of their only remaining desire.

Freedom.

"The one thing that nobody else in this fucking universe has, is you," he commanded, pointing his finger outwards like a conquering hero to no one in particular. "You, me, us. Our voice, our mind, our vision, our story."

It was as if he had the command of three hundred obeying Spartans and he was the bloody King Leonidas, ready to lead the charge against the invading army of normalcy and trite.

"So this collection right here," he waved, drawing an imaginary perimeter around the aisle of cloaked canvas portraits by his side. "This collection was created so that we can write, we can draw, we can build, we can play, we can dance and we can live life the fucking way only we know we can because the old rules? They no longer exist. There's a set of new rules now and nobody knows what they are so let's make them up as we go and conquer the fucking world!"

Almost as if it were a rehearsed segment of Jonny's wild circus of imagination, a contingent of raunchy young women – one per painting – in a rainbow-coloured line of lingerie tugged at the top of the silk cloth from behind each easel.

Each cloth fell to the floor in near-perfect symmetry, revealing a showcase of remarkable artistry behind it.

In some comparable way, the painted canvas' that sat naked in front of hundreds of watchful eyes were the true embodiments of Jonny's soul. His body of work was no longer hidden, disguised by a mask that did little to truly represent it. Each paint-coated canvas had digested itself, shedding its cloaked cocoon as it emerged liberated and graceful from its radical metamorphosis.

The art was a wondrous marvel, a natural denotation of beauty and ingenuity. But for Jonny, with such enchanting splendour came a treacherous toxicity.

Jonny's biotic mask was a picture of poison. And while such a threat was unprecedented amongst others who shared in his irreproachable history, even the butterfly family – in all its organic beauty – was responsible for the evolution of a noxious offspring.

"Woohoo, Jonny!" the crowd screamed and squealed as a stream of noisy whistles plummeted down on him.

While most paintings in *European* tradition depicted a beguiling portrayal of the masks that humanity used to disguise and conceal, Jonny's take on a transcendent and modern art rejected all of that. His subject matter documented the adventures of the mask with the unfeigned person behind it.

It was the perfect storm of contradistinction.

And it was nothing less than a true expression of undying freedom.

The eruption rivalled the pandemonium at the *Bar Marmont*, the palace's glassed walls encouraging a noise scattering as the soundwaves reflected and contained themselves off of its diagonal surfaces.

Jonny clenched his fist, transforming it into a human-hammer as he struck at the core of the blue box in Chuckie's hands. It was as if he were engaging in a real-world game of Whac-A-Mole, his thunderous strike tearing a rip-mark down the centre of the flaccid carton to reveal a pigmented compound that was as astonishing as it was taboo.

Even in a *Playboy*-inspired mansion like Tokyo's – which had been privy to everything from mass orgies to porn star fundraiser campaigns – Jonny's box of illicit Pandora-like possessions was a first.

"Ugh, Jonny?" Chuckie wobbled as he stared down at the devilry between his fingers.

Jonny offered a Machiavellian smirk.

Stay focused. Don't fuck this up. This is your chance.

Undamaged inside the broken blue box rested a traditional wooden palette, polished in high gloss as it reflected off a string of prancing light rays. The palette was indented with five wells, sculptured specifically to store and mix a wash of differing paint colours. But in the context of Jonny's grand plan, these conventional mixing wells were being used for a far more indecorous purpose.

"Is that what I think it is?" Chuckie staggered.

Each palette well was loaded with its own plastic seal bag filled with fine powder, each dyed in a unique pigment – blue, red, yellow, green, orange and white. From a distance – and under the heavy influence of every illicit matter man had created – the powder substituted as an indistinguishable substance to the solid film lubricants that ordinarily occupied each well.

"Food-coloured fucking cocaine? Are you fucking bananas, holmes?"

Chuckie wasn't sure if he was more startled by the substance itself or the notion that he had been lugging around the stimulant like a drug-trafficking roadie.

"Trust me," Jonny whispered, resting his palm on Chuckie's shoulders as he lifted the finely rounded wood from the boxed enclosure and raised it in the air with a single hand.

The food-dyed cocaine was The P-art-Y!'s elixir, a rambunctious trip into the unexplored, presented on a pertinent artist's palette.

"Tonight," Jonny hurrahed, the palette soaring over his shoulders like a championship trophy. "We're going to do exactly what we all came here to do – we're about to art… And motherfucking party!"

The crowd roared, hoisting their hands towards the heavens while a threesome engaged in foreplay somewhere amongst the horde.

Jonny pulled the palette down from its man-made pedestal and removed each plastic sealed bag one at a time before cannonballing them high in the sky.

The coloured-coke rocketed like rounds from an automatic firearm as they created an atmospheric layer of multi-balled rainbows.

Oo's and ah's filtered through the mindless chatter as the mob, with their outstretched arms, reached for the sealed bags as if they were catching falling t-shirt parachutes at a sporting event.

"Let's fucking go!" Jonny charged, fist-pumping the air as he gesticulated a 'spin-another-record' command towards the DJ booth.

"You are a bad motherfucker, my ninja," Tokyo saluted. "And to think once upon a time I thought you were just some loser kid with a lot of luck and an ego bigger than my goddamn giraffe's cock."

"That's... nice," Jonny joked in an expression of gratitude. "Thank you, man. I couldn't have done this without you."

Tokyo's white teeth fanged like Mufasa's diabolical brother as his mouth salivated at the reaping rewards the success of The P-art-Y! had to offer his shrinking pockets.

As the partners congratulated one another, Tokyo looked on towards a fuddled Chuckie, expectant of a third incoming high-five.

"But... but... the cocaine... It's... coloured?" he stuttered, struggling to qualify the legitimacy of sky-falling, varicoloured narcotics. "How the fuck did you even do that?"

Jonny was an artist's artist, the kind that picturesquely expressed his feelings, thoughts, imaginations and dreams in a singular form of self-expression. And while most of the aesthetics were reserved for his brush and paint board, Jonny had unearthed a rare, intriguing and differing kind of fine white canvas for which to paint.

"Food dye," he delineated.

"Like, as in, 'I'm going to colour my cupcakes pink for my niece's third birthday party with this 'not-suitable-for-children' bottle of food dye' kind of food dye?" Chuckie clucked in a gobbling mouthful.

"Just like that, Chuckie," Jonny reasserted as he spotted a quartet of sultry broads siphoning particles of yellow and red powder through their nostrils. "It's tinted, not flavoured. But for the hell of it, make sure you tell people that they're getting everything from strawberry to banana-flavoured blow. They won't know the difference, anyway."

"The orange one, it kind of looks like crushed up baby aspirin," Chuckie indicated, outstretching his index finger towards the plastic-packed grain.

"Yeah, well we won't be telling them that," Tokyo intervened.

"Can you tell me what flavour the orange one is?" Jonny asked, signalling towards his rose-redheaded pal.

"Ugh, 'orange'?"

It seemed like the obvious answer.

"'Bad spray tan' flavour, ideal for mostly every women on a Californian beach at sunset," he jested. "I'm fucking with you, of course it's orange-flavoured. Now get out there and turn this thing into a madhouse for me!"

Without intervention, Tokyo's Palisades paradise was already drifting down Willy Wonka's chocolate river of no return. A plethora of colour brightened the darkness in the forms of powder particles and paint as a queue developed, Jonny's semi-nude minions ushering curious guests through a makeshift walkway used to showcase his paintings like a narrowed and far less ornate Salle 13 at the Louvre.

Tokyo's visitors began to flock back to the gardens and infinity pool, setting up extemporary cocaine-inhaling benches on everything from the tiled borders of the outdoor fire pits to the glassed indoor cabinetries.

It was an anarchic, three-ringed circus of depravity and hedonistic perversion, only seen and never censored in a Seth Rogen blockbuster.

Jonny observed from up high. The marvellous mess of chaos and colour before him was his bittersweet creation.

His temporary salvation.

His guilty ecstasy.

But like all acts fuelled by unanswerable sin, a chasing consequence was never too far behind, especially for a Pennsylvanian painter who was slowly flagging.

Bang! Thud!

Cries broke from the foyer as the fourteen-foot wide pivot door slammed against its glassed enclosure.

"LAPD, nobody move!"

54

THE CASE OF CLAYTON

The crowded room ducked in unison. The commotion inside the glassed palace forced Tokyo's guests – who had been frolicking and snorting around the gardens – to return to the scene of Jonny's artsy sermon.

"Everyone, stash your shit!" Chuckie squealed through a forest of bewildered panic and orgasmic delight.

"I said 'nobody move'!" Commander Clayton Bommarito terrorised, training his weapon like a western cowboy as Chuckie ditched a clear resealable bag of orange powder beneath an artificial pot plant.

The officers stormed the living area one by one, carrying out their tactical operation with precise meticulousness.

"Tokyo van Wolfswinkel!" Bommarito summoned, his subordinates switching on the ceiling lights before yanking the power chord from the loudspeaker system. "Where the fuck is Tokyo?"

A silence surfaced, the only audible hisses coming from the faint sonic tremors of Sugar Ray Leonard's neighbouring hi fi system.

"Tokyo van-fucking-Wolfswinkel!?" the commander thundered once more, his towering stature bowing over the palace's guests like a scolding disciplinarian.

"Yo!" Tokyo answered, a little tongue-tied as he crept forward, ready to preserve his reputation.

"You are under arrest for multiple counts of disorderly conduct, disturbing the peace in a public space, possession of illicit substances and – my favourite of the lot – conspiracy to commit tax fraud," Bommarito apprised as he signalled for his subordinates to chain his detainee in metallic handcuffs.

Tokyo burst in a round of expletives as his guests gasped in a hysterical panic.

"Tax fraud!?" Jonny cried, nonplussed.

"What the hell is the meaning of this, Commander?" Chuckie intervened as a junior officer prevented him from encroaching.

"Quiet, Hooper, or you're next," Bommarito warned the feisty food chain heir as he made clear that their prior engagements had not been forgotten. "Tokyo van Wolfswinkel, you have the right to remain silent, anything you say or do can be used against you in a court of law…"

Bommarito invoked the full familiar litany as Jonny watched in horror.

"Ain't you ever heard of a warrant, my ninja?" Tokyo barked as he fought an inner-urge to resist apprehension. "A man's home is his castle… *literally.*"

Bommarito pulled a piece of paper from a document folder that was dated and signed in black marker by the judge of the municipal court.

"You know I'm a litigious son of a bitch, right?" Tokyo forewarned, his spine shivering at the chill of the metallic clamps as they tightened and toughened around his wrists.

"Perfect," Bommarito goaded. "I'm just a son of a bitch."

Bommarito offered a two-fingered salute as he directed his officers to remove their suspect from his homely castle.

"Now it might not look like it, but I'm getting *pretty* fucking lenient in my old age," the commander announced. "And I know a lot of shit has gone down in this place over the last couple of hours so I'll give you all one *very* quick opportunity…"

Bommarito paused to wipe a bead of sweat off his forehead.

"To get the fuck out of here and run back to wherever it is that you inglorious bastards and bast-ettes came from."

The bark was vicious and intimidating, the rumble in his baritone voice thundered and shook the ground heavier than the compulsive rhythm of a *Martin Garrix* tune in a basement nightclub. The once-rambunctious horde was reduced to the calm of a silent church congregation. They slowly ambled, two and three at a time like phantoms through the hollow hallways of a glassed purgatory, stumbling and swaying their inebriated bones through the palace's front door.

"What in the fuck; where are y'all going?" Chuckie choked, his buttocks submerged between two sofa cushions on account of the fierce restraint of an obeying officer. "Where are y'all going?"

"I can tell you where they're *not* going," Bommarito threatened. "Or I can *show you* where they're not going instead, if you feel so inclined as to join your little motherfucking ninja friend over there?"

"Oh, and ugh, Jonny… *Jon Jinks,*" Bommarito gloated, dangling Jonny's patronymic on a verbal thread as he taunted him with the intelligence behind the Pennsylvanian's true identity.

Jonny gasped as the commander paralysed him like a *Pokémon* with the 'stun spore' technique.

"That's right, what did you think? That I didn't know who you were?" he relished in invincibility. "Just letting you know that – Maya, was it? – Maya's been *looking* everywhere for you; even called my office a couple of times asking for our help."

Jonny was frozen but burning inside. He loathed hearing another man utter her name, especially a real-life man-wolf who was huffing and puffing and about to blow his multi-million dollar house to the ground.

"I'd give her a call if I were you," Bommarito recommended as if he were doing him a favour. "Otherwise your buddy's going to have himself a roommate at the jailhouse."

Bommarito rounded his troops, his wrinkly smirk imprinting its contours into Jonny's black-and-white memory as he signalled for the cavalry to advance for their undercover vehicles.

"I'll be seeing ya, kid," he taunted as he sauntered for the front door.

The emptiness was surreal, a prismatic hinterland of effervescent souls reduced to a red and brown pile of incredulous rubble.

Jonny was stunned, startled and sickened. He needed to rebuild with expedition if he were to have any hope of survival.

But Jonny was exhausted, his batteries zapped of all their vitality.

But most of all, Jonny was out of bricks.

55

A CURRENT AFFAIR

They stared at the screen as if it was 1954 and Jonny and Chuckie were test dummies to the first ever colour television set.

"Hey Jonny, did you hear about that painter who almost got arrested?" Chuckie jabbed in the blunt aftermath. "He had a *brush* with the law but I'm thinking he was probably *framed*!"

"Jesus, Chuckie, now's not the time for jokes!"

He cheated the system. He withheld money that wasn't his to keep. He's... a fraud.

... Just like me. And he had me fooled all along.

The syndicated newscast began with a stripped version of the bumper following the familiar tension-toned musical interlude that anyone with a free-to-air satellite had grown grotesquely accustomed to.

"We begin tonight's news bulletin with breaking news from the Westside of Los Angeles," the anchor announced, scuffling through documents on her desk as if she were unprepared for her umpteenth rodeo.

Oh boy, here we go.

Jonny's eyes synergised with the screen. It was like a masochistic bloodbath, too gruesome to turn away yet too spine-chilling to miss out. And for the first time since he and his bloodline were eulogised for their commitment to local philanthropy on a Pennsylvanian cable news network, Jonny was once again the subject, this time, of a more scandalous headline.

"Tokyo van Wolfswinkel, founder of the infamous mobile platform 'PLiNKER'…"

"That's *famous*, not *infamous* you uncultured swine!" Chuckie execrated, hawking his finger as he hurled a carton of verbal abuse her way.

"Shh, sit down, Chuckie," Jonny whispered as he pulled his red-haired pal by the hand and jerked his backside to the sofa.

"… Was arrested overnight at his Pacific Palisades home on multiple counts of tax fraud and disorderly conduct. For more, let's go to Michael Zamani who's standing by outside the van Wolfswinkel property."

Jonny's neck snapped as a palpable fright washed across his darkened skin.

"Go, go, go!" he ushered, breaking gravity as he heaved Chuckie headfirst and onwards down the corridor and towards the fourteen-foot wide pivot door.

"Thanks Rebecca," journalist Zamani chirped in his microphone, as he stood upright in the centre of the camera frame.

Jonny's hands wedged against his cheekbones as he leant forward and stared at the newscast's scenic background: a multi-storey glassed mansion engulfed in a spread of handcrafted demi-god sculptures and oriental greenery.

"Mr. van Wolfswinkel was arrested shortly after two o'clock this morning by a special investigations team who had been tirelessly following the whereabouts and activities of their suspect over the course of an eight-month period."

Eight months? What the fuck for? And I thought I was the one with the secrets.

"Now if you haven't been reading tech-industry magazines lately," Zamani apprised with a cheeky squiggle. "van Wolfswinkel privately sold his notorious social mobile platform 'PLiNKER' to robotics conglomerate 'Jellitech International' for a rumoured sixty million dollars including stock options earlier this year."

Sixty million? Is that all he sold it for?

"Now according to police reports, the company's acquisition was funded via a stock-for-stock exchange in an attempt to minimise the figure of Mr. van Wolfskwinkel's near term taxable gains," the reporter continued as Chuckie crawled on hands and knees towards the pivot door like a wombat in the perilous outback. "But after the acquisition, van Wolfswinkel's reckless spending and fruitless subsequent investments forced the sale of his Jellitech International stock options and, in the process, rendered the controversial start-up entrepreneur virtually insolvent."

He's fucking broke? Jonny gasped as he pulled at the loose skin of his wrinkling eyelids.

"And according to claims made this morning by the specialised task force's lead commander, van Wolfswinkel then engaged in wilful falsification and misrepresentation of the taxable difference between the cost basis of stock and the acquired stock price by the acquisition firm."

As the newscast reporter broke the lurid scoop, Chuckie rose from his knee-bent paws and hardened his posture, hiding the bulk of his belly behind the doorframe as he peered through the flanking windowpane. His eyes were bloodshot and his sight sluggish as a blurred vision conjoined the reporter, his camera crew and a contingent of satellite-equipped news vans in a distant and demonic glow.

"Chuckie!" Jonny bawled in hysteria, his eyes never deviating from the live simulcast on the television set in front of him as he waved his arms in a manic uproar. "Move your fucking head *now*, I can see you on TV!"

Courtesy of the television's high fidelity pixel pitch, Chuckie's spherical crown and dried candy red faux hawk could be seen beside Zamani's right ear as he reported the news like a giant with a midget resting atop his shoulder.

"Holy shit-balls," Chuckie panicked, knocking his funny bone against the door handle as he ducked from the sniper scope of a video camera lens.

The collision rumbled the pivot door as the sheer velocity shook and shimmered it in the background of the telecast.

Jonny dropped his hands across his face, cloaking everything except for his line of sight.

"Michael," the news anchor responded as the on-screen graphic converted to a here-and-there split screen. "What was the scene like upon Mr. van Wolfswinkel's arrest?"

"Chaotic," Zamani continued, apparently undistracted by the clamour behind him. "According to witnesses and this flyer recovered only fifty feet from the gates of the property, van Wolfswinkel was hosting a fund-raiser at the time of his arrest that appeared to have been part-gala-exhibition and part-deranged-party."

Jonny Jinks' heart sank somewhere deeper than the bottom of Lake Erie as the blood rushed from his face, squiggling in a scurried escape.

Gripped in the reporters' left hand was a rummaged and stampeded flyer with the decorative title 'The P-art-Y!' inscribed at its head point. The cameraman's wide framing skewed a number of bullet points and graphical illustrations from the flyer's design, concealing and preserving at least a portion of the event's secrets from the public telecast.

"Yo, Jonny," Chuckie shouted from the midpoint of the hall as he engaged in an espionage-inspired army crawl. "Did they just give you a shout out on live TV? Well what do you know, your plan worked out after all!"

"Shut... Up... Chuckie!" Jonny menaced, the blood bolting back into his threatening leer as he bit his tongue. "Get back here, man!"

As Chuckie shuffled across the liquor-laced flooring, Zamani continued his report from the centre of the television screen.

"I've been told from our sources here at the LAPD that a large quantity of cocaine and other illicit substances were also found here at the scene, causing further suspicion and investigation throughout the premises as the morning rolled on."

"Michael, how did police and special investigators narrow in on their lead so expeditiously?" the anchor asked, dragging out the sequence to accumulate a bracket count before the commercial break.

"Well this morning's arrest stemmed from an incident earlier this week at the popular Hollywood A-list hot spot, the *Bar Marmont* on Sunset Boulevard," Zamani revealed, carefully allocating his references to avoid legal scrutiny. "Where police say a private function got out of control, resulting in the damage of private property and injuries to multiple patrons."

"Oh, nobody was fucking injured, you pussy!" Chuckie roared swinging his fists from side to side with the hairy force of a vexed gorilla. "What, your security couldn't take a little paint-cum in the eyes? It was non-fucking-toxic, anyway, asshole!"

"For more on the conditions inside this lavish Pacific Palisades property," he reported as the camera's lens opened up the frame to a broader vantage. "I'm joined by Yasmine who attended last night's event as an exclusive invitee."

Zamani swang his microphone in front of the pink lips of a fine, tattooed and petite young woman with a stripe of pink in her ponytail and blotches of smothered mascara across her faultless cheeks.

"Holy shit!" Chuckie cursed, shooting upwards as he pointed towards the television screen. "I told you these hookers were no good, Jonny. I fucking told you!"

"She's not a fucking hooker, Chuckie," Jonny lied, yet again. "How many times do I have to tell you? Now sit down."

Zamani's calm promulgation was faltered by the stumbling presence of an awe-intimidating but beautifully powerful semi-naked woman as he jerked and mumbled through the awkwardness.

"Yasmine, could you provide a recount for our viewers on what you remember from Mr. van Wolfswinkel's event last night?"

The hooker-turned-witness paused and licked her lips as the camera lens balanced her silhouette at the edge of the frame.

"We were all a little shook when they came crashing through the front door," she narrated in a seductive, West Coast sociolinguistic as she turned and gesticulated to the entranceway of Tokyo's mansion.

"Oh man, she's going to rat on us all, Jonny," Chuckie panicked, knocking his knees together in a noticeable tremble. "What do we do, man? What do we fucking do?"

"She's not a fucking rat, Chuckie. I *know* her. She wouldn't say anything."

Yasmine segregated her response in sonic paragraphs, pausing and spacing out her sentences.

"But after the initial confusion, everything was kind-of civil; everyone grabbed their bags, coats, lipsticks and condoms and went home."

Huh?

"Ugh," Zamani stammered, referencing his notes for a responsive cue. "But the scene prior to Mr. van Wolfswinkel's arrest – all reports suggest that the police arrived to a wild party smothered in illicit substances which were said to have been recovered on arrival?"

A reporter only speaks in rhetoric when they don't have their story confirmed, Jonny realised.

"Not that I can remember," she lied as her body ink now became a cause for criminality and not irresistible swagger.

"You were in attendance at Mr. van Wolfswinkel's property behind us last night and into the early hours of this morning though, were you not, ma'am?"

A double negative – he's chasing his tail.

"I was," she answered as if the question itself was farfetched. "And I was one of the last people to leave – that's just how it was. There was nothing out of the ordinary to see, other than maybe a little traditional American police brutality towards a man of... *colour.*"

Yasmine looked deep down the camera's lens and into Jonny's soul, shielding his secret with verbal one-two punches as she slid the news company and the Los Angeles Police Department under a speeding bus.

"But, ugh," Zamani continued to flounder, hesitant to pose a follow-up question at the risk of further chagrin. "I, that's not, ugh..."

What... Is... Happening?

"Right. Okay guys, let's head back to you in the studio for now," the embarrassed reporter pleaded, exposing the very injurious flaws of live, unscreened and unfiltered television.

Before Jonny could relish in the fleeting feeling of short-lived relief, the television screen blacked out, offering nothing more than the mirror of his own reflection in the screen's liquid crystal display.

"What are you doing?" Jonny swang, almost offended as Chuckie retreated to a standing position behind the couch, swinging and aiming the television's remote control like an electronic lightsaber.

"What's left to see? Your hooker covered for you and Tokyo fucked us, right?" he lamented as irony instructed him to rest against

Tokyo's lavish marble kitchen counter. "I mean, the guy is fucking broke. He's dead-fucking-broker than the tooth fairy at a crack-house full of meth-heads."

"Shut-up and let me think for a second, Chuckie," Jonny scolded.

He sunk his rear-end in Tokyo's sofa, his body dripping in an inescapable quicksand. His arms jittered as he reached for his pocket to remove his giraffe-printed *Louis Vuitton* Brazza wallet.

"What are you doing?" Chuckie scorned, his snout lifting to the moon as Jonny gripped his *MasterCard* and tossed his wallet to the ground. "How is catching up on your online shopping going to help us here?"

Jonny leant forward, balancing the tip of his *MasterCard* on a glass table as he spun it clockwise with a single finger.

"Can you believe that this piece of fucking plastic caused all this chaos?" he bemoaned, his gatekeeper guard retreating as an uncontainable vulnerability bubbled to the surface.

"Jonny," Chuckie interjected in a rare flicker of perspicacity. "If Tokyo was dead broke all along, then how in the fuck has he been able to afford to pay for all of this shit?"

Jonny stared deep into Chuckie's soul as he collected the *MasterCard* and flicked it like a burnt out cigarette into the faux redhead's lap.

An uncharacteristic shrug from the artist formerly known as Jonny Cash was the only nonverbal sign Chuckie needed to decode the most basic of puzzles.

"Well, no… fucking… shit?"

56

CARAVAGGIO'S KISS OF JUDAS

The room was a plain void – empty – save for some second-hand Spartan furniture and a running DVD recorder. A table and two chairs were chained to the floor like seventeenth-century slaves in shackles as the isolated, squared room – its walls an overcast grey – offered no windows, no clock, no neutral décor, no visual stimulus and no solace.

Two mirroring surveillance cameras tucked themselves away in opposite corners of the room, creating a strangling field of view from which there was no easy escape.

The room was almost silent, the only noise generating from a climate control system switching sparingly between mild and frigid temperatures to disrupt any sense of acclimating comfort.

"Lucky it's bolted down," Tokyo uttered disingenuously, his fingertips waving towards the activated DVD recorder. "These'd make a decent dent in your head if you didn't duck fast enough."

Commander Clayton Bommarito sat cross-legged on the only chair not bolted to the ground as he smirked and whistled between his decaying teeth.

"Lucky I'm getting more and more agile by the day, then, hey?" he taunted as he wobbled his belly like a bowl full of jelly. "So let's get down to business; tell me what happened, Tokyo."

"I am sorry, I do not understand what you are meaning at the present moment," he replied like an insolent and well-programmed *iRobot*.

Bommarito dodged the provocation.

"Listen, one way or another, we *are* going to get through this," the commander guaranteed. "Now where we end up and how we get there is entirely up to you."

Tokyo submitted his chest of wisecracks to detention as he winced and channelled his focus on the navy-cloaked vermin before him.

"Ask whatever it is that you need to ask," Tokyo said, drooping his shoulders as he rolled at the wrists. "You *know* I've got nothing to hide; did you get the opportunity to meet my giraffe during your house call last night by the way? You know I've got an ownership license from the Department of Agriculture, right? Well, of course you do."

Tokyo wrestled over control as he spewed a series of unanswerable questions.

"Talk to me about the sale of PLiNKER," Bommarito inquired, avoiding the verbal vomit as he sought to seize command of the interrogation. "Why'd you make the sale?"

Tokyo paused, his eyeballs rolling as he cogitated in search for an unimpeachable answer.

"I got a good offer and I wanted the money," Tokyo answered candidly.

"But you were offered stock as compensation?"

"You've never gotten lucky playing on the *NASDAQ* before, have you, chief?"

"Commander," Bommarito corrected as he tapped at his shirt-pinned single silver star.

"Just because I traded for stock, doesn't mean I didn't monetise my assets," Tokyo divulged, unable to fence his ego. "I've got a *good* accountant, y'dig my ninja?"

The energy intensified as Tokyo could not refrain from brandishing his smugness.

"I 'dig'," Bommarito replied, mimicking the accused. "But tell me if *you* can 'dig' this."

The commander stood upright, kicking back the black chair with his horse-hooves.

Despite Tokyo's best efforts, the commander was in control as he towered over his suspect like a Pennsylvanian sycamore.

"Any attempt to evade or defeat the payment of United States taxes is one of my all-time favourite felonies, Tokyo," Bommarito chuffed. "And you want to know why? Because its sentencing can send one down two very different roads of repentance; road A: one can fork out the payment for a fine of up to two-hundred-and-fifty thousand dollars or, my very personal favourite, road B: five, wonderful, merrymaking years in a Californian prison."

Tokyo choked at the foreshadowing as he pressed his stone-like features, determined not to be tyrannised by his captor.

"But given that our research indicates that you don't have a dollar or a yen or a fucking renminbi to your name right now, I'm going to press the prosecution to serve you up a warm-boiled entrée of tar, courtesy of the never-ending highway that is road B."

Bommarito's research was valid: Tokyo *was* penniless according to his *official* financial records. But Tokyo had *unofficial* cash flow, a translucent stream of chocolate river-flowing Benjamin's generated as a subsequence of his generous – despite its deceptive denotation – patronage.

But it was a cash flow that spawned from thievery, from unsanctioned access to the ends of a hidden rainbow where only a single individual could go. It was a monetization founded on fraudulence and duplicity, a shortcut through a loophole that elevated its discoverer to a plateau of immortality.

And it was a cash flow that Bommarito should never have known about.

Tokyo's dilemma was an unavoidable minefield. An admission of a secret fortune – a fortune to which Tokyo's complicity came by means as a treacherous accomplice – would compel investigators to sniff out its actionable origin, pigeonholing the inventor in a perpetual cycle of imprisonment.

Reveal the *Monopoly* fund? Prison sentence.

Admit to tax evasion? Prison sentence.

Every remedy seemed to materialise a single, unwavering and undesirable result.

Except for *one*.

"Let me ask you something, commander," Tokyo rebutted. Tokyo's heart rate triggered to the rhythm of a flashing surveillance camera as he realigned his backside on the bolted chair. "Since you never had the chance to trade on the stock market – and believe in me, you missed the boat on PLiNKER stock *a long* fucking time ago – how about you give me a chance to make it up to you right now?"

Bommarito twitched at the nose, his fingers wiggling in a state of disconcertedness.

"I'm listening," he claimed tentatively.

"Let's make a trade, just you and me?"

"And what could *you* possibly have that I would want?"

Tokyo sniggered like an evil mastermind as the battle for power continued.

"You know what's funny, commander?" he asked rhetorically. "America is the land of taxation… that was founded to *avoid* taxation. Crazy, ain't it? And if they say that taxation without consent is robbery, the United States government *has* never, and *is* never likely to have a single, honest, godforsaken, motherfucking dollar in its treasury. But if taxation without consent is *not* considered robbery, then any would-be robber has only to declare himself a government – or a business of social and political importance – and all his robberies are immediately legalised."

Bommarito's attention peaked, his interest soaring higher with every ticking second.

"How'd you like to learn about the only bank robbery on United States soil… that nobody *ever* knew about?"

57

THANKS FOR PLAYING, BURGER PRINCE

"*... And* without boring you with every single little detail, that's basically how we ended up *here* in Tokyo's... '*fort*'."

The verbal apologia was more like a fictional narrative from a throwaway script. Jonny delineated what he could, knowing too well that Chuckie's peanut-sized brain could only withstand so much disaccord.

Chuckie's eyebrows clenched, processing the information as if he were dealing with an unavoidable stretch of constipation.

'So it's... *your* fault, then?" Chuckie intimated, evincing that perhaps everything was not *always* rainbows and butterflies in the intemperate world of the hamburger prince.

Jonny wriggled in the sofa as he shook his head.

"Nobody's at *fault* for anything, Chuckie," he argued as he dodged a softball of responsibility. "I'm going to make this right, I promise."

Jonny continued to talk the talk, his chest extending outwards towards the giraffe's artificial playground. But Jonny was out of legs – while his mouth could still move, his feet were tired of lagging behind. And although he could not openly admit to it, the mere mention of *her* name suggested with absolute plausibility that his Californian escapade was coming to a ruinous end.

"*Maya's been looking everywhere for you; even called my office a couple of times asking for our help."*

"So what now, then?" Chuckie asked. "What in the Sam fucking Hill are we supposed to do?"

Jonny pondered, juggling the alternatives on a mental scale before offering his response.

"*You* aren't going to do anything," he said as remorse swallowed him whole. "I've put you through enough of this bullshit already."

Chuckie Hooper Junior had long been considered a compelling casualty in Jonny Cash's war for self-acceptance. But this was no longer a fantasy, no longer an empirical reverie; this was real-world actuality and he had played puppeteer to the livelihoods of the ones that loved him for long enough.

It was time for *Jon* Jinks to return *home.*

"Listen to me, Chuckie," he whispered, shifting his body towards Chuckie's as if he were prefacing an incoming scene of undying love. "You've changed my life, man. For better or for worse, the person I thought I was bore no resemblance to the mad man you helped me to create and for that... I *thank you.*"

Chuckie blushed in an awkward condition of confusion as he wondered if this was a confession of sins or of hidden homosexuality.

"Call me Dr. fucking Jekyll, right?" he replied facetiously.

"I guess so," Jonny chuckled. "You were my science and your cheeseburger sauce was my serum and together, you released a part of me that I'd been suppressing all my life. But after everything I've learnt from you about this city, this kind of lifestyle; I realised I don't deserve any of it."

"The fuck are you talking about, holmes?" the pompous redhead blurted, struggling to come to grips with the notion that *he* had imparted some kind of Californian wisdom on his travelling confidant.

"I'm serious, Chuckie," he repelled. "Listen, do you remember that time you asked me for a favour? You asked if I could put a good word in to your old man for you."

"I remember," Chuckie verified, his eyes spinning in a prepubescent muddle.

"So what I want you to do now is to shake my hand, head back to the diner and tell your dad that the Pennsylvania Paint Company will do the entire Regrub Moon Hills Project... for 'free.' *Then* we'll purchase and operate the first Chuckie's Diner franchise on the East Coast... if he hands you the reigns to the empire at any time over the next eighteen months."

Chuckie raised his eyebrows and twitched at the neck as he ruminated over Jonny's proposal.

Short-term sacrifice for a long-term gain. Save Gerry and the guys; get 'em out of paint and into patties. Transfer them a bucket-load of cash to cover their losses, hide it in make-believe invoices and everybody wins. This will work. This has to work.

"Surely you didn't think you had me convinced that you were running the real-estate show all along, did you?" he teased as he gaped right through Chuckie's tinted *Ray-Bans*. "Your old man scores a crazy-good severance-slash-retirement package, the company expands and you get everything you've ever wanted – *everybody* wins.

Not everybody...

Chuckie stumbled, his brain racing at a million revolutions a millisecond.

"You'd do that for me?" Chuckie stuttered.

I need to handle my debts. It's time.

"Listen, I don't know how much pull I have but if 'Chuckie Senõr' as you so like to call him," he continued, feigning his best Chuckie-impersonating-a-Spanish-guy impersonation. "If he bites at the apple and realises that you've just brokered a deal that'll profit him hundreds of thousands of dollars, something tells me that'd call for some kind of promotion."

The cotton candy coloured redhead was being forced to handle an emotion he wasn't so familiar with: gratitude and respect.

"And what about you?" he asked in an expression of selflessness that would have made a father of discipline proud. "What's going to happen? Are you staying in L.A.? Are you going to be cool, holmes?"

So many questions. Not enough answers.

Jonny lifted his arm in a high five stance as he extended his hand and cued for a well-rehearsed handshake.

The pair connected their palms before leaning in a brotherly embrace.

"I'll be whatever I'm supposed to be next," Jonny declared as he began the voyage down the dark hallway of Tokyo's Palisades palace. "And something tells me that means... that I'm supposed to be... *myself.*"

And like that, the burger prince and the Pennsylvanian painter parted company.

58

NOJ / JON & LITTLE RED HOTELS

The disquietude was prevalent, unbeatable. Jonny had been here before like the butterflies that tumbled inside his abdomen almost four years and five – or six, or seven – months ago. But never before had he felt such anxious stimulation, such exuberant neurosis, a complete and utter disconnect with reality and an insertion into an alternate universe set yet again, in a rainbow-coloured world that looked a heck of a lot like the one from *Alice's Adventures in Wonderland.*

He heaved as if he were dragging luggage by hand from one hemisphere to the other, his breath shortening with each passing burn of the Californian fire.

For weeks, Jonny had played the conductor, the developer, and the mastermind behind a virtual reality game that mimicked a lifestyle a 'Jinks' could never lead. It brought with it a vicarious pleasure, a fulfilment of sorts that the illusionary being of Jonny – *not* 'Jon' – could indulge in.

But the guilt had begun to proliferate, compounding into a cataclysmic implosion of his soul as every fibre in his body bent and snapped at the notion of emotional injustice.

He had left it all behind – Maya, Allentown, his friends, The Pennsylvania Paint Co., his legacy – for a life of desolate fiction, a story of make-believe that featured characters too rich in both personality and materialism to ever be remotely believable. Communication had been severed like the abrupt disconnect of a phone line in a thunderstorm, Jonny adamant that a 'cold turkey' power-play could deliver him the strength to plough through the rubble, to seize the opportunity ostrich by the scruff of its cotton candy neck.

But he could not have been more wrong.

Every post-mortem step – every decision made that succeeded the extinction of 'Jon' – was a masquerading pose, a deliberate deception in a disguised dry retch, concealed behind the ghosting of a Rich Uncle Pennybags mask dripping in blotches of acrylic.

"I'm waiting on a park bench by the L.A. River, opposite Alameda Street towards E 4th," Jonny instructed into the smartphone's microphone, his right leg crossed atop his left knee as he spread his arms atop the bench's wooden backrest. "You'll find me, Sonny, you always do."

He had thirty minutes to kill. Jonny left his post, tightening his laces before pacing by Sana Fe Avenue. From this exact coordinate, the Allentown artist could sniff out the scent of titanium oxide like a police dog in a drug bust, the Arts District only a horseback stride or fifty away from where he stood.

Paint is a funny thing, he thought. *Each emulsifying pigment provides colour, changing its state from something it was into something it never knew it could be.*

Jonny tip-toed across the south side of the district, first down Mateo Street before a feisty grumble in his stomach led him towards a gas station on 8th Street.

The downtown area was baron as an empty-minded Jonathan Jinks paced by the petrol pumps and through the station's electronic doors.

Need a drink. Need to get my mind right.

The station attendant hawked him like a supercilious *Louis Vuitton* saleswoman except this time, the uncertainty was warranted. Jonny was jaded, suspect even, as he examined the shelves of the store to the discomfort of its caretaker.

"Can I help you with anything, sir?" the gas station attendant offered, his hand gently pressed against the emergency alert trigger.

"Just looking for something to drink?"

The attendant gestured to the north of the store, his index finger wiggling in the direction of a wide and illuminated grocery store refrigerator.

Gas stations were the oasis for the modern man; a jackpot-hitting pick-me-up for even the most tiresome leg of any journey. Energy drinks, donuts and scratch-off lotto tickets flooded the store like a just-for-size heaven for Homer Simpson as Jonny weaved through the aisles, interested in the purchase of anything except gas.

Jonathan Jinks was on the approach. *His* final leg awaiting as he refuelled the charisma-inflated tyres of his very own vehicle.

"What's with all the *Nascar* memorabilia?" Jonny chirped in an attempt to extinguish the suspicion-gauge as his arm brushed against a selection of *Nascar*-themed t-shirts, bobble heads and vanity plates. "I mean, are you meant to have fast cars on the brain because you're filling up your *Volvo* with some of this juicy premium unleaded?"

The gas station attendant looked on, nonplussed.

"Ugh, I just stack the shelves."

He's not going to be a problem, Jonny deduced as if he possessed the potency to take action if determined otherwise.

Jonny browsed the refrigerator's contents as a sauna of water vapour fogged the inside of the closed door like an Allentown winter.

Linings of cola, flavoured sparkling water, iced coffee and unsweetened tea occupied the refrigerator's shelves. Jonny – with an eye on each product and its price tag – scoured for a number pad as if the fridge itself were some kind of ATM-styled vending machine.

Grape juice. Seems appropriate.

Like a contestant on *The Bachelorette*, Jonny was kind-of confident with his selection. He wedged his hand around the door handle of the refrigerator, gripping it tightly before an extraordinary and adventitious obstruction paralysed him in a frozen quadriplegia.

The artificial light bulbs from the false ceiling above him fused with the natural glow of the Californian sun, forging escaping shadows and jagged reflections before a gigantic looking glass.

No way...

His throat numbed before a tickle of nausea catalysed a formation of goose bumps and levitating arm hairs. The gas station refrigerator, filled with the most innocuous of produce, offered a toxic yet omnipotent reminder, a suggestion seemingly so deliberate that had Jonathan Jinks convinced the phenomenon was an implicit and divine counsel from God.

In the refrigerator's mirrored reflection, Jonny could spy two very clear things: the first was himself, echoing movements and twitches in reverse like a doppelganger from a parallel universe. But the second, well the second was where his curiosity piqued with the vigour of a thousand crosshairs aiming at him at a 'Pennsylvanian Persons of Interest' target practice clinic.

Deep in the picture-framed distance of the mirrored reflection, a Nations of Jefferson American Bank ominously occupied the corner block adjacent to the gas station. The Nations of Jefferson American Bank – with its minimal corporate logo that accentuated its acronymic form of 'NOJ' – stood tall and unmistakable, the building's red, blue and white colour palette professing historical patriotism and leadership.

Much like the American national flag, the bank's corporate colours – and, in turn, its very policies – were synonymous with the whites of purity and innocence, the reds of hardiness and valour and the blues of vigilance, perseverance and justice. But these specific values also portrayed an eerily ironic prescience, a combustion of the burning being that would become 'Jonny' Jinks – Jonny Cash – in a transformation not to dissimilar to a naked Targaryen escaping unharmed in a ritual of a blazing flame.

It wasn't its existential presence that startled Jonny; after all, he'd driven by more than a dozen Nations of Jefferson bank precincts since that consequential night on 17th Street. It was its acronymic reflection, its very title that sent shockwaves down his spine. True to its reflective surface, the refrigerator's transparent door offered a mirrored display, a verbatim reversal of incoming light.

Everything from the gas station's illuminated 'EXIT' sign to Jonny's 'CMYK' t-shirt read back to front like a Holy Quran.

Everything including the bank's 'NOJ' building signage.

Mirror, mirror, on the fridge, who's the guiltiest son of a bitch?

It was as if Jonny had entered a warped galaxy where *Disney* films possessed diabolical connotations and Jonny was far from the knight in shining armour his reputation in Allentown suggested.

In the refrigerator's makeshift looking glass, he could no longer see 'NOJ.'

Now, he could only see 'JON.'

Now, he could only see *himself.*

* * *

my mum always told me to believe in the unexpected magic of coincidences.

I mean, sure, she was a catholic woman, a soul of pure faith and incorruptible righteousness. But it was her devout commitment to the idea of a miracle, the idea that God was omnipresent, forging these unexplored opportunities for us like a fucking Earth-controlling playwright penning his one-hundredth script that I could relate to.

I used to think that we were kind of like these engine drivers on our own 'train' of life. That each day, we'd come to a bunch of crossings, both big and small, deciding which tracks to take and which stations to stop at. But in the end, it seemed like the gear lever of my locomotive was jammed and even if I wanted to turn back or change tracks, I couldn't.

It's crazy to think that after everything I was, after all I had given, something as trivial as Los Angeles possessed the conquering power to turn me into a fucking madman. Was I reckless? Sure. I guess I was a little reckless on 17th Street, too. But from that transient moment, that blotter-blurred memory – Madison dropping a forbidden fruit beneath my salivating tongue – my credo changed and became: 'no chastity belt? No problem.'

But eventually, it became time for 'destiny' to show its hand.

Steve Jobs once said that 'your time is limited, so don't waste it living someone else's life.' But how do we know when we've strayed from our path, from our true calling? What's right for one person probably isn't right for the next, right? So when did I realise that I'd lost my way?

The truth is, I don't think I ever really did. I didn't know which 'way' was mine to begin with.

When you look in the mirror, you're supposed to see your reflection. When you look at a reflection, you see yourself in reverse.

But when you stare at a bank logo in the reflection of a refrigerator window, somehow…

gods calling manifests and you start to see yourself again as you always really were.

* * *

Outside, *iPhone* camera's flashed in fits of epilepsy as a contingent of teenage *Twitter* paparazzi swarmed before the hotel's unmistakable cobblestone in an effort to gobble up photos of their favourite celebrities.

The *Chateau Marmont*'s gothic façade was a historical and cultural landmark but Jonny's delirious partiality suggested that all he could now see was a miniature shoebox-sixed, little red hotel.

"A man pushes his car in front of a hotel and immediately realizes he's bankrupt," Jonny riddled from the *Ghost*'s backseat, his eyes fixated on the still silhouette of the *Chateau Marmont.* "How does he know this, Sonny?"

Allentown's famous son stared through the tinted passenger window of the gloss-black *Rolls-Royce Ghost* as if he were back in P.A., a cab-ride away from the towering sycamores and shady oaks that paved a landmarked lining towards his Coopersburg home.

"I really don't know, sir. How does he know this?"

Jonny knew. He had known since the beginning.

"Because all along, he's been playing *Monopoly*."

59

TRANSACTION...
CANCELLED

Jonathan Jinks rested against a brick wall like a lifeless vagrant, his legs blocking the pedestrian thoroughfare. He was exhausted – in mind and in body – as his backside boiled against the concrete.

"It's out of order," he mumbled, spooking a would-be user as she closed her purse and retreated away from the hazard before her.

Jonny sat motionless, broken like the promises he had made to his woman as passers-by drifted away to avoid both eye contact and the spreading stench.

He closed his eyes, scraping the fine hairs on his head with the rugged finishing of the machine before dropping an uncalculated handful of baby blue tablets down a river of his slushing saliva.

The feeling was mind-numbing as he compressed his eyelids with the kind of impetus that could burst a balloon. He was fading, floating away into a baron and warped orbit of dry blacks and piercing reds as the bustle of pedestrian foot-peddling and traffic pollution was but a speck of distraction to his semi-conscious condition of Zen.

Streams of perspiration dropped from his hairline and down to his nose before a familiar fragrance swarmed his senses.

Sniff. Sniff.

"C'mon, Oscar," the dog-walker implored as he yanked nervously on the canine's collar. "So sorry about that, friend."

Jonny did not budge, nor did he blink an eye. He couldn't. They were still fastened shut, but a sensory interpretation allowed him to paint the scene in his mind like a blind-man desperate for colour.

He had already stored the fragmented pieces of the visual from a multitude of homogenous meetings – the ATM on 17th Street, the brown and black Yorkshire terrier lurking in Madison's hotel room – and all he needed was to use his imagination.

"Ugh, excuse me, friend," the pedestrian trembled, this time with an added ingredient of trepidation as Jonny unlocked a single eyelid and gazed at the intolerable dog-walker. "Listen, I don't do this very often but something compels me to come to your aid."

Great. Good Samaritan 2.0. Just what I need.

The dog-walker – a virtual Poindexter in every sense of the word – knelt down to the concrete and balanced a half-empty can of cola within Jonny's arm reach.

"I'm *just* going to leave this here for you," he apprised as if he were dropping *Purina Puppy Chow* into a dog feeder before straightening his spectacles with one hand while tightly griping his dog leash in the other. "If you're thirsty, then that's great. If not, that's okay, too. Please just remember that I've performed my good deed for the day."

It became strikingly obvious that the selfless Samaritan was, in fact, nothing more than a self-serving introvert seeking in his own act of manufactured kindness.

"Let's go, Oscar, say goodbye to the nice man," he instructed as the canine barked in Jonny's direction.

Jonny creaked his neck up and down, gesturing a genuine gratitude to the self-motivated altruist before reaching for his smartphone.

The device – its touchscreen almost inoperable on account of its stains, smudges and dried body paint – rested in his lap as Jonny carefully orchestrated his final dice-roll.

No matter what happens from here, I need her to know the truth.

Jonny opened his call log and scrolled through his favourites, selecting the only option that paired its text with a love-heart emoji.

Guess I should probably change this to a broken-heart now.

He sighed, the carbon dioxide leaving his body like a toxic flush of gas as he raised the smartphone to his ear and gnawed at his bottom lip.

The ringer barely sounded for more than a second before a voice of trepidation, sorrow and perplexity answered.

"Jo–... Jon?"

He clenched his cheekbones inwards to numb the pain.

"It's me, Maya."

Jonny's voice may as well have been that of a spectre, a living revenant who had returned from the claws of death. He felt it, too, the silence interrupted only by Maya's deep and uncontrolled respiring as she tried to decode the authenticity of the phone call.

"Maya?" he echoed as he waited in limbo.

"Are you okay?" she uttered in solicitude, snapping the silence.

Maya's prosperity – her very sanity – had been bedevilled by Jonny's disappearance. But this was not the time for crestfallen criticism – not yet, anyway. This was a phone call she had been dreaming of and she was determined to syphon every last detail for as long as it would last.

"I'm fine, Maya," he whispered as the final syllable broke in a squeaky tonal pitch. "How are you?"

"Where are you, Jon?" she followed, ignoring the question altogether.

"Where I need you to be right now; I'm still in L.A."

His instructions were profound and unfeigned, filled to the brim with a vodka glass of bona fide remorse and repentance.

"What happened, Jon? What did you do?"

"I promise, baby, I'll explain everything to you when you get here," he assured her. "Just book a flight to *LAX* and call…"

Jonny pinched his own skin as he crinkled his face like a bag of empty potato crisps.

"… Call Commander Clayton Bommarito when you get here. From what he tells me you've already been acquainted. He'll tell you what to do."

The wail of a police siren oscillating in an increasing attenuation quelled his distractions, as suddenly, Jonny was very aware of his whereabouts.

"But Jon, I don't understand," Maya stressed, her voice vibrating in a frantic rhythm. "I don't understand any of this!"

The police siren screeched and inner-city dogs howled as the squad car stormed closer and closer towards Jonny's coordinates.

"I'm sorry, Maya, I'm so, so sorry," he cried as a dark cloud engulfed the common Californian sunshine, forming a secret shadow across his entire mind, body and soul.

Jonathan Jinks struck the back of his neck against the steel of the ATM, crushing his eyes together as a tear – a river of sorrow and moral scruple – slipstreamed down his suntanned cheek.

Maya was taciturn, silent, save for a suppressed sobbing. No dialogue of any sort could quantify her sorrow as her mind navigated its way through a maze of madness and incertitude.

She was shaken by Jonny's negligence and selfishness. But mostly, her heart broke with the impetus of a pounding uppercut, its pieces irreparable, unsalvageable.

"Maya," he whispered through a congested sniffle. "I'm sorry but I've got to go. Call Bommarito and get on the next plane out of Allentown."

Maya howled with all she had left.

"No, Jon... no."

And in a trice quicker than the destabilisation of everything that Jonathan Jinks and Maya Ververs had created, Jonny tapped the little red button on his smartphone, raised his head to the heavens and began to cry.

60

THE PEOPLE VS JONATHAN JINKS

The building's analogue clocks appeared to be ticking in reverse as they down-counted in unison from thirty-six hours.

The station's holding and detention cell was commonly reserved for Los Angeles' most hard-nosed criminals and mischief-makers, not painters from Pennsylvania with clean records and virtuous undertones. But this wasn't any ordinary case of suspect custody; this was the one in a million, the head-scratcher, the primetime feature on *A Current Affair* that glued its viewers to the television screen in disbelief as they tried to comprehend how it could have all gone so wrong for somebody so right.

Jonny had been photographed and fingerprinted as the city's police staff made him feel more like a modern-day John Dillinger than an olden-day Jon Jinks. And while personal recognizance was argued between his appointed council and the state, there existed no evidence to suggest that the artist from Allentown would not flee for a hideaway in the motherland.

Jonny waited behind the uninviting bars of the meagre dungeon – cloaked from head to toe in *Sunkist* orange, his feet tapping against the concrete to an internal jazz rhythm – before a familiar law enforcer with a bulky notebook tucked under his armpit made his visiting rounds.

"So *obviously* you understand why I can't let you apply for bail, right?" Clayton Bommarito said, loosening his shirt collar at the neck button as he unlocked the cell and joined him on a portable plastic chair.

"They already confiscated my wallet," Jonny replied, emptying his pockets as he tiptoed between bravado and a concession of defeat. "My credit card, too."

"Jonny... Mother... Fucking... *Cash*... It really all seems so simple now, doesn't it?"

Jonny shrugged, admitting that the sobriquet always felt more like a term of endearment than a corroborative confession.

"'Simple' isn't the word I'd use to describe any of this."

"You know, I've always liked you, *Jon*," Bommarito admitted in a passive half-truth. "Even when you were running with the Hooper kid and he was making a fucking fool of himself, I always thought you had this cool head on your shoulders – guess that's probably why my best investigative days are behind me though, right?"

Jonny wasn't sure whether to laugh or to cry. In the end, he did neither.

"So what do they call it?"

"In legal terms?" Bommarito replied. "'Larceny by finding'; it's what happens when some arguably unlucky asshole chances upon something that doesn't belong to him and takes full possession without establishing whether or not that particular something actually belonged to some other asshole in the first place – in this case, we're talking about 'assholes' of the most retributive kind."

"Any idea how that unlucky asshole actually chanced upon that thing that didn't belong to him in the first place?" Jonny asked, desperate to find a reason for his God-given loophole.

"Well apparently you sounded an incidental alarm for the NOJ," Bommarito revealed in a suppressed chuckle. "If I'm being completely honest with you, at first, they had no fucking idea what had happened."

Figures.

"But after a little digging," the commander continued. "They discovered that you were trying to record transfers during the witching hour, at a time where the NOJ's ATM systems were pulled offline for an automated maintenance. The system tries to schedule transfers but can't complete requests until reconnected to the main system. But by withdrawing your transfer at the same time, I guess you uncovered a loophole that not even the bank knew existed."

"And the 'invisible' credit card option?"

"They're still working on that one," Bommarito divulged in a 'you're-a-tricky-bastard' kind-of smirk.

In some kind of twisted reach for self-abatement, Jonny was quelled by the notion that – after all his obvious speculations – a legitimate law had indeed been broken.

"What happened to you, kid?" Bommarito entreated, proving that even the most apt of professional law enforcers sometimes needed a reason, too. "By every account, you were the best son of a bitch this side of a charity drop-off. That shit doesn't just change overnight, does it?"

The question was as loaded as Tokyo van Wolfswinkel's pistol as Bommarito wrestled earnestly, almost as much as Jonny himself, with the painter's decisions.

"Not too long ago, someone told me a little something that I'd say was life-changing," he begun, his entire soul dripping in a paint palette of remorse and regret. "They told me that life is not too dissimilar to a game of *Monopoly*. You know what the most powerful move in *Monopoly* is? It isn't even mentioned in the rulebook. It's not rolling doubles, putting hotels on 'Boardwalk' or accumulating railroads, it's the moment when you realise that it's all just a game. That the money's made up, that the lines on the board are all printed in mass and your entire identity is fictitious. It's all make-believe."

The metaphor breathed with symbolic intensity.

"You remember that at any given time, you can walk away from the game and if you do, there's a big wide-world to explore that you'd forgotten even existed while you were so absorbed by every last roll of the dice," he continued, his lips trembling like grass fields in a mild autumn's breeze as he focused on the details to keep himself from falling apart. "The moment you realise that it's all just one big game, you're free to play it however you want. As soon as you see the world for what it really is – a system manipulated by people no more or no less intelligent than you or I – you begin to establish your own system, your own set of rules. You know, every single day you can walk into a coffee shop anywhere in the world and you're guaranteed to find a scene of zombification; of people staring lifelessly into computer screens, smartphones and coffee cups while others wander around like empty bottles waiting for collection. You ask any of these people why they don't just jump on a plane and better their lifestyle and you'll get the same kind of answer, over and over again: 'I can't do that, I've got bills to pay, a boss to report to, family and friends to think about...' Basically, they're giving you *their* version of the 'I've got to pass *GO* to collect my two-hundred-dollars so I can do it all over again tomorrow' excuse."

Bommarito had been there before; coffees or donuts, they were all pawns of nourishment in the game of life, heckling the lives of powerless humans in a myriad of ways.

"The game is *real* to them and they're stuck playing with unlucky dice," Jonny suggested, his focus now stern and acute. "But what they don't actually realise is that they're *free*; free to explore, to move, to learn, to thrive, to escape from the game and make a change, any kind of change. But what if, suddenly, they stumble on a *lucky* set of dice?

What do they do then? Where do they go? What game do they play if they no longer have to commit to the one they were stuck in?"

The questions, each as unanswerable as their predecessors, screamed like fatal greeting cards from The Riddler in an animated *Batman* episode. The answers were not nearly half as important as the questions themselves.

"I made a decision," Jonny admitted, leaning his chin against his palm. "And that decision was to play a different game with the dice I was given. I decided to ditch the wheelbarrow and play as the top hat."

Clayton Bommarito sighed, his eyes rolling in an intergalactic black hole of no-return. This kind of criminality was the hardest to accept; the kind that should never have been forged by a man who had no business flirting with the damages of fate.

"… And Tokyo?" the commander moved on, the question as open and exposed as Jonny's *Louis Vuitton* Brazza wallet.

He had not intended to catapult Tokyo beneath the bus. But there *was* no bus; only a Chuckie's Diner food truck and it was steamrolling towards the Pennsylvanian painter like a part-cheetah part-locomotive.

"I suppose you won't accept 'patronage' for an answer?"

Bommarito's ripening wrinkles contoured by the minute as he huffed and shook his head.

"I was his golden goose and he was my cash cow," Jonny confessed, reading from his brain-stored, master plan encyclopaedia. "I brought the money in, he found a way to clean it; I'm sure if you go ahead and raid his palace again, you'll find a stack of invoices made out for the… 'sales' of my artwork."

To even recount their scheme aloud brought about a knife-wedging pain in his spine. That Jonathan Jinks from Allentown could be capable of something so verboten was a catastrophic realisation that even he – the crime's unlikely culprit – struggled to concede.

Jonny and Tokyo had devised the ploy over Swiss Matterhorn-crafted whiskey glasses where the pair would instantly recognise the fiscal benefits of their engagement. Jonny would continue to withdraw currency from the hapless surplus of ATMs scattered across Los Angeles while Tokyo – the brain seemingly behind any and every corporate malpractice policy in American history – would launder the bills into ostensibly legitimate income.

"Look, I know it's a cliché," Bommarito admitted, as if Jonny's entire adventure hadn't been just that. "But for my sake, tell me you regret it. Tell me you made a mistake, you fell too deep down a hole without a ladder or a rope."

Jonny released his chin from the cup of his hand as he lifted his head upright, straightened his spine and stared the commander square in his pleading eyes. This was not prototypical behaviour for a police commander, especially one with Clayton Bommarito's decorated history of service and cunning machismo. But there was something about this case, this transgression that was certain to haunt the policeman for the remainder of his days.

"Not a second goes by that I'm not remorseful, that I don't ask God for forgiveness," Jonny avowed, his head fighting the shame as he rekindled with a hidden piousness. "I've been riddled with guilt since the very moment my card made its way inside an ATM in Allentown. But this lie I created, this fantasy, it's something that – no matter how hard I tried – I couldn't erase it, I couldn't escape it. It became part of me, and I of it. And as much as I tried to *hate* myself for who I had become, I *loved* myself for it in just the same way."

Jonny's candour was admirable, his battle royal with inner-angels and outer-demons relatable to any warm-blooded male with an unpopulated bank account and a chip on his shoulder.

But Jonny's fantasy was coming to a screeching end, his rainbow of luck fading into a dark and cloudy thunderstorm of deceit and misconduct.

He had rolled doubles twice in succession and in a moment that would last shorter than the verve sparked by a serendipitous ATM jackpot, he was poised to roll them again for the third and final time.

61

DO NOT PASS GO, DO NOT COLLECT $200

there's a real good reason why the word 'art' exists in 'heart':

It's because no matter the beauty, no matter the magnificence, there's harrowing madness in every good creation. Just as God formed creation from chaos and children are born from the blood of the womb, art emerges from the pain of a broken world. If it doesn't shatter your heart or cause you to grieve just a little, then it's not *really* art.

Good art disturbs us and showers us beneath a raincloud of dark, monochromatic paint. And often, we're never equipped with an *umbrella*.

I watched a movie called *Midnight in Paris* not too long ago – I'd seen it with Maya once or twice already – and I noticed a line of dialogue that I hadn't heard before: 'life is kind of unfulfilling.'

That shit really resonated with me.

Part of an artist's job is to try to make sense of our contaminated existence, to fill the emptiness we feel as we sip cappuccinos and revel in our climb up the corporate ladder of life.

So what's my point? Not that all art is sad; I wouldn't dare be so morbid. But that melancholy is a glowing sign, a powerful and magical calling to do something great. Honest art moves us closer to a truth and those who risk being vulnerable become the voices for change.

We're all wonderful works in progress fragmented at the very core, and that's something worth embracing.

maybe in doing so, you too will discover your own passageway to paradise.

* * *

"You can go in and see him now, ma'am," the guard announced like a doctor-turned-doorman at the doorway of a hospital room as he tapered the obviousness of his weapon and buzzed the beautiful brunette inside.

Maya was certain she was entering a ward at a palliative care facility as an unsettling stomach-sink reminded her of the grim purport of her visit.

This was not apart of Maya Ververs' dream Californian vacation itinerary as the city's blue skies and penetrating sunshine were non-existent inside the chambers of a jailhouse.

She paced along the concrete, each footstep burning with the embers of an Indian firewalker.

And then she saw him.

She gasped in a kind of silence that might have woken a sleeping dog in an underground kennel, the man of her dreams kneeling before her with a face that was almost unrecognisable. It wasn't that his physical appearance had changed; it was his outer shell, his protective layering, his ghost-like silhouette, his dangerously unexplainable veil. And these were the characteristics that made him Los Angeles' version of Jonathan Jinks, a version that Maya did not wish to know.

"Hey," the inmate whispered, his voice croaky from power napping inside the insanitary hostel as his stomach began to churn.

Maya crept towards the plastic chair earlier occupied by Commander Clayton Bommarito before a draught funnelled her fragrance towards Jonny's clogged nose.

"You haven't changed a bit," Jonny hailed, knowing too well that he could not speak for himself.

Maya trudged towards him before offering her arms in a routine embrace. Jonny squeezed her like a turkey and cheese sandwich, tightly compressing his eyes shut as he savoured the rare nanosecond of home-cooked intimacy.

Maya, however, was ambivalent to any kind of reciprocation. The embrace was hollow and lifeless, her arms drooping to the side as she rubbed against a man who felt more like a stranger from a foreign land.

"What's the matter?" Jonny asked as Maya separated herself from the glue and backpedalled away from the prisoner.

"They told me what you did, Jon," she divulged. "Is it true? That night you went to Minx, was that it? Was that how it began?"

It was as if Jonny were a recent inductee in a live-action *Alcoholics Anonymous* interrogation as his contaminated moral compass fought to decipher whether a right or wrong answer even existed anymore.

"Yes, but the whole thing was all a big, stupid coincidence, Maya, I swear," he argued, boycotting any accountability. "I was the victim in my own crime and once it started, there was nothing I could do to stop it. I was on this freaking steam train with faulty brakes and carriages loaded with golden cargo."

Maya. She's not even flinching.

"But I did this all for you," Jonny rationalised, pleading his case before the only jury he cared to convince. "I did this all for *us*."

Maya, her demeanour personifying a calm before a violent storm, twitched as the colour began to drain from her skin.

And then she did it.

In a flash, she raised her right hand and massacred Jonny's merciful face, slapping the side of his cheek like a heavyweight boxing champion.

Then she cried. She cried for the imprisonment of both her lover and her own heart, for the torment and for his betrayal, for his treachery and duplicity and for the constant web of unfiltered lies he continued to spin.

"Don't you lie to me!" she howled, the ruckus forcing a precautionary peek-a-boo from the watchful guard. "You did this for *you*; you didn't *mean* to do anything and when you figured it out, you did it all *alone*."

Maya's indignation turned to sorrow, her thunderous contempt regressing into a wolf-like cry, drowning in the pain of a broken heart.

Jonny had no answer. There was no escape, no solution. The road had run out of tarmac and all that remained was a steep fall to a never-ending bottom.

"I hope that when the day comes, your *son* can look up at his father *without* shame," Maya burned, the bombshell dropping like a *TMZ* headline as she cupped her belly with the palm of her hands.

Jonny's jaw dropped, his voice box failing him at the guilt-ridden whisper of such a startling revelation. Maya had been diagnosed with endometriosis; conception was supposed to carry the odds of a Saturday night lottery ticket. But apparently the painter from Pennsylvania had been making a habit out of flirting with the improbable and this appeared to follow suit.

"What?" he stuttered in astonishment.

"Yes," Maya reaffirmed. "You're going to be a father."

A haunting desolation dominated his frozen expression as the bittersweet reveal forced an instant re-evaluation over what he had truly been sacrificing all along.

"That's… that's incredible news," he uttered, wobbling his head as a thin tear streamed down the side of his cheek. "I always knew you were going to be a mother; an *amazing* mother."

Maya clenched her eyes as they began to flush in a waterfall of pain and suffering.

"And what are *you* going to be?"

The question was as riddling as any he had asked of himself. What would he be? Who *had* he *been*?

"Apparently a convict," he jested, thinning the ice as he wiped a bead of snot from his nostril. "But that's *not* what he'll know me as."

Jonny took a moment to regain his composure before clasping Maya's fragile fingers with both hands.

"I fucked up," he cried in an unbridled admission. "I *really* fucked up, Maya. I let myself down and I let you down and for that I have no excuse. But I *won't* make an excuse for not being a father."

Maya's grip tightened and her palms perspired as a black butterfly fluttered its brittle wings inside her washboard stomach.

"Whatever happens and however long they decide they need to keep me in here," he continued, his hands glued to Maya's like wet paint. "I will be *Jon*, the Jon you fell in love with, the Jon you knew you could count on… the Jon our son *deserves* to have as a father."

Jon's appeal for clemency was real and resonant. For a man who had grossed multitudinous *wants* during his escapade across the city of Los Angeles, inside the dilapidation of a Californian cell, he had but only one *need*: forgiveness.

* * *

theres a funny thing about a monopoly chance card.

It's kind-of worded in a way that's meant to sound unambiguous, but overall, the intent always seems crystal clear: the directive on the card is meant to be carried out immediately and without detour. It sort of implies that not only have you failed, but you've failed *right now* and you're shit out of luck if you're ever hoping to receive the kind of benefits ensued by virtue of atonement.

You know, Picasso once said that 'we artists are indestructible; even in a prison, or in a concentration camp, I would be almighty in my own world of art, even if I had to paint my pictures with my wet tongue on the dusty floor of my cell.' You could almost say that he was being prophetic and that I'm his reincarnation.

Okay. That's a bit rich. But you get where I'm heading.

Funny story about Picasso: in 1927 he hit on a pretty blonde named Marie-Thérèse Walter with the old 'excuse me, Madame, you have an interesting face, I would like to paint your portrait; I am Picasso' routine.

She'd never heard of him.

But after a colourful love affair and a child born out of wedlock, she became his *ultimate* muse.

What I'm trying to say is that's basically all I've got left now, until the timing is right again. I'll paint pictures of my unborn child, pictures of Maya's galaxy-covered hand, pictures of destructive ATMs and spicy burger sauces and pictures of a perfect family portrait. I'll paint without a brush because it's all I know to do. I'll paint without a brush because it's all that I have left.

I guess you're wondering what happened to Tokyo, right? You guessed it: he *sold* me out. Ironic, given he was fucking broke and all. But empty pockets make damaged men do dangerous and selfish things.

That much I can *absolutely* admit to you.

And now, this leaves me with only one immediate, highly

unfavourable and irreversible outcome. A harsh cliché for which I now know I deserve.

I will *not* pass go.

I will *not* collect two-hundred dollars.

I will *not* change who I am.

i will go straight to jail.

thanks for reading

Your support is incomparable and I truly hope you enjoyed every last page. I know you don't owe me anything (heck, you just spent your hard-earned dollars on a paperback when you could've just as easily spent that money on a night out, a burger, a craps table, seventeen *Chupa Chups* or a couple of months of *Netflix*) but I thought I'd let you know that *Amazon* totally encourages customer reviews.

I wouldn't be mad in the slightest if you left one.

james sismanes

facebook.com/thejamessismanes

twitter.com/jamessismanes

www.jamessismanes.com.au